COFFEE AND GHOSTS 3: NOTHING BUT THE GHOSTS

THE COMPLETE THIRD SEASON

CHARITY TAHMASEB

COLLINS MARK BOOKS

COPYRIGHT

CONTENTS

Author's Note   v
Coffee and Ghosts, The Season Lists   vii

COFFEE AND GHOSTS 3

Part I
GHOSTS AND CONSEQUENCES
Chapter 1   5
Chapter 2   13
Chapter 3   25
Chapter 4   37
Chapter 5   45
Chapter 6   59
Chapter 7   75
Chapter 8   81
Chapter 9   95
Chapter 10   105
Chapter 11   115

Part II
A FEW GOOD GHOSTS
Chapter 1   123
Chapter 2   129
Chapter 3   133
Chapter 4   141
Chapter 5   151
Chapter 6   161
Chapter 7   171
Chapter 8   183
Chapter 9   191
Chapter 10   201

Chapter 11   207

Part III
NOTHING BUT THE GHOSTS
Chapter 1   215
Chapter 2   227
Chapter 3   237
Chapter 4   243
Chapter 5   249
Chapter 6   255
Chapter 7   263
Chapter 8   269
Chapter 9   281
Chapter 10   289
Chapter 11   299
Chapter 12   307
Chapter 13   313
Chapter 14   325
Chapter 15   331
Chapter 16   339
Chapter 17   345

What the heck is Coffee & Ghosts?   359
About the Author   361
Also by Charity Tahmaseb   363

AUTHOR'S NOTE

COFFEE & GHOSTS is a cozy paranormal mystery/romance serial told in episodes and seasons, much like a television series. Think *Doctor Who* or *Sherlock*.

I've recently consolidated the episodes into three season bundles. This makes the episodes easier to find and—I hope—more enjoyable to read.

If coffee hasn't yet topped your list as the most versatile substance on Earth,
consider
"The Ghost in the Coffee Machine" by Charity Tahmaseb.
~ **Lori Parker, Word of the Nerd**

COFFEE AND GHOSTS, THE SEASON LISTS

Season 1:
Episode 1: *Ghost in the Coffee Machine*
Episode 2: *Giving Up the Ghosts*
Episode 3: *The Ghost Whisperer*
Episode 4: *Gone Ghost*
Episode 5: *Must Love Ghosts*

Season 2:
Episode 1: *Ghosts of Christmas Past*
Episode 2: *The Ghost That Got Away*
Episode 3: *The Wedding Ghost*

Season 3:
Episode 1: *Ghosts and Consequences*
Episode 2: *A Few Good Ghosts*
Episode 3: *Nothing but the Ghosts*

COFFEE AND GHOSTS 3

THE COMPLETE THIRD SEASON

PART I
GHOSTS AND CONSEQUENCES

COFFEE AND GHOSTS SEASON THREE,
EPISODE 1

CHAPTER 1

My business partner is kissing the back of my neck. Since we spent the night together, this isn't much of a surprise. I'm curled next to Malcolm, his arm draped over my waist, his rich, nutmeg scent warming the air. I want to laugh at the audacity and joy of it all, but don't dare make a sound, don't dare move. His kiss is a soft, shivery thing. I don't want him to stop. So I remain absolutely still as morning light filters through the drapes and bounces off dust motes in the air.

I'd be lying if I said I didn't love this.

I'd be lying if I said I wasn't worried.

But I am. This is new. Our business is still new, not quite a year old. Beneath the joy is a thin wire of dread that insists this happiness can't last. We've made a huge mistake mixing business with pleasure, and once I confess what happened at Nigel and Sadie's wedding reception last night, it will change everything; it will change *us*.

I will confess. I know I must. But not before coffee. No one should talk about business or pacts with (possibly) demonic entities before coffee.

Malcolm's lips continue to explore the nape of my neck. I'm pretty sure he's awake. True, he's an expert kisser. Even so, no one has so much skill that they can execute what he's currently doing while asleep.

I've vowed not to move, but my toes begin flirting with his. They find the sensitive arch of his foot, and I'm rewarded with his exhale against my neck.

"You awake?" he says, voice low and still warm with sleep.

"I'm guessing you are," I say.

"How are you?"

The simple question betrays so much with its tone: *Are you okay? Was last night okay? Did we make a mistake?*

I'm sure there must be other doubts I'm missing, other things he's feeling. I go with a single word reply.

"Good."

"Hm. You were that last night, too, if I recall."

Now I turn to face him. I'm rewarded with that sweet, dark-roast smile, his eyes, shining at the sight of me. I can't help wondering: how did I get so lucky?

"I think I promised you some Kona blend," I say.

"You did, and I plan to collect. But first, I think I need my morning kiss."

Morning kiss. Evening kiss. It's how we juggled being business partners and a couple, although that was before we moved the arrangement into my bedroom.

"Well, we turned the lights off after midnight." I peer up at him, trying to school my face into absolute seriousness. "Technically, that's morning, so we've already had our morning kiss."

"Doesn't count unless the sun's up." Malcolm tugs me closer, folds me into his arms.

It is, by far, the longest morning kiss on record.

~

I'M NOT sure how many pots of coffee I've brewed. Thousands, certainly. On most days, I do it without thinking. Unless we're up against a truly powerful ghost, I don't need to pay attention to the particular blend (although Kona works best to eradicate ghosts) or how precisely I measure the water.

This morning? My hands tremble—just a bit. I'm in Malcolm's tuxedo shirt. The tails skim my knees. Even with the cuffs rolled, the sleeves knock against things with a sweep of my arms. When I sprinkle coffee grounds all over the counter, I set down the scoop, close my eyes, and try not to cry.

"Hey." Malcolm's voice is gentle in my ear. He moves behind me, wraps his arms around mine, and then cradles me against his chest. "Don't worry. I think it's impossible for you to make a bad cup of coffee."

"I could if I tried," I insist.

"That's just it. You gotta *try*. Just toss in some Kona blend. You could make brewed mud this morning. Trust me. I wouldn't notice."

"You sound like you're in a good mood, Mr. Armand."

"I'm in a very good mood." He turns me in his arms and places a kiss on my nose. "I've never been in a better mood."

Something inside me loosens. Tension drains from my shoulders. I eye the coffee scoop and vow to make Malcolm the best damned cup of coffee he's ever had.

Only now I realize that it's okay if it isn't.

By the time the scent of Kona blend fills the kitchen, and Malcolm has two cups and the half and half ready to go, I feel like myself again. We'll drink our coffee, clear our heads, and then we can tackle the big problems left over from last night. We can do this, I'm certain.

Just as I think this, footfalls sound above our heads. Malcolm and I glance upward and then, at the same moment, our eyes meet.

"Belinda?" he says.

I give my head a little shake. "I didn't hear her come in last night. Did you?"

He opens his mouth as if to answer, then shuts it tight. I take that as a no. Because treading above our heads is more than one pair of feet. We could make a dash for the stairs, but we'd only meet whoever is on their way down. We could hide in the living room, but that seems cowardly.

Malcolm studies me, then he glances down at the T-shirt and boxer shorts he's wearing. His lips twitch. Before I can say anything—or toss him one of my grandmother's old aprons—Belinda charges into the kitchen.

"Okay, okay." Her words come out rushed, like she's trying to convince me of something she knows is wrong. "Before you say anything, I just want to say that I'm not..."

She stutters to a halt. Her gaze flits to Malcolm and back to me. For a brief moment, her mouth hangs open. But this is Belinda Barnes, so the shock is quickly replaced by an impish grin.

"Well, it's about time. High five?" She holds up a hand. "I think this deserves a high five."

Malcolm snorts. I scowl.

"There will be no high fives," I say, willing my cheeks not to flame. They do, of course. My entire face is on fire. Even my knees feel hot.

This only makes Belinda laugh. "Fist bump?"

I tilt my head and glare. It's then I noticed her attire, remarkably similar to my own. The man's dress shirt is a pale blue, and since she's six feet tall, hits her mid-thigh.

Then the shirt's owner clears the kitchen doorway, and the whole situation goes from slightly awkward to fairly mortifying.

Jack Carlotta stumbles over the threshold, not that there's anything on the floor to trip him up. To his credit, he swallows his shock almost immediately. Maybe that's a lawyer thing. Before he does, I see a flash of ... something in his eyes. I can't tell if it's regret or guilt or simply shame.

Once upon a time, Jack, Belinda, and I attended high school together, and once upon a time, Jack and Belinda were *the* couple. You know the kind—star athlete and homecoming queen. That was also before the ghosts started tormenting Belinda, before the drinking, before Jack left for college.

And before he started asking me out on a regular basis. By text message. I still have one on my phone from only a few weeks ago. I've never said yes. He's never stopped asking.

After last night? I'm guessing that might change.

Along with the warm scent of coffee, the air is thick with embarrassment. It's my kitchen, which I suppose makes me the one responsible for starting a conversation, offering my guests breakfast. I glance at Malcolm, but his brow is clouded with a low-grade glare aimed in Jack's direction.

They've never really liked each other.

"I have Kona blend!"

I blurt the words, and they ricochet in the tiny space. Then Belinda tips her head back and laughs. The sound of it slices through the embarrassment to the point where even Malcolm cracks a smile.

"Pour us some coffee," Belinda says, pulling on one of my grandmother's aprons. She winks at me. "And then get out of here. Jack and I will make brunch."

MALCOLM and I do end up hiding in the living room. A racket comes from the kitchen—the clatter of pots and pans, the sizzle of veggie bacon, and the aroma of biscuits baking. I cradle a cup of coffee, and if the steam doesn't do much to cool my cheeks, at least it clears my head.

Malcolm paces. He's set his cup on the mantelpiece and pauses after each lap around the living room for a sip.

"You know," he says, after he's logged at least a quarter mile.

"This isn't the way I pictured the next morning. I was hoping to cook you breakfast in bed."

"I still had to get up to make the coffee," I point out.

He makes terrible coffee. For the life of me, I can't figure out why since he's so good at everything else.

"I make okay coffee," he says.

"No, you don't."

"I do. Ask Nigel."

"But—"

"I've been faking."

"Why would you...?" I trail off, my mind whirling at this new bit of information. "But we've spent hours in the kitchen."

A sheepish expression lights his eyes while that dark-roast grin spreads across his face. "Yeah, that was kind of the point. At first, you know, before ... everything." He waves a hand toward the ceiling and the general direction of my bedroom. "I just wanted an excuse to spend time with you."

I tilt my head and go for stern. "And then it got too complicated to explain."

He raises his hands in surrender. "I know, I know. Bad habit."

I grumble a sigh, and he laughs.

"Forgive me?"

"I'll think about it."

I'm expecting him to log another quarter mile around the living room while I do. Instead, he shakes his head as if he's shaking away a thought—and the laughter that goes with it.

"What?" I ask, bracing for another confession.

"I was just thinking that we should text Gregory and Terese and invite them over for the most awkward morning-after brunch ever."

Now, I do laugh and pat the spot on the sofa next to me. "Sit?"

He does, and not too much later, I'm snuggled in his lap. His chin rests on my head, and I'm flush against his chest. His heartbeat is a strong, steady thing against my back.

"Am I forgiven?" he whispers.

"Still thinking about it."

His laughter rumbles beneath me. I'm a terrible liar, and he knows it.

I contemplate the front lawn, the spring morning. I let my gaze drift. At first, the shadow doesn't register. At first, that's all I see, a shadow stretching across my lawn. It takes a few moments before it attaches itself to the man who is so clearly casting it.

He stands on the sidewalk midpoint between my house and Sadie's. In the past months, I've seen so many necromancers stand in that very spot that I'm pretty sure he's one as well.

True, he isn't pulled together as most others I've met. His canvas trousers are the color of damp sand, worn and patched. His hair is shaggy, dipping beneath his collar, and far more gray than black. He carries a backpack slung over his shoulders. But there's something in the way he tilts his chin, tucks his hands so casually in his trouser pockets that pings sudden recognition.

I don't know him. Certainly I've never seen him before, but he's familiar in a way I can't pinpoint.

"Malcolm?"

"Hm?" It's barely an answer. His lips are too busy brushing against strands of my hair, and his fingers are intent on caressing my arms through the long sleeves of his shirt.

"I think there's a necromancer on my sidewalk."

The caressing comes to an abrupt halt. His fingers curl around my arms, and he holds me steady.

"Where?"

I part the shutters to give him a full view of my front lawn, the sidewalk, and the necromancer whose gaze is doing a slow and steady survey of my house.

Malcolm doesn't speak. He doesn't move. He is so still that dread curls in my stomach. Up until now, a necromancer on the front walk has been a harbinger of bad things. Still, this particular necromancer doesn't look all that dangerous.

"Am I right?" I prompt.

"Yeah." He exhales. "You're right. That's a necromancer." With his grip still on my arms, he eases me from his lap. "That also happens to be my father."

CHAPTER 2

I'm uncertain how long we stand in the living room; Malcolm's gaze is focused on the outside, while mine flits back and forth between him and the man on the sidewalk. Now that he's said the word, called this man *father*, I see the resemblance. In fact, I can't believe I didn't before. It's there in the tilt of the chin, the solid jawline, and the stance. More than once I've seen Nigel tuck his hands into his pockets and affect that very pose.

It's a deliberate move, one designed to make him look harmless.

The man doesn't budge, but then, neither does Malcolm. There are the wards, of course, the one around Sadie's house that Nigel put into place, and then my own that surrounds my property.

Malcolm's father hasn't dared to cross either. In my case, that makes sense. He's a stranger, and my ward is particularly strident when it comes to stranger danger, especially of the necromancer variety. But he's also Nigel's father. From what little Malcolm has told me, I know they had a falling out.

One so big he won't cross the ward and knock on the door?

"Should I invite him inside?" I ask, pitching my voice low so he can pretend not to hear the question.

Malcolm's mouth is nothing but a grim line, but he gives the slightest of nods.

I head for the door. I'm about to pull it open when I realize my state of dress—or undress as the case may be. I consider rushing upstairs to pull on some clothes. But really? That doesn't change the situation. Besides, Malcolm is still in his boxers and T-shirt and shows no signs of panic or embarrassment.

The porch is cool beneath my toes. A breeze catches the shirt-tails and chases them around my knees. I grip the rail for support and call out.

"Excuse me, Mr. Armand? Would you like to come in for some coffee?"

He abandons his contemplation of Sadie's house and turns toward me. He walks a careful line along the sidewalk until he reaches the walkway to my house.

"Are you granting me entry?" he asks. His voice is deep, a rich bass with a hint of an accent.

"I am."

He nods and continues up the walkway. At the porch, he pauses. He has the same eyes as Malcolm, dark and piercing, but where Malcolm's are so often filled with warmth and humor, his father's are flinty. Up close, I can see the years spent outdoors written on his face—entrenched grooves around his mouth, crows feet that deepen when his gaze takes me in.

"You're a Lindstrom, aren't you?" he says.

"I am."

His lips compress into a line. In that moment, he definitely resembles his son. "I was afraid of that."

I'm not certain what to say to this. I'm not certain I should even invite him inside. But he's here, on my porch, and whatever happens next, it's probably better if it happens inside.

"Malcolm's in the living room," I say. "I'll go get you a cup of coffee and be right there." I gesture toward the living room with the vain hope Malcolm will appear and do something about his father. He doesn't, so I'm reduced to asking, "How do you take it?"

"I don't suppose you have any tea."

I open my mouth, but before I can respond, he speaks again.

"No, I don't suppose you would. Extra sugar, no cream."

I give a numb sort of nod. My pulse is thrumming in my throat. My feet feel awkward and clumsy, and I'm afraid my next steps will send me tripping into the kitchen. I have no idea why this man is judging me—well, other than the fact I'm wearing his son's rented tuxedo shirt and not much else—but his gaze is not kind.

So I jut my chin forward and say, "I'm Katy Lindstrom, by the way." I hold out my hand.

He stares at it for a long moment. "Darien Armand." With what feels like reluctance, he takes my hand. "Short for Katrina?"

"It is."

He drops my hand as if he's just discovered it's covered in slime. "Like the hurricane. Seems appropriate."

Without another word, he turns toward the living room and vanishes inside.

I tiptoe a few steps closer, but nothing but silence comes from the room. I wasn't expecting a tender father-son reunion, but the absence of any reaction makes my stomach tighten once again, the dread heavier than before. There's something worse about no emotion at all.

THE KITCHEN IS A WARM, safe refuge. I'm tempted to pour that cup of coffee for myself (no sugar, just half and half), sit at the kitchen table, and send Belinda eye messages while she prepares brunch with Jack.

She's standing at the stove, clutching the spatula almost like a sword, as if she's ready to do battle. But it's Jack who speaks.

"Who the hell is that?" He's at the kitchen sink. Plump raspberries sit in a colander, their juice staining the white porcelain. He looks as if he's ready to charge into the living room, but his state of dress isn't much better than Malcolm's.

"That's Malcolm's father."

Belinda exhales and swears. "You're kidding."

"I wish I were."

A sardonic smile twists Jack's lips. "Well, that's awkward."

I spear him with a glare. "It's been an awkward morning."

A blush streaks up his cheekbones. He turns back to the raspberries.

"He's one of those badass necromancers, isn't he?" Belinda says.

I nod, slowly. "I guess so, but I don't know for sure."

"I do," she says. "He's got that vibe."

"What vibe?" There's a vibe? If so, it's news to me.

"You all have it." She turns back to the French toast on the griddle and starts flipping the slices of bread. A sizzle fills the kitchen, its steam scented with vanilla and a hint of cinnamon.

"We do?" I touch my fingers to my chest. "I do?"

"Sure. I mean, I never realized it until recently. I just thought it was something special about you and your grandmother."

"My grandmother wasn't a necromancer."

She raises an eyebrow but doesn't contradict me. "Then when Malcolm and Nigel came to town, it made sense that they'd have it too. But now I can tell it's different for each necromancer."

"I don't get that vibe." I frown, wondering if I simply haven't noticed it or if it's something I *can't* notice.

Belinda's sense of ghosts is as good as mine, even if she can't catch them. When she was little, ghosts—mostly harmless sprites—were even her friends. She chatted and played with them. Her parents chalked it up to imaginary playmates. But the fact she's so receptive makes her a target for the nastier spirits, the sort that will corner you, taunt you, truly haunt and torment you until they've drained all they can from you.

I know my grandmother tried to teach Belinda how to capture ghosts. While we've been roommates, so have I. I don't understand why she can't.

And I really don't understand what a necromancer vibe is.

I pull two cups from the cupboard and start in on the coffee. I suspect Malcolm will need a fresh cup. I'm dumping a couple of heaping tablespoons of sugar into the second cup when Jack makes a gagging sound.

"Whoa. Really?" His face puckers. "That's a lot of sugar."

"He said extra sweet." I pick up both cups and head for the door.

I can't help but wonder if this is the only sweet thing about Darien Armand.

AGAIN, I pause outside the living room entrance and soak in the quiet. Any other time, I'd say the space was empty. Except this silence feels spiteful. I glance at the cups in my hands. Kona blend can solve a multitude of problems.

I'm not sure it's up to this one.

Malcolm is at the fireplace, elbow propped on the mantelpiece, fingers rubbing his temples. Darien Armand is standing in the center of the room, his backpack at his feet.

I don't know what to make of this. I never knew my parents; they died before I was old enough to have even a fleeting memory of them. I don't understand the intricacies of a father-son relationship. I *really* don't know how to bridge the gap between these two men.

I know ghosts and coffee, so I will start there and hope something happens along the way.

I offer the extra sweet to Malcolm's father. "It's Kona blend," I say.

He takes the cup and inclines his head in what might be an acknowledgment.

"It's a favorite of ghosts." I cross the room to Malcolm and hand him the second cup. When I do, the pained expression leaves his eyes for a moment, but it returns far too quickly.

I turn so I can keep both men in my sights. "We use it on all our eradications—well, most of them. Some ghosts like tea, but you probably know that. Malcolm makes wonderful tea." The words pour from me like sugar might pour from an upturned canister, and I can't seem to stop them. They sound loud—and a little bit desperate—in this space. "We own a business together. Did you know that? K&M Ghost Eradication Specialists."

"Really?" Darien takes a sip of the coffee.

No face scrunch, despite the amount of sugar I dumped into his cup. Instead, he presses his lips together. His expression is deliberately bland as if he doesn't want to betray even a hint of admiration.

"So that would make you business partners," he says.

It's not his words so much as his tone that rankles. Malcolm lifts his head and stares at his father.

"Yes, we're partners," Malcolm says, and there's a force to his words I've never heard before. "Katy's my partner."

"I see." Darien takes another sip, and in that simple gesture is a world of condemnation.

Then it hits me. I remember Malcolm telling me about the Armands, how they've always been free-agent necromancers, how not so long ago, even Malcolm and Nigel were in competition with each other. Could that be it? Could their father disapprove of our partnership—and of me?

"You'll forgive my confusion," Darien continues. "I could've sworn it was your brother who was on his honeymoon."

A flush invades my cheeks, hot and unrelenting. Something

flashes in Malcolm's eyes, something fiery and unforgiving—and flinty. In this moment, the two men are so alike that I'm scared of what might happen next.

"That's enough."

The measured tones come from the living room's entrance. I turn to find Nigel standing there, framed by the threshold, hands tucked in his pockets. I gape, wondering at his prescience, when I see Belinda over his shoulder.

She's holding up her cell phone and gives me a little shrug.

Nigel and his father stare at each other.

"You could offer me your congratulations," Nigel says.

"Yes." Darien lets the word hang in the air. He takes another sip of coffee before adding, "I could."

Are all father-son relationships this fraught? The air is thick with unspoken accusations. Beneath that, something else simmers, not so much anger, but a deep and relentless hurt. There are wounds here that haven't had the chance to scab over.

The racket from the kitchen makes me jump. I hear the timbre of Sadie's voice, and I know she's followed Nigel and has just commandeered my kitchen from Jack.

"Katy has graciously offered you her hospitality," Nigel says. Again, it's his tone that catches me.

It catches Darien as well. His skin is too weathered to truly show a blush, but his posture shifts, he nods in my direction and almost looks contrite.

"And my wife," Nigel continues, and when he says *wife*, his eyes light up, and he can't hide his smile. "My wife is a wonderful cook. Let's talk over breakfast."

I want to point out that, technically, it's brunch, but I suspect that those are only more nonsense words that won't help this situation. Before I can make things worse, Belinda darts into the living room and grabs my hand.

"Come on," she says.

We slip past Nigel, who raises an eyebrow and then winks.

"Trust me," Belinda says as we head up the stairs. "It's always better to meet the parents when you're fully dressed."

"And you know this how?"

She merely laughs and when we reach the landing, shoves me into my room.

EVEN WITHOUT INVITING Gregory and Terese, Belinda and I have managed to host the most awkward morning-after brunch ever. Malcolm has pulled on his tuxedo trousers, and the outfit looks stylish and deliberate. But he squirms next to me in his chair like a small boy who's nervous about the next words that might come from his father's mouth.

Belinda is breezy in a sundress. I opted for jeans and one of the few blouses I own. I usually pair it with a blazer when we visit the one and only law firm in town. (Lawyers end up haunted more often than you might guess.)

If not for Sadie, I suspect the entire meal would have disintegrated into sullen silence. She sits next to Darien and has somehow kept the conversation going despite everyone else's monosyllabic responses.

In fact, she's in her element. I imagine that back when she was married to Harold that she must have hosted dozens of awkward dinner parties. What's one brunch with a wayward father-in-law?

"Nigel tells me you've traveled all over the world," she says to Darien now. "That must be fascinating."

"It is."

"Do you have a favorite place?"

"Each region has its merits."

Malcolm nudges me in the ribs. When I glance at him, he rolls his eyes.

Sadie is undeterred. That, I think, is her strength. She continues as if he's just regaled us with a tale of scaling the Andes.

"Nigel and I will be leaving soon on our honeymoon." She pauses to beam at her new husband. When she does, Nigel loses the sour expression and smiles in return. He gives her a nod of encouragement before bringing his fingertips to his lips and blowing her a kiss.

"It's not much of a trip," she continues, "but we plan to stay in a bed and breakfast up north, perhaps do some antiquing. I like to restore old things." Sadie gives a little shrug. "It's a hobby."

Darien slices a thin strip of French toast, his silverware making the barest clink against the china. "I prefer not to be weighed down by material possessions," he says before taking a precise bite.

Malcolm pokes me again. Before he can treat me to another eye roll, Nigel tosses his napkin on his plate. He stands and plants his palms on the table.

"Stop being rude. You're a guest in this house. The least you could do is behave."

Darien tilts his head in Nigel's direction. "You sound like your mother."

Sadie places a hand on Nigel's arm. "He meant no harm. Everyone's allowed their opinion on subjects. I like to restore antiques. Your father does not."

"That's just it. He did mean harm. He meant to be rude." Nigel glares, but Darien doesn't return the gesture. Instead, his gaze is fixed on Sadie.

"Oh," Darien says, as if making a sudden discovery. "You're a sensitive, aren't you?"

Her brow crinkles. "A what?"

"He means you're sensitive to ghosts," Nigel says. He relents under the steady pressure of Sadie's hand and sinks into his chair. He turns to her, his expression gentle. "That you can sense them when others can't. Like with your sprites. You know when they've snuck in before I do."

"Yes, it's true. I do sense ghosts quite easily," she says to

Darien. "Just ask Katy." She shoots me a quick look before returning her attention to him. "So I guess that makes me a ... sensitive."

"Nigel's and Malcolm's mother is one. It often works out that way, a necromancer pairing with a sensitive. It's a mutually beneficial arrangement." Darien gives Nigel a sidelong glance. "Given your ... predicament, I suppose this makes a certain amount of sense."

Nigel's eyes narrow. "You mean my addiction."

Through all this, Malcolm's hand has found mine. He laces our fingers together and tugs me just a bit closer.

"Your hand is cold," he whispers.

Both my hands are cold and have been ever since we sat down to eat.

"You okay?" he adds.

I nod, but I'm not certain that's a true answer.

"I guess that would make me a sensitive, too." Belinda gives us one of her homecoming queen smiles, looking anything but sensitive. "Just ask Katy," she adds, echoing Sadie. "So do necromancers always pair off with a sensitive, or do they ever marry or partner with each other?"

As if on cue, I feel everyone's gaze land on Malcolm and me. His fingers tighten around mine. I think the blush that started in the living room will become permanent.

"Usually not," Darien says.

"But it's not unheard of," Nigel adds, his words quick.

"I suppose it isn't, but necromancers are far too competitive. There's too much risk of betrayal. The Armands have learned that the hard way." Darien gives his head a shake as if he's shrugging off old regret. "Such arrangements never last."

Tension radiates from Malcolm's hand into mine. He leans forward, on the verge of jumping up. I'm poised to do the same arm-calming maneuver that Sadie performed on Nigel a few moments before.

Instead, Sadie stands and breaks the spell that has settled on all of us. "I think it's time for some coffee. Katy, that's your specialty. Will you help me in the kitchen?"

Malcolm gives me a quick nod. With his hands at my waist, he propels me to my feet. Belinda hops up, grabs the empty French toast platter, and rushes after us.

"I'll help too!" she sings out.

On my way to the kitchen, I peer over my shoulder at Malcolm. Despite everything, he gives me one of his sweet, dark-roast grins. It's meant to reassure me. I return the smile—or try to—but Darien's words ricochet through my mind, clouding my thoughts with words like *betrayal*.

And I wonder if he's right.

CHAPTER 3

I n the kitchen, Sadie leans against the sink, hand pressed to her chest, eyes fluttering closed for a moment.

"Oh, my," she says. "He's a cool customer, isn't he?"

"He's an ass," Belinda says.

Sadie directs a pointed look at Belinda, but there's humor beneath the reprimand—and a sigh.

"At least this explains much about the boys," she adds. "Nigel's told me some, of course, but it's a sensitive subject." Sadie pauses, her mouth twisting on the words *sensitive*. "At this point, he sees Reginald as more of a father figure than his actual father. I'm beginning to see why."

"He doesn't like me."

I blurt the words without thinking, but I know the truth of them. Darien Armand does not like me.

Sadie crosses to me. "Katy, no. It isn't personal. I doubt there are many people Darien Armand does like." She pauses and considers the ceiling. "I think it's clear that he has a great deal of hurt he hasn't ... processed yet. It has nothing to do with you."

Except, I'm pretty sure it does, but I can't pull the threads together to explain why. According to him, I'm a hurricane and a Lindstrom. The latter might be the worst of the two offenses. I can't say why he doesn't like me, only that he doesn't.

"More coffee?" Belinda says. "Seriously, the man simply hasn't had enough of your coffee."

I get to work brewing a fresh pot by pulling out the one hundred percent Kona. Even the rattle of the beans sounds expensive. It's the coffee equivalent to Dom Pérignon.

Forget Darien Armand. We have a newlywed couple to toast.

WE EMERGE FROM THE KITCHEN, a tray of cups and saucers jangling, the aroma of rich, sweet coffee paving the way for us. At least, that's what I hope it's doing.

Everyone is milling about in the living room. I peer into the dining room and see the dishes neatly stacked on the table and all the chairs pushed in.

Malcolm, I think, is responsible for these feats. Now, in the living room, he paces—or does when his father doesn't toss him a glare and halt him in his tracks. He looks desperate for something to do, and his face lights up when he sees us enter. He rushes forward and takes the tray from my hands.

"How's it going?" I whisper.

Malcolm's gaze darts toward Nigel and Darien. "Tense. It's tense, but civil. Probably because there are witnesses." He nods toward Jack, standing at the mantelpiece, who's managing to look both grim and grateful.

Belinda sets cream and sugar on the table and then crosses the room to him. Jack tucks her in the protective curve of his arm, and she snuggles next to him. Momentary worry pings at me, but this isn't high school. Belinda might be a sensitive, but she's nobody's pushover.

Malcolm sets the tray on the coffee table, and I pour two cups—

one extra sweet and one with half and half. I hold out the cups as I approach. The slightest tremor in my hands ripples the coffee's surface, but I don't spill a drop.

I haven't spilled a drop since I was eight.

Darien inclines his head again, which makes me think that's all the acknowledgment I'll get from him. Nigel cradles his cup, his smile warm.

"Thank you, Katy," he says, the words directed more at his father than at me. "Katy makes the best coffee," he adds.

"The Lindstrom women always do." Darien takes a sip. He likes the coffee; I can tell. Also? It's killing him to admit it. "It makes one ponder nature versus nurture."

"Wait," I say. "Did you know my grandmother? My mother?"

"I grew up in the necromancer community," Darien continues. "Even though the Armands like to hold ourselves apart." His gaze scans his two sons before he returns his attention to me. "A community is still a community."

"But—" I'm about to protest that my grandmother wasn't a necromancer when a revelation pops into my head. "You knew my mother."

It's not really a question, but the silent answer plays across his features before he speaks.

"Everyone"—he clears his throat—"knew your mother."

Again, it's not so much what Darien Armand says, but how he says it. The words make my cheeks sting. I don't even know what he means by those words or his tone, but when Nigel's eyes go flinty, I do know this:

It was on purpose.

Nigel gives my arm a quick squeeze before he turns on his father. "Why are you here?"

"You sent a ghost, son. You invited me to your wedding."

"Which was yesterday."

Darien shrugs, the barest lift of one shoulder. "Blame the messenger."

27

With his words, all three of us look at Malcolm. He's the one who sent the ghosts since Nigel, with his addiction, can't interact with them.

"This isn't Malcolm's fault," Nigel says, "and you didn't travel halfway around the world simply to insult someone you've never met."

"Have I insulted anyone? I certainly didn't mean to. I can't be held accountable if they took offense."

Malcolm's hand comes to rest on the small of my back. His other hand wraps around my upper arm. I feel a tug, a precautionary sort of gesture, like he's moving me out of the way of an oncoming train. I brace for what comes next. Certainly, something comes next, what with the way Nigel is glaring and Darien is studiously ignoring both his sons, his full concentration on the rotation of his teaspoon in his coffee cup.

Nigel opens his mouth. Malcolm's grip tightens. The doorbell rings.

At the sound, Sadie lets out a little gasp. I feel a wave of relief. I don't know who it might be, and at this point, don't care.

"Excuse me," I say.

In fact, I flee the room with so much relief that it's probably obscene. It feels like escaping on the last day of school, or breaking out of jail, or something. Malcolm follows right behind me, although I'm perfectly capable of answering my own door.

The bell rings again.

"Why don't you let me get it," he says.

"It's my door, Malcolm. No one is on the other side, trying to hurt me."

"I know, I know." He scrubs his face with his hands. "I'm just edgy, okay?"

I wait. After a moment, he peeks through his fingers at me and cracks a smile. Then I take his hand, and together we answer the door.

On my porch stands a girl of maybe eleven. Her hair is a riot of braids, each secured with a plastic clip in the shape of a cat. I love them immediately and wonder if I'm too old for cat clips, then realize that yes, I probably am.

"You're Tara," I say. "Aren't you?"

She nods and her braids bounce.

"You sell me cookies every year."

She nods again.

I still have several boxes in the freezer. Malcolm is patting his trouser pockets. He glances around, almost in a panic.

"I left my wallet upstairs."

My eyes meet his. I know the moment we both remember *why* his wallet is upstairs, in my bedroom. A blush burns my face—yet again—and a flash of pink streaks up Malcolm's cheekbones.

But yes, he wants to retrieve his wallet because he's the reason my freezer is so full of cookies. He can't help himself. He will buy as many cookies as he can afford and I can stuff into my freezer. He's been in town for barely a year, and already the neighborhood kids know he's a soft touch.

"I'm not here selling cookies," Tara says.

It's only now I notice how somber she is, her dark eyes sad and serious. She clutches a little purse, one of blue and yellow and in the shape of a cat.

"I want to hire you," she adds.

I send Malcolm a questioning glance. He gives his head a little shake and mouths, "Why not?"

"Okay." I exhale and check the house behind me. It's filled with tension and stranger danger. "It's too nice to be inside. Can we talk out here?"

Tara nods and the three of us settle on the steps. The wood is warm beneath me, the breeze on the cusp of losing the morning chill. The scent of lilac fills the air. My nose twitches in response.

"I know it's Sunday," Tara says, "and you were closed for the wedding—"

"Wait," Malcolm says. "Did you walk downtown?"

She bites her lip. A *yes* if I ever saw one.

"We're not closed," I say, "because most ghosts don't take Sunday off. They really can't tell time."

That almost earns me a smile, but something is wrong. I can feel the weight, the burden this little girl is carrying around with her.

"They won't stop fighting," she says, all at once, blurting much like I do at times.

"Who won't?" I lean forward, not certain where this is going.

"My parents, but they don't make any sense, and it's cold in there."

"Where?" Malcolm asks, his voice gentle.

"The living room. It's like a movie, like they're actors saying lines. They don't sound like themselves. I mean, their voices do, but not the words."

My gaze meets Malcolm's over the top of Tara's head.

"Possession?" he mouths.

I don't nod. I don't shake my head. Despite the sun warming the porch step, my limbs are like ice. I'm cold, from my toes to the pit of my stomach. I've never dealt with a possession before. That's a caliber of ghost way out of my league.

I swallow hard. My grandmother fought a possession once, all on her own. She never told me what happened or what she did to separate the ghost from the person it had inhabited. The entire family moved from Springside not long after. I remember how my grandmother came home haggard and worn, how she crawled into bed and slept for nearly twenty-four hours.

How she refused to speak of what happened when she woke.

"I can pay." Tara opens the cat purse. Inside coins glint in the sunlight. A few dollar bills rustle. She holds the purse up to Malcolm. "See? I have enough ... I think."

"More than enough." He takes the purse and snaps it closed before handing it back to her. "But consultations are free. We won't know what to charge you until we see what's going on. Sound fair?"

She beams at him. So do I. For a moment, I think we both forget our troubles—possessions and entities and estranged fathers —and just admire how the sun makes Malcolm's ebony hair gleam, how sweet that dark-roast smile is, and the way his lashes reach his cheekbones when he closes his eyes.

Yes, we both have a crush.

"Is there any coffee left?" Malcolm asks, effectively breaking the spell.

"Yes, but..." Mentally, I ransack my cupboards. What I need is my field kit—my lost field kit. "I'll need to dig out some old thermoses."

"You do that, and I'll let everyone else know they'll have to get along without us." He grins at Tara. "We have a paying customer, after all."

THE THERMOSES JANGLE and jostle inside a reusable grocery sack. A small bag of sugar thumps against my thigh. I miss my canvas field kit. I miss my collection of precision-made German thermoses and their matching cups.

Tara lives only a few blocks away. We've opted to walk, although now I'm rethinking that decision. Malcolm stops every few feet, adjusts his shoes, tugs at the tuxedo trousers. He's pulled on the shirt, but it hangs loose and unbuttoned. Despite everything, he's managed to make the outfit look intentional.

"Sorry, sorry," he says after the fourth or fifth time. "These weren't meant for hiking." His stare turns grim as he considers the shiny black dress shoes and then the expanse of sidewalk ahead of us.

"They're not," I agree, "but you *are* rocking a James Bond thing."

His expression lights up, and I swear, a bit of a blush stains his cheeks. "I'll take that as a compliment."

"But you can run home and change," I add. "I'll go on ahead and meet you there."

"No, no. If this really is a possession, you shouldn't go in alone." His gaze flits to Tara. "No one should."

He's right. I know he is. Besides, I like having him at my side, even if he's still squirming like a preschooler.

A block later, he apologizes again.

"Sorry," he says. "I mean about this morning."

I'm about to tell him it's fine, that nothing about this morning is his fault, but his eyes are dark and sad. In this moment, he looks almost lost.

"It's funny." He scrubs his face again and then runs his hands through his hair. "I promised myself that the next time I saw my father, I wouldn't completely shut down. What happens?" He casts me a sidelong glance. "I completely shut down."

"You were ambushed."

"We sent the ghost, so I'm not sure why we were both so surprised he'd show up—except we didn't think he would. We even joked about it." Malcolm shrugs. "He didn't come for my graduation from the U of M. He didn't even respond when I asked for help with Nigel's addiction. It's like we send ghosts and expect nothing in return."

What they found to joke about escapes me, but then maybe it's easier to joke than to be constantly disappointed.

"How does sending a ghost work?" I ask, in part to change the subject—he looks so miserable—and in part because I'm curious. "I mean, we count on the fact that ghosts aren't very good at navigating."

"It's ... a necromancer thing." His mouth curves into a half smile.

Ah, yes. *A necromancer thing.* "I knew you were going to say that."

"Remember when you showed Selena how to find me?"

Yes. Unfortunately.

"It's like that, only inside." He taps his head. "A ghost can glean all the information you have on someone. So I knew my father was somewhere in South America or maybe the Falklands. I grew up with him, which provides even more information. The ghost takes all that along with some navigation points and heads off."

"So sending a ghost to someone in a known location would be much easier."

"Even then you need a reliable ghost. This isn't a job for a sprite. I wouldn't trust a sprite to get a message across the room."

Tara walks ahead of us, her steps slow enough I can tell she's eavesdropping. It's a trick I used when I was her age. I was so often in the company of my grandmother and other adults, working instead of playing, that it became something I did without even thinking.

"Are you interested in ghosts?" I ask her.

She stumbles to a halt before picking up her pace.

"It's okay to be interested in ghosts."

Her pace slows. She turns around and takes a few steps backward. "It is?"

"Of course. I'm interested in ghosts."

"Yes, but you're..." Tara pauses, brow furrowing as if she can't find the right word.

I want to say: *I'm the girl who catches ghosts*, because that's what I've always been. But Tara's next words take me by surprise.

"You're a grown up."

"I am?"

Malcolm snorts a laugh. It isn't the rich, full-throated laugh that tells me he's happy. Still, a laugh is a laugh, and the sound reassures me. He nods in my direction and then rolls his eyes at Tara.

"She's been a grown up for so long she doesn't even realize it."

"I don't feel like a grown up," I protest.

Tara nods like she understands. "Because your grandmother died."

At that moment, an eleven-year-old girl speaks the truth and strips everything away. That hollow space opens up inside me, a tender ache like a fresh bruise. I want to resist the urge to touch it, but of course, I can't.

"Yes," I say, "because my grandmother died."

"I miss her," Tara says.

"I miss her too."

"She would listen to me about ghosts."

"She would?"

"When she was out working in her garden or sweeping the sidewalk," she says. "I would talk to her sometimes on my way home from school."

"My grandmother had a thing about sweeping the sidewalk," I tell Malcolm. "It was weird."

"Maybe she was using it as cover for placing a ward," he says.

I open my mouth, but nothing comes out except exasperated air. I feel as if the wind has been knocked out of me, twice in a matter of minutes. I grip his arm.

"She was placing wards." I speak the words and feel the certainty of them. "Right in front of me."

How many other things—necromancer things—did she do right in front of me? Why didn't she ever tell me, show me, explain? I have no answers, and Tara is staring at us, wide-eyed. I give myself a mental shake. We have a job to do. Maybe I can't change the past —in fact, I know I can't—but I can help this little girl with her present, and possibly her future.

"You can always talk to us about ghosts." I point to Malcolm and then myself. "We'll listen."

"I thought that might cost money." Tara's grip on the cat purse tightens.

"Or," Malcolm says, drawing out the word. "Maybe it pays money."

Her face brightens. "It does?"

"Well, it has to be good information."

We fall into step with her and continue down the sidewalk.

"Can you sense ghosts?" I ask.

Tara nods hard enough the cat clips in her braids clack together.

"Can you see them?" Malcolm pitches his voice a bit lower, like this is a serious job interview.

Tara pulls herself up tall. "Sometimes. There's a shimmery outline." She waves her hands in the air.

"Have you ever tried to catch one?" I ask.

"With Tupperware," she says. "My mom got mad because I lost the lid. And I never ended up with a ghost, anyway. I always wanted one, for a friend. But now, now that I see ... I'm sorry I ever even wished..."

One tear, and then another. She stops walking, hangs her head, and I know she doesn't want us to see her cry—she especially doesn't want Malcolm to see that. I shoo him away and kneel in front of her.

"You didn't do this to your parents. Ghosts don't work that way. They're not ... smart enough. They only have room inside them for so many thoughts, and those thoughts are about them-selves, usually something from before they were ghosts."

She nods, but her eyes still brim with tears.

"That's why it's so hard to catch them. You have to be able to sense them and be a good detective."

"And coffee," she says, the words thick with those tears.

"And you need coffee," I say.

"They really don't like instant," she adds.

"Not even sprites like instant," I confirm. "Have you tried that?"

"That's why my mom got so mad at me and told me to stop talking about ghosts." She peers up at me, the tracks of her tears staining her cheeks. "I stained the carpet."

"I've stained lots of carpets," I say. "Still do. I've been catching ghosts since I was five, which means you're old enough to help. In fact, Malcolm and I will need your help since we don't know your parents very well. So, will you?"

Tara nods again. The salt remains on her cheeks, but her eyes are filled with determination rather than tears. We start toward her house, a gray two-story with a bright blue door.

After a few steps, her small hand takes mine and we walk the rest of the way together.

CHAPTER 4

W e don't barge in. Not only is that bad manners, but ghosts are unpredictable, even on their best days. I stand with Tara on the porch while Malcolm does a circuit of the house. Gingerly, I test the door with a brush of fingertips.

The wood is warm, the brass handle gleams from sunlight, not frost. At least we don't need to battle a full-on ghost infestation along with a possible possession.

"Things look normal from the outside," Malcolm says as he rounds the corner of the house.

And no raised voices come from inside. That could be good, or it could be very bad. I reach out and ring the doorbell.

Other than a soft chime, nothing happens.

Tara regards me with the contempt only a preteen can muster. "It's my house." She rolls her eyes for good measure, opens the door, and walks inside.

Now I can hear the voices, angry and cold, although the words are indistinct. I glance at Malcolm.

"Should we?"

"It's better than letting the whole neighborhood in on this." He takes my hand. "If it's truly a possession, we'll need to be careful."

"There's only been one in Springside that I know of," I say.

"What happened?"

"That's just it. I don't know. My grandmother handled it on her own. The family moved away." I shrug. "There hasn't been one since."

"Until now."

Yes. Until now. Until Orson Yates came to town. "Do you think—?"

"I don't know what to think." He shakes his head. "Not yet."

Together, we step over the threshold. We are only halfway through the foyer when Malcolm halts.

"Feel that?" He licks his lips like he's tasting the air.

The otherworldly presence is thick, cold and penetrating. I doubt my puny offering of coffee will even make a dent. Malcolm's brow crinkles, and he glances around.

"Something about this feels ... familiar."

"Does it?" I ask.

"You don't feel it?"

"No. All I feel is cold and sorrow and..." I raise my chin to sample the air. "Deliberate, like when you know someone well and know what exactly will hurt them."

We take a few more steps toward the raised voices and the source of the cold. The farther we move into the house, the colder the air gets. The skin on my arms prickles with goose bumps. Malcolm laces his fingers with mine, and it's the only warm, safe thing in this space.

In the living room, Tara's parents rage in front of a fireplace. Closer to the entrance, there's a playpen. Inside that playpen is a little boy who can't be much more than two. He has wild, loose curls and deep, black eyes, the sort that lend his baby face the seriousness of an old soul. His arms are outstretched, but Tara's shaking her head, telling him he's too heavy.

He lobs a stuffed bunny at her.

I kneel next to the playpen. "He's more trouble than a sprite," I say.

Despite the cacophony from the other side of the room, she smiles. "He can be."

"Will he let me pick him up?"

"You can try."

So I do. He is sticky and squirmy but comes to me without complaint. I sometimes think that toddlers are very much like sprites, or sprites like toddlers—I'm not sure which.

"Hey, little man." Malcolm holds out his pinky for the baby to grasp. "What's your name?"

"Thomas Junior," Tara replies.

Thomas Junior gurgles at the attention. He releases Malcolm's finger and takes a firm hold of my hair.

I settle Thomas on my hip and study his parents. Their father is stony, arms crossed over his chest, his eyes dark like his son's, but lacking any depth. They are flinty and cold. I understand now what it means to cut someone with your eyes.

Tara's mother is on the receiving end of that. Her hair is loose and wild, with curls to match her son's, only hers seem to coil, almost snake-like. She is saying something, something passionate, but it's like her words are bubbling up from underwater.

"Man, this is brutal," Malcolm whispers in my ear.

"You can understand them?"

He pulls back and gives me a wary look. "Can't you?"

I give my head one slow, firm shake. "No."

"Really?"

"It's all garbled. Like the words are filled with static, or they're speaking underwater."

"That's weird."

It is. It really is. Unease unfurls in my stomach. Only a ghost with tremendous strength could manipulate reality so that I hear one thing and Malcolm another.

"Usually a possession like this needs direction from a powerful necromancer," he says.

"We've had several of those in town recently." And still do.

"That's what's worrying me."

"Are all possessions caused by necromancers?"

"They start that way," he says, "but some ghosts take to them and keep on possessing people ... well, forever, I guess, or until another necromancer stops them."

"What do you think this is?"

"Personal."

The word comes from Malcolm with so much force and feeling, I'm taken aback. I'm usually the one who blurts things with Malcolm following in my wake, connecting the dots of my thoughts and intuition, turning them into something logical.

I focus on Tara's parents again, thinking about what I can't hear and what Tara said. I touch her shoulder.

"How do they sound to you?"

Her lower lip juts out. "They don't fight like this."

"Do you understand their words?"

She casts me a look, one filled with relief. "Not ... really. It's a jumble. I mean, the words are real, but they're all out of order."

Well, that's more than what I'm getting from the conversation. Next to me, Malcolm has tensed. He stares at Tara's parents, not blankly, but with resignation, like he's shut down. Thomas is warm and solid on my hip. I adjust him so I can place a hand on Malcolm's upper arm.

Nothing.

"How is this familiar, Malcolm?" I keep my voice gentle.

"They always do this," he says. "They fight. He'll make her cry. He always does. He blames her for everything."

In his words, I don't hear Malcolm, my self-assured business partner, but a little boy who wishes desperately that his parents would stop fighting. Yes, this is personal. I glance from him to Tara's parents. But ... how?

I take a knee and let Thomas bounce on my thigh. I nod at Tara to come closer. When she does, I whisper.

"When did this start?"

"Late last night ... early this morning."

Up close, I can see the circles beneath her eyes and a hint of red that's more than from just tears.

"And this is new, right? They don't normally fight like this."

She nods.

Personal, I think. Familiar. Family. Could Darien Armand have brought this ghost to town with him? I can't fathom a reason why he would, and why he would unleash something like this on an unsuspecting and unrelated couple.

Thomas kicks his legs and jostles the thermoses in the grocery sack that's still slung over my shoulder. I ease him to the floor and consider where to set up. I'm not sure coffee will help. At the very least, it might clear Malcolm's head—and mine.

Thomas tugs at my shoelaces. We generally don't eradicate with toddlers underfoot. I wonder what my grandmother did all those years ago before I was old enough to help. Sprites as babysitters, perhaps? No. That could only end badly.

"Can you watch him," I say to Tara. "I need to get the coffee out. It's hot."

She clutches her brother around the waist. He flails against the confinement. A moment later, when she retrieves the stuffed bunny, he settles in her lap, content for now.

I scan the living room, searching out childproof ghost eradication sites. The mantelpiece is the most obvious place; it's also the most hazardous. Tara's parents haven't budged from the hearth. Her mother is gesturing, arms and hands wild. Her passion is no match for his stony silence.

Bookshelf, I think. I'll deploy a few cups there and work my way around the couple. Perhaps the steam will be enough to distract this ghost, so it releases its grip, if only momentarily.

Everything's a jumble in my sack, but I retrieve cups and thermoses and start pouring. The scent helps me, at least. The steam travels on the air, more around the couple than toward them. This, too, is odd.

I step forward, hand outstretched, testing the air for a possible barrier. Could a necromancer do that in addition to unleashing a ghost? Or is this simply proof of how strong this ghost is?

I don't have enough experience with necromancers or possessions to tell. My gaze darts to Malcolm, who certainly does have enough experience, but he hasn't glanced my way in minutes, hasn't reacted to the coffee. I decide I need him and cross the room with a cup laden with half and half.

He won't take it. I stand there, steam wafting beneath his nose. I touch his shoulder, gingerly. I don't want to startle him. I don't want him flinging his hands and sending the coffee flying.

Nothing. Panic grips my throat so for a moment, I can't speak, can't breathe. Dread is heavy in the pit of my stomach. I can't fight this thing without Malcolm. I'm not even sure that I can snap him out of this trance, or whatever it is.

I turn back to Tara. "You still with me?"

Her eyes are huge and worried. "Is he okay?"

"I don't know." I see no point in lying to her. My grandmother never lied to me. Well, no, that isn't true. She never lied while catching ghosts, at least, not to my knowledge. For now, that's good enough.

"It's like a trap," Tara says.

"It is, isn't it?"

"Don't fall in!"

Her plea almost makes me laugh.

Tara's mother breaks free of the hearth. She shakes out her hands as if Tara's father has been gripping her wrists this whole time.

"This is about the Lindstrom woman, isn't it?" she says.

These words shatter the air around us. These words I understand. These words make me flinch with guilt, although I can't explain why. I only know Tara as the little girl who sells me cookies every year. I've glimpsed her mother standing on the sidewalk behind her; I've never met her father.

"You're obsessed with her," she says, "with *it*. You can't go back. It's time to stop."

"I'm not the one who broke my vows." Tara's father is like granite in his response.

I don't know why I can understand the words now. I glance toward Malcolm and meet his questioning gaze.

"Katy?" He reaches a hand toward me; I set down the cup and take it. His fingers are frigid, and that, too, is strange. "What's going on? Why are they talking about you?"

Are they? Aside from a wave of irrational guilt, I don't feel like I'm being talked about. I shake my head, unable to answer. But now that he's here, with me again, maybe we can solve this together.

The coffee is cooling. Already the scent has left the air. Fresh cups, all around, I think. I'm about to suggest this to Malcolm when the tread of heavy boots sounds behind us.

Reluctantly, I turn. Over the past several months, I've come to recognize that stride. And yes, behind me, flanked by Officer Deborah Millard, is Police Chief Ramsey.

CHAPTER 5

Malcolm and I stand on the sidewalk. We stand there even as a car pulls up and a woman with the same wild curls as Tara's mother rushes inside. We're still there when she emerges minutes later with both children and an overstuffed diaper bag slung over one shoulder.

Tara breaks from her and dashes toward me. She clutches me tight around the waist and slips something into my hand, a crumpled bit of paper. She presses a finger to her lips so that I won't betray a thing; this is our secret.

She races to the car, and before she ducks inside, turns to wave. Thomas squeals a goodbye from his car seat. The woman—an aunt, I'm guessing—gives us a cold stare. She leaves us in a cloud of exhaust.

I smooth the paper, frown at the row of numbers on it, and then tuck it into my pocket.

We remain in place as if there's a ward around the house. I cast a furtive glance at the neighborhood, looking for rustling curtains in living room windows or eyes peering from a kitchen door.

Someone called Chief Ramsey at home. I'm certain of it. But we remain there, on the sidewalk, because he told us to.

At last he lumbers down the front porch steps. Behind him, Tara's mom carries an overnight bag, and Officer Millard is speaking to her in quiet, soothing tones. Chief escorts them to one of the patrol cars and sees them off. Only then does he turn his sights on us.

Malcolm's hand grips mine, but he does no more than that. He hasn't spoken since Chief Ramsey showed up. My mind has been such a jumble of thoughts that I haven't said much either. But now that strikes me as odd. We always talk things through, even when all we do is talk in circles.

Chief comes to a halt directly in front of us. "This is a domestic disturbance. You have no business here."

"But Tara—" I begin.

"I let you do your job within the bounds of the law." He points at the house behind him. "But this is not part of your job. It's part of mine."

"Does this happen often?" I doubt Chief will tell me, but I'm hoping something will give him away.

His gaze flickers, briefly, toward the house before he schools his face. No, I think, he wasn't expecting to spend his Sunday like this.

"That's none of your business," he says.

"You're right," I say. "It's not. I'm sorry. I wanted to help Tara." And catch a ghost; I still plan on catching that ghost, but Chief doesn't need to know that.

The crinkles deepen around his eyes. Chief doesn't smile, but then, he hardly ever does.

"She reminds me of you," he says. "Always trying to fix things on her own." His gaze darts toward Malcolm and the soft look vanishes. "Why are you still in your tux?"

Malcolm and I exchange glances. He opens his mouth, but Chief holds up a hand.

"Never mind. I'm better off not knowing." He shakes his head. "Go. Get out of here. Don't worry so much. Go ... be young."

With that, he heads for the remaining patrol car and leaves us there, on the sidewalk.

In the silence that comes after, Malcolm finally speaks.

"I did it again, didn't I? I completely shut down." He swears. "I can't believe I did that." His mouth goes grim, and he stares up at the sky.

"It was more than that, at least for a little while. It was like you were in a trance."

"A trance?"

"I was trying to give you a cup of coffee. You wouldn't take it."

"You were?"

"You don't remember that?"

He swears again and rubs his eyes as if they're sore or tired. "No. I don't."

"Do you remember telling me that you thought this possession was personal?"

I study him carefully, searching for any shift in his expression, any glimmer of recognition. He blinks. The clouds clear from his eyes.

"Almost? Does that even make any sense?"

Under the circumstances? As much as anything does. I hate to bring up my suspicions, but better they're out in the open now rather than festering inside me all day long. Besides, I'm not certain I can face Malcolm's father and be civil if I don't know for certain.

"Your father," I say, picking my way through each word with care. "He wouldn't—"

"Blow into town and unleash one of the most powerful ghosts we've ever encountered?"

"Yeah. That."

"He could. I mean, he's fully capable of doing that."

"But in this case?" I venture.

Malcolm scans the house, from the brick chimney to the rose bushes along the front and sides. The petals cast a rosy glow on the gray paint. From this far away, I can't feel the presence of the ghost.

"It doesn't feel like him. All necromancers have a signature." Malcolm raises his chin as if to taste the air. "Actually, this doesn't feel like anyone at all."

"Except familiar. You said it felt familiar."

"I think what I meant was the dynamic, the fighting, but not the ghost or its necromancer."

The living room curtains shift. I sense more than see Tara's father—or rather, the ghost possessing him—scrutinize us.

"We should probably leave," I say.

Malcolm nods and heaves a sigh. "Yeah. I ... it's like I'm not totally free of whatever it is."

The sun is bright on the sidewalk, and I dread going home. "I don't want to go back to my place."

It's wrong, I know, to shirk my hostess duties, but the last thing I want to do is field questions from Belinda, play referee between Darien Armand and his sons. And while I should really apologize to Sadie for ruining the first day of her honeymoon, I don't have the words for that, either.

Malcolm lifts one foot and then another. "My feet are killing me."

"We could go back to your place," I suggest. "It would be quiet, and you could change, and then we could talk this thing through."

He doesn't respond. At last, the silence forces me to turn from my contemplation of the sidewalk. He's standing there, one eyebrow raised, the smallest of smiles curving his lips.

"Are you trying to get me alone?" he says.

I laugh, and he holds out his arms.

"Come here."

So I do.

He holds me close, and I can feel his heartbeat beneath my

cheek. It's warm and safe in his arms. I hang on tightly, like I'm clinging to a life raft.

"That's better," he murmurs into my hair. "Together. We'll figure out who did this together."

Perhaps it's the warmth of Malcolm's embrace, or the fact I'm secure here as nowhere else, but my mind whirls, pulling in pieces from the last forty-eight hours. I think of the necromancers who have been in town. I consider Malcolm's words, how this haunting feels familiar. I think of my name—or at least, my last name—tossed about.

"Prescott Jones?" I venture, the suggestion quiet and easily batted away.

"Maybe he doesn't care about me, but he loves Nigel," Malcolm says. "He would do a great many things, some of them ... questionable. But hurt Nigel? No."

"So that"—I nod toward the house—"hurts Nigel?"

Malcolm pulls back, holding me at arm's length. "Oh, you're brilliant."

Well, not really, but I nod again so he'll keep talking.

"This was meant to hurt Nigel," he says. "I'm certain of it."

"And whatever this thing is, it also hurts you because you're related."

"See," he says and tugs me close again. "Brilliant."

"Not Carter Dupree." This is another improbable suggestion. The last time I saw Carter, he was about to run for his life. He's out of the state by now, possibly the country.

"Not a chance. If I'm not strong enough for something like this, there's no way he is."

Not that there's a rivalry there or anything. I refrain from rolling my eyes.

"What about...?" I'm about to suggest Orson Yates when a memory flashes across my mind.

The warehouse—and all those empty rooms with their sticky, psychic residue. An abandoned torture chamber would contain less

49

horror. I think of how Orson cornered me in the kitchen at the wedding reception, and in particular, his taunts. I grip Malcolm even tighter.

"Hey," he says. "What is it?"

"It's Orson. At the reception, when Harold's ghost was choking me, Orson was telling me how he planned for Nigel to relapse, and oh, God, he has a ghost for Belinda too, and you. He has something planned for you."

"Shh." Malcolm's whisper is gentle against my hair. "Don't move, don't make a sound. As far as anyone knows, we're just engaging in a little PDA."

"Do you think he has spies out?"

"There's a chance." He shifts and pulls his cell phone from his pocket. "I'm warning Nigel. My father might not like anyone, but he won't let an attack ghost hurt Belinda. And Reginald's still in town. They'll be okay."

"So this? This was meant for Nigel?" I ask the question simply to ponder out loud. Malcolm still has me in his embrace, his fingers texting furiously against my back.

"It might take a possession at this point," Malcolm says. "It would be a guaranteed way to force him into a relapse."

"How well does Orson know your family?"

Malcolm gives his head a little shake. "I never met the man until he came to Springside, but I grew up in the necromancer community—it's odd that I hadn't met him. True, my father isn't all that social."

Really? I hadn't noticed.

"He doesn't think much of the necromancer community in general," Malcolm adds. "He steered me away from it. Free agents and all that." He rolls his eyes. "And my grandfather respected that while training me. So here I am, left in the dark."

"Same with me," I say.

Where the words come from, I'm not sure. At that moment, I know: everything my grandmother did was deliberate. Malcolm eases back, tucks the phone into his pocket, and trains his gaze on my face. He touches my cheek, the left one, the one that still has the entity's blue cast to it.

"I think your grandmother went to great lengths to make sure that you wouldn't have any contact with the necromancer community."

"But why?"

His fingers rest on my face. He taps the blue spot gently as if he's afraid my cheek might shatter. "This is why. Mind catching me up on what happened last night?"

WE WALK to Malcolm's apartment in silence—or as silent as someone can be while his dress shoes are tapping against the sidewalk. Malcolm has his fingers laced with mine. With each step, his skin warms. I can feel the trance loosen its grip on him until—at last—he is fully Malcolm again.

We will need to consider how to eradicate that ghost. The thermoses jangle at my side, a reminder of how impenetrable this possession is. I can't fix this on my own; I can't afford to lose my partner, either.

At the door to his apartment, he fishes around in his pocket, and then with the key in the lock, turns to me.

"Would you like to come in for some tea?" His words are overly polite and formal, but his eyes glint with humor. His expression is open and warm like it was in my bedroom this morning.

At the thought, yet another blush attacks my cheeks. I nod, suddenly shy.

"Good."

He kisses me, swings open the door, and the force of the otherworldly smashes into us. An invisible hand yanks Malcolm from me and shoves him across the room. He crashes against the living room windows and the glass shakes.

I brace, certain it will crack or splinter, explode into tiny pieces. It merely wobbles, and so does he. Relief washes through me. I unsling the sack with the thermoses and try to track the ghost. Coffee hasn't done us much good so far today, but I can't imagine it will hurt.

Assuming I can pour even a single cup, that is. The ghost rolls toward me. It's like a tumbleweed, picking up bits and pieces of the apartment—junk mail and flyers for pizza delivery, receipts and bills. The thermoses spill from my bag and shoot in all directions across the floor.

The unearthly presence slams me into the front door.

"Katy!"

I sink to the floor, clawing the air for my breath, blinking hard to regain my vision. Malcolm reaches me in a flash, kneels at my side. He gathers my hands in his.

"Katy, are you okay? Say something."

I nod, unable to tell him I simply had the wind knocked out of me. Before I can stand, the ghost swoops in. I manage to point, all the early warning that Malcolm gets.

He ducks, yanks us both to the ground and covers my body with his.

"Coffee ... tea." Two words. That's all I can force out.

We work so well together that he knows what I mean. I'll distract with the coffee; he'll brew some tea. Will it be enough? If this is one of Orson's attack ghosts, I'm not certain it will.

Malcolm eases off me. He points. One thermos is under the futon, another by the flat screen television. The TV looks expensive and like it would make an excellent projectile for a ghost this strong. I opt for the thermos beneath the futon. Ghosts get enough ideas on their own.

Malcolm rummages in the kitchen. The metal clank of the samovar reverberates through the small space. I'm on my stomach, arms stretched beneath the futon, fingertips grasping for the thermos. I secure it just as an otherworldly wave washes over me. I'm flat on the floor, so other than a layer of cushions landing on top of me, I'm fine.

"Water's heating," Malcolm calls out.

Time. He still needs time. I grasp the thermos, pull up to sitting using the coffee table, then realize I have a single cup—the thermos's built in cover. That's not going to work. A strong ghost is also a thirsty ghost.

"Cup?" I send the plea toward the kitchen, which is on the other side of the breakfast bar.

Malcolm ransacks the dishwasher, pulls out something that's clearly breakable, and mouths, "Catch?"

Do I have a choice? I hold up my hands, certain this will sting, or I will drop the cup, and it will shatter.

He pitches it toward me. The cup flies through the air only to hit an invisible wall. It bounces, picks up speed, its trajectory on a collision course with Malcolm's head. He swears, ducks, and the cup explodes against the kitchen backsplash. Tiny fragments rain down into the sink.

"I'll just use the one cup," I say, my words small and contrite.

"Good idea."

I crack the thermos and release the scent of Kona blend. I yearn to close my eyes and inhale. The coffee's still hot, still fresh despite the rough morning. I don't dare lose sight of the thermos, its little cup, or the swirling fog above my head.

I pour the coffee, and steam rises from the cup. I decide not to cap the thermos. Instead, I let its steam join that from the cup. The extra amount might be enough to entice this ghost.

Oh, I have its attention. The ghost swirls above my head, its form still thick and foggy, but all its focus is on the coffee. From the kitchen, I hear a gurgle and a click. I catch a whiff of exotic spices. Until I met Malcolm, I never knew some ghosts like tea. We can only hope this is one of them.

The combined aroma absorbs the chill from the air. This ghost is still strong, still forming weather patterns on the ceiling, but we've drained some of its power. It wants something hot; it's tempted.

All at once, it swoops down. I yelp, cover my head with my hands. The ghost drains the contents of the cup in mere seconds and then does a lap around the coffee table before diving into the thermos.

The thermos clanks and rattles. It wobbles along the surface of the coffee table. Each time I try to catch it, it slips through my fingers.

Before I can yell for help, Malcolm charges across the room. He's gripping a Tupperware container and launches himself at the thermos. The Tupperware hits the coffee table, captures the wayward thermos, and skids across its surface. Malcolm lands with a thud on the floor, thermos and ghost trapped. The air clears, the ghostly fog dissipating as if sucked up by a vacuum. The Tupperware rocks in his grip, so I join him on the floor.

The container surges upward. Lukewarm coffee splatters everywhere. The thermos spins across the floor. We crash down. The ghost bucks again, and again we crash. I can only imagine what his downstairs neighbors are thinking.

But the coffee and Tupperware do their trick. The fight drains from the ghost. The air in the apartment grows warmer. What sounds like a plaintive cry comes from within the Tupperware itself. Something about it sounds familiar and tugs at my heart.

"I thought this might be an attack ghost," I say when I catch my breath.

"Yeah, but it's too ... nice."

Nice being one of those relative terms.

"It was almost too easy." Malcolm scans the coffee-splattered living area and heaves a sigh. "Almost. I'm buying the tux, aren't I?"

I peer over his shoulder and inspect the damage. He now wears a white dress shirt that's been polka-dotted with dozens of coffee-colored splotches. The tuxedo trousers are damp. I bite my lip, uncertain how to break it to him.

"That's what I thought," he says, and his sigh chases strands of my hair from my cheeks. "I'm buying the tux."

"Sorry?"

"It's not like you unleashed this ghost."

"Are you sure?"

I think back to the warehouse, to all the rooms sealed with containment fields, all those rooms filled with Springside's ghosts. I set them all free. Most were grateful, but clearly not all of them were.

"Are you a Springside ghost?" I aim my question at the container.

The Tupperware rocks.

"Did I set you free from that warehouse?"

The container rocks some more, but this ghost is losing its strength—and its anger. I'm not certain it was angry at all, maybe just scared or alone.

"Are you lost?" I ask.

From inside the container comes a pinging as if the ghost is ricocheting off the sides. The sound isn't violent. If anything, it's filled with relief.

"So which one is it?" I ask Malcolm. "Can you get a sense of it?"

"I don't want to lift the Tupperware," he says. "It still feels too wild."

Wild? I consider the swirling mass beneath the plastic. Wild is the perfect description.

"You're brilliant," I say.

"I am?"

"This is one of the wild ghosts that haunt the old barn." I bring my mouth closer to the container. "Am I right?"

The ghost thumps its response.

Malcolm sags. He doesn't release the container, but his hold relaxes, the white draining from his knuckles. I hop up to find the lid. We can't release this ghost—not yet. It's still in a mood. But now that it's made its point—it wants to go home—I can snap on the lid.

I kneel and ready the lid. We'll have to finesse this. But Malcolm is still slumped over the container. He's shaking, and panic grips me. Maybe we've underestimated this ghost.

"Malcolm?" I place a hand on his shoulder. "Are you okay?"

I get a nod—and nothing else. He continues to shake.

"Malcolm?" The panic has moved into my voice, and his name comes out as a squeak.

He holds up a hand. "Sorry … sorry." He gulps a breath, and the sound is full of laughter. "If you unleashed this ghost, then it unleashed the twelve-year-old boy in me."

He pushes off the container to reveal the ghost inside.

It's mooning us.

"Oh, very funny," I say to the ghost. "Aren't you clever." This is why we use Tupperware with opaque sides. Ghosts can manifest all sorts of images, especially when contained. At least this one is keeping it PG-13.

Malcolm is still chuckling as we snap on the lid. Once we do, he holds the container at eye level.

"You behave," he says. "Or I will personally drive you up north and paddle you into the boundary waters."

The ghost shimmers and then settles at the bottom of the container.

"So." He offers me his hand and pulls me to standing. "We're adding a trip out to the old barn to our agenda?"

"You could change first," I say. "And I think you promised me some tea."

"I did." He tugs me closer and folds me into an embrace. I snuggle against his chest, his T-shirt damp beneath my cheek. He smells of nutmeg and Kona blend.

"You know," he says, and I can feel the rumble of another

laugh. "This really, *really* isn't the way I pictured the next morning."

"But it's ours, right?" I'm so relieved to have a next morning—going on afternoon—that I'm almost grateful to the troublemaking ghost that's gently rocking its container.

Malcolm's laugh is warm against my hair. "It is, isn't it? I guess it means we're still—"

"K&M Ghost Eradication Specialists?"

"Exactly." He gives me a quick kiss, no more than a mere brush of lips. "Let me change, let's have some tea, and then we can take it from there."

I pour the tea while he changes. When he emerges from the bedroom, I do a double take. He's wearing a pair of basketball shorts and a University of Minnesota T-shirt, one with fraying at the neck, its gold faded to a pale yellow. It looks soft and like it must be his favorite.

Not that I've seen it before. Malcolm is always so pulled together. Even when he helped me rake up all the leaves last autumn, he paired some high-end skinny jeans with a fancy fleece jacket.

He's confessed to me that when he can't sleep at night, he goes running. I know he jogs a couple of miles before work each morning. Still? I'm having trouble reconciling this.

"What?" he says, turning around as if he can see his backside. "Did I forget something?"

"I just haven't seen you so ... underdressed."

His smile starts slowly, barely a tug at the corners of his mouth. Then he treats me to that sweet, dark-roast grin. "Well, except for last night."

The blush attacks once again. He laughs and then takes my hands, pulls me to the futon. We settle in, a glass of tea for each of us.

"We should talk," I say when we've both reached the bottom of the second glass.

"I don't want to, not now. I want to do this." He takes the tea glasses and places them on the coffee table.

With the pillow plumped behind us, he tugs me down, spooning me.

"This is how I pictured the next day," he says, his words a mere whisper against the nape of my neck. "Some tea and an afternoon nap."

My eyelids are heavy despite the two glasses of tea. I don't want to talk either. I want to simply be with Malcolm, no thinking, no planning, no doing.

"We'll talk later," he adds. "We always do, right?"

"We always do."

I let the warmth and safety of Malcolm's arms lull me. I don't forget about the entity, or Orson Yates, or Malcolm's estranged father. I doubt he does either. But at this moment, those things don't matter.

All that matters is how content I feel right now. I fall asleep to the rhythm of his heartbeat against my back and the soft thump, thump, thump of a ghost inside a Tupperware container.

CHAPTER 6

A persistent buzzing wakes me. I'm not sure where I am, exactly. A large, flat-screen TV looms over me. It might be threatening if I couldn't see my reflection and Malcolm's in the darkened screen. But I can. I like the picture so much that I consider buying my own television.

The buzzing continues, pauses, then starts up again. My phone. On silent. I always turn the ringer off when we go out on an eradication. The last thing you want is the ringtone blaring right as you're about to make a catch.

"What *is* that?" Malcolm murmurs against my neck.

"My phone. It's ... somewhere." Not my back pocket, where I usually tuck it.

"Did it fall out when the ghost threw you against the door?"

Oh, of course. I push to get up only to have Malcolm capture my arms.

"Stay put," he says. "I'll get it."

He tumbles up and over me. When he lands on the floor, his eyes go wide. He paws the coffee table, which is empty—no tea glasses, no ghost.

I scan the floor and point. Two glasses have rolled to a stop next to the television stand. The ghost has vanished, Tupperware and all. I'm about to panic when Malcolm lets out a laugh.

"Take a look." He nods toward the end of the futon.

There, settled by my feet, is the ghost in its container. It appears to be snoozing contently, like an ethereal golden retriever.

"We need to get that thing out to the barn," I say. "It's nothing but a troublemaker, worse than a sprite."

"Let me find your phone." He scoops up the glasses and heads toward the kitchen area. "Ah ha! Found it." He holds the phone above his head so I can see it. "It's Nigel," he adds.

A pang of guilt hits me. "How long have we been gone?"

"Too long, I'm sure, and I'm sure I'm about to hear all about it." He balances the tea glasses on top of a stack of dishes in the sink and answers the phone.

"Hey," Malcolm says and then pulls the phone away from his ear. "Hold on. I'm putting you on speaker so you can yell at both of us."

"Where the hell have you been?" Nigel's normally measured tone is taut, filled with worry and laced with anger. "It's been hours. You can't leave to investigate a possible possession and not check in. You both know that, right?"

Well, we do now.

"Sorry, sorry," Malcolm says between outbursts. "We came back to my place so I could change and ran into another ghost."

For a blissful moment, the line goes silent. Then Nigel clears his throat. "Another one?"

"A stray from the warehouse. It couldn't find its way back to its usual haunt."

"You're certain," Nigel says. "Because I wouldn't put it past Orson to deploy a spy or a decoy or—"

"Positive," I chime in. "It's one of the wild ghosts from the old barn. We're going to drop it off there on the way home."

"Be careful, because that could be where the spy or decoy or actual attack ghost is waiting."

My gaze meets Malcolm's, and a chill washes over me. I hadn't even thought of that. I feel as though I've swallowed some of Nigel's worry. What else haven't we thought of?

"We'll be careful," Malcolm says. "We're heading out now and will be back at Katy's in half an hour."

"You guys okay? Have you been fighting it this whole time?"

The quiet that follows Nigel's question stretches long and guilty. I stand and check the little clock on the kitchen stove. It's late afternoon, and we've been gone much longer than it takes to change clothes and catch a ghost.

Malcolm coughs. "We ... also took a nap."

Now the silence is incredulous.

"A nap," Nigel says, his voice full of disbelief. "Really. A nap. Never mind that Dad's in town, Orson Yates just released an untold number of attack ghosts, and I'm supposed to be on my honeymoon, you two decided to ... *oh*, you took a nap."

Wait. I don't like how Nigel's voice has gone all sly. A wash of pink stains Malcolm's cheekbones. I feel as if I'm missing something, something crucial.

"Look," Nigel says, his voice softer now and highly amused. "I get that it's ... new for you guys, and it's great that you're together, but under the circumstances—"

"We took a nap," Malcolm snaps. "Really, it was just a nap."

"Sure it was. Stop arguing and get back to Katy's. It's your turn to babysit Dad."

With that, Nigel hangs up. Neither of us moves. We simply stare at the phone resting in Malcolm's palm.

"What does he think we did, then?" I ask.

Malcolm purses his lips, and his gaze darts toward the bedroom.

So it takes me another moment, but—at last—I connect all the dots. My face grows hot, and I wonder if I'll ever stop blushing.

"He thinks we—?"

"Yep, he does." He hands me my phone and then tugs me close. "Kind of makes me wish we had."

I cast a glance over my shoulder. The ghost is rocking in its container, the motion propelling it across the futon.

"Not in front of a ghost," I say.

"You're right." He threads his fingers through my hair, easing his mouth toward mine. "They gossip way too much."

WE APPROACH the old barn cautiously, leaving Malcolm's convertible on the gravel shoulder of the county road. Although the sun won't set for several hours, a hush has fallen over the area, as if everything around us is holding its breath.

"Sense anything?" Malcolm whispers.

I shake my head. The air tastes serene. Sunlight dapples the tree-lined path in front of us, glinting off rainwater that remains in some of the deeper ruts. Even the hum of insects has faded to something soft, a lullaby of a sound.

"I don't like this." He holds the Tupperware container at eye level and peers into it.

The ghost floats, neither agitated nor happy to be home. I nod toward the barn.

"Let's just release it and run back to the car."

We both glance behind us. It's like we're worried the path back to the road will vanish, swallowed by the trees and underbrush.

"I don't like this," he says again. "It's too quiet."

Other than the copse of trees that leads up to the barn, the area is wide open. Behind the structure, fields stretch for miles. Corn this year, as far as I can tell. There's something reassuring about the pattern of bright green and dark, rich earth.

"It's kind of hard to haunt corn," I say.

"You haven't seen many horror movies, have you?"

I point to the fields. "This sort of corn. Does that look haunted to you?"

"It doesn't." He glances up, and his gaze fixes on the barn. "This, on the other hand?"

The old structure stands sturdily. My grandmother always said that it had good bones. I've taken that to mean that it's architecturally sound. The breeze turns to a moan through the open doors, and the mottled paint—of an indeterminate color—makes me think she meant something more.

"Things ... happened here," Malcolm says.

"We almost set the barn on fire once, my grandmother and I, that is."

"What?"

"It was an eradication. A new ghost was wilder than usual, causing problems over at the farm. I think it started a barn fire or maybe couldn't save the horses in one—during its life, I mean. I don't know." We're at the doors now, and I trace a smudge of gray that remains after all these years. "All ghosts want something, right? This one wanted to put out the fire."

"And save the nonexistent horses?"

I nod. "I caught it in some extra-large Tupperware."

Inside the barn, the air is cool against my cheeks and tastes dry on my tongue. Spring hasn't reached this far inside, not yet. By July, the place will feel like an oven, but right now a chill races down my spine and makes me wish I had a jacket.

"Here," I say when we reach the center. "Let's release right here." I peer into the rafters, searching out this ghost's compatriots. There are three, at least, that regularly haunt this spot.

"I still don't like this," Malcolm says, but he readies the Tupperware.

"Maybe you better let me."

He grimaces at the container. "Yeah, you probably should, but I got your back."

I smile at him. "You always do."

Before he can pass me the container, before I can crack the lid, the Tupperware shoots from Malcolm's grip. The container flies into the air with so much force that it crashes against the ceiling.

Malcolm's arms wrap around me, and he tugs me to the ground. We crouch there, hands over our heads and peer upward. The container bounces from rafter to rafter with no set pattern. A wail comes from inside the plastic, but there's nothing we can do except watch it volley back and forth.

"Do you sense anything?" Malcolm asks. "See anything?"

I raise my chin—well, as much as he will let me. Is there an otherworldly presence besides the one we brought in? Possibly. Then why haven't we detected it before now?

A hollow laugh reverberates through the space. The container makes a final pass among the rafters before bulleting toward the ground on a collision course with us.

Malcolm grips my arms even tighter and rolls me just as the Tupperware hits. It kicks up dust and hay and comes skidding to a stop at our feet. A thick coat of grit covers my lips, and an equally thick mist hangs in the air around us. I sneeze, once, twice, three times. From inside the container comes hammering and keening.

"Very funny," I say to the two ghosts that now surround us. "I suppose you left him behind at the warehouse too."

The outline of two shimmering figures appears. The ghosts bounce once and then sink to the floor as if they're dejected by my scolding. It doesn't last. With ghosts it never does.

Malcolm stands, brushes himself off, and then offers me his hand. I pick up the Tupperware, but before I crack the lid, I skewer the two ghosts with a look.

"Be nice," I say.

They dance about in anticipation. Tonight there will be all sorts of howling and goings on now that their brother has returned. I ease open the lid, and all at once, the ghost streams out.

It does a victory lap around the space before doubling back and cuffing Malcolm on the side of the head.

"Hey!" His fingers investigate the spot, and he winces. "What have I ever done to the ghosts of Springside?"

"You're a stranger," I say.

"After nearly a year?"

"I don't know. Maybe it's because you exist?"

He snorts. "You might be onto something." He takes the Tupperware and then my hand. "And I caught their ghost catcher after all." He aims his next comment toward the rafters. "Sorry, guys."

We walk from the barn, hand in hand, the ghosts dancing behind us.

IT'S close to dinner by the time we reach my house, and Sadie is in my kitchen. Honestly, I'm not certain she ever left. The air is moist, filled with the gentle slosh of the dishwasher. The counter-tops gleam. She has commandeered several of my Tupperware containers. They sit on the kitchen table, filled with chocolate chunk cookies, gooey brownies, and homemade pita chips.

I shoot a look of dismay toward Malcolm and try to muster a smile for Sadie. I'm certain it's nothing but guilty.

"There you two are!" She wraps me in a quick hug and Malcolm bends down so she can kiss his cheek. "I told Nigel not to worry. He's in the living room with your father."

This last she directs toward Malcolm, whose entire face puckers. He's teetering on the edge of shutting down again. I can feel him pulling away from all of us, not just his father.

"And"—I wave a hand at my kitchen—"This?" I can't fathom why she's been in my kitchen, baking all day long.

"Nigel doesn't want to grant our father access to Sadie's house," Malcolm says.

Sadie opens her mouth as if to deny this, but no words come out. She purses her lips and gives the barest of nods.

"So even though they're related," I say, "your father won't cross Nigel's ward?"

"Not this particular ward, and not unless he's specifically asked."

"That sounds..." I pause, trying to conjure up the right words, or at least, polite ones. I fail. "Passive aggressive."

Malcolm shrugs. "It pretty much is."

"Does your father plan to stay here?" I have a spare room, but I'm not certain I want Malcolm's father in it. I'm not certain I have a choice.

"No, if he can't find a place to camp, the most he'll do is ask to pitch his tent in your backyard."

"You're kidding," I say.

An evil sort of delight lights Malcolm's eyes. "Not at all."

"There's the campground out by the nature preserve," I offer up.

"That would be perfect. Maybe we could ask a sprite to act as an early warning system, let us know when he's on his way here. That way, we can be out on a call." Malcolm draws little air quotes around *out on a call*.

"Really," Sadie scolds. She slaps his shoulder with an oven mitt. "You're as bad as Nigel. Your father has ... issues, but he's traveled all this way to see both of you, and that says something."

"It might say something," he mutters, "but I don't think either of us is interested in listening."

Sadie rolls her eyes at me. I don't think I've ever seen her do that. Right then, I know: it's been a long day for her, too. I'm about to offer to cook dinner, but I'm grimy from the old barn. Besides, the kitchen timer rings, and her face brightens at the sound.

"The rice is done. Go." She shoos Malcolm out the kitchen door. "Katy can stay to help, but I think it's time you joined the others."

He casts a single glance over his shoulder, mouths a curse word, but heads off to the living room.

Sadie sinks against the counter but rallies quickly. "It will be the five of us for dinner."

"Belinda?"

"With Jack and Reginald. He's keeping an eye on things, and once Darien leaves for the evening, she'll come back here."

"He *is* planning on leaving."

She opens her mouth and then closes it. "I believe so." She shakes herself and laughs. "Of course he plans to leave. Dinner is almost ready. Why don't you set the table and then brew up some coffee for dessert."

I do, pulling my grandmother's wedding china from the cabinet in the dining room. I set the table, a sudden pang of loss hitting me. Maybe it was Tara's words this morning, but the ache of missing my grandmother has grown over the past few months.

I wish she could've met Malcolm. I wish she were here to tell me about necromancy—or at least explain why she never told me about it in the first place. If she were here, I suspect Darien Armand would already be out at the campground, cooking his dinner over a fire.

But she's not here. Even with Sadie in my kitchen, Belinda staying in a spare bedroom, and Malcolm in the living room, I feel inexplicably alone.

DINNER IS A TENSE THING, full of clipped words and overly polite requests for the butter and salt. By tacit agreement, we limit our conversation to Sadie's cooking, which is fantastic. She even conjured up several of Darien's favorites, although his gratitude consists of inclining his head in her direction—and little more.

Nigel grips his fork, and I worry he might snap it in two.

Coffee in the living room afterward isn't much better. Steam from the Kona blend fills the air, but it's like the aroma has lost its ability to entice or soothe. Darien clears his throat once, twice. He sets his cup on a side table, leans forward. For a moment, I think he's planning to leave, and my heart leaps with an inappropriate amount of joy.

"I suppose we should address the elephant in the room," he says instead.

I glance about, almost expecting to spot a real elephant charging across the floor.

"Elephant?" Nigel says, and he takes a sip of coffee. "Really? There's just the one?"

Darien inclines his head toward his son, an acknowledgment of sorts. "I'm speaking of the most recent transgression."

I dart a look toward Malcolm. He's standing at the mantelpiece, perhaps because it's the most neutral territory in the room. I'm perched on the edge of my grandmother's old rocker. Sadie and Nigel have the sofa. Darien has claimed a hardback chair.

In the silence that follows, it's clear no one else knows what transgression he's referring to. He sighs, clearly put out that he must explain himself.

"Once upon a time," Darien begins, "your grandfather"—he nods at Nigel and then Malcolm—"partnered with another powerful necromancer."

"Wait a minute," Nigel says. "The Armands have always been free agents."

"Not always, and not consistently." Darien directs this toward Malcolm, who appears absorbed by the bric-à-brac on the mantel-piece. "The truly powerful ghosts and the entities of this plane require more strength to control than one necromancer can muster on his own, even one as strong as your grandfather was."

Darien shifts in his seat. "And he was quite powerful." He says this to Sadie, whose eyes are wide with trepidation.

She nods, curls bouncing. The motion catches Nigel's attention. He releases her hand to capture one of her curls and lets it wrap around his finger. The tender move plants an ache in my heart.

"In this particular case, your grandfather had hoped that

together they could use their combined strength to trap an entity of considerable power."

My head jerks up at this. An entity? Of considerable power? Dread fills my stomach. For a moment, I'm afraid I'll have to dash from the room because I can't hold onto all this dread and my dinner. I don't because I know who that other necromancer was, even if she never claimed to be one.

"That was my grandmother," I say, "wasn't it?"

Darien raises an eyebrow as if the dimmest student in school has surprised him with a correct answer.

Both Nigel and Malcolm protest at once, and their replies merge into one: *Katy's grandmother wasn't ... that's impossible ... what are you saying?*

Darien casts them both a disappointed look. "You've been believing the stories Ms. Lindstrom has been feeding you."

I open my mouth in shock. "My grandmother wasn't a necromancer, at least, not in my lifetime. I didn't even know about necromancy until Malcolm explained it to me."

Across the room, Malcolm cringes. Yes, that wasn't one of our finer moments as partners.

"Do you mean to say that Lena Lindstrom gave up the practice of necromancy, and yet here you are, strong enough to capture and control that very same entity?"

Darien shocks the words from me, obliterates all my thoughts. My mind whirls as I try to process these new pieces of information. My grandmother as a necromancer? My grandmother partnering with Malcolm's grandfather? Once again, my gaze darts toward him, but he isn't looking at me. His entire focus is on his father.

"Katy doesn't lie," he says.

At least not very well.

Malcolm's eyes go flinty, and his lips twist with what looks like disgust. "That's what I do."

I'm starting to understand why.

"She grew up without knowing anything about necromancy," he adds.

"Then why does the aura of the entity surround her?" Darien sits back as if he's just delivered the final piece of evidence that will convict me. Of what, I'm not certain. "She's been deceiving you, all of you. It's only a matter of time before she betrays you."

Now Malcolm's gaze meets mine. "You were going to tell me, weren't you?"

I nod.

"But not last night?"

"I wanted last night to be about us." I don't care who hears it. I would gladly climb to the roof and shout it across the whole of Springside.

Despite everything, his expression warms. His eyes glow, and he gives me that sweet, dark-roast smile. "That's what I thought." He turns toward his father and his expression cools. Flint returns to his eyes; it's icy and sharp.

"Because Katy has a pact with the entity, she was able to save my life," he says, his words clear, distinct. "More than once. She hasn't deceived me, and I don't think she's capable of betrayal."

"That's because you're young and not—"

"Not very smart? I'm nothing more than a second-rate necromancer? At least I'm not bitter."

The hostess inside me flutters with panic. This is not polite, after-dinner conversation. Sadie is biting her lower lip as if she, too, wishes she could reel the discussion back to safer topics. Nigel, on the other hand, glances from Malcolm to his father, a hand on Sadie's as if to stop her from doing just that. The corner of his mouth tugs into a smile he aims at Malcolm, one filled with approval and admiration.

"If I'm bitter, then I have cause to be," Darien says.

Malcolm rolls his eyes.

"In the past two days alone, Katy's saved my life, at least

twice." He shoots a questioning look my way. "Orson had a gun at the reception, right?"

Sadie's eyes widen in outrage. Nigel leans toward her, whispers in her ear. Her brow furrows, and while I don't know what he said, I do know this: there will be words later.

"And then before," Malcolm says, "at the warehouse."

I manage a single nod, even as I try to push images of Malcolm, wounded and near-death from my mind.

"You see?" Malcolm turns to his father again. "Twice."

"Three times, actually, but it's gauche to keep score," says a voice that isn't mine and certainly doesn't belong to anyone currently in the room.

A chill invades the space, and the words themselves tremble the floorboards, the walls, the wood of my grandmother's rocker. I stand and hold up a hand as if that will somehow stop this thing from appearing. Because I know that voice, recognize the chill.

I'm not the only one. The cool arrogance drains from Darien's expression. Nigel appears wan. Malcolm grips the mantelpiece, but his gaze searches the room.

"Thank you," he says to the air.

"Acknowledged, although it's Katy who deserves the gratitude. You're a lucky man, especially since she's so willing to overlook your rather obvious flaws."

I don't know how Malcolm will react to that, but his laugh surprises me. He scans the ceiling as if he can zero in on the entity.

"Yes, I know. I'm lucky."

"There, you see, Darien? Your youngest isn't as dimwitted as you believe him to be."

I step forward, hands on hips. Since the entity hasn't appeared, I direct my outrage toward the sky. "But I didn't invoke you."

"No, my dear, you didn't. Call it boredom, or perhaps I'm a bit miffed you didn't invite me to your dinner party."

A spot in the center of the floor begins to swirl, a whirlpool of motion that—if you stared at it too long—might hypnotize you.

The form that emerges is not the craggy beast from the warehouse. It's humanlike again, almost benign. If someone were to peek through my window, they'd only see an extra guest, one dressed in pressed slacks and shirt. Maybe you wouldn't remember the face, and maybe the white in the shirt blazes a little too brightly.

The faded spot on my left cheek pulses in recognition—this is my entity. It commandeers the center of my living room, standing there, adjusting the cuffs of that snow-white shirt as if it doesn't realize it has captured our attention.

Then it glances up, and I'm caught in the swirling void of where its face should be.

"You don't need to invoke me in order for me to make an appearance."

That's going to put a crimp in my social life.

The thing has the audacity to laugh. Really, it isn't fair that it can read my thoughts—and always could.

"I'll limit my appearances when you're"—it pauses and shifts its attention toward Malcolm—"occupied with certain matters."

"You said three times?" As much as I don't want to, I cast my thoughts back to the warehouse. "Did I miss one?"

"In a sense. You were busy. Do you remember when I promised to guarantee Malcolm's safety if only you ran?"

I nod.

"Then here's what you missed." The entity holds out its hand, and inky smoke rises from its palm.

It has done this before, shown me scenes of Springside. This time, a portal opens up, one that looks out onto the warehouse barely two days before. I feel the tug of the past. I want to resist, hold up a hand to stop whatever happens next. Even as I wish this, I know we don't have a choice.

All at once, the portal swallows us up. The entire room plunges through mist and into the dark recesses of the warehouse. Stale air invades my mouth. My wrists sting from where the zip ties bit into my skin. My leg muscles protest the sudden speed. I run from the warehouse because it's the only way to save Malcolm.

Then it's as if a force yanks my spirit from my body. I see it retreat, dust kicking up in the wake of my strides. I'm so amazingly fast that all I want to do is watch myself run, but the scene in the warehouse grabs my attention.

Sometime during my escape, Malcolm managed to sit up. He collapses, this time onto his back. His head strikes the concrete floor, and I cry out. But a smile fights through the pain on his face, and his eyes are alight with what looks like triumph.

He shouldn't be so happy that I left him behind.

Prescott Jones and Orson Yates circle each other. The others in the warehouse keep their distance. Prescott holds up his hand, and his fingers glow with an otherworldly presence. I've seen this before, and I think he's about to unleash an attack ghost.

Before he can, Orson's face contorts, his expression both cruel and crafty. He swings around and aims the pistol at Malcolm.

The rapport leaves my ears ringing. The shot must go wide, since Malcolm still breathes, and there's no evidence of a wound. Orson fires again.

This time, I see it. Something deflects the bullet, one that would've struck Malcolm in the throat. Everyone ducks as the bullet pings off the shield. It embeds itself somewhere in the ceiling.

In the noise, Prescott slips away. The sedan outside the warehouse rumbles. By the time Orson stumbles to the door, the car is halfway down the dirt road that leads to the highway.

Orson wastes another bullet firing after it, but he is agitated, or has lousy aim. The shot plows into the ground and sends debris into the air.

And then all is quiet.

Orson turns from the retreating car. "Time to decamp," he says, tucking the pistol into his suit coat pocket. "This space has served its purpose, but it's been compromised. Leave all the ghosts in the main hallway. They aren't worth much anyway. Contain the ones in the back rooms. I'll be around to collect them shortly."

He steps into the warehouse. The space is thick with the stench of gunpowder and blood. He walks to the support pole where I'd been tied up and yanks what looks like a digital recorder from a spot about six feet up.

Again, he smiles that crafty, cruel smile. His fingers curl around the recorder, and he pockets it.

"Put him in one of the back rooms," Orson barks. He aims the toe of his shoe in Malcolm's direction.

"But—" One of Orson's flunkies cringes as the word leaves his mouth.

"As long as you don't ... damage him, no harm will come to you." He levels his gaze at the young man. "Or don't you trust me?"

The man swallows hard. He doesn't nod; he doesn't shake his head. His gaze darts to Malcolm as if he's weighing his options— an absent entity or a very real gun.

"Besides," Orson continues, "he'll only last as long as the pact does, but let's not make him easy to find."

Four men surround Malcolm. I want to cry out. I want to race across the floor to stop them. I'm strangely immobile. Despite the speed that carried me from the warehouse, I can't move my feet. No words emerge from my mouth.

Two men cradle Malcolm's legs, the others his head and shoulders. They are so very gentle, as if they know their lives depend on carrying him like one might an injured child.

They ease him to the floor of the room where I found him later. The last man to leave flicks off the light.

Everything fades to black.

CHAPTER 7

For a moment, that black is all I see. Slowly, my living room comes into focus. The sofa with Nigel and Sadie—he has her pulled close, tucked in his arm. Darien in the hardback chair, his expression like granite. Malcolm at the mantelpiece. And the entity, holding us all in its thrall.

"So you see," it says, its tone self-satisfied, "three times."

I draw in a deep breath. My legs ache as if I've just completed the run from the warehouse. I can almost taste the salt of my sweat, the grime from my time spent tethered to that pole, and the fear that burned the back of my throat.

"You can ... do that? Take us into the past?" My words are breathless, but even I can hear the curiosity in them. This is a notion that's both amazing and terrifying.

The entity brushes some imaginary lint from its shirtsleeve. "When I choose to."

"Three times then," Malcolm says. "I owe you, Katy."

I shake my head. "You don't owe me anything. I left you behind."

"And don't go thanking me again." The entity sighs, and its

75

breath turns the air icy, devoid of scent. "It was the only way to get her to leave."

"She's stubborn like that," Malcolm says.

The entity swings its head toward Malcolm. For a moment, he can only stare. His eyes don't glaze over, but he appears caught in the void where the entity's face should be. Something passes between them. Malcolm's expression shifts, determination settling on his features.

"Yes." He speaks directly to the entity. The cold, stale air absorbs his reply. A moment later, he adds, "I will."

His words are so soft, I'm not certain he's said anything at all or even what it means.

"We'll see about that," the entity murmurs.

"Parlor tricks."

The verdict comes from Darien, and an icy pit forms in my stomach. I once accused the entity of that myself.

It was an incredibly stupid thing to do.

"Ah, Darien, you doubt what I am, my power?"

"No," Darien says. "I doubt Ms. Lindstrom is truly strong enough to hold you, which makes this"—he gestures toward the center of the living room—"a sham."

The entity places a smoky hand on where its chin might be, assuming it had a face. Darien won't meet my gaze, so I look toward Nigel, who does such a convincing act of avoiding my eyes that I almost believe him. I try Malcolm. He merely shrugs.

I'm glad I'm not the only one who doesn't know what's going on.

Then Nigel clears his throat, prompted, I think, by an elbow nudge from Sadie.

"What my father is trying to say is he doesn't believe you've truly captured the entity since you haven't..." Nigel trails off.

"Haven't what?" I ask.

"Sent him away, say back to the Falklands—it was the Falklands, right?"

Darien gives a single nod.

"Or shown any concern about the three attack ghosts he has at the ready." Again, Nigel turns toward his father. "Did I miss any?"

"Your instincts, as always, are impeccable."

Only now do I see Darien's fingers glow with that unearthly light. A bit of static fills the air. In it, I taste the otherworldly. These ghosts are strong, but I can't count them, not like Nigel has. He's right. Until he mentioned it, I had no idea. The ability to hide ghosts like that is the mark of a powerful necromancer.

"But if I don't have a pact with the entity," I say, picking my way through this minefield of a conversation, "then why is it even here?"

"That's what I'd like to know," Darien responds. The light in his fingers fades, probably because Nigel called him out.

"You know, I am right here," the entity says.

"Would you tell us?" I ask.

"Well, no, but you don't need to talk around me."

I snort.

"And you're a terrible hostess. Have you even offered me a cup of coffee?"

What compels me, I can't say, but I cross to the coffee table, pour a fresh cup, and then hold it in my hands.

"Cream?" I've served this thing coffee once before, although I've never asked its preference.

"Add a little sugar as well, my dear," it says. "I'm feeling rather sweet tonight."

I do. Then I march the cup across the room and hand it to the entity. So far I'm the only one who has dared approach it. The cup slips from my grip and into the entity's, all without it brushing my skin. Even so, the vastness of this thing leaves me breathless. It holds the cup despite its ethereal form. I can see the outline of the window through the facsimile of the shirt it wears—or pretends to wear.

The moment the exchange is complete, something shifts. I feel lighter, somehow, like when I check my bank balance and see enough money to cover all the bills.

"Did I just ... pay for something?" I venture.

"Ah, you are astute." The entity doesn't so much sip the coffee as make it evaporate. "Nothing wrong with putting a little something away for a rainy day, is there now?"

I turn from the entity and face Darien Armand. He regards me, skepticism warring with shock in his expression.

"You treat it so casually. That's ... unwise."

The entity chuckles. The sound is hollow in the air and rumbles beneath our feet. "Katy and I have always had a casual relationship. Isn't that right, my dear."

The damned thing sounds so gleeful. I refrain from rolling my eyes. My focus is still on Darien.

"I could ask it to send you back to wherever right now, couldn't I?"

Darien tilts his head as if he's been expecting this threat.

"You could, my dear," the entity chimes in, "and I would gladly comply."

"I could get rid of the ghost haunting Tara's father and find the other ones that Orson has unleashed in town. Right?" My gaze remains locked on Darien.

"In mere seconds or we could draw it out, have a little fun. That part is entirely up to you."

"But that all costs something." I turn to include Nigel and Malcolm. "It's like having a credit card with a huge limit. It would be so easy to fix everything." I think of Tara and Thomas Junior. I think of Belinda and what we'll have to do to protect her. "But then you have to pay the bill."

I wonder if this is something necromancers don't understand. Even now, all three men stare at me like I'm talking nonsense. Only Sadie nods as if what I say makes any sense at all.

"And who knows what that bill is going to look like?" I add.

I already know what it's like to have impossible bills to pay. It wasn't so long ago I spread them all out on my dining room table and considered which was the better option: paying the electric company or the property taxes.

Oh, but it would be fun. That's my promise to you, assuming you decide on that path.

I shake my head and try to shake the entity's insidious words from it. "I might lose everything I was trying to save." In fact, I'm certain of it.

We would still have fun.

I turn back to the entity, arms crossed over my chest. "Really?"

It raises its hands in a gesture of surrender, although I doubt this thing has ever surrendered to anyone. "You can't blame me for trying. You, my dear, would be a delight to corrupt."

"I remain unconvinced." Darien. Again. "She's had no training. She can't even deploy a ghost. By any measure, she isn't even a necromancer."

Malcolm spins from the mantelpiece, eyes stormy and dark, and aimed at his father. I'm immobile, shock rocketing through me. Why is Darien provoking the entity? I can't imagine what proof he needs beyond this manifestation in my living room.

"She isn't even second-rate," he adds.

The entity stands in the center of the room as if it hasn't heard these words. It tilts its head toward the cup as if admiring both the container and the contents. Its form expands to surround the coffee. I know the second the last drop has evaporated, and I'm compelled to pour yet another serving.

"Thank you, my dear."

I stare into the void that should be its face. There's no expression. No telltale hint of feeling or emotion. Slowly, it nods at Darien then returns its contemplation to me. Its amusement fills the air. I suspect that—if it could—it would wink at me.

Malcolm looks ready to charge. Nigel leans forward as if he wants to leap from the couch. It's only Sadie's calming hand on his arm that holds him in place.

Then I know: Darien is not provoking the entity at all. He's provoking me—or trying to—the way he might his sons. But I'm not an Armand; I've never been anyone's son. His words don't strike me the way they so obviously do his own flesh and blood.

"I don't know what she's done, but the two of you"—Darien points, first at Malcolm and then Nigel—"have fallen for it. The gossip is ... distressing, at best."

"You're worried about gossip?" Nigel tries to shake off Sadie's hand to no avail. "Malcolm nearly died three times yesterday, and you're concerned about what a handful of necromancers are saying? Why do we even care? We're free agents."

"What one Armand does effects all of us. My business has been ... down as of late."

I want to ask what it is Darien does for a living, but Nigel glares at his father. I look first to him, then Darien, and at last toward Malcolm. I feel as if I'm missing something in all this. I suspect that missing piece might be something Darien is hiding, and that it has to do with my grandmother and Malcolm's grandfather.

I'm going to open my mouth and ask—what, I'm not certain. But I'm tired of talking around the subject. Before I can, the entity speaks.

"Yesterday almost ended very differently—for everyone involved. Would you like to see that, Darien?" The entity's words are soft, coaxing, like he's offering a wild thing a treat before springing a trap. "Would you like to see? Would you?"

Darien stares straight into the void where the entity's face should be. His eyes glaze over, and his mouth goes slack. He gives the entity a single nod.

And in that moment, I feel as if he's condemned us all.

CHAPTER 8

This time, there's no portal or preamble. I'm plunged into the stale air and grime of the warehouse. Behind me, I hear the retreating footfalls, the sound of Carter Dupree running away. At my feet, the zip tie, a few feet farther, Malcolm.

My eyes meet his. He tries to push to his elbows, but his arms tremble, and he collapses. It takes all my willpower not to rush to him, gather him close, and find a way to get us out of here. For a moment, I contemplate doing just that. What happens if we walk out the door and not look back? Even as the idea crosses my mind, I know it isn't possible. Whatever this is, we must see it through.

I take a step forward, compelled not toward Malcolm but the entity.

He shuts his eyes and shakes his head. "Katy, don't."

I don't know if he says these words or if I merely hear them in my head. And while part of me knows I could choose a different path, I'm drawn forward.

"I have to," I say, and the truth in those words strikes me hard. I have to. I must.

"Please." He tries to push up again, but he's far too injured.

"Goodbye," I whisper. "I love you."

Then I turn toward the entity and break into a run.

My hiking boots clomp against the cement floor. First Orson and then Prescott turn at my approach. Despite the dim light of the warehouse, Orson's face appears bright red. Prescott holds up a hand as if he means to stop my advance.

"Katy, no! You don't know what you're doing." Prescott takes a step, a move meant to block my access to the entity.

This is where Orson launches himself at Prescott. This is where I bypass both of them and capture the entity. This is where I run away to safety.

Instead, Prescott catches my arm. My momentum whirls us around. I stumble, missing the entity by several feet. Prescott grips my elbow. I don't know if he means to pull me away from the entity or Orson.

Except there is no entity. The warehouse holds no trace of the craggy, lava-eyed beast, the air devoid of its presence. In front of us, Orson stands, the pistol pointed in our direction. The barrel flits first toward me and then to Prescott.

"He's not going to shoot us." Prescott's whisper is hot and urgent in my ear. For once, he doesn't sound convinced of what he's saying. "He wouldn't dare. Too many questions from the necromancer community, too messy."

Despite the reassurance, I can't swallow back the thick panic in my throat. My limbs are icy with dread because Orson Yates has already killed. I'm not sure how I know this, but the moment the thought passes through my mind, I know it's true.

Orson's expression shifts, that crafty, cruel look lighting his eyes. That's when I catch movement in my peripheral vision. That's when I see Malcolm sit up, attempt to stand. I want to yell at him to run, but I know he won't. Like always, he's trying to come to my rescue.

Orson swings around. I know where he's aiming the gun. I know what he plans to do. Without thinking, I launch myself forward. With luck, I'll have enough time. With luck, I'll be able to block the bullet or cause the shot to go wide. I slip from Prescott's grasp with no effort at all. A few more steps and I'm in between Orson and Malcolm.

For one second, I think someone has punched me in the back. But the sensation is too hot, too precise for that. Orson's bullet pierces us both, me through the spine and Malcolm through the shoulder. The rapport echoes, the sound bouncing off the warehouse walls and inside my head.

Malcolm stumbles backward, knees buckling, and he falls onto the floor. A cry lodges in my throat; my breathing stops. For a moment, my body hangs suspended in the air. Then I come crashing down, tumbling on top of Malcolm.

I can't feel him, but I sense his warmth; I'm grateful for it because I'm cold, so very cold. He holds me, one hand anchored at the small of my back, the other cradling my head.

In all of this, his murmur plays in my ear.

"Katy, Katy, Katy."

It sounds like a prayer.

Something inside me releases its grasp. I float upward, leaving my body behind. Malcolm still embraces me; he still chants my name, but I can see us now, there on the gray and dusty warehouse floor. A pool of blood spreads beneath him, growing ever wider.

Orson Yates stands a few yards away, pistol lowered but clutched so hard his knuckles are white. I wonder if this means I'm a ghost now. If so, I will haunt him until the day he dies.

A hush falls over the space. In the distance comes the rumble of a sedan, of tires churning up gravel. I don't need to look to know Prescott is gone. Everyone else is silent.

Except for Malcolm. Each time he says my name, his voice grows weaker, the syllables come slower. His fingers slip from my hair in a final caress. He mouths my name one last time. Then the light leaves his eyes.

No one moves. Outside the warehouse, a songbird warbles.

Inside, wails echo in the hallway where all the ghosts are locked behind containment fields.

Orson shakes himself as if waking from a dream. The pistol slides from his grip and strikes the floor. The clatter shocks everyone else into action. They scurry about, frantic, gazes darting everywhere except where Malcolm and I remain crumpled on the warehouse floor. Orson walks to the pole and yanks the digital recorder free. He lets it rest in the palm of his hand before his fingers curl around it.

He looks up, stares through the very space where I'm floating. With deliberation, he tucks the recorder into his suit coat pocket.

Then, he smiles.

AIR RUSHES INTO MY LUNGS. The cry lodged in my throat emerges, and I sound like a wounded animal. I choke and gasp before doubling over. Instead of concrete, I see the living room's worn carpet and the floorboards that need to be refinished. The scent of Kona blend warms the air, and a hint of lilac sneaks in through an open window. I hold still because if this is an illusion, I don't want to break it.

Across the room, Malcolm coughs so hard he must grip the mantelpiece to remain standing. Sadie weeps against Nigel's shoulder. His eyes are damp, mouth a grim line. Darien holds himself rigid in his hardback chair like a man waiting for execution.

"A very different ending," the entity says. Its voice remains soft as if it has just finished telling us a bedtime story. "Imagine the gossip were this to have happened, Darien." The entity shrugs. "Ah, well, at least you would've arrived in time for the funeral."

Darien remains stoic. I can't tell if he's even heard the entity.

"You can ... show us things that didn't happen?" The words feel rough against the back of my throat, and the taste of the warehouse is stale on my tongue.

"If I am more prescient than mere mortals, it's only because I collect and synthesize a great deal more than they can. But in this instance, the outcome came down to a moment's hesitation on the part of Prescott Jones. So unlike him." The entity shakes its head. "If you ever see him again, my dear, you must ask him why."

"Can you show us things that will happen?" I ask.

"I can show you possibilities, but that is all." The entity spreads its arms. "The future depends on so many tiny actions made in the moment, as you've witnessed."

That makes sense, not that I plan to ask the entity for such a favor. That, I suspect, comes with too high a cost. Besides, no one here needs to be clairvoyant to guess what Orson Yates might do with any entity, never mind this one.

"Katy."

My heart leaps at the sound of Malcolm's voice. It has the same tenor, that same prayer-like quality as it did in the warehouse. In the warehouse that never was, I tell myself. Except I can't convince myself of that. Even though I'm standing here in my own living room, alive and whole, part of me knows that somehow, somewhere I died, that Malcolm died.

I meet his gaze. His eyes are dark, unfathomable. He grips the mantelpiece, but I think now it's keeping him in place rather than holding him up.

"Katy," he says again, like he can't believe this is our reality. He pushes from the mantelpiece and charges across the space.

Like before, I don't think. I run to him. I will always run to Malcolm Armand. There is something about him that feels like home; he is home. Even so, fear grips me, because before we touch, I doubt he's truly here, that he's still alive.

He is. He takes my head in his hands. His gaze is so intense that it steals all my words, my thoughts.

"Katy, don't, just … if it ever comes to that, don't do anything like that again."

I shake my head as much as his grip will let me. Tears dampen my eyes. I can't promise him that because if there's ever a chance I could save him, I would.

He pulls me close and kisses me then. The feel of it is dark and dizzying, like we've plunged into the blackness again. Everything falls away until it's just the two of us, alone. And I wish with all my heart that it would stay like that.

Someone clearing their throat has no effect, although I register the sound in the back of my mind. I should probably ask everyone to leave, but can't muster the will. All I can do is hang onto Malcolm, ever fearful that if I let go, I'll lose him forever.

"Hey, you two." Nigel's gentle voice intrudes. He's there, next to us, although I don't remember him standing, walking. I don't remember Sadie, either, but she's there with him, her eyes swollen and worried.

Malcolm eases his mouth away from mine, but he doesn't let go. Nigel grips us both by the shoulder.

"We'll talk more in the morning, but for now, take care of each other." He squeezes and pulls us closer. "You." He gives Malcolm a tap on the head. "Stop being such a hero." He turns to me. "That goes double for you."

Nigel steps back to let Sadie hug us close. Sobs shake her body, and she plants a damp kiss on each of our cheeks.

Then it's just Malcolm, Darien, and me.

Malcolm's father doesn't speak. He doesn't embrace either of us. He does, however, give Malcolm a nod of what might be approval. I'm not sure it extends to me, but I doubt that matters.

At the front door, he hefts his backpack onto his shoulders.

We don't ask where he's going; he doesn't tell us.

The door closes behind him with a soft click. A moment later, Malcolm throws the deadbolt.

"I don't want to leave you," he says, but his hand still rests on the lock. I worry that he thinks too much has happened, that it's better if he does leave.

"Just because everyone else left doesn't mean you have to."

He turns then and sinks against the door. He curls his fingers in a come-here gesture.

I do.

"I don't have anything here," he whispers.

"I gave you a toothbrush."

"I mean clothes, pajamas."

"You have clothes." I pluck the hem of his shirt. "And do you really need pajamas?"

"I don't know." A warm, sweet smile tugs at his lips. "Will I?"

"I doubt it."

"If you say so." He buries his face against my neck. "Jesus, Katy, I can't shake the idea of it. I'm afraid this is an illusion, and if I move too fast or do too much, I'll shatter it."

I'm afraid that if I speak, I'll shatter this as well. So instead, I take his hands and urge him toward the staircase.

We climb the stairs at a glacial pace. Malcolm stops to sweep strands of hair from my face. I pause to tuck the tag of his shirt beneath its collar. I touch his cheek, find the pulse in his neck, press my palm against his chest and feel the rise and fall of his breath.

When we reach the landing, I realize the entity vanished without my noticing. It's just Malcolm and me, the two of us alone —the thing I wished for with all my heart. Something shifts in the air, a balancing of sorts.

My heart's desire, all for a cup of coffee.

Something tells me that, next time, the exchange won't be quite as easy.

I'M NESTLED in Malcolm's arms. Everything is warm and safe here, just as I wished for. A breeze flutters the curtains. The night outside the bedroom window is quiet except for an occasional cricket or dog bark.

I should sleep, but my mind whirls. I struggle to piece together everything I know and test it against everything I believe, but the gaps between the two are vast.

"What are you thinking about?" Malcolm's voice is a low rumble beneath me. The sound is rich and warm, and his breath chases those wayward strands of hair across my forehead.

"You're awake?" It's an inane sort of question, but he only laughs.

"Your thoughts are so loud that I'm surprised the entire neighborhood isn't awake."

I sigh. "Sorry. I'm just trying to pull everything together."

"I figured as much." His fingers stroke the line of my brow. "Don't think so hard."

"Can't help it. I'm just so ... I was wondering about everything, like back at the mausoleum. Remember when you said you were getting a vendetta vibe from the entity? Were you—?"

"Lying?"

I cringe. "Yeah. That."

"Given my track record, it's a fair question." Malcolm shifts and I roll to see his face.

In the dark, it's hard to discern his expression, but I detect no guile.

"I was telling the truth, at least about the vibe. I mean, I thought it was about you, which makes sense considering its actions back then. But I wonder. Maybe it just *involves* you somehow."

"How?"

He tugs me close for a quick kiss. "If we knew that, we'd probably know everything."

I suppose we would.

"I thought maybe tonight was part of a vendetta," I add, "putting us through that alternate reality."

"I suspect it was more of an object lesson for my father."

Or for me. I ponder this and the entity in general. I'm here, right now, alone with Malcolm, because of the entity, because I captured it, and because now I'm its necromancer—or so it says. I'm not cold and dead on a warehouse floor, and neither is Malcolm. Yes, I think, this evening was a not-so-subtle reminder of all that.

"I don't understand the entity, what it wants. It haunts me, it marks me, and now it does me favors—for a price—and it talks to me like—"

"Like it's trying to seduce you. Yeah, noticed that, don't like it." His chest heaves with an exhale. "This entity doesn't have a morality like humans do, but it does honor its agreements, and it's made one with you. But it's still going to get as much from that deal as possible."

"Sounds like a stockbroker," I say.

"Hey!"

"Or a necromancer. No wonder every last one of you is chasing it down. That's what you were doing, right? When you came to Springside."

"Yes, and no. I did come to speak to your grandmother, and rumors had surfaced about this entity. That must have been about the time she died, and it was free of the pact your grandmother made with it."

We're quiet for a moment, my mind filled with missing my grandmother. Malcolm strokes my hair as if that alone can take the sadness away.

"At first it was all about me," he says, his voice quiet. "Yeah, surprise, right?"

I can't help it. I laugh.

"Then I thought if I could catch it, I could make a bunch of money and impress you and then, you know, other stuff."

"Basically what we're doing now."

"Pretty much," he says and pulls me in for another kiss. "But the entity was right. My attention shattered. You shattered it. I could've caught it before Nigel did, but I think even then, I knew I wouldn't be able to hold it. Real life with you was better than my imaginary one."

Real life with Malcolm still astonishes me. I couldn't have imagined it, and some days can't believe it's true. I have no idea what my life would've been like if he hadn't zoomed into town in his cherry-red convertible.

"I think it goes back even farther," I say after a moment. Malcolm's fingers play up and down my spine. As distracting as that is, my mind is buzzing too hard to concentrate on anything other than the entity.

Well, almost.

"Something happened with my grandmother and your grandfather."

"I wouldn't trust anything my father says."

"Something happened, and..." I fight to put the thoughts I have into actual words. "And maybe instead of you chasing the entity, it lured you to Springside."

Malcolm bolts upright and sends me tumbling toward the edge of the bed. He swears. I flop back to wait until he works through most of his vocabulary.

"Christ, you're brilliant, you know that?" He reaches for me and settles us among the pillows again.

"Not really. If I were brilliant, I would've figured that out months ago."

"This changes things. This feels like we're onto something."

"Maybe. There's more, maybe something to do with my mother as well," I say. "Remember at Tara's house, and her mother talking about the Lindstrom woman? Let's assume she didn't mean me since I don't even know Tara's father."

"So, that leaves two Lindstrom women, right?"

Enough lamplight filters through the curtains that I see a curious smile curve Malcolm's lips. "Do all Lindstrom women keep their maiden name?" he asks.

"It's tradition. My grandmother made me promise that if or when I ever got married I wouldn't take my husband's name."

"You know that's a necromancer thing, right?"

"What?" This time, I bolt upright and nearly clock Malcolm in the jaw. "I can't believe you're telling me this now."

"I never really thought about it until now. Female necromancers ... I wouldn't say they're rare, but those who practice the craft keep their maiden names. Like your grandmother. And your mother."

"That's the second thing your father said to me. He asked if I was a Lindstrom."

"What did he say when you told him yes?"

"He said, 'I was afraid of that.'"

Malcolm's body shakes, but his laughter is a dark thing I don't much like.

"My father, always the diplomat. Jesus."

"Forget your father for a moment—actually, don't. I have the feeling you'll need to think about him if we're going to eradicate the ghost possessing Tara's father. Remember what Tara's mother said?"

Malcolm exhales. "Something along the lines of you're obsessed with her, with *it*."

"The entity?"

He falls silent.

"What does your father do? I mean, as a necromancer."

"He's an expert at tracking and capturing very powerful, very elusive ghosts—usually for a very high price." He meets my gaze then, but his eyes are shrouded both by his lashes and the dark. "These aren't Springside ghosts. These are ghosts who live in the jungle or the Sahara or wherever because they want zero interaction with humans."

"Could he catch the entity?"

"I don't know. Possibly? Probably?"

"Do you think he maybe wanted to at one time? Do you think maybe my mother did?"

"Huh. That's an interesting way to look at it."

"Maybe she hired him?" I suggest.

"Or maybe they were working together." His fingers continue to explore, caress, as if he could pull answers from my skin. "I mean, clearly, the Armands aren't the free agents we like to claim we are." He pauses, stares at the ceiling. "But why would they work together?"

I never knew my father; I didn't grow up with a grandfather. But I feel the loss of my grandmother acutely. Some days, the pain stabs as sharply as it did on that morning I found her. What if you felt that every day, but there was something you could do about it?

"My grandmother never had a funeral for my grandfather. There's a plot—an empty one—in the Springside cemetery that was supposed to be his. I don't know what she told everyone. I could ask someone, Mr. Carlotta or Chief Ramsey maybe. What if she—or my mother—wanted to get my grandfather back?"

Malcolm falls silent again. His mouth isn't grim, but it's lost its smile.

"I don't suppose that's something your father would tell us?" I prompt.

"You suppose right."

Just what Springside needs: yet another necromancer with an agenda. Malcolm's fingers thread through my hair. I know it must be late, but the night seems to stretch before us endlessly. He kisses my forehead and then my nose. I have so many thoughts about everything that I'm certain they'll all burst out at once.

I blurt the first one that feels the most crucial. "Orson Yates."

Malcolm snorts. "If you're trying to turn me on, that's not the way to do it."

I laugh and burrow closer to him. "I'm curious about what he might know about your family, or really, your parents' marriage."

"Everyone in the necromancer community knows enough, so that includes Orson. Their breakup was epic. We're talking drama on the level of a soap opera. My mother is ... dramatic. Imagine the polar opposite of my father."

Yet another person I can't wait to meet.

"And Orson doesn't much like Nigel," I say. "I mean, even before all of this, at least not from the sound of it."

"You didn't know Nigel before the addiction. Katy, he was amazing. His strength rivaled my father's. He was going to do great things."

"I can't imagine Orson liked that."

"No, not at all."

After only six months, Orson knows me well enough that, to hurt me, he stole all of Springside's ghosts, and then kidnapped and nearly killed Malcolm. How well might he know the Armands? What could he do with that knowledge?

"Why did this ghost attack Tara's family?" I ask.

"Orson ... left in a hurry." He shakes his head and laughs softly.

Yes, and Malcolm was a big part of that.

"He probably unleashed the ghosts he had with him and went somewhere to lick his wounds," he adds. "You know how bad some ghosts are at directions. Some can't find their way across town."

Or back to the old barn.

"And this ghost picked Tara's family because?"

Part of me wants to jab Malcolm in the chest, prod him to think harder on this. I scowl as if I can help him do that thinking.

He sighs. "Because there's something about her family that looks an awful lot like mine."

"And that would be?"

He takes my head in his hands and cups my face. "Katy, I just don't know."

"Or maybe you don't want to think about it."

"That. Exactly."

"You need to. You need to think about your father."

"No, no, I don't. The world is a better place when you don't think about my father. Trust me, I've had years of practice not thinking about my father."

He tugs me closer still. I open my mouth to protest, but he swallows my words with a kiss. He hooks a leg around mine, and we roll. I can't help but laugh again. There's something so wonderful about being with him like this.

He nuzzles my neck, kisses the hollow of my collarbone. So gentle. So soft.

"What are you doing?" I whisper, afraid to break the spell.

"Not thinking about my father." He peers at me, and we're close enough that I can see the warmth and humor in his eyes. "Doesn't this night feel like a gift?"

It does; it really does. On the breeze, I catch a whisper of something that sounds almost like an admonishment. My heart's desire, and I'm squandering it. I push away the fear of what might come next. Instead, I thread my fingers through Malcolm's hair and pull him to me.

"You're right," I say. "Let's not waste it."

CHAPTER 9

Everyone should wake up to the scent of cinnamon and a hint of lilac in the air. I haven't opened my eyes, but the mattress shifts with Malcolm's weight. The clean aroma of Ivory Soap joins the one from the cinnamon rolls.

At least, I hope it's cinnamon rolls.

The urge to open my eyes nearly overwhelms me. If I don't, then it's still, technically, last night. If I don't, then I can keep the problems of today in the recesses of my mind, if only for a few more moments.

But when the smell of coffee—real, percolator-brewed coffee—reaches me, I nearly fall out of bed.

The only reason I don't tumble to the floor is Malcolm, sitting on the edge of the bed, all pressed and gelled. He's immaculate, of course, white dress shirt and creased khakis. In comparison, I'm ... rumpled.

"Morning, beautiful." He holds up a tray. "Look. Breakfast in bed."

"You made me cinnamon rolls?"

"Well, sort of. I popped them from a can, but—"

"That counts."

"And I also made you some..." He lets the sentence trail and reaches for an insulated carafe. He pours and then hands me a cup. "Coffee."

The cup warms my fingers, and the scent fills the pocket of space between us.

Malcolm sits back, hands planted on his thighs. "Okay. I'm ready for your honest opinion."

I roll my eyes, but I do sip, tentatively at first. The dark roast is bold, with a hint of cocoa. And it's good. Really good.

"My grandmother would be proud."

"You're just saying that."

To prove my point, I down the entire cup and then hold it out. "More? Please?"

"So it passes muster?"

I merely nod because, by this time, I've snagged a cinnamon roll and my mouth is too full of cream cheese icing and flakey layers for actual words. The second cup clears away the gooey sweetness and the fog from my head.

"These are the best cinnamon rolls I've ever had."

"They're not really homemade."

"They're still the best," I say, and I hope he takes my meaning.

The smile he gives me is almost shy. "You win. They're the best."

"And this?" I say, waving a hand at the whole package that is Malcolm Armand, ready for business. "Does this mean what I think it does?"

"Probably. If you hurry, we might be able to eradicate this ghost in time for Thomas Sr. to make it to work."

We eradicate at all hours of the day—and night—it's true. An early morning one like this? It feels right. The ghost won't expect us back so soon and neither will Chief Ramsey. I plant a sticky kiss on Malcolm's cheek on my way to the shower.

Just before the door closes behind me, I hear his murmur.

"It's about time I started thinking about my father."

THE BLUE DOOR of Tara's house glows in the sunrise. The sight is hopeful—almost. Since yesterday, the color has faded a shade or two, but at least the paint isn't peeling. Not yet, anyway.

"Does it look like a full-on infestation to you?" Malcolm whispers.

I can't tell, not from this distance. The grass sports patches of brown that weren't there yesterday. Several of the roses droop, heads bowed as if in mourning, petals scattered along the ground.

"I don't know," I say. "It may not bother until we're committed."

That would trap us inside.

We continue to stare at the house, putting off that moment of commitment, probably because our plan is sketchy, at best. I carry a percolator and everything to brew coffee, but I don't think we'll need it. In this case, I think it will be the samovar and the tea that will make the difference.

"My grandfather showed me how," he says now, an echo of our previous conversation.

"Do you think you can?"

His mouth is grim. "If I can draw out the ghost, it will be up to you to catch it."

I shift the bag on my shoulder. The Tupperware containers rattle. Malcolm's never even witnessed a possession, but his grandfather did instruct him on what to do. That's more than what I know.

The sound of a car door shutting punctuates the air. I don't think much of it. Springside has its share of early risers. It's only when someone clears his throat behind us that I make the connection.

"Do you even have a plan for getting inside the house?"

The words are calm and measured, but they send my heart racing. I whirl at the same moment Malcolm does. Behind us, Nigel and Sadie stand, arms linked. An amused smile plays on Nigel's lips. Sadie has the look of a soldier going to war.

"What are you doing here?" Malcolm says. "Are you crazy?"

"No more than you." Nigel studies the house as if he can calculate the risks from the sidewalk. "I might be an addict, but I'm still a necromancer."

"World-class," Malcolm says, his voice soft, full of admiration.

"Neither of you have faced something like that." Nigel points to the patches of brown, bricks in the chimney that have turned gray. "The entity notwithstanding. Not only is this thing stronger than Harold's ghost, but this is also a possession. You have no idea what that means."

He's right, of course. Still. "And it was sent here to possess you," I say.

"Which makes me the perfect bait."

Malcolm gives his head a violent shake. "Oh, no. Not that."

"You think tea is going to work, baby brother? Amateur move. This thing already has substance and heat, in the form of a human body. Tea isn't tempting it. Even Katy's coffee won't tempt it. But its original target? It was sent here for me. It's the least I can do."

"It might be the least, but it's also the stupidest," Malcolm shoots back. "I already lost you once. I don't want that to happen again. I saw what happened when you couldn't stop swallowing ghosts."

"And I watched you die yesterday. I think that makes us even."

Their voices are rising with the sun. I cast a hasty look up and down the street, watch for curtains fluttering in windows and people peering out of doors. The last thing we need is a concerned neighbor calling the Springside Police Department yet again. I send Sadie a pleading look.

"Nigel." Sadie pats his arm. "Malcolm is only concerned. And

Malcolm? Why do you think I'm here? I'm not losing him. Neither of us is."

They both scowl. Nigel makes a face. Malcolm rolls his eyes.

"Honestly," I say in disgust, "I sometimes think you two just like to fight."

"Yes, Katrina Lindstrom. They do."

My heart leaps again. Sadie lets out a little gasp. Nigel's eyes widen, more in recognition than surprise.

How Reginald Weaver came to be standing next to us I may never know. But he's here, sturdy and calm, his form casting a long shadow across the lawn.

"What are you—?" Nigel begins.

"You're quite predictable, my friend." Reginald nods toward Sadie. "Plus, your lovely bride was concerned."

Nigel glowers, but the look washes over Sadie. Instead, she beams at Reginald. His appearance eases the worry inside me. I step back and consider our little group. There's Malcolm, who's always at my side. Nigel, who was once addicted to swallowing ghosts, and Sadie, who has a lifelong fear of them. Add an enigmatic and reclusive necromancer? We're an unlikely team. Even so?

We might be able to do this.

"Who's coming inside with me?" I ask.

Nigel blinks. "You have a way in?"

From my pocket, I pull the crumpled piece of paper Tara shoved into my hand yesterday. "I do."

"Do you also have a plan?" he counters.

I give him a pointed look. "Isn't that why you're here?"

Nigel rubs his temples. "You're worse than Malcolm."

"Actually," I say, "I don't think we should all go in at once, or through the front door. I think it should just be me."

"Katy," Malcolm begins, "I don't think—"

"It put you in a trance yesterday," I say and then point toward

Nigel. "He's this thing's target. It knows me, but it can't hurt me the way it can the two of you."

Reginald nods. "Yes, that is our best option. There's an alleyway around back. You can let us in through the kitchen door."

I tilt my head, curious about how he knows this.

"I, perhaps, did some reconnaissance last night." He nods in my direction. "You be careful, Katrina Lindstrom. Get to the back door as quickly as possible. Remember, the ghost will try to stop you."

Malcolm cringes as if the last thing he wants is to send me in alone. But he takes our makeshift field kit and slings the bag of Tupperware over his shoulder before tugging me in for a quick kiss.

"Let's do this," he says.

And then I'm alone, feet planted on the walkway, staring at the gray two-story house with the fading blue door.

A CHILL SHROUDS the front porch. It's not a full-on ghost infestation, but the house is rapidly aging, becoming haunted. It has the feel of a place long abandoned and unloved.

I study the series of numbers scrawled on the tiny piece of paper in my palm. The keypad barely registered yesterday. Despite my bravado on the sidewalk, I'm not one hundred percent certain I can get in.

I test the door with a brush of a fingertip, just in case I'm wrong about the infestation. The surface is cool, but not so cold I'll risk frostbite. Each key beeps as I press it. A light flashes. The deadbolt churns in the mechanism.

So far, so good.

Then, on its own accord, the door creaks open.

Or not so good.

The foyer is dim. The air is cold and stale and makes the back of my throat ache. This is what anger might taste like. And while I know Reginald told me to hurry, I can't force my feet to move any faster, not even when the door groans closed behind me.

I test out each step as if I could move through the air without disturbing it. I don't know where this ghost might be, except it must still possess Tara's father. That means it must be somewhere physical. Upstairs in bed. On the living room couch. But not in the ventilation system or floating along the ceiling.

A clatter echoes through the house, of someone ransacking cupboards or pulling items from a bookshelf. I freeze and try to gauge where the sound is coming from, but the noise clouds my head. It's everywhere and nowhere all at once.

Kitchen. I need to get there, let everyone in. A sliver of icy air curls around me. I inch forward, and it grasps at me again, twists around my ankles and knees. I don't trip, but each step I take is slower. My lungs must work harder to pull in a full breath. An icy tendril worms its way higher until I feel it caress my throat.

I grab onto the wall and drag myself forward. This thing knows my fear, that awful sensation of not being able to breathe. I close my eyes—briefly—and focus. But my heart still pounds; my breathing is ragged.

Frantic thoughts ping in the back of my mind. I'm not going to make it to the kitchen.

A menacing force builds behind me. I glance over my shoulder to no avail. I can't see this thing, but I sense it, and it's poised to pounce. Kitchen, I think. Get to the kitchen.

Up ahead is the living room, and beyond that, the entrance to the kitchen. I keep it in my sights, even as the hallway plunges into darkness. I go on instinct, clawing my way forward. I yank and jerk and pull free of the tacky air and burst into the wintry light of the kitchen—and nearly crash into Thomas.

I stumble backward, hands held up as if that will ward him off. He looms in front of me. Overnight, his hair has turned pure white. His skin looks as if it's been coated in wax. There's a human somewhere beneath all the layers, but he doesn't have enough warmth or strength to fight his way out. His lips are cracked and pale, fingers thick and clumsy.

But his eyes. Oh, his eyes aren't his own. Those belong to the ghost, and they regard me with perverse delight and cunning.

"Well, if it isn't the Lindstrom woman."

His voice slides through the space, adding a layer of frost to everything. Above our heads, icicles grow from the kitchen rack. They glimmer, their points deadly. Beyond Thomas, I spot the back door, its window obscured by thick fog. I can't see out. I doubt anyone can see in.

I contemplate Thomas again. Who am I supposed to be? My mother? My grandmother?

"I have a first name," I say.

The air in this space sucks all the moisture and strength from my words. I'm not even sure they reach Thomas, except for the smile that distorts his lips.

He laughs, the sound rippling through the air. The kitchen rack shudders, shaking loose several icicles. They shatter against the granite countertop, shards flying everywhere.

I duck behind my arms. The cuts come, quick and tiny, a series of searing pain along my forearms and the back of my hands. Compared to this kitchen of grays and whites, the blood that bubbles from my skin is so red.

So the ghost refuses to take that bait. Blood streams along my skin and I shake out my arms, speckling the floor with splotches of red. I don't know who I am in this strange reality, or what my mother or grandmother may have done—except for one thing.

"I didn't betray you."

These words come out with more substance. They're warmer, stronger. They meet the cold air in the center of the kitchen, and clouds form. Light flashes, and moments later, the room quakes with what can only be thunder.

The storm clears the fog from the back door. Through the

windowpane, Reginald appears. Then he vanishes. I think I see the top of Malcolm's head.

Something flies at the window. I duck, instinct taking over once again. Glass splinters. The window explodes, and the kitchen door crashes against the wall.

"Get Katy," Reginald says. "Hide in a bathroom and tend to her wounds. Meet us in the living room."

"But—" I begin.

The four of them charge into the kitchen and overwhelm my protest. Reginald and Sadie shield Nigel from the ghost while Malcolm dashes for me, grabs my hand, and yanks me from the room.

"But—" I try again.

He doesn't even glance my way. We race through the downstairs hallways until Malcolm pulls me into a powder room. He locks the door behind us and starts pawing through the cabinets.

"I hope they have something in here, otherwise we're going to be ruining some fancy towels."

"They have two kids," I say. "There must be something. But I don't really need—"

"Jesus, Katy, look at your arms." Malcolm flings open the medicine cabinet and lets out a sigh of relief.

I do as he says, holding my arms out in front of me. Sheets of red rush toward my fingertips. I'm dripping blood onto the floor, so I move toward the sink. As I do, a wave of dizziness sweeps over me. I knock into Malcolm.

"Easy there," he says. "Let's clean you up. You okay?"

I nod and hold my arms still.

Water stings. Soap stings. The antibiotic spray Malcolm spritzes all over my skin stings.

"I'm not sure there are enough Band-Aids for this." He rattles a box and then dumps the contents on the edge of the sink.

"Gauze?" I suggest. Now that my arms are clean, I can see all the cuts—so small, so precise, so deadly.

"It will have to do." With gentle fingers, Malcolm wraps my arms, using an entire roll of gauze from the first aid kit. His mouth is grim, and his eyes focused on their task. I want more than anything to make him laugh.

"I look like a mummy," I say.

He swears. Not the response I was hoping for. Then he cups my face with a hand.

"Katy, just..." He trails off, and I can't tell if he's heartsick or angry. Before I can try something else, the smallest hint of a smile warms his face.

"Just be careful," he says.

And then he kisses me.

CHAPTER 10

A grayish light filters through the hallway. It's not the blackness of before, but it's not natural, either. We've only been inside for half an hour, at most, and I acutely miss the sunlight. I'm starving for something natural and warm. I grip Malcolm's hand tighter since he must be the warmest thing in this house.

"Our presence is draining some of its power," he whispers. "If the ghost doesn't keep its guard up, Reginald will be able to capture it."

"Even while it's still possessing Tara's father?"

"It's ... messy, but possible."

We pause near the kitchen. The space is a disaster of pink-tinged puddles and splatters of red everywhere that make me think of crime scenes and serial killers. A light fog remains, clogging the skylights, barring the sun from entrance.

Malcolm shakes his head. "Nothing in here." He eyes me. "Except for your blood."

We move on, inching our way along the textured wallpaper. I glance behind me, but it's too dark to tell if I'm leaving bloody prints in my wake. We pause outside the living room. Malcolm presses a finger to his lips, and I nod. We hold still. We listen.

We hear absolutely nothing.

We wait in silence for ten seconds, thirty, a whole minute. The muscles in my legs begin to twitch. An urge—to rush in and confront this thing—nearly overwhelms me.

"It wants me in the living room," I say, my voice barely a whisper.

"I feel it too, only—" He breaks off and shakes his head.

"What?"

"Different. That's all."

Slowly, I inch my head so I can study him. He hasn't shut down, not yet anyway. But where I want to rush in, hands on hips, and scold—much like my grandmother might—Malcolm's reaction is wholly different. He glances at me, and I see the heartache in his expression.

He has the look of a little boy who knows he's going to lose his family. The hurt in his eyes is deep, and I want nothing more than to make it go away.

"What would you do when your parents fought?" I ask.

"Freeze, shutdown, hide."

"What would Nigel do?"

"Sometimes come get me, take me outside. We'd go somewhere or ride our bikes."

"In the winter?"

The moment I say the words, I realize that's where we are—or maybe it's *when* we are. Winter. Ice. The gray quality of the sunlight. Everything suggests the longest night of the year, of being trapped inside.

"Basement, or our rooms. When he was older, Nigel started trapping ghosts and letting them loose. My mother would sense them immediately, and their presence would distract my father. Funny thing is, when they realized he was doing it? He got nothing but praise. He was what? Eight, and already deploying attack ghosts—more or less."

That isn't the whole story. I hear it in his tone. Malcolm isn't telling me something, and I'm not sure what that something might be. But it will have to wait. The urge to storm the living room is strong. I can't imagine what Reginald is doing, but he probably could use some help.

I brace against the wall, ready to push off and barrel into the living room when an otherworldly presence anchors my shoulder in place.

"Not yet, Katrina Lindstrom." The voice—an ethereal version of Reginald's—echoes around us.

Malcolm manages a low chuckle. "He has a ghost watching you."

"He can do that? How does he do that?" Despite everything I've seen this morning, this may be the most surprising.

"He's a powerful necromancer. If he says not yet, then he means not yet."

"And he can deploy a ghost to say it to me?"

"Exactly."

So we wait. In the quiet that follows, another question occurs to me.

"Is eight young for a necromancer?"

"For directing them, the way Nigel was? Yes. He was considered a prodigy. But by eight, a necromancer should at least be able to capture ghosts."

"I started working with my grandmother when I was five."

"See?"

"And you?"

"What?"

"When did you start deploying ghosts?"

He falls silent. "I never did," he says at last. "Never have."

"But you and Selena—"

"Selena and I had an arrangement. I never deployed her or sent her on errands. Ghosts were my companions. I sensed them early, possibly earlier than Nigel did. There was a time when everyone thought I was simply a sensitive."

"And not a necromancer?"

"Exactly. Everyone thought I had inherited my gift from my mother, but none of the skills of my father."

I consider this—and all the things I know about the necromancer community—and the power and prestige that comes with being a necromancer. I suspect sensitives aren't granted the same status.

"Nigel was the smart one," he adds. "I was the pretty one."

"But, Malcolm, you're smart."

He gives his head a little shake.

At the moment, I don't have words to convince him otherwise. A reverberation comes from the living room. That otherworldly presence whips around my head.

"Soon, Katrina Lindstrom. You will need to catch the ghost once I've drawn it out and before it can enter Nigel."

I nod, although whether Reginald's ghost can relay this to him, I have no idea. Malcolm unslings the bag with the Tupperware and hands me the largest container. He hangs onto the lid.

"How did you find out you were a necromancer?" I ask.

"Nigel caught one of my ghosts, one of my friends, and it got mad. So when he unleashed it on my parents, it went crazy. It wasn't more than a sprite, really, but no one could catch it."

"Except you?"

The barest hint of a smile plays on his lips. "Except me."

"And that changed things?"

"Sort of."

In those two words, I hear it all: he was still the pretty one, the baby of the family. I think of Nigel, being so good at such a young age. Would the pressure of that build to a point where you couldn't take it? I glance at Malcolm and wish he could see himself the way I see him.

A buzzing fills the air, a crackling static that makes me want to drop the Tupperware and clamp my hands over my ears. Before I can ask what it is or what we should do, a single word rings out.

"Now!"

Malcolm grabs my hand, and we rush into the living room.

Nigel stands near the hearth. In front of him, Sadie is stationed. Her lips are pale, eyes wide and scared, but her curls are wild, fierce things. She stands in front of her husband like a sentry.

In the center of the room, Thomas Sr. shakes. Reginald is at his side, a palm on Thomas's forehead, a hand bracing his shoulder. Sweat runs down Reginald's face. His arms tremble. His stance is wide, but every few seconds he readjusts it, as if this ghost is on the cusp of overwhelming him.

I worry that maybe it is.

Malcolm points to the sofa and then to the bookcase opposite of it. I nod, let his fingers slip from mine as we take up a position in between Thomas and Nigel. We can't block the ghost's view of him. It's the only thing tempting it from its current home. But we can't be so far away we miss making the catch.

Reginald lets out a terrific roar. A wail comes from Thomas, unearthly and loud, but the sound diminishes as the ghost peels away from his body. Thomas slumps into Reginald, and the ghost that so recently occupied his body now occupies this space.

It fills the living room with its rage and power. The walls shake. Glass rattles in the windowpanes. Pictures swing on nails and crash to the floor. The ghost swirls, its form like winter itself, so cold and barren. Despite its ethereal form, the force feels like a blizzard, like icy snow striking skin.

The ghost rotates, tighter and tighter. It shoots across the room, a frigid arrow. It bounces off one wall, the next, building up speed. It ricochets off a family portrait, and this time, I know its target.

It's heading straight for Nigel.

Malcolm leaps, but the Tupperware lid slips through this ghost without slowing it down. It flies too far above my head for me to even attempt a catch. The ghost skitters along the ceiling, but its aim is clear.

Nigel doesn't crouch or flinch. He merely stands there, his hands locked on Sadie's waist. Her expression loses all its fear. The moment before this thing plunges into Nigel, the moment before it destroys the man she loves, Sadie raises her hands, like a center fielder, and deflects the ghost.

It careens straight for me, knocked off course and off kilter. I lunge, Tupperware clutched in front of me. I land on the floor with a thud. The container beneath me rocks. My fingers slip along the sides, and I'm desperate to keep a seal with the living room floor.

I think of what Orson Yates—of all people—once told me: that every time I catch a ghost, I commit an act of necromancy. The seal is more than physical. I concentrate on that, on not letting go, not with my hands and not with my mind.

The ghost bucks like it might throw me off. Before it can, before my arms give out, Malcolm joins me, his grip covering mine, reinforcing it.

The ghost quiets—or rather, it can't fight the two of us. We won't risk snapping the lid on anytime soon, but for now, everyone is safe.

At least I think so. I glance up. Thomas is stretched out on the sofa. Already the glossy black is returning to his hair, and the layers of wax are melting away. His eyes are closed. My guess is he's unconscious.

Reginald is slumped on the floor next to him, rumpled and worn. He must see the question in my eyes because he nods, touches his fingers to his brow as if in salute.

By the fireplace, Nigel cradles Sadie. He cups her head in his hands. From my spot on the floor, his murmur reaches me.

"My brave and beautiful wife."

When Orson orchestrated this attack, I don't think he counted on Sadie's quiet fierceness, or love overcoming fear. Orson understands weaknesses; he miscalculates when it comes to strengths.

Late morning sunlight streams through the windows, chasing away the fog and warming the air. The scent of roses alone gives me hope that we've truly banished this thing, even if Malcolm and I can't move from our spot on the floor.

"Katrina Lindstrom, young Malcolm, can you continue to contain the ghost?" Reginald's voice quavers.

I dart a look at Malcolm and then peer at Reginald. He's still slumped against the sofa, legs stretched out in front of him, and his skin has a waxy cast to it that worries me.

"Are you—?" I begin.

"Yes, I will be fine, with time."

How much time? Worry eats away at my relief. The kitchen is a disaster, the living room not much better. Malcolm and I are planted on the floor. If anyone happens inside—Tara's aunt, her mother, Chief Ramsey—the consequences will be both real and otherworldly.

We need a necromancer, a ghost catcher, someone to secure the lid. Nigel can't, and at the moment, Reginald isn't strong enough.

"You're bleeding again," Malcolm says, his voice low.

Spots of red now dot the gauze along my arms. With the blood comes the pain, that stinging sharpness, and an itch that's nearly impossible to ignore. I want nothing more than to let go and scratch at my arms.

"It's okay." I close my eyes and take a deep breath. "It'll stop."

Maybe.

We hold on tight as sounds invade the space. Birdsong, the rumble of an occasional car, a bicycle bell ringing out in greeting. As long as we hold still, hold onto this ghost, everything will return to normal.

I don't relax my grip, but I let my head rest on Malcolm's shoulder. His lips brush strands of my hair. A bit of hope sparks inside me. We caught the thing, after all. The rest? The rest is easy.

The second that thought crosses my mind, I hear the front door rattle. Malcolm swears softly. He clutches the container tighter. Footfalls echo along the hallway. My back is to the living room's entrance. I don't see who shadows the doorway, but when Malcolm swears again, I'm certain it can't be good.

Except his tone is all wrong. He sounds almost amused and exhales a half laugh.

"I don't believe it," he says, the words low and quiet against my ear.

"What—?" I begin and crane my neck.

Standing at the threshold is Darien Armand.

He scans the mess, judgment sparking his expression. Oh, he does not approve—that is clear.

"As business models go," he says. "This seems to be a losing proposition."

Darien crosses the space, removes the lid from the floor, and takes a knee next to Malcolm and me.

"Do you accept my assistance?" he asks.

This must be one of those necromancer things. My gaze meets Malcolm's, and he gives me a slight nod.

"I do." Honestly? At this point, my arms ache too much to refuse. At this point, it would be foolish to refuse.

With the utmost care, Darien slides the lid beneath the container. The Tupperware snaps into place. The ghost rockets about, but a seal created by three necromancers is too much, even for it.

"I will also dispose of this ghost." Darien stands, bringing the container to eye level. "I have an interested client."

Just like that, he leaves, without a goodbye, or really, a hello. And without my permission to take the ghost—not that I want it. Still. Before Malcolm can stop me, I spring up and run after Darien.

I catch him on the sidewalk. He turns at my approach, but remains silent, a hand on each side of the Tupperware container.

"Can I assume your client isn't Orson Yates?" I ask.

"You can assume anything you like, Ms. Lindstrom."

I sigh. "What about your sons?"

"What about them?"

"Don't you want to know how they are?"

"They're both relatively unscathed. That's obvious. What's also obvious is the very large mess they must now clean up." He nods toward the house. "You might want to assist them with that."

My throat tightens with outrage. Words. Oh, I have words. Dozens of them, but I can't seem to push any of them out of my mouth.

"This is one of the reasons I left the necromancer community. I was forever cleaning up after everyone." Darien tips the container in my direction. "Of course, in this particular case, you can put an end to things before they become even worse."

"I don't see—"

"Don't you?" He raises an eyebrow. "A necromancer with the sort of powerful ally that you possess?"

"It doesn't work like that."

"Of course it does. You simply need to be willing to pay the price. Consider, Ms. Lindstrom, whether my sons are worth that price."

He leaves me with that. I don't follow him down the sidewalk; I don't argue. There's no point. So I stare after him, the sun beating down on my head. Without thinking, I unwrap the gauze from around my arms. The notion that the sunshine might heal the cuts is strong, if irrational.

"Katy ... Katy." Malcolm jogs up the walk. "What's going on?"

I shake my head.

He halts next to me, his gaze scanning my arms. With gentle fingers, he pries the wadded up gauze from my grip and swears softly. "What did he say to you?"

"Nothing I don't already know."

"Come on." He wraps an arm around my shoulders and urges me back up the walk. "Sadie has half the place cleaned up. There's not much we can do about the back door window. Nigel thought about making it look like some kids and vandalism."

Malcolm continues talking. I nod, burrowing deeper against his side. In this moment, I want nothing more than his warmth. The chill from the house, from this ghost, still haunts me. It's like I'm shrouded in that wintery ice.

But if I'm honest with myself, I know that it's more than just the house or the ghost. It's the words of Darien Armand.

I steal a look at Malcolm, and I know this:

He is worth that price.

CHAPTER 11

Tuesday morning, I sit on my front porch steps, a cup of coffee warming my fingers, the sun doing its best to warm my arms. The cuts are healing, but the only time I don't feel chilled is in direct sunlight.

Reginald assures me this will pass once every last cut has healed.

I sip my coffee and wonder if that's true.

The clacking alerts me long before I see Tara. She skips down the sidewalk. While I'm clearly her destination, she clutches a thin whip of a willow branch that needs to touch everything in her path.

She stops at the end of my sidewalk, braids swaying.

"Hi." It's a tentative greeting. The willow branch twitches nervously.

"You can come sit," I say, "unless you need to get to school."

"Summer vacation."

"Really? Since when?" I check the position of the sun as if I can glean that information from it.

"Yesterday." She takes careful steps up my walk, placing one foot directly in front of the other while, at the same time, avoiding all the cracks in the concrete. It's quite a feat.

She settles at my side, and the cat clips in her braids clack again.

"Thank you," she says, quietly, like this is a secret between just us. "I know it was you and Malcolm who got rid of the ghost."

"We had some help."

"But it was mostly you and him."

I decide not to contradict her since she's glancing around, searching for him, hope in her eyes.

"He's not here right now," I say.

She slumps. "He should be."

I bite back a laugh because that's how I feel most of the time. "Malcolm doesn't live here."

"He should. He really should. Then you wouldn't be alone."

"I'm not alone. I have a roommate."

"I mean here." She touches the left side of her chest, the spot that can only mean the heart.

Again, she shocks me with how cleanly and clearly she cuts through everything.

I sigh, and so does Tara. Then we eye each other and laugh. I tilt my head and consider her. As I do, she drops the willow branch and pulls that blue and yellow cat purse from her pocket.

"I need to pay you," she says.

I hold up a hand. "Hang on for a minute."

She shakes her head, jostling the cat clips. "My parents won't. They won't even believe me about the ghost."

"A lot of people won't, even when they've seen one." Or have been possessed by one.

"Why did that ghost pick us, my family?"

I've been pondering this, turning over what little I know about Malcolm's and Nigel's childhood, how my family and his intersected at some point.

"That ghost was sent to hurt Nigel," I say at last.

"Why would anyone want to hurt Nigel?"

I go with the truth, or as much of it as I can for an eleven-year-old. "That's a long story, but some people use ghosts in ways they shouldn't. In this case, I think there was something about your family that made the ghost think of Nigel."

As much as ghosts truly think. Was it the volatile relationship between Tara's mother and father? Or maybe Tara and Thomas Jr. somehow confused this ghost. I cast her a look—yes, the clever, precocious one and the beautiful baby. I consider what Malcolm said, about sending ghosts as messengers. Could you deploy an attack ghost in the same manner? Load them up with information about your target and send them on their way?

"I still need to pay you." She digs around in her purse.

I shake my head, wishing I had a set of cat clips that would clack and help me make my point. "How about this. Are you doing anything this summer?"

"No. We're having 'cash flow' problems." She draws little quotation marks in the air, and at that moment, she reminds me of both Nigel and Malcolm. "We're stuck here in Springside."

"That was me, every summer. It's not so bad, especially if you have a job."

"A job?"

"It's been almost a year," I begin, and the words catch in my throat. Even after all this time, I miss my grandmother with a fierceness that takes me by surprise. "And I never figured out the gardening and the weeding, and someone should really sweep the front walk."

"I could do that!" She shoots her hand in the air as if I've made this offer to her entire class at school and might miss her in the crowd of volunteers.

"Not only that," I say, "but it might be good if someone else in town knew how to catch ghosts. What if I get hurt?"

Tara frowns at the cuts on my arms.

"Okay, what if I get the flu? Who's going to catch Sadie's sprites?"

"I could do that?"

"I think you could."

Her entire face scrunches. "But I don't like coffee."

"Want to know a secret?" I wait until she leans close. "For the longest time, neither did I."

She laughs. The sound is like sunshine and ice cream and summer in Springside. I think it might be time to train the next generation of ghost catchers.

I think we might need them sooner rather than later.

Before I can down the last drops of my coffee, a shadow falls across the walkway. Tara sucks in her breath. There, on the sidewalk, stands her mother, Thomas Jr. on her hip. At the sight of his sister, he kicks his pudgy legs, lets out a squeal, and tugs one of his mother's gleaming, black curls.

"Tara! What are you doing?"

Tara bites her lip in response. "Just visiting Katy is all."

Her mother charges up the walk. "I'm so sorry. She's been talking about all this ghost nonsense, and..." She trails off. I see the moment the realization hits—that she's speaking to someone who makes her living from ghost nonsense. A hint of pink invades her cheeks. She averts her gaze.

"Actually," I say, "I was talking to Tara about a summer job."

"A job?"

I wave a hand, indicating the ragged hedges around my house, the shaggy lilacs, and the fact I'm cultivating more weeds than flowers.

"It could use some serious help," I add, "and Tara's perfect for the job."

"I don't know." Tara's mother shakes her head.

"Please, Mom! Please! I'll do my chores at home, too. Please!" Tara clutches her hands together, almost prayer-like.

"If you need references." I nod toward the Victorian house next to mine. "You can talk to Sadie."

Doubt still clouds her expression. So maybe my neighbor, friend, and best customer isn't a stellar reference. I ransack my thoughts, certain the only other references will confirm that I'm the crazy girl who catches ghosts.

Then the obvious hits me.

"Or Police Chief Ramsey. Talk to him. He's known me all my life." And scolded me for at least half that time.

Her look softens. She switches Thomas to her other hip and holds out her hand. "I'm Celia Davenport."

"Katy Lindstrom. Would you like to come in for coffee? I was just about to brew a fresh pot."

Celia hesitates. "I've been working from home all morning." She laughs softly, eyes darting first to Thomas and then Tara. "Or trying to."

"Then you could probably use a cup," I say.

"If it's no trouble."

"Of course it isn't," Tara chimes in on my behalf. "It's what she does."

I shrug. "It's true."

Celia pushes a curl from her forehead. "All right then."

I hold open the door and let Celia and Thomas in first. Tara skips behind them, and when she passes me, I whisper, "I'll show you how to brew Malcolm's favorite coffee."

Her eyes light up. Now this is an offer she can't refuse.

"It never fails to bring him around," I add.

"Really?"

"Really," I say.

But once inside, I send him a text—just in case.

PART II
A FEW GOOD GHOSTS

COFFEE AND GHOSTS SEASON THREE,
EPISODE TWO

CHAPTER 1

My business partner, Malcolm Armand, leans across the table and kisses the maple syrup from my lips. We're sequestered in a cozy booth inside the Springside Pancake House. They make the best breakfast for dinner, even today, when it's served with a side order of worry.

Malcolm would kiss away the worry, too, if he could. It's there in the way his thumb rubs the faded blue spot on my left cheek, the way his mouth curves against mine. His hands come to rest on my arms, and his skin is so warm against mine. With the utmost care, he traces the scars that remain on the backs of my hands and along my forearms. The wounds aren't tender, and when he strokes them, it doesn't hurt. Instead, it's almost like these scars are greedy for his touch, for his heat and his vitality.

"You okay?" he says.

I nod.

"Not too tired?"

I narrow my eyes at him.

"Sorry, sorry." Malcolm raises his hands in surrender. "I sound like a mother hen."

He does. But truthfully? I don't mind too much. Also? I *have* been tired ever since we exorcised the ghost sent to possess Nigel. The scars left in the wake of that are so tiny, and yet, unless I'm in direct sunlight, I can feel them draining me. It's a slow drip that fogs my thoughts and weighs down my limbs.

Malcolm nods toward the window. Across the street, his cherry-red convertible is sitting in front of our office. The gold lettering that reads *K&M Ghost Eradication Specialists* glows with the setting sun.

"I'll do the rounds," he says. "See if any of our usual suspects are up to anything."

"Be careful." I want to remind him that an attack ghost with his name on it could be lurking anywhere in Springside. Before I can, he scoots from the booth, holds up a finger, stopping my words, and then casts a look toward the ceiling.

Yes, he knows what I'm going to say.

"*You* be careful. I'll be back in an hour to pick both of you up." His gaze darts toward the rear of the restaurant. "Don't let her walk home again."

"I'll try."

It's a promise I might not be able to keep. Belinda Barnes is a force unto herself—all six feet of her.

I track his progress from the Pancake House door and across the street. The sunset paints Main Street in bands of pink and gold, and Malcolm's convertible gleams so brightly it could be on fire. He doesn't bother with the door. He simply launches himself up and over and into the front seat.

A low whistle sounds behind me. "Sometimes I think he just strolled off a movie set."

Sometimes I think that myself. "He has his faults."

Belinda snorts and starts clearing dishes from the table. She lifts Malcolm's plate and sends a twenty-dollar bill fluttering. Her sigh is tinged with exasperation.

"He already paid." She holds up the twenty, inspecting it with a critical eye. "He can't keep tipping me—us—like this." She nods toward Annie, the other waitress on shift. "He'll go broke."

"See?" I say. "He does have faults."

Belinda shakes her head as if she could shake away my words. "You know I'm closing, right?"

Of course I do. It's why I'm here, in this booth, nursing an orange juice. "I know."

"It's been a week. I don't think—"

"Well, I do."

"What if this ghost doesn't exist? What if Orson Yates was lying? What if it's lost and haunting someone else?"

We've considered all of that—Malcolm, Nigel, and me. Malcolm, who is out looking for otherworldly evidence; Nigel, who has postponed his honeymoon and is scouring the internet for any and all ghost sightings; and me. Tonight, my job is to make sure Belinda doesn't walk home—or to make sure she doesn't do it alone.

I've fought a couple of Orson Yates' attack ghosts, and I know this: we won't see it coming. If it's as strong as the last ghost, we might not be able to defeat it. All our precautions might add up to nothing.

This is why my orange juice is spiked with worry.

Belinda clears the table, scooping up the glass once I've downed the last drop. Annie waves a goodnight as she leaves. The front doors whoosh closed. Then it's the clatter of a few dishes, the swish of the mop, and row upon row of empty booths.

It's just a bit creepy. Also? I feel utterly useless simply sitting here.

"Can't I help?" I've asked this before. In fact, I've asked this every night for a week.

"And get me fired? No."

I sigh and turn my attention toward Main Street. I long to see a flash of cherry-red. Instead, my phone buzzes with an incoming text. If I can't have Malcolm here with me, at least I can have him on my phone.

Malcolm: All quiet at the old barn.

Katy: Too quiet?

Malcolm: I got showered with hay when I stepped under the loft, and there's a shredded cornstalk in the front seat of my car. Tomorrow you should check on them. They miss you.

I laugh. Cornstalks and mischief—it sounds like a routine summer haunting. If not for the threat hanging over us, if not for the possession of last week, I'd say things were normal in Springside, that none of us need to worry, least of all Belinda.

A clatter comes from the kitchen, followed by Belinda swearing. Her vocabulary is nearly as creative and extensive as Malcolm's is.

"Something wrong?" I call out.

"The door to the cold storage is stuck."

"Need help?"

I don't wait for an answer. I slip from the booth and make my way toward the back, past the counter with its swivel chairs, the short order cook area, and then the prep area.

I'm partway through the kitchen when a sensation washes over me, faint and shivery, like I've walked through a spider web. I halt, hold absolutely still, and breathe in the air. I tilt my chin in an attempt to taste what might be the otherworldly.

The presence is so slight, I'm nearly certain it isn't there at all, except for the goose bumps on my arms and the prickle of hair at the nape of my neck.

"Belinda?" I go for casual, working to keep the tension from my voice. With my gaze straight ahead, I pull out my phone and send Malcolm a quick text.

Katy: Can you come back?

A moment later the phone buzzes in response, but I don't look at the screen. Instead, I inch forward. Belinda hasn't answered me. It's possible she didn't hear me. It's also possible that she can't, that there's something in between us, something otherworldly.

I try again. "Belinda?"

The space feels so empty, like I'm the only living thing inside the restaurant.

My phone buzzes a second time. Logically, I know all incoming text messages sound alike, but Malcolm's seem to contain an extra hint of panic. My silence is making him nervous.

Malcolm: What's up? Something wrong?

Malcolm: Katy, don't go silent on me. What's wrong?

Katy: I don't know. Maybe nothing.

Malcolm: On my way.

I pocket my phone and touch the stainless steel worktable. A second later, I jerk my hand back, my fingers stinging from the bite of cold metal. I exhale; my breath fogs in front of my face.

And yet, the otherworldly presence is thin, the sort that suggests nothing more than a naughty sprite is in residence. Everything else points to a full-on ghost infestation.

I call for Belinda one last time. The space swallows my words. Nothing lingers from the day's dinner rush—no scent of warm maple syrup, no bacon thickening the air, no hint of coffee. (Which is just as well—the Springside Pancake House serves the worst coffee in town.)

The air is cold and stale against my tongue. I take small, quiet steps forward, willing my sneakers not to squeak against the freshly mopped floor. The lights above my head flicker and then dim. I pull out my phone and take a surreptitious peek at the battery life. That, too, is draining.

The cold storage is near the back of the restaurant; this I know from an elementary school field trip to the Pancake House. In my mind, I hear the echo of us all those years ago, the chatter and the noise, and Belinda's voice rising above it all, declaring that someday, she would work here.

Now the only sounds are the stainless steel racks creaking from the drop in temperature. I feel as if I've stepped outside in mid-January. The otherworldly presence is elusive. Tendrils of it slip through my grasp. I can't find its source, don't know where it is. I don't know *what* it is.

When I reach the cold storage unit, I realize I don't know where Belinda is, either.

CHAPTER 2

I indulge in a full sixty seconds of panic. I abandon any form of stealth and race around the kitchen, through the restaurant. I try every door that has a handle—the cold storage unit, the back and front doors, the restrooms. These last open for me, yielding up a blast of icy disinfectant and nothing else.

Fog creeps up the front windows, eats away at the view of Main Street, obliterates the rosy hues from the sunset. A full-on ghost infestation. It has to be. Everything points to it—except for the fact that I'm missing the ghost.

I pull out my phone. The battery life is currently at twenty-five percent. It was fifty only a few minutes ago. I should go look for Belinda, but this might be the only chance I have to let Malcolm know what's going on.

Katy: I'm trapped inside the Pancake House. Feels like an infestation.

I wait, but if he's driving, he won't see my text. With reluctance, I tuck my phone away. If I'm lucky, it'll still have power when he has the chance to reply. I steel myself against the cold emptiness of the restaurant and go in search of Belinda.

I do a quick circuit through the front. I peer into all the booths, kick open the stalls in the restrooms. I'm fairly certain I won't find her here. That leaves the kitchen area, where I do ridiculous things like opening up all the long metal cabinets to reveal the industrial-sized pots and pans. On tiptoe, I check top shelves.

The cold mounts. My phone is stubbornly silent. My options dwindle. Unless Belinda somehow slipped out the back before the doors froze shut, she should be here somewhere.

Then it hits me: the one place I haven't looked is *inside* the cold storage. I approach the unit, dread churning up the pancake special in my stomach. The taste of sour orange juice burns the back of my throat. I brush my fingers across the handle, fast enough that the icy burn doesn't quite register.

This is where the ghost is, inside the unit. My guess is, Belinda is in there too. I consider my options and start with the obvious. It's always good to start there—keeps you from overlooking it, as my grandmother always said.

I find a roll of paper towels and snag enough sheets to insulate my hand against the door handle. It moves, but the door doesn't budge. That, I suppose, would've been too easy. But it isn't locked, which means the only barrier is an otherworldly one.

I pull out my phone. Twenty percent. No text from Malcolm.

Katy: I think the ghost has trapped Belinda inside the cold storage unit. Ideas for getting inside?

I turn and survey the space. Normally, I'd be brewing coffee right now. Kona blend or, for a ghost this strong, possibly one hundred percent Kona. My gaze lands on a series of coffeemakers and the stove. The idea strikes just as Malcolm's text arrives.

Malcolm: You're in a kitchen, Katy. Start brewing.

He's right, of course.

Katy: You read my mind. Also, the ghost is draining my phone battery.

On my way to the coffeemakers, I pull a few of those industrial-sized pots from a cabinet and clank my way toward the sink. Water from the faucet sputters at first, but soon I've filled two huge pots. My arms protest as I waddle them to the stove. I waste precious moments puzzling out how to use it, but I need steam and lots of it, so I keep puzzling even as my phone buzzes at me.

At last I switch two burners to high and set the pots on top. I confront the coffeemakers then, more confident, even if they are automatic drip. Not my preferred method of brewing. I pull out the coffee only to find it comes pre-ground and in large packets, the topmost ones flirting dangerously close to the "Brew By" date. I tear one open and recoil from the sad aroma that greets me.

It's anemic, at best.

A sign above the Springside Pancake House marquee boasts fresh coffee all day long, brewed in small batches. Technically, I suppose that's true. In practice?

I'm not certain the coffee's going to help. I swallow back my despair and check my phone.

Malcolm: Alerting Nigel and Reginald.

He doesn't mention his father, which is just as well. Darien Armand hasn't left town. What he's done—or plans to do—with the ghosts at his disposal, I don't know. Unless ...

I cast a glance toward the cold storage unit. No; Darien Armand may dislike me, but he has no reason to hurt Belinda. This is Orson Yates' attack ghost, and it has found its victim.

The screen of my phone dims. I blow out a breath—fifteen percent—and text Malcolm again.

131

Katy: I think it's Orson's attack ghost. My kingdom for some Kona blend.

I consider the row of coffeemakers, all lined up like soldiers ready for battle. Well, if the coffee won't help, it can't hurt. I pull out filters, rip open packets, and consider all the tricks my grandmother used for turning bad coffee into something drinkable.

A pinch of salt or a dash of cocoa in the grounds, and eggshells—something about crushed eggshells. The first two I have in bulk. The last? This is the Pancake House, after all. I'm certain they buy eggs by the truckload. I turn slowly, my gaze lighting on the cold storage unit. The eggs—and the half and half for the coffee—would most likely be in there.

Then I spy the refrigerators. And, for the first time since Malcolm left, I manage a smile.

I have no finesse when it comes to cracking eggs. The whites leave traces of slime on my fingertips. Bits of shell litter the countertop and float among the yolks, but I have what I need. I set all the pots brewing, one with cocoa, one with salt, one plain, and one with the eggshells.

The water on the stove is lukewarm, so I do another circuit of the kitchen area, spending extra time in front of the cold storage unit. I inspect the seams of the door and try the handle again. I wonder how airtight the room is and whether Belinda has enough oxygen.

She's fine, I tell myself. That would have to be some sort of safety violation. Right? I nod, reassuring myself. I'm about to return to the coffee and my pots of water when my phone buzzes again.

Malcolm: Katy? Are you sure you're inside the Pancake House?

CHAPTER 3

For a moment, I can only stare at the screen. What does he mean, am I sure? I glance around, taking in the flickering lights, the gurgle of the coffee starting to brew, the huge pots of water standing sentry behind me. Of course I'm sure.

Then my phone rings. I jump, heart soaring. When I answer and hear Malcolm's voice on the other end, I all but collapse against the counter.

"Katy, you okay?"

"Sort of."

"Are you hurt?"

"No, no, I'm fine. Worried, is all. I'm brewing coffee and heating water, but I don't know if it will help."

As I talk, I make my way from the kitchen to the front of the restaurant. Fog has completely obscured the windows. Shadows play on the other side, but I can't tell if that's Malcolm or merely an otherworldly illusion.

"Well, I'm standing right outside," he says, "and everything looks normal."

"You can see inside? You can't see the fog?"

"What fog?"

"The fog that's keeping me from seeing you."

He swears. "This is bad."

He doesn't need to say how bad. Any ghost that can conjure this sort of illusion during a full-on infestation is powerful indeed, maybe even more so than the ghost that possessed Thomas Davenport.

I slip into the booth that sits in the exact center of the restaurant and scoot all the way to the window.

"I'm underneath the N in *Pancake*," I say. "Can you see me now?"

Gingerly, I brush the window with my fingertips. The glass is cool, but not so cold it will give me frostbite. I press my palm flat and bring my nose close, willing the fog to clear.

Shadows continue to play on the other side. One grows darker and closer, the shape menacing.

I nearly jerk back. My fingers twitch as if they long to push away from the glass. I remain at the window because I know the only thing on the other side is Malcolm. I blow out a long breath, certain that won't help.

But, for a moment, it seems like it might. The glass clears. The menacing shadow solidifies into Malcolm. He's standing opposite me, his hand pressed against mine with the thick glass separating us. His gaze locks with mine. A smile lights his face even as his eyes fill with concern.

Then another thick cloud rolls in, icing the window. Fractured crystals form beneath my palm. The sting is like nettles, the frost sharp and thick. Malcolm fades into shadows once again.

"This is serious," he says, voice low.

I steal a glance at my cell phone. Ten percent. I know I should end the call and conserve the battery, but Malcolm's voice is the only warm thing in this frozen world. I don't want to let that go.

"It's draining my cell phone battery," I tell him.

"Hang up. We'll do this by text for as long as possible."

Before I do, I ask one last question. "What happens in the morning, when they try to open for business?"

"We'll have this fixed by then. I promise you. We'll have it fixed."

With that, he ends the call.

～

IN THE KITCHEN, the scent of coffee greets me. The water on the stove hasn't started to boil yet. When—if—it does, I'm not certain it will help. The only reason I can smell the coffee is that I've brewed four pots at once.

I pour half and half into one of the adorable cow pitchers the pancake house uses and then set about giving each pot a taste test.

I immediately wish I hadn't. I contemplate licking the sleeve of my T-shirt to remove the flavor from my tongue. I'd reach for an orange juice chaser, but I've already used supplies that aren't mine. I'd hate to add to that.

Only the last pot, the one with the eggshells, holds any hope. This coffee is weak but lacks the aggressive bitterness of the others. I pour it into an insulated carafe and switch the others off —nothing good can come from cooking the coffee any longer.

Then I confront the cold storage room's door. I stare at my reflection warped in the shiny metallic surface. I appear ghostly, or at least ghoulish, my head pinched in the center like an hourglass. My nose is huge; my feet are tiny. My hair is frightening, but that might be from the ride in Malcolm's convertible. The rest is getting a supernatural boost.

"I don't have Kona blend," I say, "but I do have coffee, and I can make some more. Lots more."

My voice echoes around me, the false notes in my promise grating against my ears. I uncap the carafe and hold it next to the seam in the door. I doubt the aroma can sneak in, and if it does, I doubt it would tempt even a sprite.

Steam mists the stainless steel surface. On impulse, I draw a smiley face on the foggy canvas. Then I add the word *please*. When the fog evaporates, I hold the carafe close and try again. I write *coffee* and *hot* and *steam*. This last sparks another idea.

I run back to the stove and find the pots of water on the verge of boiling. I lug one down and drag it across the kitchen, the tile floor screeching a protest.

Ghosts like coffee because the steam gives them substance. The flavor gives them so many other things—a link to their previous life, memories of that time, a sense of who they once were. But steam alone can attract them. I've witnessed more than one sprite dance on steam from a teakettle or float near a laundry room vent.

No matter how powerful this ghost is, I doubt it's enjoying the cold storage unit.

I do a quick calculation of the door's trajectory and place the pot out of its arc. The last thing I need is a scalding. Steam coats the metal surface with even more fog. I dart forward and back, writing notes to this ghost.

When the handle rattles, I'm torn between dashing back to brew more coffee and staying put to rush the door when it opens. Indecision causes me to take a step back. As I do, the door flies open.

An otherworldly presence bursts forth. Clouds of it stream from the room. Its form rumbles above my head, swooping around the restaurant. It locates the coffee pots and collides with each in turn.

The carafes go flying, each one crashing and cracking against the floor. When the ghost finds the second pot of water simmering on the stove, I consider whether the cold storage unit might be the safer place to be.

I use the pot of water to prop open the door and venture inside. It feels like winter. Frost covers the racks. Icicles hang from the ceiling. The air is stale, but breathable—for now, anyway. I scan the floor, peer into corners. With each step, my heart thuds a warning.

Venture too far from the door, and I might find myself permanently inside.

"Belinda? Are you in here?"

My words echo even though I've only spoken in a whisper. I creep forward. The back of my throat is raw with cold. Every step away from the door makes my heart pound even harder. This could be a trap.

Finally, near the back, I spy the toe of a sneaker.

Belinda has wedged herself into a far corner between two tall racks filled with crates of oranges. They look like snowballs now, thanks to the cold and the frost.

"Belinda?"

She doesn't budge. Her knees are pulled up to her chest, her head buried against them. She's clutching herself, hands pale from the effort and the cold. I know this pose. When I was younger, I watched my grandmother coax Belinda from it so many times. In high school, I did the same.

"Can you hear me?"

It's possible she can't. It's possible this ghost has already taken up residence inside her head, and the only words she can hear are the ones it speaks. Horrid, cruel words. I kneel next to her and touch the back of her hand. My own fingers aren't much warmer than hers are.

"Hey, let's get out of here, okay?"

I ease my fingers beneath her grip. Immediately she clenches my hand so tightly I let out a yelp. In an instant, I'm transported back to high school—a girls' bathroom, the locker room, the orchestra room with all its music stands serving as silent witnesses.

"Kind of ... like old times." Her voice is soft, barely there, but it's her own voice, not that of the ghost.

"Yeah, just like old times." I brace so I can help her stand.

First things first: I need to get us out of the cold storage unit before the ghost figures out how to move the pot of water and lock us both in here. I consider the coffee. I'll need to brew some more. At the very least, it will warm up Belinda. The warmer she is, the better she can fight off the ghost.

"It knows things, Katy," she says.

We're inching our way out of the unit. Belinda takes shuffling steps. The urge to push or pull her along nearly overwhelms me, but that isn't the answer. That might tempt this ghost to shut her down completely.

"It's been in your head," I say. "It's going to know a lot."

"No, not like that. Different things, things I can't know, about you, and Malcolm, and even your grandmother."

"It's warmer in the front of the restaurant," I say, trying to keep my voice steady while my thoughts whirl. I'm not certain what Belinda means, but I do know that the nastier ghosts are adept at tailoring their taunting. And when it's an attack ghost?

"I bet it's only stuff it knows from Orson Yates," I say. "Don't give in to it."

"It's more than that." She sags against me, her free hand clutching one of the metal racks for support.

We're nearly at the door, which is still propped open by the pot. Steam is no longer rising from the water's surface, and this worries me. A giant pot of ice water makes an excellent weapon for an irate ghost. The moment I think this, the pot starts to wobble.

"Can you keep walking?" I cast a look toward Belinda and back at the pot.

She nods and shuffles forward, the sound of her footfalls swallowed by the thump of metal against tile. Water sloshes over the edge of the pot. The wobbling increases to spinning. The silver of the pot's sides blurs into white—though whether it's from speed or frost, I can't tell.

All at once, the pot shoots into the air. I have no choice. I let go of Belinda and leap forward, my shoes skidding on the wet floor. I slam into the door and push. A clanking echoes through the restaurant, the sound of the pot striking the tile floor. Then, a force shoves the door back toward me. Its surface strikes my palms, stings the flesh, and snaps my wrists backward.

My arms ache from fingertips to elbows, but I press them against the door and hold my ground. The thing on the other side would—if it could—slice me in half between the door and its frame.

It can't, but it can make this hurt. The frame digs into my spine, the door itself into my hipbone. I press all my weight against the door, but can't budge it even an inch.

And then Belinda is there, next to me. Her skin is alarmingly pale, but her eyes are fierce. She adds her weight. Together, we move the door half a foot.

"On three," she whispers.

I nod and keep my eyes on her as she mouths the count.

"One ... two ... three."

We shove, our combined strength taking the ghost by surprise and giving us those few precious inches we need to escape. I slip again, my arms flailing, just as the door slams shut behind us.

We both cling to it despite the ice-cold surface. I pant, my breath clouding the air in front of my face. My hands and wrists are tender, and I let the frosty door numb the ache.

"The front," I say to Belinda once the pain has subsided. I don't trust my grip, so I loop an arm around one of hers and tug her gently from the door.

We don't run; we *can't* run. Our feet slosh through puddles and crack thin layers of ice. We make it to the front of the restaurant without slipping or sliding or encountering the otherworldly presence.

This, I realize, isn't a reprieve. A persistent, otherworldly mist hangs in the air. We are in a full-on ghost infestation. We're here for the duration—something this ghost already knows. It's biding its time, content to let us have these few moments until the next round.

I raise my chin and taste the air. Now that it's no longer

hunkered down in the cold storage unit, I can get a sense of its personality. Conflicting feelings bombard me, everything from anger to anguish. But beneath all that is something else, something that's both calculating and gleeful, something that feels deliberate and cruel.

I settle Belinda in a booth and pull out my phone to give Malcolm an update. It's odd that he hasn't sent me a single text since we last spoke.

Then I see why. The battery is completely dead.

CHAPTER 4

I decide the best course of action is to brew a fresh pot of coffee —or rather, several fresh pots. We need what little heat the coffeemakers can generate. I sweep up the mess the ghost made— all coffee grounds mixed with shattered glass—and pull out new carafes.

The water on the stove makes an effort to simmer, but the cold rolls through the restaurant in waves, sucking up all its warmth. It's better than nothing, and when the aroma of the coffee joins the steam, my thoughts don't feel quite as frozen, although when I blink, I can feel the cold against my eyes.

I grab a cow pitcher of half and half and an order pad. I find two cups and, with deliberate steps, make my way to Belinda's booth.

She has her legs pulled up onto the seat cushion, but her wan smile suggests she's still with me.

"You might want to add some cream." I nudge Belinda's cup across the table. "And some sugar. It's hardly my best brew."

I take a sip, and my face puckers. Malcolm once compared restaurant coffee to a brown crayon dipped in hot water.

This tastes worse.

"It's hot," I add. "That will help. It will make you feel better."

Mechanically, she reaches forward and goes through the motions of adding cream and sugar and then sipping. I wait, gauging her reaction. She closes her eyes, and a small sigh escapes her.

"Better?"

She nods.

"Is it inside your head?"

"It's gone silent, but that's not necessarily better. I know it's there. I can feel it ... lurking."

So can I, although I don't hear ghosts the same way Belinda does, and never have. I hardly ever use the necromancer trick of talking to them the way Malcolm sometimes does. This ghost is so strong that its presence is a tangible thing. It flavors the air, shrouds the lighting, pollutes the space it occupies.

I squirm in my seat. The small hairs on the nape of my neck prickle. I swipe a hand across the collar of my T-shirt. I'm tempted to turn, to see what's behind me, but I know nothing's there.

It's a trick, a garden variety one at that. This ghost is capable of so much more. I study the mist and wonder what's holding it back.

I press a palm against the window beneath the letter N and wonder if Malcolm is on the other side, if he can sense me. Everything feels so empty, so isolated. I look toward the door. Oh, to simply walk out of here and be done with this. I could return with reinforcements, with real coffee. I could ...

A thought strikes me. There might be a way we could leave. Even trapped inside a full-on infestation, I'm not without resources.

I push to stand. "I think I should—"

"Oh, no, you don't," Belinda says. She eases back, sitting upright now. She hugs her knees, but her gaze targets me. "You're not invoking the entity."

"But how—?" How did she know when I barely knew myself?

"It's all over your face—literally. That stupid blue spot is brighter."

Without thinking, I touch my left cheek and the place the entity marked so long ago. It's numb and slightly waxy. The entity has always read my thoughts. Now I consider whether this mark is one of the ways it does so. I cast my thoughts upward, testing, probing. Can it hear me? Would it come to my aid even if I didn't invoke it?

I'm greeted with silence that's as cold and hard as the air around us. No, if I want its help, I must ask. The cost of that? I probe again. Something shifts in the air, almost like a whisper of an answer. While I can't articulate what it wants from me, I do know this:

I'm not ready to pay. Not yet.

"Plus, they've been chattering." Belinda unclenches her grip long enough to hold up her hands like they're talking puppets. "You know how sprites are, and they love to talk about you."

I'm about to respond when her words sink in. "Sprites?" I glance around, sampling the air. "Is there more than one ghost?"

Her eyes go wide with the notion. "I hear them, and yet..."

I scoot from the booth as if standing will help me gauge what we're up against. I don't get too far before pouring myself a second cup—I need something hot to hang on to. The caffeine might help me think, even if the taste is like licking a chalkboard.

"One ghost or many?" I scan the kitchen area behind the short order cook stove. The space looks arctic, like it's been in a deep freeze for months.

"I try to count them," Belinda says, "and they melt into one, but I'm telling you, there are several I recognize."

I turn from my contemplation of the kitchen. "From where?"

"Everywhere," she says, and her voice holds a plaintive note I haven't heard in years. "It's like every ghost that has ever haunted me is here, inside the restaurant."

∽

IT TAKES another full cup of coffee for me to sort through what Belinda has said. I know I shouldn't drink so much. If the ghost— or ghosts—decides to freeze us out of the restroom, we'll be in trouble. Then again, ghosts do love toilet humor.

Either way? I don't plan to visit the restrooms anytime soon.

I return to the booth and start jotting on the order pad.

"What are you doing?" she asks.

"Making a list, an inventory of supplies I used, so I can reimburse the Pancake House."

"Are you kidding me? You're eradicating. They should pay you."

"They didn't hire me."

"I bet Malcolm's already alerted Samia and Jim." She reaches across the table and pulls the order pad from my fingers. "They'll understand."

I'm not so sure. I'm equally unsure about how we'll escape, and whether the Pancake House can open for business in the morning. But most of all, I'm uncertain about this infestation.

One or many? Now that Belinda's mentioned it, I get a sense of the other personalities—it explains the anguish and the anger. Then they all vanish into a single behemoth, and its presence is so overwhelming, it steals my breath.

"All the ghosts?" I say to her.

"A lot of them, at least."

I point to the pad she stole from me. "Make a list. Write down every last ghost you remember and every last one you sense here."

"And then what?"

"And then I'll go find them. I got rid of them once, right?" I raise my cup and down the last drops. "I can do it again."

Belinda chews the end of the pencil—it probably tastes better than the coffee—and scribbles a few lines. I decide on a little reconnaissance. I check the front door of the restaurant again, simply because it's foolish to overlook the obvious.

In this case, it's more than obvious that we're in a full-on ghost infestation. The entire front entrance is frosted over. The indoor-outdoor carpet crackles beneath my sneakers. I can't even see shadows through the windows. I certainly can't tell if Malcolm is on the other side.

"My sprites are here," Belinda calls.

"Your sprites?" I emerge from the entryway. I've eradicated a lot of her ghosts, but I don't remember any sprites.

"From when I was little," she adds. "They would play with me, keep me company. They were my friends."

"Then, why would they haunt you now?" I investigate the cash register for no other reason than it's the sort of item a ghost—or ghosts—would love to launch across the room.

She tilts her head as if considering both my question and the otherworldly presence in the air. "I'm not sure they are, not exactly." She glances at me, brow wrinkled. "Does that make any sense?"

"About as much as everything else," I say. "I think we can assume this is not a typical haunting or infestation."

Cash register secure, I move along the counter. Beneath it, the storage areas are open, filled with cups and saucers, placemats, and packets of crayons for children. As soon as I've taken this all in, I pretend it doesn't exist. No reason to give these ghosts any ideas.

Something breezes through the front of the restaurant. Belinda grips the cow pitcher, but packets of artificial sweetener fly about, striking the windows, the tables, the countertops—and me. I duck behind my hands, but this attack isn't so much malicious as it is mischievous. In its wake comes the hint of a giggle.

Belinda's mouth quirks into a half-smile.

"Your sprites?" I ask.

"Yes, but ... not. It's more like my memory of them."

Sprites have such a slight presence that detecting them is tricky, sometimes impossible. I usually can, and more often than not, they want that attention. But they're gone now, assuming they were here at all.

I point to the order pad. "Any others?"

"The one from Ms. Callahan's geometry class?"

The suggestion itself seems to cause the lights above our heads to fizzle and pop. Another otherworldly breeze scoops up paper placemats and scatters them throughout the restaurant. By rote, I chase after them. They slip through my fingers. I can't catch or collect any of them. As soon as I realize what I'm doing, I halt, breath ragged.

"I still say that one was trying to help you."

Belinda shrugs. "Maybe, but geometry was my best class—I actually wanted to take that test."

In the quiet of the restaurant, I hear the echo of that day—the screeches and cries, the laughter and cheers as the tests went flying across the room and eventually out the window.

"Like a memory," I say to Belinda now.

"Exactly."

"Any more that you sense?"

"Do you remember that one—totally horrid—in my Family and Consumer Science class? And it threw you..."

Belinda trails off, eyes widening in horror. I scamper toward a booth, my feet slipping on the slick tile floor. Too late. An ethereal fist catches me in the stomach, propels me toward the kitchen, and tosses me against one of the refrigerators.

I slide to the floor, hip smacking against that icy tile, my jeans crunching broken glass and pieces of eggshell. I fight for breath, and my vision tunnels to a single point before expanding again.

"Katy!" Belinda springs up and skids to a halt next to me. "Are you okay?"

I nod, barely.

"Did you get the wind knocked out of you?"

I nod again.

"Are you hurt?"

I gasp a breath and hold up a hand, stopping her questions. "It's like we're ... following a script." Word for word. I remember this ghost, and it *was* horrid. I remember this conversation as well. "You mention a ghost, and we relive its eradication."

Belinda sinks down next to me and leans against the refrigerator. "You're right."

"Don't say anything about the one in the boys' locker room."

"Promise. I won't."

The tile is so cold that my hipbones ache. After a moment, I nod toward the front of the restaurant. Before I can stand, Belinda clambers to her feet and offers me her hand.

Back at the booth, I pour more coffee. We both need another cup. At this point, I'm so cold that the coffee tastes, if not good, then passable. By tacit agreement, Belinda continues her list, and I double my reconnaissance efforts.

"Oh, God, I'm sorry, Katy."

Belinda's words are pitched low, filled with something other than fear or anxiety. I want to say guilt, but none of this is her fault. She's staring at her list like it's an exam with a failing grade.

"You didn't cause this," I say.

"I'm talking about back in the day, high school and all that."

"You didn't cause those hauntings, either."

I inspect the rack above the short order cook stove. The Springside Pancake House prides itself on being low-tech. The wait staff uses pencil and paper, and they stick each ticket to the spinning order wheel. This, at least, is secure.

Mostly.

"That's not what I'm talking about."

I turn to look at her. The otherworldly fog has rolled through here as well, and the air is thick and full of mist. But there's something else, something more between us.

"What are you talking about?" I ask.

"I'm making this list, right?" She waves a hand at the ghosts who will not be named. "And it's making me think of all the other things from high school, the things I didn't invite you to, the parties—"

I laugh. "Like the ones at the old barn?"

That was a spectacularly bad idea. Then again, eighteen-year-olds with a keg nearly always have bad ideas at some point. For a while, though, the parties were epic, and the wild ghosts that haunt that space behaved themselves—right up until they didn't.

It took my grandmother to eradicate everyone from the barn—the kids, not the ghosts. If the parties were epic, her scolding topped them. No one left unscathed, including Belinda. I might have been embarrassed, but I was too busy clutching Tupperware and chasing down a contingent of sprites to worry about it—too much.

"It wasn't just those kinds of parties." She ticks the items off on her fingers. "It was the sleepovers, the birthday and swim parties. It was prom—"

"I didn't want to go to prom, and I really didn't want to go with Jack."

"Would you, though, if I hadn't gotten back together with him?"

"If I truly thought he couldn't get a date? Maybe. But that's not Jack." I plant my hands on the counter and lean forward. "Belinda, what's this about?"

She shakes her head, ponytail swaying from side to side. Then she musters her homecoming queen smile. "I'm a lousy friend."

"You're a great friend. We were just ... different then. You did your thing, and I did mine."

And mine was catching ghosts with my grandmother. By then, I did all the chasing and the capturing since her fingers were too stiff and her legs too slow.

"Except when I needed you," Belinda says, "and then you were always there."

"It's what I do. Really, could you picture my grandmother letting me go to all those parties, anyway?"

"It's not like any of us had permission." She snorts. "My

parents didn't know. Half the time, I told them I was going to your place to study."

I drop my gaze as if the countertop has become utterly fascinating.

"Wait a minute ... are you saying they knew?"

"Actually, I didn't say anything."

"Ha, ha. Seriously. What gives?"

I don't want to talk about this. Nothing good can come from this discussion. There are certain ghosts here that shouldn't be disturbed. But Belinda has me locked in her gaze and won't let go.

"It was my mom, wasn't it?" she says. "It would be just like her to put you up to it. Did she bribe you? Threaten you? Say the word, and I'll—"

I hold up a hand, cutting her off. Belinda and her mother have a rocky relationship. As easy as it would be to pin this on her, I can't.

"Your dad," I say at last. "He asked both me and my grand-mother, but mostly me, to keep an eye on you, to let him know where you were, what you were up to. He was ... worried."

And it's difficult to deny a dying man that sort of request.

"You spied on me?" A curious look lights her eyes, like she's both incredulous and hugely pissed off.

"Not really."

"The ghosts did?"

"I didn't talk to them back then." But it's entirely possible that my grandmother did. "Your dad was worried," I add, "about the hauntings and the drinking—"

She swears and drops her head to her knees.

Viewed from the outside, Belinda had one of those charmed high school existences that everyone envies—homecoming queen, star athlete boyfriend, amazing wardrobe, indulgent parents.

But they barely spoke to each other. The ghosts would crawl inside her head. They would whisper their lies and fill her mind with so much chatter she couldn't think. When her father died of pancreatic cancer two months after high school graduation, she let the ghosts in for good.

"So, you spied on me." This time, her words come out as an accusation rather than a question.

I've always been a terrible liar, so I respond with the truth.

"Yes. I did. Because he asked me to."

That was enough for both my grandmother and me. Springside High was—and is—small enough that even if you weren't invited to all the parties, you knew where they were, who went, and what happened.

It wasn't that hard to let Belinda's dad know where she was at any given time. It was all over social media; I'm not sure you could really call it spying. Except, of course, it was.

A chill washes across my neck, the sensation filled with the supernatural. Speaking of both ghosts and spying, they must be loving this, or at least the meaner ones are. This sort of emotional discord gives some ghosts a charge. Some people might speculate that the ghosts feed on negative energy.

My grandmother always said that a cruel person in life makes for a worse ghost in the afterlife.

A chill also rolls off Belinda. I can't repair the damage I've done, not in the middle of this infestation. I need to get us out of here, then maybe I can salvage our friendship.

I push strands of hair from my face and consider my next tactics. I could use some help. I could really use Malcolm and his ability to talk and charm and brew tea. I survey the restaurant. The entryway is in ghostly lockdown. No one is coming in or out. But there's a kitchen entrance, an emergency exit ... and a window. Not the big bay windows that look out onto Main Street, but one I've seen in the alley behind the Pancake House.

"I'm going to look around," I tell Belinda, not that I expect her to answer.

She doesn't.

CHAPTER 5

In the kitchen, I add water to the pot and start on another round of coffee. The aromatic steam seems to help. At least it doesn't hurt.

Unsurprisingly, the kitchen door is glazed over. I'm not even tempted to try the handle or test the deadbolt. The emergency exit appears benign. Only a light dusting of frost covers the silver handle. As I stand in front of it, the urge to reach forward, to push the door open, nearly overwhelms me.

Why? I wonder. I yank my hands back before my fingertips brush the handle. The answer is staring at me from a sign in the middle of the door:

Alarm will sound.

That's all we need: nonstop sirens, the police, the fire department.

These ghosts are devious and bent on making us as miserable as possible.

The last option—really, the only option—is the window. Which is where? I scan the walls, matching them to landmarks outside. Then I realize why I've never seen the window from the inside.

It's in the men's restroom.

I retrace my steps, switch out the old coffee for the new, and set the fresh carafe on the table in front of Belinda. I get nothing for my efforts. I swallow back the dread with a few sips of hot coffee.

"Don't let them in," I whisper. "You're stronger than that."

Then I head off to inspect the men's bathroom.

The otherworldly presence in the restroom is thinner, the air easier to breathe. Disinfectant mixes with the aroma of the coffee I'm holding. My stomach rolls in response, and the combined flavor coats my tongue. I gag before dumping the rest down the drain and taking some quick, shallow breaths to keep my breakfast-for-dinner on the inside.

Then I spy the window. It's at the end of the row of stalls. High up, so I'll need to perch on the radiator to peek outside. When I do, I can see the brick of the neighboring building, Springside Hardware and Tools.

No frost covers the glass—not yet. The metal latch feels cool, but turning it won't give me freezer burn.

When a hand appears on the opposite side, I yelp. My feet skid on the radiator, and I tumble backward. I smack against the tile floor, the ache spreading from wrists to elbows once again. The spike of pain in my tailbone leaves me breathless and gulping for air.

What I saw registers. A hand! A hand that belongs to a person, a person who is most likely Malcolm coming to my rescue like he always does. I claw to standing, and then I clamber back onto the radiator.

My fingers are numb, but I work the latch. I push on the frame, but it barely budges, creaking a protest. From the other side comes the sound of scraping and scrabbling. Someone swears. Malcolm— it must be. From all the noise, it sounds like we have reinforcements as well.

No one has opened this window in ages. The layers of dried paint are as strong as super glue. A knife from the kitchen would help, but I don't want to alert the ghosts to what I'm doing. I dig in with my fingers.

Slivers of the dried paint stab beneath my nails. I push. The person on the other side tugs. The hinges screech, and a thin crack appears between frame and window. Warm air rushes through the opening. It smells like damp wood with a hint of rotted vegetables, but I breathe it in because it's real. Beyond the stench, I sense the summer evening and all the promises it holds.

A pair of hands grips the window frame. The hinges squeal a final protest before the window swings up and open. I jump down from the radiator as first an arm and then a leg poke through.

He comes tumbling down, much like I did earlier. It's an awkward, uncoordinated sort of entrance that's unworthy of Malcolm.

It's that thought that stops me from rushing to him. It's that thought that has me teetering on tiptoes, on the verge of falling forward.

"You're not Malcolm." I can barely believe the words I'm saying.

"No. I'm not." The honeyed drawl hangs in the air, almost seems to thicken it. "Sorry to disappoint. Again."

When he looks up, the force of it strikes me.

I'm here, in the men's restroom, with Carter Dupree.

MY FIRST IMPULSE is not to berate Carter or even to thank him, but to rush past him. I do, scrambling back up to the window. For a moment, I can see the alleyway below. There, standing in its center, is Malcolm. He's peering up at me, his gaze worried.

"Malc—"

Before his name can fully leave my mouth, the window slams shut. It freezes over, crystals forming on the glass before a solid wall of ice shrouds my view. It's thick and opaque, and I can't even detect shadows or shapes on the other side.

I teeter again, but this time, hands at my waist keep me from crashing to the floor. I don't want to say thank you. I really don't. So, I go with the other question pinging around in my head.

"What are you doing here?"

Carter raises his hands as if I've accused him of something. "Trying to help?"

"Wouldn't you be better off in Mexico or Canada or somewhere Orson isn't?"

He gives a little shrug. "He's not in Springside."

"Not at the moment."

Carter inclines his head. "No, not at the moment, which is why I figured it would be the last place he'd look. Besides, he's busy with other things."

"Like what?"

"You."

"Me?" I suppose that isn't a stretch, although I also suspect it isn't me—exactly—that Orson Yates is after. "He wants the entity."

"He wants you, or, more accurately, wants to take you down."

This makes me laugh. Maybe it's because I'm stuck in the middle of a full-on ghost infestation and talking to Carter Dupree in a restroom, but the whole thing strikes me as ludicrous.

"You make it sound like I'm a kingpin or a crime boss or something."

"Actually, that's the way he's making it sound. He's put out a general call to all necromancers in the Midwest region."

"And that means what?"

"Retribution."

I've heard about that before, from Nigel and Reginald. It's what keeps necromancers from going rogue, as far as I can tell. And as far as I can tell, it's Orson Yates who's gone rogue.

"And you know this how?" I ask.

He holds up his hand like a talking puppet—very much the way

Belinda does. "Sprites like to gossip." He tilts his head as if he can hear them whispering now. "And I like to listen."

"Did they tell you anything useful about this infestation?"

"They didn't have to," he says. "I helped build it."

"You helped..." I lose the thread of my response. Honestly, what would anyone say to that? Thanks for all the ghosts?

"I know. It was a shitty thing to do. In my defense, at the time, I thought I was doing the right thing."

"The *right* thing?"

"Okay, the most vengeful thing." He studies me. In the dull yellow of the restroom, his blue eyes look gray. He's sporting at least three days' worth of growth on his jaw. He's a far more tarnished version of himself than he was a few weeks ago.

"You're not supposed to be as good as you are," he says. "You know that, right?"

"So everyone's been telling me. But if I were really that good, I'd know how to deal with that." I fling a hand toward the door and the hallway that leads to the main area of the restaurant. "Are you really here to help?"

"I am."

I nod toward the door. "Then, let's go."

NEVER IN MY life have I imagined that I would be grateful to Carter Dupree even once, never mind twice. But I am. The air in the main area is heavy with ghosts—those from the infestation and those that still linger after my conversation with Belinda.

The moment her gaze lands on him, her eyes widen. She sits up straight and sheds her despondency. She utters several curses that rival Malcolm's.

"Yeah, it's nice to see you, too," Carter says.

"What are you doing here?" She shakes her head, ponytail swishing back and forth as if she could sweep him from her sight.

155

"He's here to help. He knows about that." I point toward the kitchen. "He helped ... build it." I turn to Carter now. "Did you build it? I mean, what is it, exactly? One big ghost, or lots of ghosts jumbled together?"

"Yes." A smirk lingers just beneath his bland expression.

"Oh, that's it." Belinda shoves herself from the booth. "He's just messing with us. Let me at him."

Carter holds up a hand as if to stop her, then turns it toward himself as if he's inspecting his manicure. "Please. Like you could make me if I didn't want to help."

Belinda plants a hand on her hip. "I know I can."

Something passes between them, an odd sort of exchange full of challenge, animosity, and something more, something that looks like compassion. Theirs is not a relationship I want to contemplate.

"Guys, please. We need to get rid of the ghosts. Ideally, we need to do that and clean up the place before Samia arrives to open for the morning shift. Right?" I turn to Belinda. "When does she usually get here?"

"It's insane, like four in the morning."

I glance around the restaurant. The bacon and eggs wall clock is ticking toward ten. I consider the mess I've already made—and the one that's sure to follow. Ghost catching is a sloppy business. Six hours, give or take. I bite my lip hard enough that the warm, coppery flavor of blood and the quick stab of pain clear my head.

"Okay," I say to Carter. "How do we fight this thing?"

"I'm not sure," he admits.

Belinda throws her hands in the air. "See? He's only here to mess with us."

Carter glares at her.

"Can you tell me what it is, exactly?" I ask. "One minute, it feels like a really powerful ghost, and the next, I can sense sprites and personalities, and..." I tilt my head. In that instant, I sense a chorus of spirits, as if the ghosts have been eavesdropping and want to send this particular point home.

I catch Belinda's eye. "High school."

"Yeah." Her gaze searches the air. "Just like high school."

We both turn and lock our sights on Carter. He mouths something indistinct and then rubs the stubble along his jaw.

"It's a necromancer thing," he says.

Of course it is.

"It's kind of like a Frankenstein monster version of a ghost. What you do, or really, what a powerful necromancer does, is take a collection of ghosts—any kind of ghosts, from sprites to really strong ones—and stitch them together."

"Stitch them together." I say the words more to myself than either of them. I try to picture it—ghosts, a needle and thread. I'm at a loss for how someone might do that.

"Yeah, it's not easy. It's not something I can do."

"But Orson can?" I say.

Carter nods. "It was ... he was ... teaching me the technique. After I got a lapful of orange juice"—he throws a scowl at Belinda —"I decided it might be fun to get a little revenge."

"You're nothing but charm," she mutters.

I send her a quick shake of my head. At the moment, we need Carter, whether we like him or not.

He continues as if he hasn't heard her. "Since I was collecting Springside ghosts anyway, I separated out those that had haunted Belinda. It wasn't that hard. Sprites like gossip and praise, so they were more than happy to tattle on the less forthcoming ghosts."

This I can see. Sprites love attention. They love shiny things. Not too long ago, Carter was nothing but shiny.

"And then what?" I ask. "You have all these ghosts, so how do you ... stitch them together?"

"That's the part I can't explain. The rest is Orson's doing." He holds out his hand toward the kitchen as if he's detecting an invisible force. "Do you sense him? He has a distinct signature. Most necromancers with his kind of power do."

I hold out my hand and will my fingertips to discern something different about this haunting. I detect that undercurrent of cruelty, but like earlier, I can't put a name to it.

"Nigel could," I say, dropping my hand. "But I can't."

Carter scrutinizes me, his face scrunched up not in disgust but what looks like genuine curiosity. "You make no sense as a necromancer."

"Well, I keep telling people I'm not one. Nobody listens."

He snorts and continues. "What this is, essentially, is a big knot of ghosts. A strong enough necromancer should be able to slice through the knot. And then, poof." He holds up his hands. "No more knot."

"But a bunch of ghosts on the loose," I say.

"Most will want to leave."

I tilt my head toward the kitchen. I don't need to strain to pick up the wailing, the cries. Carter's right. The large majority of ghosts want nothing to do with this haunting.

"How, exactly?" I ask.

Carter once again stares as if my ignorance astounds him. "You broke the containment field in the cemetery, right?"

I nod.

"And the ones in the warehouse?"

"I did."

"Same idea, except instead of visualizing breaking through something, you concentrate on cutting through something."

"And that's it?"

"It's a precision sort of move, takes a certain amount of finesse."

Which I clearly don't—or at least shouldn't—have.

"Is this something you can do?" I ask.

Carter glances away as if the cash register has absorbed all this attention. "I'm not strong enough," he says, "but you are."

"I am?"

"It's why we didn't bother to deploy it sooner. Orson knew you could slice through it pretty easily, and then we'd lose all those ghosts."

"But now it's something to keep me busy while he's off planning retribution or whatever it is?"

Carter shrugs. "Whatever works, right?"

"So, what should I do? Find the knot and cut it in half?"

"More or less." Doubt clouds his expression. "I guess."

"Where is it?"

He raises his chin. It's a familiar move, one I've done and watched Malcolm do so many times before. Carter rounds the cash register and heads into the kitchen area. Belinda and I follow, walking the same wandering path that he does.

We pass the coffeemakers. He glances over his shoulder, nose wrinkled.

"That smells awful."

"Thanks," I say.

"When this is over," Belinda whispers in my ear, "let me at him. I'm telling you, I need an hour, tops, to ruin his life."

"I'm not even going to ask how you plan on doing that."

We move deeper into the kitchen, past the racks and the prep areas, and mounting dread tells me where this journey will end. Belinda's fingertips brush my hand, and then she grips it tight.

Our sneakered feet meet the ice-slicked tiles. The pot remains on its side, embedded in the slush around it. Carter skids, and his arms flail, but he catches himself. Then, he halts our trek.

In front of us is the door to the cold storage unit.

CHAPTER 6

For a long moment, none of us speak. I don't relish the idea of going back in. But Carter's right. The knot is here, behind the stainless steel door.

"How are we going to get in?" Belinda whispers.

Before I can answer, the handle rattles, and the door creaks open. A gust of cold air rolls from the space, chasing strands of hair from my cheeks and making Belinda's ponytail sway. The breeze ripples through the kitchen, and the stainless steel racks shudder in its wake.

"Oh, this is bad," Carter mutters.

Inside the room, clouds hang in the air from ceiling to floor. I catch glimmers here and there—something in the shape of a sprite I once caught, a more robust ghost lurking near the back. In the center, a huge cluster of ghosts is gathering.

At least, I think they are. One moment, I can count dozens. The next, all I see is one large mass, roiling with rage and sorrow.

"Do I imagine a sword?" I ask him. "A pair of scissors?"

"I don't think it matters, as long as it works."

"Did Orson ever—?"

He gives his head a quick shake before I can even ask my question.

"Orson didn't work like that. He parceled out instruction. It kept us ... dependent on him."

"I'm guessing you didn't make it this far in the lesson."

"Sorry." The single word is laced not with sarcasm, but with regret.

"Yeah, me too." I survey the mass in front of me. No one has attacked or thrown anything our way. That, in itself, is a small miracle. I pull in a deep breath. "Okay. I'll try."

I think back to when I broke the containment field in the cemetery, only instead of chipping a virtual hole with a tire iron, I now imagine a sword, like something out of *The Lord of the Rings*. I picture myself holding it above my head, bringing it down...

A cry rends the air. Belinda grabs my arm.

"What was that?" we both say.

Carter glances away as if he suddenly finds the prep area fascinating. He won't meet my eyes.

"They're crying," Belinda says. "My sprites. I can hear them. My sprites are in there."

I nudge Carter. He starts but turns to face me.

"What happens to the ghosts when you slice through them?" I ask.

He stares as if I've asked a ridiculous question. "They're just ghosts, Katy."

"But what happens to them? I need to slice through some of them, so what happens to those ghosts in particular? Where do they go?"

He shrugs. "I don't know. When the knot is cut, most of the ghosts go free."

"And the others?" The frustration in my words is as thick as the ghosts hanging in the air.

"They ... vanish."

"Do they die?"

"They're *ghosts*," he says as if I'm dimwitted. "They're already dead."

"It hurts them," Belinda declares.

She's right; it's an honest hurt, one I sense in the pit of my stomach.

"Is there another way to do this?" I ask.

"There is no other way." He gestures toward the mass of ghosts. "You slice through. How else are you going to untangle everything?"

Another cry goes up. The shelving inside the cold storage unit rattles with the force of it. Even the meaner ghosts, the ones harboring cruel intentions, quiver at the suggestion.

"How else?" I consider the entwined mass. "By unraveling them?"

"I don't think that's possible," Carter says.

"Have you tried?"

He shakes his head, in warning rather than in answer. "That's part of this, the purpose behind this trick. Not only can you tie up all of a necromancer's ghosts, but you force him—"

"Or her."

"Or her." He sighs. "To sacrifice some to free the rest."

"What a terrible thing to do," I say.

"I didn't say it was nice."

"But in theory, I could go in there." I point. "And untangle each ghost from the others, right?"

"It will drain you. It will leave you vulnerable."

"To what?"

"A necromancer with an attack ghost."

Like Orson Yates or Darien Armand? I flirt with the idea of conjuring up the sword again, but I lack the will to even imagine myself imagining it.

"I could go in with you," Belinda says, her voice low.

I give my head an emphatic shake. "Oh, no, you couldn't."

"I could, and besides, you need me. Can you tell where one ghost ends and the other begins?"

I squint into the churning crowd of them. Even now, I can only catch the suggestion of a form, and certainly not several, distinct forms.

"Can you?" I ask Belinda.

She nods. "I'm a sensitive, remember? And this is what I do." She swings toward Carter. "Right? You guys use them all the time, I bet."

An odd half-smile lights Carter's face. "Huh. Orson has a couple of friends"—he draws little air quotes around *friends*—"that he consults on a regular basis. We always thought it was, you know, for a different kind of favor."

Belinda snorts. "In his case, it's probably both." She nods toward the cold storage unit. She looks fierce, but beneath the homecoming queen smile, uncertainty lurks.

"Want to give it a try?" she says.

Do I? I can't imagine the sword any longer. I don't want to slice or cut or damage these ghosts, not even that truly vile one near the back. I don't want to be like Orson Yates, so I do the one thing I'm sure he wouldn't.

I plunge in.

THE FOG of ghosts swallows us immediately. Carter is a shadowy figure backlit by the kitchen. His form morphs, growing fatter, then tall and thin. His nose stretches, Pinocchio-style.

Belinda breathes a laugh. "They're making fun of him," she whispers.

Why, yes. Yes, they are.

"Where do we start?" I ask. "Can you find a thread or a ghost to begin with?"

She extends a hand in front of her. Ghosts swarm and then

retreat. One slithers by me, ruffling my hair, but when I try to follow its path, it fades into the cloud once again.

"Here," she says. "Let's start here with this one. Do you recognize it?"

She sweeps her hands around and around until the outline of this particular ghost takes shape. It shimmers except for those spots where it's stitched to the other ghosts in this tangle. And I do recognize it.

"Ms. Callahan's geometry class."

"You were such a troublemaker," Belinda says to it.

The ghost squirms, mewing in a way more suitable for a sprite than a full-fledged spirit capable of short-circuiting the overhead lights. For this sort of work, a sword—imaginary or otherwise—won't do. Even a pair of sewing scissors feels too brutal. I don't want to cut; I want to pull.

Hands, then. Fingertips and nails.

"Will you let me?" I ask the ghost. "I think I can set you free, but you've got to hold still."

The ghost floats between Belinda's cupped hands while I get to work. It's like grasping soap bubbles. The ghost is just substantial enough for me to touch it, but oh so fragile. I pluck at the seam between it and its compatriot.

The more I tug at the seams, the more I can sense them. As with containment fields, once I start to work, I can distinguish what is the otherworldly and what is courtesy of a necromancer.

I don't want to rip. I soon realize that the stitches holding these ghosts together are very much like those that hold fabric—and Orson is a master tailor who has stitched these ghosts together with a strength that's daunting. I free a section only to have a tangle emerge within the tangle. The ghost squirms, shoots away from Belinda. Its outline fades. I step back and exhale a long breath.

"Be good," she tells it. "We're trying to help."

I glance around the cold storage area, trying to follow the line of ghosts into the center of the knot.

"It's endless," I say. So many ghosts, and all of them so tangled together.

"It's not. I've been counting them in my head. Don't worry about the others. Just concentrate on the next one."

It's good advice, for ghosts and life.

"Thanks," I tell her. "Thanks for coming along."

"What's a sensitive for?" She reaches into the cloud of ghosts. "This one. Do this one next."

I do. I work, and the outline of each shimmers and fades, but my fingertips start to recognize the feel of the thread—for lack of a better word—that holds them together.

My shoulders cramp; my fingers ache. This is going to take all night. But the ghostly chatter has died away. The vile ghost in the corner pouts—there's no mistaking that—but it hasn't taken a swipe at either of us.

Because if I don't untangle them? They're stuck with each other. For eternity? This, I don't know, but they want to be free, and they're letting me work.

For now, that's enough.

Images flash through my mind as we get closer to the center of the knot. Scenes from past eradications, from all the mischief these ghosts have caused, but there's more. I pause, scanning the air, not certain what I'm viewing is in my mind at all.

"Can you see that?" I ask.

Belinda nods, loose hair from her ponytail hiding her face.

It's like a ghostly version of television, or the portal the entity once used. The scene plays out on a misty screen. There, a pre-school version of Belinda is laughing with three frisky sprites. They swoop and dart around her princess-pink bedroom, ruffle her blonde curls, and float above her pillow at night, casting a muted, otherworldly glow to ward off the dark.

"Are those yours?" I know the answer, but I ask anyway.

"My sprites," she says, her voice as insubstantial as the mist around us. She raises a hand toward the image, then lets it drop. "I should've never sent them away."

"You did? When?" I don't remember my grandmother eradicating sprites when it came to Belinda; I certainly haven't.

"I was four, maybe five. My mother said I was too old for imaginary playmates." She shakes her head, but I think she's shaking her hair loose so I can't see her face. "She doesn't have a sensitive bone in her body."

In more ways than one. I squelch the thought and barely manage to swallow back the accusation. Belinda's father was the one who made the calls, paid for the eradications. When he died, I thought the ghosts would move in for good.

"What about your dad?" I venture.

"I think he must have been." She peers through the fringe of hair at me. "Don't you?"

Around us, scenes play out as if in response to her words. The foggy image of Belinda's father on a cell phone, his face worried. That vile ghost in the corner tormenting Belinda. My grandmother pointing and directing as I slip through a crawlspace after it.

Then a scene appears that doesn't feature Belinda at all, but her father. He's standing in our living room, even though my grandmother has urged him to sit more than once. He balances a cup of coffee in one hand, one I've just given him.

"I wish," he says, and then sighs, the sound of it so heavy, I'm not certain how he can stand under the weight of it. "I wish I could get through to her."

"It's the age," my grandmother says, "and nothing more. Give her time."

"Yes. Time." Belinda's father sips the coffee and closes his eyes.

My grandmother winces, and I see her mentally chastising herself for the careless words.

"I could help."

It's strange to hear my own voice come through the mist. I remember now. Mr. Barnes didn't ask me to spy.

I volunteered.

The scene fades. But the ghosts aren't through with us, because the next thing to appear is a hospital room, one equipped with monitors and IVs and drawn shades.

Belinda's father is so thin, barely a presence beneath the woven hospital blanket. Belinda sits at his bedside, and there's a stack of books on the nightstand. She's been reading to him and now closes the book and grips it in her lap.

"Mr. Bauer will be so proud I finally finished *To Kill a Mockingbird*." She gives her dad a practiced smile, although it looks as if it might shatter. She looks like she might shatter.

"You always did things in your own time, and that's okay. Remember that."

"Dad—"

"Shh. Just remember that, pumpkin, okay? And don't worry about the rest."

The room darkens. Hours must pass by, but the next thing I see is Belinda resting her head on his bed, hand gripping his, the heart rate monitor switched off. If grief has a sound, it's not wails and sobs but the low hum of ventilation, of overhead lights, of a world where you can't hear the soft breathing of the people you love.

This scene, too, fades. My heart is pounding hard in my chest. The corners of my eyes are damp and hot. Belinda is trying to hold the ghost we've been working on, but her fingers are trembling. I tug her hands from the ghost. It dips and dives and ruffles her hair in an attempt to give her a ghostly kiss.

She doesn't bat it away. She doesn't shove me away, either, for which I'm grateful.

"I wasn't there for him," she says, and her voice is so small, it's nearly swallowed by the mist.

"Were the ghosts lying, then?" I ask.

She raises her head, but locks of hair shroud her face. "What?"

"You were with him at the end."

"Only the end. I was a terrible daughter."

"He never thought so, and that's the part that counts. He gets to decide that, not you. He thought the world of you. That's why he came to us. If he didn't love you, didn't think you worthwhile, why would he bother?"

The ghosts hang cold and motionless in the air, and their hush surrounds us.

"I thought I might find him here." At last, she pushes the hair from her face. Her cheeks sparkle with tears. "I thought maybe he'd come back and haunt me." Her gaze tracks the line of ghosts, all jumbled from our efforts to untangle them. "I'm pretty sure I'd sense him if he did."

Her determination to follow me in here starts to make sense, as does her drinking. I wonder what's harder to live with, the voices or the silence.

"Not everyone ends up as a ghost." I consider the ones floating around us. "My best guess is, not everyone needs to. In your dad's case, I think he knew you'd be okay, just in your own time."

Belinda hiccups a single sob and throws her arms around my neck. I rock her and let her cry. At some point, three spirits join us. They're tethered to the long line of ghosts; they're not going anywhere without all the others. But they're free enough now to push their way to us.

"I don't think you truly sent your sprites away," I say to Belinda before turning my face toward them. They're hovering about her, all chatter and concern. "You three were there, in the hospital, weren't you?"

In answer, they bob up and down.

"And you've always kept an eye on her, right?"

More bobbing.

Belinda eases from me. She pushes tears from her face and reaches out to push a few from mine. Then she turns her attention toward the sprites.

If they weren't knotted together, they'd probably do backflips. As it is, they shimmer and bounce and begin to dance as best they can. They're clumsy, like puppies, and career and collide into each other.

"You know," I venture. "You're not a necromancer. It's not like you could end up addicted. You're not like Nigel."

"What are you trying to say?"

"That maybe you don't need to send these three away."

"I don't?"

"Do they scare you?"

"No."

"Do you like them?"

"Yes."

"Can you put up with their antics?"

She tilts her head and considers the trio. "Maybe."

"Then, there's no reason they shouldn't stick around." I pull in a breath, an odd weariness settling on me. "Of course, we have to untangle them first."

I scan the storage unit. Before, these ghosts resembled a large ball of otherworldly yarn; now it looks as though we've strung the shelves with strands of supernatural tinsel. Ghosts are everywhere, a little less tangled but not free, not yet.

Belinda pushes to her knees and then stands. I don't remember when, exactly, we landed on the floor, but the tile is frigid beneath my legs. My muscles ache with the cold. Belinda offers me her hand.

"Come on, ghost catcher," she says. "It's time to get back to work."

CHAPTER 7

An hour later, I decide that unraveling ghosts must be the most tedious task ever. At least, I think it's an hour later. There's no clock in the cold storage unit, but when I ask Belinda about the time, a couple of ghosts form an impromptu clock.

It's an ethereal two in the morning, assuming these ghosts know how to tell time. This I doubt. I do know we've been in here for a while. Fog shrouds the doorway. Carter's shadow wavers, but whether he's been there the whole time, I can't say.

I tug and pull at the seams that hold these ghosts. Each stitch is like its own containment field. My fingertips are numb, my thoughts as hazy as the air around us. Despite the cold, sweat trickles down my spine.

I swipe a hand across my brow. "No wonder most necromancers cut through the seams." I'm about to add something else to this when a whirlwind kicks up in the center of the room.

All at once, I'm thrown to one corner and Belinda to the other. Two spirits of surprising strength tether my arms. My hands are locked so far apart that I can't pull at the seams, never mind free myself.

"I didn't mean it, guys," I say. "But if you don't let me go, I can't finish. Unless you want to be stuck with each other for eternity."

The air roils around us. So much otherworldly chatter fills the space that I want to clamp my hands over my ears.

But, of course, I can't.

Some sort of supernatural debate rages and then simmers. The shackles evaporate. I rub my wrists, although there's no mark or bruise—just a ribbon of cold that stings and throbs.

"Belinda, too," I say, "or I'm not pulling out another stitch."

The ghost in the corner—the vile one—lets go so suddenly that Belinda flies forward and crashes into the metal racks. Something tumbles to the ground—something that sounds an awful lot like a dozen eggs.

She props her hands on her thighs and gasps.

"You okay?"

"Just ... get ... back ... to ... work," she manages between breaths.

The more I tug, the more I'm led back to Belinda's three sprites. Over and over again, I follow a line of ghosts only to return to them. The obvious strikes me; I feel foolish for not realizing it sooner, for not seeing what Orson has done.

Belinda's three sprites are at the heart of the tangle. I kneel in front of them and consider what Orson gleaned from them—from all these ghosts—and how he used that knowledge against both of us. How, if I had decided to slice through this tangle, I most certainly would've destroyed them.

I marvel at that, at how well he picks his targets.

"What if I worked from the inside out instead of the outside in?" I say this not only to the sprites but to the room at large.

The air quivers with excitement. Yes, I'm on to something. I inspect the stitches holding the three sprites. They're tighter, closer together, sometimes looped through all three sprites at once.

Even so? I'm certain that if I untangle this particular knot, all the rest will fall away.

Belinda sits across from me, her hands cupping the sprites. Despite their predicament, they're positively giddy with the attention.

"Hold still," I tell them. "This is tricky. I don't want to hurt you."

"He's a real bastard," Belinda says. "Why would a ghost even go near someone like Orson or Carter?"

"Maybe they don't have a choice. Most people aren't as sensitive as you or Sadie. The hauntings are just that—random and scary."

"And when you're lonely..." She lets the sentence trail. "I guess some attention is better than none."

Yes, I think. Lonely. Maybe that's why I feel such a kinship with these ghosts, no matter the trouble they cause me.

I return my attention to the three in front of me. They're subdued now, much like five-year-olds with splinters, bravely submitting to the grown-up with the tweezers.

These three have been so loyal to Belinda that I don't want to damage them in any way. I gnaw on my lower lip in the hope that the pain will keep me alert. Bit by bit, I obliterate Orson's stitches. Bit by bit, their range of motion increases.

Then, at last, I tug the final thread, and it evaporates. For a moment, the sprites simply hang in the air as if they can't believe they're free.

Then, the unraveling begins. There's a popping and a shredding, a chain reaction where first one ghost and then the next is free. They zip around the cold storage unit, their joy contagious.

Belinda laughs. I want to, but exhaustion is weighing me down. It's hard to breathe with all the fog and mist that lingers.

"Go on!" Belinda shouts. "Get out of here. You're free!"

I expect a mass exodus, a rush for the door. If Carter is

anywhere in their path, they'll flatten him. We'll be catching ghosts for weeks.

Instead, they spin in tandem, creating another whirlwind. The metal racks around us start to fade. The floor beneath our feet turns rocky. Above our heads, the ceiling vanishes, revealing bright sunlight and blue skies. I blink, the glare of the day hitting me, and raise a hand to my eyes.

The Pancake House slips away, but we're not on Main Street, and it's not the middle of the night.

It takes a moment, but I recognize the warning sign with the curvy arrow. I've taken the turn in this road a thousand times. A few miles farther on is the nature preserve where Malcolm and I do our releases.

Below our feet is the ravine. Several yards away, someone is standing, someone who looks like Orson Yates.

BELINDA GRABS my arm and yanks me down. We crouch at the side of the road, our gazes locked on Orson.

He's partially hidden from the road by a cluster of saplings, his eyes trained on the approach from town. He stares straight ahead, straight past us ... straight through us?

The sun is beating down, warm and bright after the cold storage unit. I blink once, twice, and then rub fingers across my eyelids. There's something odd about Orson, something I can't quite place.

"Does he look different to you?" I whisper.

"Younger?" she says. I sense more than see Belinda take in his full measure. "Definitely younger, like our age. I hate to say it, but he's actually kind of hot."

"Ew."

"In a retro kind of way. Look at him. Hello, it's the 90s calling, and they want their stone-washed jeans back."

I can't help it. I snort. Loudly.

We both freeze, but his gaze remains on the road. It's as if he can't even hear us. I turn to Belinda again.

"1990s?" I venture.

"Totally. I mean, look at that..." Her words fade. She pats the earth with both hands, the move frantic. "It feels real." She picks up a handful of dirt.

The gravel appears solid enough in her palm, but when she lets it slide from its perch, the image wavers until the pebbles and dust settle once again.

"What is this?" she asks.

"Like before?" I suggest. "In the Pancake House? The ghosts are showing us something."

"Why?"

I open my mouth to respond, but no words come out.

"And why is it so real?"

This, I have a sense for. Underneath the illusion, I catch a hint of the otherworldly, the echo of memories stitched one to the other. "They're working together, and they're just strong enough to make this feel real."

I think of how strong the entity must be, then, to have transported the group of us to the warehouse.

"They're your ghosts," I add. "Maybe they—"

"No, they're *our* ghosts, Springside ghosts."

Yes. Springside ghosts, every last one, not a single interloper in the group.

"And this is something they think we should see?" I ask.

"Maybe. Maybe they're thanking you for not slicing them to bits like a scary necromancer." Her gaze moves from Orson to me. "What happened back then that they'd want you to see?"

"I don't know. I was just a..." My lips go numb. The word I was about to say lodges in my throat. I don't even want to think the word, and I give my head a vigorous shake as if that will dislodge it.

It doesn't. No matter how much I don't want the thought in my mind, it takes up residence there.

Baby.

I leap forward. Belinda makes a grab for me, but I'm too quick. I dash into the center of the road.

"Katy, get back here. He'll see you."

"He won't. He can't." I spin in a circle, arms wide. "This isn't real. It's a memory, or several memories."

Pieces of the scene around us flicker in and out. The trees across the ravine are a fuzzy green, their leaves imprecise. Even though the ghosts of Springside have pooled what they remember into one collective memory, they don't remember everything.

"Guys, don't do this." I speak to the sky, to the air, to anywhere the ghosts might be. "I don't need to see this. Really, I don't. Okay? Can we go back now?"

"Katy, he's looking right at you."

"He isn't looking at me or for me."

"Then..." Belinda pulls herself up and inches to the side of the road. "What is he looking for?"

"My parents."

I turn, face Orson, and wave my hands over my head. I jump up and down. He keeps the vigil, his gaze focused straight ahead. It's unnerving to be caught in his unrelenting glare, even if I know he can't see me. Orson from the past can't be aware of Katy from the future.

At least, I don't think he can.

From behind me comes the roar of a motor. Something flickers in Orson's gaze. I whirl and face in the direction of the oncoming car.

"Katy, what're you doing?"

"Waiting."

"Get back here."

I purse my lips and shake my head.

"Katy, don't do this."

"I'm not doing anything."

"You can't stop this, whatever this is."

"I know."

Up ahead, sunlight glints off the car's windshield.

"Katy, come on."

The road beneath my feet rumbles. The roar grows louder, the noise of it shaking the air. The car is taking the turn much too fast. I know; a mere four months ago, I nearly skidded through this turn and pitched into the ravine below.

A screech fills the world then, one so loud I feel it in my lungs, my heart. The car flies around the corner, heading straight for me, the left two wheels lifting from the asphalt.

Belinda screams. A cacophony resounds; past and present merge. Light explodes before my eyes. For a moment, I'm in the dark, surrounded by the fog and mist of the cold storage unit.

Then bright sunlight fills my vision.

The car, the one that's carrying my parents, is behind me now.

Belinda sobs with relief. She races from her spot at the side of the road and captures me in a fierce hug. Together we watch the car smash through the guardrail and plunge into the ravine.

The sound of it guts me. The crunch is like nothing I've ever heard before. I rush forward but collide with an invisible wall. Fog covers the deepest part of the ravine, obscuring my view, and I feel as if I've had the wind knocked from me.

"I don't understand." I step back and address the wispy clouds flowing in random patterns. "I thought you wanted me to see this."

Silence greets my plea, from both the ravine and the ghosts below. Then, I hear it. Light steps on asphalt that break into a jog.

Orson Yates runs past us until he's teetering at the edge of the ravine, one hand gripping the branch of a tree. He scampers down a few feet only to crawl back up again. He frowns in the direction of the car, and an odd play of emotions flickers across his face.

I'm expecting that cunning and cruel smile of his, but it never materializes. In some ways, Orson looks as gutted as I feel. He slides down the ravine only to change his mind and claw his way back up. He does this once, twice, enough times that I lose count. He's a man caught in a trap of hesitation and doubt.

In the distance, the thin wail of a siren rises up. The sound draws closer until it's all we can hear. Orson freezes, near the top of the ravine now, his grip so tight on that tree branch he's bound to snap it in two.

A Springside patrol car draws up. An officer steps out. The bulk may be a little less, but the shoulders are just as broad, and there's no mistaking the towering frame of Police Chief Ramsey.

Make that Officer Ramsey. Like Orson, he looks so young. Too young, really.

"Sir, did you see what happened?"

"A car, it ... I mean—" Orson points. "Broke through the guardrail and..."

Chief is already on his radio, calling for support, an ambulance, the fire department. Orson appears jittery. He unclutches the tree branch and skids several feet down the ravine.

"Sir, stop!" Chief scans the area. He lifts his chin almost like I do when I'm sensing ghosts. "I smell gas. Let—"

It isn't an explosion, not like in the movies, but there's a crackle of flames. Smoke snakes up from the center of the ravine. I can't see the crash site, have no idea what it looks like.

I think that's just as well.

More sirens fill the air. Orson takes one last look at the ravine, his gaze hollow, nearly vacant. Then he pulls himself up the incline to the road. Chief Ramsey offers him a hand and tugs him the rest of the way.

Then, inexplicably, Chief lets go. Shock, rather than anger, fills Orson's expression. Chief whirls and starts down the road. Somewhere beneath the wail of sirens and the snap and pop of the fire, a plaintive cry echoes.

It sounds like a sprite, tiny and lost.

At first, I don't see what's making the sound. Chief kneels at the side of the road where the gravel meets a soft patch of grass. He freezes there except for one massive shuddering of his shoulders.

"I don't believe…" His words trail off, swallowed up by the snap and sizzle of the fire and the approaching wails of the sirens. He crouches, and when he does, I see what has caught his attention.

A baby is sitting in that soft patch of grass, one that's not quite as old as Thomas Jr., but not an infant, either.

All my rational thoughts stop. I can only stare at the scene. Belinda comes up behind me, grabs me around the waist, and holds on tight. It's as if she knows I need the support to stand.

Chief remains frozen in place. The baby clutches and unclutches one of his fingers. She blinks at him, in wonder, perhaps. He must fill her entire view, shading her from the sun. Although she's tiny, she probably shouldn't see the carnage in the ravine.

It's something she won't remember.

Orson comes up behind them. Chief surveys him over his shoulder, very much a guard dog sizing up a threat. His gaze sweeps over Orson, and the man halts.

Orson's brow furrows. "What is it?"

That's when Chief rouses himself. With gentle hands, he scoops up the baby and tucks her into his arms. He keeps Orson in his sights, but grooves line his mouth and anguish fills his eyes. He looks more like the Chief Ramsey I know than a young patrol officer at the start of his career.

Orson is a man petrified. He stands there staring at both Chief Ramsey and the baby. "That isn't … I mean, it can't be. It isn't—"

"Possible?" Chief supplies.

"Was she in the car?"

"I don't see how she could've been." Chief rocks the baby

gently in his arms, swaying slightly as he does. He and his wife never had children. A sudden sadness strikes me in the midst of everything else—he would've made a wonderful father.

"Then, how...?" Orson's mouth opens and closes as if he's struggling to breathe.

"You tell me," Chief says. "You saw the accident?" This is more a statement than a question, less of a friendly inquiry and more a detective across the table from a suspect.

Orson nods, but the gesture is absent-minded. He searches the air, the ravine, scanning the space, back and forth, back and forth. Clearly, he's searching for something. A glimmer sparks in his eyes. He takes a step away from Chief, and then another, intent on something.

"Sir, as a witness, you need to remain here. I need to take your statement." Chief jangles the handcuffs at his side. How? I'm not sure, not with his arms full of baby.

The light in Orson's eyes dims. He mutters a curse that Chief pretends not to hear. Before either man can say another word, a second patrol car pulls up, followed by a fire truck and the state troopers.

Chief points a finger at Orson in the way you might tell a dog to stay and heads for the second patrol car. He walks straight through Belinda and me. She gasps, but I'm too numb to feel anything.

The edges of the scene fracture, and the sphere of what we can see grows smaller and smaller. The green in the grass and the blue in the sky fade to pale imitations of color.

Only the center of the vision remains, the smoke-filled ravine. This, too, is quickly changing to mist and fog. The cold from the storage unit invades my bones.

Before the scene vanishes completely, the smoke clears from the ravine. On the other side, a man is standing. For a moment, my heart leaps. I recognize that ebony hair, the set of the jaw.

But the man is too gaunt, not quite tall enough to be Malcolm. No, it isn't Malcolm at all.

The man on the other side of the ravine is Darien Armand.

CHAPTER 8

Belinda and I collapse onto the hard tile floor. Ghosts fill the room. In fact, not a single one has escaped. They swirl above our heads, and although I'm not listening—at least, I'm trying not to—their chatter is nearly deafening.

"Shh." Belinda holds a finger to her lips. It's an admonishment most choose to ignore.

Her three sprites crowd around us. They're unusually bold, shoving the other ghosts away and letting us catch our breath.

"Huh," she says, and the corner of her mouth turns up into an almost-smile. "They're worried about you."

"I'm fine."

"Yes. Of course you are." She rolls her eyes, a move meant for her sprites, and then points at me. "Yeah, I know. She's stubborn."

From somewhere deep inside me, I manage a laugh. At the moment, it's better than tears. Those can come later, preferably when I'm not on the floor of the cold storage unit.

"We need to get out of here," I say. "Right?" I aim this at the ghosts. "You guys want to go home?"

As a mass, they stream for the door. The whoosh ruffles our hair, and the sound of it is like an approaching train.

"I hope Carter isn't on the other side," Belinda says. Then she gives me an evil grin. "Actually, I kind of hope he is. Come on. Let's go see."

We find Carter outside the door, flat on his back in a puddle. He's craning his neck and scowling at us—and the world in general. Without hesitation or reluctance, Belinda offers him her hand.

He shakes out his limbs, wrings water from his shirt, and mutters a few curses for good measure.

He nods toward the cold storage unit. "What happened in there?"

I'm not certain we should tell Carter anything about what we saw. Before I can throw Belinda a warning glance, she gives him her patented homecoming queen smile. Then she runs her fingers through her hair, secures it in a ponytail, and says, "What didn't?"

Carter seems to have forgotten he even asked a question. I tilt my head and study Belinda. I'm pretty sure this is a trick I can never attempt, never mind master.

"Want to get out of here?" She wraps an arm around my waist, and together we take a few steps into the main kitchen area. "Are we good?" she adds, her voice so low, it's barely a whisper.

"We're always good."

"And you? After all of ... that? Are you okay?"

"Are you?" I counter.

"I'm not sure." Her gaze flits upward, toward where the three sprites are dancing along the ceiling. "But I feel better now that I have my sprites back."

"So do I." I'll worry less about her with these three keeping vigil.

She gives me a sidelong glance, and I muster a grin.

But I sigh with dismay when we pass the mess we made during this eradication. The coffee has brewed so long that a burnt odor lingers in the air. It's almost enough to put me off coffee for good. No wonder some people think it tastes terrible. In this case, they're right.

Through the windows, the lights of Main Street glimmer. It's probably my imagination, but I'm certain I see the gold lettering on the storefront of K&M Ghost Eradication Specialists. My heart beats harder at the sight. Because, even though it's technically night, and we'll be cleaning for the rest of it, somewhere on the other side of the door, Malcolm is waiting.

Carter reaches the entryway first. He rattles the handle. He rattles it again before jerking it back and forth. Then he plants a shoulder against the door and shoves.

"Come on," Belinda says, annoyance tingeing her voice. "Not funny at this point."

"Not a joke." Carter's voice is so tight that I think he might growl. "Trust me, I want to be as far away as possible from here."

Behind us, the ghosts are gathering. I'm pretty sure we haven't lost a single one. They jostle and swirl, each jockeying for a spot close to the door. All at once, they whirl, creating an otherworldly battering ram.

I call out, but it's too late. They smash into the door—and Carter. He's knocked to the floor for the second time in minutes. He sits there, knees bent, head in his hands.

"Hey, guys," I say to the thick fog obscuring the ceiling. "I know you don't like him, but—"

"Mutual," Carter says.

"And you're not helping," I tell him.

Ghosts are capricious. They'll keep us trapped in here out of spite, or because they think it's fun to watch the humans snipe at each other.

I brush my fingertips across the door, although since Carter was just yanking on the handle, I doubt we're in a full-on ghost infestation.

The wood is smooth, cool but not cold, and definitely not frosty. It locks from the inside, and nothing's engaged.

"Why can't we get out?" I wave a hand at the ceiling. "Why can't they?"

Carter lifts his head from his hands. His eyes are wide with fear. It might be the dim light in the foyer, but I swear, he's turned a sickly gray. He shakes his head, hard.

"No, no, no," he mutters. Then he turns his gaze on me, the look full of desperation. "Remember the cemetery?"

I nod, dread thickening in my throat.

"We're inside a containment field."

"So, a necromancer can trap humans along with ghosts?"

"Sort of. A necromancer can break free easier than ghosts can, but with enough necromancers, you can detain someone. It's how retribution is ... meted out." Carter peers upward. "Or, with enough ghosts, it creates its own sort of lockdown."

"Like an infestation?"

"They can't leave." He shrugs. "We can't leave."

"So, which one is this? Is there a group of necromancers outside the restaurant?"

"Not that I can see." Belinda's voice comes from the seating area. She's in a booth, leaning up against the window, hands cupped around her face.

"In this case, it's just one," Carter says. He slumps against the door, and his head thumps the wood. The sound is defeat itself. "I recognize the signature."

I'm glad someone does. "Orson?" I ask, although his posture alone has already told me the answer.

He gives one miserable nod.

"I thought you said he wasn't in Springside."

He shuts his eyes and groans. "I'm an idiot."

I'm tempted to agree. "Do you think he's close by?" I say instead.

"He must have been, probably while you guys were in the cold

storage unit. That's why the field is so strong. He's been reinforcing it."

"But I'm sure Malcolm, and Nigel, and Reginald... They would,
I mean—"

I don't know what I mean. Would they sense him? Is that
something necromancers can do? I certainly didn't, and neither did
Carter until a few moments ago. I don't even know if Malcolm had
the chance to alert either of them.

"I suppose Reginald could deploy a ghost or two to keep
watch," he says, "but Malcolm doesn't do that sort of thing."

No, he doesn't, and Nigel can't.

"So, the sneaky bastard slimed his way through the alley and
trapped us?" Belinda suggests.

A laugh nearly chases the fear from Carter's features. "Yeah,
that's exactly what he did."

"Then maybe we don't want to leave right now." I'm not sure
what possesses me, but I lean down and offer Carter my hand.

He stares at it as if it might have some of that slime from the
alley. Then he takes my hand. He looks toward Belinda and then at
me again.

"No, we need to get out of here. This sucks." He gestures
toward the ceiling and the ghosts churning there. "For everyone."

I point to the door. "And if Orson is on the other side?"

"Then I take a bullet or an attack ghost or whatever he has
planned for me."

"I won't let that happen."

"We won't," Belinda echoes.

He doesn't say anything, but something shifts in his expression. "So, in the cemetery—" He coughs and clears his throat. "Do
you remember what you did?"

I nod.

"This is a stronger field. Can you feel it?"

I lift my chin. At first, all I get is a wave of ghosts clamoring for
attention. Oh, they're loud. Beneath the racket and chatter, I sense

the containment field. It surrounds the restaurant, almost as if the Pancake House is contained in an industrial-sized snow globe.

"I do," I tell Carter. I probe it with my thoughts, the way Nigel showed me on that snowy February night in the Springside Cemetery. I can't detect a single crack, a flaw, a fissure. "I'm not sure I can break it."

"I can't either, not by myself, but there might be a way."

I wait for the explanation. Carter stares at the floor, then up at the ceiling. Something near the cash register catches his attention. He scowls and jabs a finger at the ghost floating there. "Yeah? Well, you're an asshole."

"Language," I say. "Remember the sprites."

He rolls his eyes. "You don't hear them?" He rubs his temples. "It's nonstop chatter."

I do, but it's all white noise to me, the words indistinct. I have no idea what that ghost said to Carter. I look toward Belinda in question.

She nods and casts her gaze toward the ceiling and the thick layer of ghosts there. "Yeah, they can't shut up. Most of them want to leave, but some want to stay and talk, and every single one has an opinion."

I tilt my head. I catch bits and pieces, a word here, a comment there, but only if I concentrate. It's easier to tune them out.

"It's probably why you're such a good necromancer," he adds. "Despite everything. No distractions."

I'm not certain how to take that—as a compliment? If it is, it's a backhanded one. Belinda mutters something and sends a look toward the bevy of sprites floating above her head. They shake with ghostly laughter.

Carter still doesn't say anything about the containment field.

At last, frustration overtakes me. "This way to break out?" I prompt. "Are you going to elaborate?"

"We have to hold hands," he mumbles.

"What?"

Behind me, Belinda snorts.

"We have to hold hands," he repeats, louder this time.

"That's it?" I sigh, the long night catching up to me. My limbs feel heavy. Keeping the fog from my thoughts is becoming a full-time job. "This isn't elementary school, and I don't have girl cooties."

"Yeah, well, I don't want your boyfriend charging in here and knocking me into next week."

"He won't." At least, I'm pretty sure Malcolm won't.

"I got this." Belinda scoots past us, giving my shoulder a squeeze. "You guys do your necromancer thing. I'll run interference." She plants herself in front of the door, hands on hips. She throws a glance over her shoulder, one aimed at Carter. "Better now?"

He glowers. I can't help it; I laugh. Then I hold out my hands, palm skyward.

"Ready?" I ask.

He murmurs something that might be *yes*, and then Carter and I link hands.

"There's a point near the back entrance," he says. "That's where Orson began the field, and it will be weakest there."

I close my eyes. Perhaps it's the combined power, Carter's and mine, but the image of the containment field pops into my mind. Near the back door, I sense the weak spot. It isn't much, not even the width of a hairline fracture.

"The field at the cemetery was kind of sloppy," Carter says. "Orson's good, and he had time to build this one and reinforce it."

"Nigel said that eventually the ghosts would find a way out."

"They would, but in this case, it would probably take weeks."

Of their own volition, my fingers tighten around Carter's. We don't have weeks. We don't have hours. I concentrate on that spot near the back entrance. A shadow is hanging over it, one that's the same size and shape as Orson.

I yelp, but Carter grips my hands before I can jerk away.

"It's an aftereffect," he says. "Don't let it spook you."

"Is that how you sense another necromancer?" If so, it's really creepy.

"It's one way."

"Uh, guys?" Belinda says. "Any luck?"

Both Carter and I remain silent.

"Because we might have a problem."

I don't want to ask, but I do anyway. "What sort of problem?"

"Samia's here."

CHAPTER 9

Even the ghosts go quiet. The chatter around us dies. The only sounds are the sizzle and pop of one of the coffeemakers and the rumble of Samia's minivan.

Then that cuts off as well.

"Is Malcolm outside?" I ask.

I hope and pray that he is. Malcolm can sweet talk and work his charm. He can convince Samia that all is well; I'm certain of it.

"Actually," Belinda says, her voice hesitant, "no one's out front. Well, except for Samia."

"Where is he?" I say this mostly to myself. It isn't like Malcolm to wander off in the middle of an infestation this large. It isn't like him to wander off at all. In fact, I'm surprised he hasn't been pounding on the doors and windows, trying to get in.

"Maybe something better came along." Carter. Of course.

Before I can say anything, before Belinda can, an otherworldly whoosh sideswipes Carter and sends him into the newspaper rack. He crashes to the floor, and the rack teeters and falls on top of him. The ghosts erupt, whirling and nattering and making a ruckus once again.

Hands on thighs, Belinda peers down at him. "What? You diss Katy in a room full of Springside ghosts? You really are an idiot."

"Nice." He makes no move to stand or even push the rack from his ribcage. He almost looks content there on the floor. "You know, I really wish I never came to Springside."

"We're all wishing that right now," Belinda says.

The room shakes with ghostly glee. Even I manage a laugh, but it catches in my throat when I glance toward the restaurant's front door. My eyes meet the dark, concerned ones of Samia.

I gape, wishing I had words to fill my mouth, words to explain to her what's going on in her restaurant. Even if I did, I'm not sure she could hear me through the closed door.

Belinda notices my stare and jerks around, and her shoulders slump in defeat. Then she gestures widely, something I'm sure means, *We can explain all this.*

Not that we can.

Samia's face vanishes from the window. Belinda rushes forward and peers out.

"What's she doing?" I whisper the words, which is ridiculous. It's not like Samia can hear us.

"She's got her cell phone out."

That's not good.

"I can think of two people she might be calling," Belinda adds. "Jim or Chief Ramsey."

Either way, I suspect I've seen the last of the all-you-can-eat pancakes, and Belinda may be out of a job. If only Malcolm were here to...

The thought strikes me so hard it hurts. I stare down at Carter, and I must look fierce, because he recoils.

"You said Orson was in the alley, right?" If he were standing, I'd grab him by the collar and shake the answer from him—that's how desperate I feel. "That's where he created the containment field?"

In response, Carter gives a single nod, and his Adam's apple bobs. I force back a wave of nausea.

The alley is also the last place I saw Malcolm.

I BOLT, jumping over Carter and the downed newspaper rack. My name echoes after me, but I don't glance over my shoulder. If I'm wrong, there will be plenty of time to explain later. And if I'm right?

I don't want to think about that.

With both palms, I shove open the door to the men's restroom. I dash to the window and scramble to the ledge. I kick my feet, trying for purchase. An otherworldly force pushes from behind, so I end up half in and half out of the window.

The ledge bites into my stomach. I wince, fight for a full breath, and scan the alley. It's not quite sunrise. The only light comes from a streetlamp near the alleyway's entrance. I breathe in that damp wood scent, catch a hint of rotted vegetables. To my left is a dumpster, the most likely source of the stench.

I grip the windowsill and lean out even farther. In front of me, the air wavers. Orson's containment field runs down the center of the alley. I stretch an arm and brush fingertips against the barrier. I scan the darkness below, searching for Malcolm.

Something shoves from behind—a ghost, no doubt, trying to be helpful. I teeter on the window ledge. My arms flail, and I let out a yelp.

Then, from below, comes a voice.

"Katy?"

"Malcolm?" Relief and fear course through me all at once. He's here, he's alive, but he doesn't sound like himself. "Are you okay?"

"Katy? Is it really you?" He sounds dazed, like he's just woken from a dream. "I was afraid you were dead."

Or a nightmare.

"I'm right here. I'm fine. I was worried about—"

"When I saw Orson—"

"You saw him?"

If Malcolm responds, I don't hear his answer. At that moment, the overly helpful ghosts at my back give me one last shove. I lose my perch. My stomach and then my thighs scrape along the sill. I tumble from the window.

I'm pretty sure I scream. At least the sound of it echoes in my head and burns my throat. Then something warm and solid stops my fall. My breath leaves me just as a solid oomph leaves Malcolm, and we crumple to the ground. His embrace is fierce and protective, and it's the only reason I don't panic.

"Katy, Katy." My name sounds like a prayer, and now I let in some of the panic. This isn't Malcolm. This isn't right. "I thought you were dead," he says again. "I thought Orson ... did something, and you—"

"Same," I manage, trying to banish all the images of Malcolm lying dead in this alleyway. My head is tucked in the crook of his neck, and his pulse is pounding erratically against my ear. I don't know whose heart is thumping harder, his or mine.

He holds me, an arm wrapped around my waist, a hand cradling the back of my head. We have so much yet to do, but we can take this moment, I tell myself. It isn't wrong to take one small moment.

I nuzzle closer. Despite his hours in the alley, he smells warm, like nutmeg, but like something else as well, something with a coppery tang. His fingers are oddly damp against my skin.

I pull back enough to peer up at him. I know worry must be reflected in his eyes, but the alleyway is so dark, I can't see it. That's just as well. I think it might undo me. Instead, I take one of his hands and study it.

I tug it into a thin beam of yellow lamplight. His fingers are stained, warm and sticky, his knuckles swollen. I take his other hand and inspect that too.

There's no mistaking blood.

"What happened?" I ask. His face is unmarred as far as I can tell. It doesn't look like he was in a fight. "Did Orson do something?"

He shakes his head. "That's just it. He didn't, at least not to me. I don't think he realized I was here in the alley until he was done creating the containment field."

So, when he trapped us, he trapped Malcolm as well. I reach a hand out and test the barrier again. Still there. Still intact.

"He came up behind me," Malcolm says. "I was busy trying to find a way up to the window." He points to the dumpster. "That wasn't budging, and the crates wouldn't hold my weight."

Splintered boards litter the alleyway, and there's a foot-sized hole in the side of a nearby orange crate.

"I didn't even notice him until he was standing right there." He gestures to a spot across from us. "I thought he might shoot me or unleash an attack ghost." Malcolm reaches out and taps the containment field. "This actually saved me. He couldn't do either without destroying this in the process."

"What did he do?" My gaze darts to Malcolm's hands. The wounds, the swelling—it all speaks to some sort of desperation.

"He just stared at me. Then he smiled that creepy smile of his and said, 'You're too late to save her, but that's the Armands for you—always too little, too late.' And then he left. I was trapped, my phone didn't work, and you were inside with Carter and who knows what."

He stares at the space where Orson must have stood and then slumps against the wall beneath the window. He pulls me closer, and I wrap my arms around his waist as tight as I dare.

"I went a little crazy," he whispers into my hair. "I tried to climb up the wall."

I think of how scraped his fingers are. "Climb or crawl?"

"Both. I tried to break through the containment field. When I couldn't, I started hitting it."

That explains the bruised knuckles.

"I thought I failed you." He utters this final confession in a voice so low that I barely hear it.

"You could never fail me."

A sigh makes his entire body shudder. "I thought we'd been set up. Carter came breezing in, all apologetic and with all the answers, and I was stupid enough to trust him because I didn't know what else to do. Then Orson showed up, and I really thought—"

"For the record, Carter's been helping."

Well, mostly, when he's not being passive-aggressive.

"Good." Malcolm heaves another sigh. "I'm in no shape to kick his ass."

I allow myself to simply rest against his chest and listen to his heartbeat, steady and sure now. In a bit, I'll tell him about Samia and how we need to break the containment field. In a bit, we'll get back to work.

Instead, Malcolm shifts. He takes my face in his hands, and I can feel the tacky residue of blood against my skin.

"Katy, I want this to stop. This thing with Orson is only going to get worse."

"I want it to stop, too, but I don't know how."

He stares at me. Even in the low light, I sense the force of it, the significance. I scramble to my feet and take a step back. There's a request in that look that I can't fulfill. I ask anyway.

"Do you want me to invoke the entity and order it to stop Orson?"

Malcolm stands. For a moment, he braces a hand against the wall. Then he reaches for me, but I slip from his grasp.

"You have to tell me that this is something you want. I won't do it any other way."

My throat tightens around a thick swell of what must be tears. I can't breathe. It feels as if that one solid, sure thing is crumbling beneath my feet.

He sags against the wall, hands slapping the brick. I wince because that's got to sting.

"Yes ... no ... I don't know." He clenches his fists, once, twice, frustration radiating from him. "I only know that if it were me, I would've made the deal by now, given the entity whatever it wanted, and—"

"Lost everything."

My words stop him. He shakes his head as if he doesn't believe me.

"Why, then?" he says. "Why have something like that and not use it?"

"Think about what you might have to give up. Think about what that does to you, to me, to Springside."

The silence stretches between us. He rubs his eyes, scrubs his face with his hands. His jaw tenses, and then he blows out a breath as if he's just considered several ideas and dismissed each one.

"There isn't one scenario," he says, his voice quiet, its frantic edge smoothed with what sounds like shame, "where I don't lose you." He swallows hard and peers skyward. "Maybe that's its gift to me. There's no way around that. I lose you, without a doubt. But if this keeps going, I'm afraid I'll lose you anyway."

"Then?" My throat remains tight, thick with tears on the edge of spilling over. I wait.

Malcolm curls the fingers of one hand, a barely there *come here* gesture. I'm wary, but I inch forward. When I'm close enough, he takes my hand and kisses the palm.

"I want this to stop so we can start." His lips find my palm again, and the eruption of butterflies in my stomach is fierce. "But I won't ask you to invoke the entity, no matter how tempting it is. It might be easy, but it's not the answer."

He pushes a few strands of hair from my cheek with a feather-light touch. It must hurt his fingers, but he doesn't even wince.

I hold on to him with all my might. I don't know who had the worst night, him or me. A thought flits across my mind: what would I have done, trapped in the alley with no way out? What would I have done if I thought Malcolm might die or already be dead? How long could I have resisted temptation?

I don't want to think about it, so I push those thoughts from my mind. I concentrate instead on the here and now. And right now?

We have a restaurant to restore.

I ease from his embrace and hold out my hands to him. He takes them without hesitation. "Are you up to breaking a containment field?" I ask.

He surveys the alley, his gaze zeroing in on the back entrance. "Weak point by the door?"

"That's the one. We were trying to break it when Samia showed up."

His grip tightens on mine. Malcolm closes his eyes and swears. "I'm sorry I wasn't out front. I would've—"

"I know, I know," I say. "Let's just do this and go home."

There's nothing awkward or weird about working like this with Malcolm. His skin is warm, his grip is secure, and the weak point comes into focus. Already I can sense a few fissures that weren't there moments before.

"This is so much better than holding hands with Carter."

Malcolm's grasp tightens imperceptibly. When I open my eyes, I find him looking at me, one eyebrow raised.

I bite my lip because, suddenly, all my words have fled. I try anyway. "What I mean is—"

He laughs, and it's nothing but amused. "You can explain later."

We resume our task. Within seconds, the containment field around us starts to shake. It's a low reverberation at first, one that penetrates the soles of my shoes. Fissures turn into cracks, and those travel across the surface of the field, branching in multiple directions.

The tremors grow, the vibration flowing through the space,

through us. A sound like ice cracking fills the air, and then, all at once, the field shatters.

The helpful ghosts from the restroom flow from the window and circle around us. One ruffles my hair. Another plants a kiss on my cheek. Yet another bops Malcolm on the head. Then they stream from the alleyway, their numbers so great, it looks like early-morning fog.

We make our way from the alley, stumbling over smashed orange crates and tripping on discarded trash.

The doors to the Pancake House are wide open. Belinda is standing outside, waving to someone—or possibly something otherworldly. Samia is gaping at her restaurant. Amazingly, Nigel is there. I wonder who—or maybe what—alerted him. He has a hand on her shoulder. He gestures toward the entrance, and I can almost hear his comforting words.

We're sorry about the mess. Of course we'll help clean up.

Reginald is in quiet conversation with Carter, who seems reluctant to step from the man's shadow. I wonder what they're talking about, but most of all, I'm grateful we're free, that all the ghosts are free.

I turn a grin on Malcolm. His lips twitch. He's about to smile himself when something darkens his expression.

"Katy?"

He halts, and since we're holding hands, I do too.

"Are you okay?" he asks.

"Why wouldn't I be okay?"

Sure, I'm tired, but I don't think that's odd. It's been a long night.

"You look ... wrong."

"Wrong?"

Maybe it *is* exhaustion, or the power of suggestion. Or maybe it's something more. A wave hits me, one filled with cold nausea. My leg muscles go rubbery. I hold still, certain if I take a step, I'll collapse under my own weight.

The world narrows, the edges of my vision growing dark. I suck in a deep breath. At the moment, it seems very important that I keep breathing. I turn toward Malcolm. At the moment, it seems very important that I don't lose sight of him, either.

His mouth moves, but I can't hear any words. My legs go out from under me. I brace for impact, for asphalt bruising, scraping. Instead, I land in Malcolm's arms. He scoops me up and plants a gentle kiss on my cheek.

And then my world goes black.

CHAPTER 10

The sun is bright against my eyelids. I don't have the strength yet to open them. I've tried, several times. I want to reassure Malcolm that I'm fine. But since I can't speak—or even open my eyes—I'm probably not fine at all.

It doesn't stop me from trying.

I'm resting in his arms. This I know for certain. I'm too warm and secure to be anywhere else. His fingers thread through my hair. Occasionally, he murmurs my name. I hear shouts, the rumble of a car. Then Samia's voice breaks through the fog in my head.

"Honestly, all of you," she says in her soft, lilting accent. "Bring her inside."

Once again, Malcolm scoops me up. I want to help. At the very least, I could loop my arms around his neck, but it feels as though lead weights are anchoring my wrists. I can't raise my hands. I can't do much of anything.

I'm not certain there's anything more frustrating.

Malcolm settles us in a booth. At least, the squeak of vinyl suggests this. I rest against his chest, his arms around mine.

"She is dehydrated, perhaps," Samia says. "Some water?"

Malcolm eases a straw between my lips. I sip, but the ice water is so cold, I recoil.

"Hey, there you are," he says, his voice low and hopeful against my ear. "I knew you were in there somewhere."

I manage the barest of nods. His chest rises and falls with a sigh of relief. Then, at last, I open my eyes.

Around me, everyone is hovering—Belinda, Samia, Nigel, Reginald, even Carter. Five pairs of intent eyes have me shrinking against Malcolm again.

"Maybe some of you could back off," he says.

"Of course," Samia says, and she beams at me. "Once I thank Katy."

For what? Not totally destroying her restaurant? Even now, the scent of burnt coffee lingers in the air. I don't detect any ghosts, but the aftereffects of the infestation remain.

"I'm sorry," I begin. "Especially for the mess—"

"Is nothing, not compared to what a ghost can do to the breakfast rush."

I concede she has a point.

"We will clean." She nods toward Belinda and points to the parking spaces outside the restaurant. "And Jim is here to help."

Belinda herself leans in and gives me a quick peck on the cheek. "We will clean," she echoes before lowering her voice. "And thank you. Thank you for being my friend."

She turns toward Carter, and I know she's assessing his damp clothes, the stubble along his jaw. Most of the shine has left him. What remains is possibly far more interesting.

"And you," she says before giving him a light kiss on his cheek. "You might make a decent human being after all."

"Nice." The scowl is back, but for a second, a wash of pink paints his features.

With that, Belinda heads toward the kitchen area, scooping up coffee cups as she goes.

Reginald studies me with concern. He's been quiet this entire time, but now he clears his throat.

"Katrina Lindstrom, can you tell us what happened in there?"

I do, as best I can, from the initial infestation to Carter's appearance to deciding to unravel the ghosts.

"Wait." Nigel holds up a hand and halts my words. "You didn't slice through them?"

"I didn't want to hurt or destroy any of them. Orson tied up Belinda's sprites at the very center. I didn't want to ... I mean, not kill them, but—"

Nigel whirls on Carter. "And you *let* her?"

"Whoa, man. I tried to talk her out of it. I told her it would leave her vulnerable." Carter folds his arms over his chest, and the frown is back. "Besides, have you tried talking her out of something?"

I push to sit up even though that takes me away from Malcolm's warmth. "No one *let* me do anything. I decided for myself. I didn't want to hurt the ghosts, especially since they were all Springside ghosts."

"You don't understand." Exasperation fills Nigel's voice, and he shoots Carter a quick glare before continuing. "It's not something necromancers do. It could take you weeks to recover."

I glance at Malcolm, who gives me a little shrug, and then turn toward Reginald. "What have I done?"

"Something most necromancers never attempt," he says.

"But why? It's not like the ghosts are—"

"Expendable?" Nigel says. "That's the thing, Katy. They are."

"No, they're not," I insist.

This, I think, is why I don't like necromancy. It's so casual in its cruelty. I know the ghosts are no longer human. I know they aren't even like pets (except for maybe the sprites). Still, they exist. They laugh. They wail. They celebrate. They mourn.

Even Reginald, despite all his kindness toward them, would've sliced through the tangle of ghosts that Orson created. I see that in his eyes even as he averts his gaze so I won't.

"To put it bluntly," Reginald says, "the ghosts feasted on you."

That *is* blunt. And untrue. I'm fine, or at least, mostly fine. If I could push up from the table and march out of the restaurant, I'd prove it.

"Feasted?" Malcolm sounds as skeptical as I feel.

"Her warmth. Her humanity." Nigel points at me. "Look at her. Really look at her."

Malcolm's gaze shifts toward me. He's already said himself that I look wrong. To be truthful, there's a hollowness inside me that I can't seem to shake off.

"It's often referred to as necromancer flu," Reginald adds. "And, like the flu, bed rest, fluids—especially hot ones—will help. No ghost catching or even interacting with them for a while."

"But she'll be okay, right?" Malcolm asks.

No one speaks. It's this, rather than the earlier scolding, that feeds my dread. My limbs are cold, my fingertips like ice. A pinprick sensation rushes along my scalp, followed by a shudder, but I stop it before my body can start to tremble.

"She'll be okay," Malcolm says again. This time, it isn't a question.

"It would be better if she weren't still healing from the previous encounter." Reginald nods at me, indicating the scars that remain on my arms. They've begun to ache, a dull sort of pain radiating from each cut.

"But, yes," he adds in what sounds almost like an afterthought. "With time and rest, she should make a full recovery."

The problem, I think, with being sick—even with something as ridiculous as necromancer flu—is that people talk about you rather than *to* you.

My gaze is drawn toward the window and Main Street beyond. The sun is rising, and in its glow, Springside is coming to life.

From my vantage point, I can see the police department and

what looks like the bulky shadow of Chief Ramsey. I can't see his face, but I imagine he's studying the commotion at the Pancake House, and I imagine that he doesn't approve. Not so long ago, he spoke of my parents' death. He told me that he was the first officer to arrive at the crash site, and it was clear the pain of that hadn't faded.

Now I know he didn't tell me the whole story.

"Nigel," I say. "Is there some way you can access the police report of my parents' accident?" My non sequitur stuns everyone into silence, which gives me time to add, "And the newspaper reports, as well. I mean—" I look up and confront their stares once again. "I'm guessing there was something in the Springside news-paper, at least."

Nigel purses his lips and nods.

"Katy?" Malcolm's voice is gentle, his hand steady on my shoulder.

I turn to him. "Will you take me home?"

He gives me one of his sweet, dark-roast smiles. "You know I will."

He eases me from the booth. I can walk under my own power, but just barely. His arm around my waist keeps me upright until I'm secured in his convertible.

When we reach my house, however, he won't let me try the stairs.

"You won't make it," he says, "and you don't want to add broken bones to the list."

He's right; I know he's right. Even the idea of the porch steps is enough to exhaust me, never mind the ones that lead to my bedroom. For the third time that morning, he scoops me up.

"Under different circumstances," he says, pausing at the threshold, "this could be romantic."

His words ease the dread in my chest. I laugh. "It *is* romantic. Just having you here is."

He kisses me then. When he speaks, his voice is as soft and tender as his kiss. "I think so too."

With that, he carries me into my house and shuts the door with his foot, cutting us off from the world.

CHAPTER 11

W hat wakes me, I'm not certain. The air is rich with spice. I'm buried beneath my grandmother's down comforter. The sheets feel luxurious, as if I've just slipped between them after a long day—or night—of ghost catching. But I sense that I've been here for hours. Through the windows, light is streaming into the room, and its glow is gold with the sunrise.

I open my eyes and find Malcolm sleeping in an easy chair next to the bed, his feet propped on a worn footstool. His mouth is soft, but a furrow mars his brow, as if even in his dreams, he's worried.

I push to sit up—or try to. I have all the strength of a baby bird, and my biggest accomplishment is rustling the covers.

This is enough to wake Malcolm. His eyes flutter open. When his gaze finds mine, some of the worry melts from his brow.

"There you are," he says. His grin is warm and sleepy, but full of that dark-roast sweetness. "How are you feeling?"

I simply nod, since I'm still figuring that out. "How long have I been asleep?"

Malcolm taps his cell phone on the nightstand and studies the screen. "About twenty-four hours."

I don't bolt upright. I try, but I can't. It's like the air itself is heavy. Even so, the news is enough to get me into a sitting position.

"Hey, easy." In an instant, he's at my side, one hand supporting my back, the other adjusting the pillows. He settles me in and then takes a seat on the edge of the bed. "Better?"

The sight of him here, in my bedroom, leaves me dumbfounded —or maybe that's the necromancer flu. He's warm and rumpled, his faded U of M T-shirt wrinkled from a night in the chair. A few of his fingers are sporting bandages, and his knuckles are wrapped in gauze. It makes him look like he's been in a prizefight.

I nod toward the chair. "What are you doing there?"

He brushes the back of his hand along my forehead. "Keeping an eye on you."

"No, I mean instead of there." I let my gaze stray to the empty half of my bed.

A hint of pink highlights his cheekbones. "Well, you know, I always make a point of having an explicit invitation."

I muster all my strength and pat the space next to me.

He chuckles. "There's also the fact that Reginald's been checking on you every few hours, and that's—"

"Awkward?"

"Yeah. That." He shifts, pulling an insulated carafe and a glass mug from the nightstand. "But now that you're awake, maybe a little tea?"

He unscrews the cap, and the source of the aroma I smelled earlier becomes clear. It's Malcolm's fire spice tea. It's like drinking liquid Red Hots—without the sugar coma and mouth-scraped-raw aftereffects. Of all his tea recipes, this one's my favorite.

He hasn't made any since winter; just inhaling the steam is enough to make you break out in a sweat. Even now, perspiration dots his forehead. But I'm so cold—even sequestered under a down comforter and an extra blanket—that I can't wait to hold the mug in my hands.

"Easy," he says again, wrapping my fingers around the glass.

I force my hands not to tremble and hope my arm muscles will kick in. The glass is heavy, or rather, I'm inordinately weak, but the first sip sends a surge of warmth through me. I sink into the pillows and sigh.

"Good?" he asks. "Is it helping?"

"I think this is the best batch you've ever made."

The tea heats my stomach, the fire spreading from there. It's beating back the cold that's both freezing my limbs and sapping all my strength.

"I had some help this time. I've been chatting." He picks up the phone. "With my mother. She's nursed more than one necromancer through the flu. I have some necromancer stew going in a crockpot downstairs for when you feel like eating something."

"Necromancer stew? It's not made from actual necromancers, is it?"

Malcolm snorts a laugh. "It's more like turbo-charged chicken noodle soup, although I made this batch with vegetable stock. Prem swears by it."

"Is that your mother's husband?"

He gives his head a little shake.

"Partner?"

"Not really."

"Then what is he ... she...?"

"He." Malcolm heaves a sigh. "My mother likes to refer to Prem as her lover."

He's so uncomfortable—squirming like a little boy—that I laugh. The hot cinnamon spice slices through the layer of fog in my head. It sparks my curiosity, and I want to know more about the woman helping me. "What do they do in Paris? I mean, aside from the obvious?"

He squirms some more and throws me a scowl, but it's in jest —mostly. "They run a tour company."

"Tour company?"

"Haunted Paris."

"Oh! Ghosts?"

He grins. "Exactly. They cater mostly to tourists, but they also help necromancers in tracking down ghosts as well. And when the ghosts don't cooperate, Prem deploys the ones he keeps in reserve."

"Haunted Paris," I echo. My feet twitch as if they want to jump up and rush to the closet so I can start packing.

"You'd love Paris, Katy."

"You've been?"

"I lived there for a few months while I was growing up."

"Do you speak French?"

"Enough to order a decent meal."

I'm dumbfounded again, but maybe I shouldn't be. This might explain why Malcolm is so suave and pulled together. I can picture him in a café or catching ghosts along the Seine.

"We'll go someday," he says, and nods at my glass, urging me to drink. "But not until you're better."

I comply even as I narrow my eyes at him. "I don't think—"

"What? That we'll have enough money? Didn't you count all those ghosts you released? We're already getting calls and texts."

"We are?"

"Belinda helped me with an inventory, and it's clear Orson and Carter have been collecting them for months. This goes beyond the ones they had in the warehouse. No wonder business has been so bad."

This surprises me more than it should. I swallow down another gulp of tea as if that alone will return my strength. We have so much to do—and I have something important to confess.

I open my mouth to do just that, but Malcolm places a finger on my lips. "We can talk about your parents' accident later."

"Then—?"

"Belinda told me—and just me. It's not that I don't trust Nigel or Reginald, but for now, I think it's better if only the three of us know."

I shake my head, not to contradict him, but because there's more to this story.

Belinda didn't see Darien Armand. Only I did.

"It wasn't just Orson. Your father was there."

I blurt the words—it's the only way. If I wait too long or think too hard about it, I won't say them at all. Dreams of Paris will keep me from that.

Malcolm pauses in his reach for the carafe. For a moment, I don't think he'll move or say anything at all.

"What?" he says at last.

"The ghosts showed him to me. He was standing on the other side of the ravine. Belinda didn't see him. I don't even think Chief Ramsey or Orson saw him. But"—I shake my head as if that might shake away the image of Darien Armand—"he was there."

"My father was there." Malcolm's voice is a cold, hard thing. His lips form a thin line. "Of course he was."

For an instant, I think he's being sarcastic. The words have that sort of bite to them. Then he laughs, the sound of it so harsh and bitter, it steals the warmth from the tea. I almost wish he'd defend his father or refuse to believe. This acceptance fills me with icy sorrow.

"We could ask Chief," I say. "I mean, about me. I don't really know if I was there. What if the ghosts are playing a prank?"

"I don't think they are." He eyes me. "Do you?"

I give my head a quick shake and then lift the mug for another sip. There's nothing but a swallow left in the bottom, but I finish it off.

Malcolm's gaze lingers on my face, and his mood shifts. The bitterness leaves his eyes, and his mouth turns up in a smile. "The pink's coming back to your cheeks. That's good. That's real good."

I touch my face. And, yes, even though my fingertips no longer feel like ice, the skin beneath them is also warm.

He steals my glass and refills it. "Drink up," he says. "Because we have a trip to plan."

"I think we have other things to do first."

He nods as if conceding the point. "True. But the trip? That's pretty important. I've wanted to go back for ages, and I've always thought Paris would be the perfect spot for a honeymoon."

I freeze with the mug halfway to my lips and peer over the rim. "What does that mean?"

His hands join mine, and together we hold the mug. "Whatever you want it to."

In turn, we each take a sip of tea. Then Malcolm places the glass on the nightstand.

He kisses me, and it's a kiss to set the world on fire. Hot cinnamon spice mixes with his warm nutmeg scent. The combination may sweep me away. The combination may have me saying yes.

Not that he's asked. Not that he needs to.

I close my eyes and try not to dream too hard about Paris. It's a fragile thing, one that too many wishes might break.

I close my eyes and try not to dream too hard about Malcolm.

PART III
NOTHING BUT THE GHOSTS

COFFEE AND GHOSTS SEASON THREE,
EPISODE 3

CHAPTER 1

A week ago, my business partner, Malcolm Armand, may—or may not—have proposed marriage. This is something I'm not quite sure about, because, in truth, he merely proposed a trip to Paris.

But he claimed it was the perfect spot for a honeymoon.

Now, Paris at dusk fills the screen of my laptop. Buildings glow. Lights twinkle and throw stars on the water. It's enough to steal your breath. I'm not sure how much money you need to earn to own a view of the Seine. Apparently Malcolm's mother and the man she refers to as her lover, Prem, make more than enough. Even through the webcam, I'm mesmerized.

Malcolm's mother, Arianna, returns to her balcony and settles in the chair. "Yes, here it is." She thumbs through a hardback journal, one worn with age and use. "My grandmother kept meticulous notes."

I sometimes wish *my* grandmother had.

"Open," she says.

I comply, opening my mouth and leaning forward so Arianna can peer inside.

"Now the eyes."

I pull back my eyelids so she can examine the skin beneath.

"Still too pale." She presses a finger against her lips in thought. This doesn't mar her perfectly applied lipstick in a red so fierce it probably stops traffic. Her precision-cut bob sways, her hair a glorious silver. With the silk scarf knotted at her neck, she *is* Paris.

"I still don't like how slowly you're recovering," she adds. "You're young and healthy." She tilts her head, and the bob cascades along her cheekbones. "Show me your arms again."

So I do, holding each arm in front of the webcam so she can examine the scars that still linger.

Arianna frowns. When she does, the family resemblance is so strong that it startles me. Both her sons wear that same scowl.

"I'm feeling better." I'm hedging my bets. I've been locked inside my house for a week now. I'm allowed onto the porch, but only in full sunlight. Otherwise, it's cup after cup of tea and bowl after bowl of stew. "I could probably go on a few calls with Malcolm."

"No, you can't. You don't have the strength."

"I feel like I do. I'm going stir crazy."

"You *think* you have the strength. The moment you encounter anything stronger than a sprite, you'll undo everything we've done in the past week. No ghost catching, no interaction at all."

"Not even with sprites?" I venture.

"Not even that."

A thump comes from the living room, followed by a muted cry of, "I got it!" Tara's voice is triumphant, and Belinda's laugh is indulgent.

"Do it again," she urges.

My gaze flits toward the living room. I hope Tara doesn't decide to show me her latest catch. Back on the screen, Prem strolls into view. He has a full head of black hair, and his skin is a lovely shade of olive. I've speculated on the age difference, but Malcolm refuses to play along. No matter. It's clear from Prem's expression that—

even after five years—he is dazzled by Arianna. Even so, he gives me a smile in commiseration before heading off screen to prepare for his evening.

"I'll send Malcolm another recipe to try," Arianna says.

"More tea?" I love Malcolm's tea—it's as warm and exotic as he is. His samovar now keeps my percolator company in the kitchen. I like the way it looks there on the counter, the glint of gold warming the cooler silver of the coffeepot.

But I've consumed gallons of the stuff in the last week. I'm not certain I can drink another cup.

She eyes me as if I've asked a silly question. Of course it's more tea.

Before I can protest, another crash comes from the living room, the sort that shakes the floorboards.

"I got them! I got them! Let's go show Katy!"

Oh, no. I open my mouth, hold up a hand, but Tara's only eleven, and these sorts of social cues zip right past her.

Belinda's eyes go wide. She lunges to catch Tara, but it's too late.

"Look!" Tara lands next to me, the cat barrettes in her braids lightly clacking. She holds up a Tupperware container. Inside, three mischievous sprites are swirling. "I caught them all at once!"

"You sure did!" I say, although I suspect the sprites might have had something to do with that. They're a friendly trio and probably think this is a game. Even so, it's good training, if only to learn the mechanics of catch and release. "Want to head into the backyard and let them go?"

She nods with more clacking from her braids. She takes Belinda's hand, and they rush out the back, the screen door thumping in their wake.

When I turn back to my laptop, Arianna's scowl greets me.

"What did I say about no interaction?"

"But I'm not the one interacting. I'm only training Tara how to catch them." When her scowl deepens, I add, "From a distance. It's

217

all"—I place a hand on my hip and use the other to point—"like that."

Something softens in Arianna's expression. She regards me for a long moment, and in the silence, I can hear Paris at night. "You look so much like your mother."

My heart thumps a strange beat. In the week I've been video chatting with her, Arianna's alluded that she knew my parents. But with Tara and sprites about, Belinda hovering over my every move, and Sadie visiting several times a day, I haven't had the chance to ask her about them.

Honestly? I haven't had the courage.

I bite my lip, which earns me a finger wag from Arianna.

"No, no, stop that. It will absolutely ruin the look of your lipstick."

Yes, like I wear lipstick.

"I'm sending you some," she adds as if reading my thoughts. "Every woman should own a never-fail tube of lipstick."

I stop biting my lip—if only so I can bite back my reply. I like Malcolm's mother, but the woman could steamroll right over you. I'm glad there's half a continent—not to mention an entire ocean—between us.

The kitchen door opens. I turn, expecting Tara and Belinda. Instead, Malcolm steps through. I start at the sight of him. True, he's dressed impeccably—pressed trousers, a dress shirt. But he's also wearing what must have been a long day of ghost catching.

The white dress shirt is splattered with coffee, his loafers look as if they've been soaking in tea, and a series of grass stains has ruined his khakis.

Even the smile he gives me—one of his sweet, dark-roast ones—appears worn and tired.

I really need to get better.

On the laptop screen, Arianna lights up. "Oh, there's my baby boy."

Malcolm struggles to keep the grimace from his face. "Hello, Mother."

Arianna rolls her eyes and offers a cheek. "Kiss."

Dutifully, Malcolm air kisses first one and then the other cheek. It's very continental and sophisticated, even if it is through a webcam.

"I'm glad you're here," Arianna says. "I need to speak to you later, probably about midnight your time." She waves a hand toward the balcony doors. "It's tourist season, and we have two groups booked tonight. We won't make it back until morning."

"I—" Malcolm begins, but the Arianna steamroller bumps right over his protest.

"I want to move some of my investments around and ask your opinion on a few things, and I don't want to bore Katy."

He tries again. "But I—"

"There's a good boy. Well, I must be off. I need to help Prem prepare for this evening."

For an instant, it seems like all of Paris fills our view, and then the screen goes blank.

Malcolm's lips twitch, and he swears softly. "My mother doesn't need my help investing," he says.

"It sounds like she wants it," I offer. "That's good, right?"

This last week has been hard on Malcolm. Arianna is chatty, and I like her, but I sense a certain amount of strain when it comes to Malcolm and Nigel. Her affair with Prem was part of the reason behind her divorce from Darien. The aftershocks of that linger. I can see them in the vulnerable crinkles around Malcolm's eyes.

"Yeah, it's good. Technically, she was my first customer." He reaches a hand toward me, and I hop from the kitchen stool and step into his embrace. "But it means I have to sleep at home tonight."

"You can't talk to her here?"

"All her paperwork is at the apartment." He casts a look

upward, toward the ceiling and the second story, where my bedroom is. "I'm sure she's guessed and everything, but it's—"

"Awkward?"

"Yeah. That. It's stupid. I shouldn't mind, but—"

"It's fine," I tell him. "I can survive a night on my own. Besides, Belinda is down the hall, and Sadie and Nigel are next door. It's not like I've been alone lately, anyway. "Plus," I add, patting the splotches on his shirt, "you could do some laundry."

He laughs and pulls me in closer. "You're right. I probably could."

"I should start going on calls with you. You've been working overtime all week." I wave a hand, indicating the number of stains he's currently wearing. "Was it bad today?"

"They're frisky, is all," he says, but his words emerge with a sigh. "Truthfully, I think they miss you and resent me. My wardrobe will survive, and so will I."

I peer up at him. "I don't like that you're going out alone. You're next on Orson's list."

That's the real reason I need to get better. We've faced two of the three threats Orson made at Sadie and Nigel's wedding reception—a possession meant for Nigel, and all the ghosts ever to haunt Belinda. I don't know what he might have planned for Malcolm, except that it must be deadly.

"Orson had his chance," Malcolm says. "In the alley. He could've broken his containment field, but he didn't." He cups my face with a hand. "It's you, not me, we should be worried about."

Maybe. I can't convince myself of it. If Orson truly wants to hurt me, he'll go after Malcolm. This is something he already knows.

"Speaking of which," Malcolm says, "are you ready to try some new tea?"

Am I? I heave a sigh. "Bring it on."

IT'S ONLY LATER, when I'm snuggled on the sofa with Malcolm, that regret truly starts to eat at me. I don't want him to leave. It's a purely selfish thought. If nothing else, he really does need to do some laundry. His wardrobe may be vast, but I suspect it's reached its limit. And it's not like I've never been on my own. I've become so used to having him here so quickly that the idea of giving him up for a night rankles.

"It's like the good old days," he says as if reading my thoughts. "Remember evening kisses?"

"It wasn't that long ago."

"I guess not." He shifts and settles me closer. His hands come to rest on my arms. Somehow, he knows without looking where the scars are. With his fingertips, he strokes each one as if that might heal it. His warm nutmeg scent is laced with Kona blend and a hint of Earl Grey. He smells like a long day at work.

"How are the ghosts?" I ask. "I mean, really."

"Like I said, they're frisky. I—" He breaks off, and I hear the echo of his next words. *I could really use your help.* "Maybe they're just happy to be away from Orson," he says instead. "Who wouldn't be?"

Yes, who wouldn't be? I fall silent, considering that, and what it might be like for the ghosts to be free, really free.

"Hey." Malcolm's voice is hushed. "What's up?"

"I was just thinking."

Beneath me, his chest rumbles with amusement. "When aren't you thinking?"

"I'm serious."

"So am I, and it's one of the things I love about you."

All the words melt in my mouth. My thoughts spin, and my heart thumps hard against my ribs. I want to say those words back, but I have a hard time making them leave my mouth. Every once in a while, I'll squeak it out. Malcolm doesn't seem to mind. His affection doesn't have a scorecard.

"So, what are you thinking?" he prompts.

This I have words for, so I tell him. "What's a necromancer without any ghosts?"

"Is this a riddle? Because I've never been very good at those."

"My grandmother always said it was better to separate ghosts from people, and she even told me she'd show me how after she died. I always thought she meant the people were better off." I shift so I can gauge his expression. "What if she meant the ghosts?"

"What's a necromancer without any ghosts?" He considers for a moment. "Unemployed?"

"What's Orson without any ghosts?"

"A bully without any reinforcements?" He eyes me. "I have other words for Orson, but I'll spare you."

I laugh and snuggle closer. "What does it mean to be free?"

"Okay, riddles are one thing, but existential questions are way out of my league."

"For the ghosts, I mean. My grandmother never even hinted at necromancy. I still don't talk to ghosts the way you do. It makes me feel like I'm violating one of her rules."

Malcolm shifts again so he can look at me straight on. "The ghosts would love it if you did. They adore you."

"Not all of them," I say.

"Most. Even the malicious ones have a certain amount of respect."

"She didn't want me to be a necromancer," I add. "That's pretty clear. But why?"

Concern replaces the warmth of Malcolm's gaze. He studies me, then brings a finger to my cheek and traces the faded blue spot that still lingers there.

"This is why," he says, his words solemn.

"But it happened anyway."

"Maybe she hoped it wouldn't."

"And left me unprepared." I strive to keep the grumble from my voice. I've worked so hard not to blame my grandmother for this. I miss her so much. Her death left a hole inside me that I haven't been able to fill—although having Malcolm in my life helps.

"Or not," he says, almost as an afterthought.

"Or not what?"

"Unprepared. You've been beating Orson at his own game."

"I've had a lot of help," I counter. "Plus, I'm not playing his game."

Malcolm grins at me. "That's why you're winning."

With both hands at my waist, he propels me from the sofa. He's about to stand when he flops back. He raises a hand with what looks like gargantuan effort.

"A little help?"

Oh, he's so tired, but, Malcolm being Malcolm, he wears even that with style. I help him to his feet and walk him to the door.

"Be careful," I say after one last kiss.

"Aren't I always?"

"I'm serious."

"So am I, which means you lock the door behind me."

I do. I also stand vigil until he's pulled his convertible from the curb and is heading down the block. I wait until the taillights have winked from view and then head into the kitchen.

Only the light over the stove illuminates the space. The air is still warm and fragrant with exotic spices. The samovar is switched off, but the gold sides glimmer—with something otherworldly.

I step closer and peer at the samovar. There, in the residual heat, floats one of Belinda's sprites.

"Shouldn't you be upstairs?"

The sprite swirls, crashing into the samovar and making it rock. I steady it and can't help inhaling another burst of that spice. I lean closer and sniff again. Then I pull the thing apart and inspect the tea leaves.

Beside me, the sprite bobs, puppy-like and curious about what I'm doing. I'm not exactly sure what I'm doing, except I know this:

I'm wide awake.

"What did Malcolm put in here?" I ask the sprite.

It flips over backward, apparently overjoyed that we're conversing.

"Actually," I say, "what did Arianna tell him to put in here?"

The sprite shoots toward the spice cabinet, slips inside, and then rattles the contents. The force of its effort flings the cabinet door open. Jars of spice and containers of herbs rain down on the counter.

"Stop! Stop!" I brace a hand on the door and use the other to collect the rolling jars. "You'll wake Belinda."

This subdues the sprite enough that I can clean up the mess. I consider dumping the tea leaves in the garbage. I consider texting Malcolm for the ingredients. Both can wait until morning.

"Come on," I say to the sprite. "It's time you were in bed."

I walk upstairs, the sprite weaving through the banisters beside me. At Belinda's room, I shoo it beneath the door.

"Go on. Take care of her."

I catch the telltale hint of a cry when it joins the other two. After the initial greeting, the room grows silent, the sprites now content. They'll keep an eye on Belinda, and certainly one will alert me if Orson sends another attack ghost her way.

Something tugs at me—regret again. It's so quiet up here, so lonely. I almost knock on Belinda's door. I consider waggling my fingers near the crack to coax out one of the sprites.

I opt for a heavy sigh instead.

There's no need to be alone, my dear.

I freeze halfway to my room. Then I give my head a vigorous shake as if that will knock the voice out of it. Because I know that voice, and I have no intention of inviting it in. Not now. Not when I'm alone.

I hold still while the house around me settles. If I stay this way, don't make a move, don't even allow myself to think, then everything will be okay. I wait, and all I hear is the pounding of my pulse in my ears.

Bit by bit, I relax. The voice in my head has faded. I take one step and then another toward my bedroom.

At the entrance, with my hand on the doorknob, I freeze again.

The bed I left rumpled is pristine—comforter smooth, pillows plumped. The clothes hamper has righted itself, and all the wayward socks have found their way inside. The blinds are drawn, and the windows have been opened just enough to let in the night breeze.

In the chair, the one Malcolm has occupied this past week, sits the entity.

CHAPTER 2

The entity is in the form it thinks I like, that of a well-dressed man. And while it's true that Malcolm is almost always well-dressed, that's not the reason I like him. I'd like—I'd love—him no matter what he wore, even torn flannel and frayed jeans.

Would you, my dear? Would you really?

I scowl in the entity's general direction, but then turn my mind's eye toward Malcolm in torn flannel and frayed jeans. I try to bite back a smile, but it's no use.

I would very much like Malcolm in torn flannel and frayed jeans.

So predictable. It's always the pretty ones who get all the attention.

I ignore that. "What are you doing here?"

The entity spreads its arms wide. *I can't visit my necromancer?*

"I didn't invoke you."

True, but I think I mentioned that you don't necessarily need to.

"Plus, I'm not a necromancer."

Not true, but we're arguing semantics now.

Yes, we probably are, not that I plan to admit it.

I cast a glance down the hall. A hush has fallen over the rest of the house. It's as if the entity has created a bubble around my room, where there's light and sound and endless night.

I shut the bedroom door, although I suspect I don't need to. Belinda won't hear me—no one will.

Except for me, my dear. You're always forgetting about me.

Hardly. I try again. "Why are you here?"

The entity raises its hands in supplication. *To chat. We never get to chat. You're always busy with other things—being kidnapped or shot at or untying ghosts. You should consider a sabbatical.*

I skirt the bed to put it between the entity and me. Not that it's much of a barrier. In fact, it's a silly and obvious thing to do. I expect the entity to laugh at me.

It doesn't.

So I ease onto the comforter and then grab one of those perfectly plumped pillows as a talisman. I need something to hold on to, something that feels real, especially if we're going to chat.

Nothing good can come from that.

Oh, come now. Honestly? True, we've had our ups and downs, but you're my necromancer now.

I touch the faded blue spot on my cheek. I don't need a mirror to know exactly where it is. The skin there is slightly waxy, always cooler than the rest of my face, even now, when my fingertips feel like ice.

The entity tilts its head, conceding the point. *Yes, well, like I said, ups and downs. All relationships have them. Speaking of which, you might want to rethink your choice of partners—in and out of bed. Bit of a mama's boy, that one.*

I shoot it a look and several nasty thoughts.

It merely laughs. *So fierce. I wonder, does he know how lucky he is?*

The entity pauses and turns its head toward the ceiling as if in contemplation. It doesn't have a face, or, at least, it's never given this incarnation one. There's only a swirling void where a face might be.

Ah, the jury's still out. I guess time will tell.

I don't know what it means by that. Something about Malcolm? About me? The one thing I do know is, the entity won't tell me.

Another thing I know?

When it comes to Malcolm, I'm the lucky one.

You sell yourself short, my dear.

"So, we're going to chat?" I say, because I don't relish an endless night with this thing in my bedroom. Giving it what it wants is the only course of action.

But even as the thought crosses my mind, I notice how the lamplight is muted to a perfect glow. The air tastes sweet, and the breeze touches my cheeks in a way that's impossibly soft. It's all manufactured and gauzy, like a Hallmark card commercial, and yet...

You doubt my abilities?

"I don't, actually. That's the point."

I've been around for a very long time. It flicks a hand. Sparks light the air, ones that look like fireflies. They glow before winking out, the last one twinkling in front of my nose. *I've picked up a few tricks along the way.*

I consider what I might ask the entity. It would know everything, wouldn't it? From who assassinated JFK to the real reason Darien Armand is in town. In front of me, the entity glimmers as if in anticipation.

Excellent. We are going to chat.

Then it morphs—or, rather, its outfit does, from impeccably tailored suit to a velvet smoking jacket in midnight blue. A pipe appears in one hand, although, since it doesn't have a mouth, I'm not sure what good that will do.

Still, I can't help it. I laugh.

I'm simply getting more comfortable.

I almost hate to ask. "For what?"

For our chat, of course. You ask. I answer.

"For a price." I know how this works.

Not all answers come with a price—at least, not an exorbitant one.

It's almost like a game of truth or dare, sparring with this thing. Only it knows all the truth, and dares always have consequences.

You are far too cautious.

Maybe I am. Nearly everyone has urged me to use the entity, to make a deal, extract promises, take the easy way out and keep everyone safe. I want nothing more than to keep everyone safe.

I'm not convinced using the entity is the way to do it.

Why not, my dear?

I sigh. "Can I at least have some thoughts to myself?"

Not when they play so wonderfully across your face. I wasn't even eavesdropping. So, why not use me, when I'm here and oh so convenient, not to mention willing?

"Are you? Are you, really?"

Convenient? Why, yes. The entity raises a hand, indicating its form in the chair. *I'm right here.*

"I mean willing."

Excuse me, my dear?

"Are you truly willing?"

You're my necromancer, so, yes, of course I am. That's how it works.

"So, if Orson Yates were your necromancer, you'd help him ... do whatever—to me, to Springside, the world?"

The entity flickers. It has no face, so trying to gauge how my words affect it is a fruitless task. Still, it pauses a bit too long before filling my head with more of its words.

There are rules to how this works, Katy, ones that are far older and much deeper than you can possibly understand.

"That's not an answer." I know this thing is powerful. I know poking at it with a virtual stick is a stupid thing to do.

In my defense, it did say it wanted to chat.

The entity rumbles something that sounds almost like a human snort. *I did, didn't I? Here's my question for you, then. Why don't you trust me?*

Oh, for so many reasons. I could list them out. I could write an essay about all those reasons.

The one that pops out of my mouth surprises us both. "You're not my friend."

You wound me.

"I'm serious."

Apparently.

I crawl off the bed and leave the pillow behind. I no longer need the talisman.

"There isn't any bargaining between friends."

Are you certain about that? Isn't there a bit of bargaining going on between you and that so-called partner of yours? He's quite the charmer, but he isn't always ... how shall we say? On the level.

I cringe, because, yes, Malcolm has some issues with the truth. "We don't keep score."

Perhaps, and perhaps not. With him, who knows?

"But this isn't about Malcolm. I know him, and I trust him. All I know about you is that your loyalty depends on which necromancer currently has a pact with you."

A fairly straightforward proposition. You have no reason to doubt my intentions.

"But..." I open and then close my mouth, frustrated that I can't articulate my thoughts. They aren't even thoughts, really. What I want to say is more of a whisper than actual words.

"It isn't fair to you." I blurt this, not caring that it might not make sense.

The entity's form roils with laughter, the sound of it rich and indulgent, a parent amused by a toddler.

Unfair? To me? Could there be anything further from the truth?

"No, it isn't fair to you," I say again, warming to my subject. "You don't get to choose your necromancer, do you?"

Choose? No. Influence? Ah, now, that's a distinct possibility, and frankly, far more fun.

"But what if someone you despise catches you?"

That rarely happens.

"But it could."

There are rules for how I can interact on this plane. I abide by them because every once in a great while, they bring me someone like you.

Should that flatter me? Maybe. I think it's meant to distract me instead. Despite all the power the entity has, it needs a human conduit to do everything it might want to do. On our first encounter, it claimed to want simple things: the ability to drink a cup of coffee, to touch a cheek.

These aren't the desires of the power-crazed. Orson Yates doesn't want those things, or, at least, he just doesn't crave them.

"You're lonely," I say.

I know something about loneliness. I'm a girl who catches ghosts, raised by her eccentric grandmother, after all. Even when someone like Belinda included me, I always felt outside the circle, like there was a barrier between everyone else and me.

The entity flicks some imaginary lint from the cuff of its jacket. *Really, my dear? I've been around for ages.*

"Okay. Make that very lonely."

I know about that, too. That time still stretches out in my mind, the dark space between when my grandmother died and Malcolm and I became partners. What would it be like to have that same darkness without end?

I never thought I'd feel sorry for the thing that has haunted and tormented me for nearly a year. I never thought I'd understand it.

Your pity is wasted on me, my dear. As for your understanding? You have no more a chance of comprehending me than a sprite has of mastering calculus.

"Are you sure?" I ask. "About the sprite, I mean."

This time, the laughter is more muted, a warm chuckle. *See? It's things like this that make our exchanges more than equitable.*

The entity stands and walks forward, its strides fluid. It halts mere inches away from me. Its proximity buzzes the air, and its power is tangible, sharp and electric. The tiny hairs on the back of my neck stand on end. The urge to step back nearly overwhelms me.

I hold my ground.

Have I convinced you yet?

I shake my head.

Why ever not?

"The first thing you said to me tonight. 'There's no need to be alone.'"

You were mooning about, missing that partner of yours.

"You seem fixated on Malcolm."

That's because he takes up so much space in here. The entity gestures toward my head. *You sound rather lovesick most days.*

I ignore that. Behind me, the curtains rustle with the breeze. The air is cooler, as if the night has released the last bit of the day's warmth. The void where the entity's face should be swirls, the pattern shifting and changing to something more shrouded.

The bubble around us shatters. I feel the late hour in my legs, and it presses against my eyelids. And I consider: maybe it wasn't the tea at all.

I was wondering when you'd figure that out.

Without another word, the entity vanishes.

MY PHONE RINGS just as I reach for the lamp on the nightstand. The sound startles me, and I switch the light off, on, and then off again. My heart thumps a hopeful beat. No matter how tired I am, I want to talk to Malcolm more than anything. It must be him, calling to grumble about his mother.

The number is one I recognize, because I've seen it pop up on the screen several times this week. But it's not Malcolm.

It's Arianna. Calling me. At one thirty in the morning. And she wants to video chat. I decide to leave the light off.

"Oh, good, you're awake," she says the moment the connection goes through.

I want to say, *You just called and woke me up, so of course I'm awake.*

Except that isn't true. I cast my thoughts toward the entity. Did it keep me awake and alert on purpose? For this?

I strain for a telltale hint—a rumble or a sigh or something in the air. The breeze kicks up again, and the curtains flap.

I'm not sure that's an answer.

"I apologize for the late hour and the ruse, but I simply must speak to you alone." She waves a hand, the gesture dismissive, and her mouth quirks into a knowing smile. "Like I don't know the two of you are sleeping together."

I don't want to talk about that, not at one thirty in the morning. And I really don't want to talk to Arianna about it, especially since she's as fresh as the Paris morning I can see behind her.

"This is important, Katy." She pauses and takes a sip from a white porcelain cup that could double as a soup bowl. Her lipstick leaves behind a perfect impression. "Before I say anything, you must promise never to tell Malcolm or Nigel what I'm about to tell you."

A secret? Oh, I hate those. I'm a terrible liar. Malcolm will know I'm hiding something. So will Nigel, for that matter.

I give my head a vigorous shake. "I don't think—"

"You need to know this, for their sake, if for no other reason."

"Their sake?"

"Will you promise me?"

I open my mouth, hoping for the right words, or any words, to come out. "Arianna, I can't. I mean, without knowing what—"

"I know you love my son."

If I'd hoped to find words, that declaration blows away any chance of it. She laughs, the sound light and airy. True, it's morning in Paris, but it's still far too early for this sort of conversation.

"I've been chatting with you all week long," she says by way of explanation. "It's fairly obvious, and I..." She trails off and becomes devoted to her cappuccino again. After a long sip, she continues. "I approve. You're good for him, and vice versa."

I give a numb sort of nod.

"Which is why you must promise, for his sake, and the sake of your partnership—both in and out of bed."

The echo of the entity's words shoots through me. That isn't a coincidence; it can't be. Once again, I'm wide awake. I feel as if I've downed a giant cappuccino like the one Arianna is drinking.

I push the pillows—still perfectly plumped—behind me and settle in. This, I suspect, will be a long chat.

"All right. I promise. I won't tell Malcolm."

"Or Nigel."

"Or Nigel," I add.

I wait, certain Arianna will launch her first volley. Instead, she brushes a few strands of hair from her forehead. She has, of course, an impeccable French manicure. She sips the cappuccino again. At last, she pushes back from the table and stands. For a brief moment, she vanishes from the screen. I hear the scrape of the balcony door, and she reappears in front of me.

"Prem knows this," she says, settling into her chair, "but I want to spare him the rerun." Arianna smiles, not the dazzling expatriate smile she so often wears, but one that's much sadder, more worn around the edges. "I'm sure someone has informed you about my affair by now, the one that ended my marriage to Darien."

I nearly bite my lip before remembering that it will earn me a scolding. "Malcolm mentioned it," I say. "He was trying to explain ... things about the family." I give in and gnaw my lip anyway. "Around the time of the wedding."

"Oh, my poor baby boy," she says. Her gaze darts to my chewed lower lip, but she ignores it. "Yes, that's exactly the sort of thing he'd do, and, of course, you've met Darien."

I nod.

"Some people wear their hearts on their sleeves. Darien? He likes to display all his wounds for everyone to admire."

Oh. Yes. No animosity *there*.

"I don't blame him," she adds. "Not when it comes to this. Because it wasn't my first."

Arianna falls silent, and I consider her words, trying to piece together the puzzle that is Malcolm's family.

"We did everything couples do when small children are involved: marriage counseling, fighting, more counseling. It wasn't until I met Prem that I realized how miserable we all were. And since, by that time, the boys were nearly grown and Darien traveled constantly." She raises a hand and lets it fall. "It was a step that, had I more courage, I would've taken years ago."

Arianna comes across so fierce, so sure of herself, that I can't imagine her a coward.

"But that's merely background." She glances away from me, toward the Seine. "I hate to burden you with this, but current circumstances dictate that I do." She returns her attention to me, staring at me straight on. Her gaze is like an arrow, and it pins me in place.

"About the time of your parents' deaths, I embarked on an affair with Orson Yates."

CHAPTER 3

T he phone slips through my fingers and lands on the bed,
screen down. How long I leave it there, I'm not certain. It
doesn't matter. I don't have a single coherent thought in my head,
never mind words to form into sentences and questions.

Malcolm's mother and Orson Yates? I don't need to worry
about keeping this a secret from Malcolm. If I told him, he
wouldn't believe me, not when *I* don't believe it.

I wonder if the call is still connected. Then I wonder if it would
look too obvious if I brushed my thumb over *Cancel* and discon-
nected it. My stomach is a bundle of knots, and my chest feels
tight. I don't want to talk about affairs and broken marriages. I
don't want to know how it all relates to my parents' deaths.

Because clearly it does.

At last, I retrieve my cell phone. Arianna is still there, cradling
the oversized cup in her palms.

"I'm sorry," she says. "An in-person chat would've been so
much better."

Not really. This way, at least, I can hide most of my shock and
all of my disgust.

"Orson Yates?" I mean it as a question, but the name comes out as an accusation.

"Orson was a much different man back then." Arianna regards me through the screen. "I know, it doesn't seem possible to you. For me? It doesn't seem possible he's changed so much. Or, rather —" She sets the cappuccino down and taps her lips with an index finger. "He's nurtured some traits at the expense of others."

I cast my thoughts back to the road and the ravine on the way to the nature preserve, or, rather, the version of it Springside's ghosts showed me. Orson was obviously younger, but there was something else about him, a kind of vulnerability. He was someone who, on the surface, appeared capable of both compassion and curiosity.

I peer at Arianna, and her expression shifts, a glimmer of approval lighting her eyes.

"I see you understand. Not everybody does. For some people, the world is black and white."

I wonder if that includes Darien Armand.

"The necromancer community was hit hard by your parents' deaths. In fact, I'm willing to say that it fundamentally changed the community. Things were never the same after that. Many of us left —not right away, of course." She pauses and contemplates the Seine. "But when we left, we left for good."

"I don't remember my parents." My voice sounds small and insubstantial, and I think the night breeze might be able to sneak in and steal the words away.

"I'm sorry for that. They were ... they were quite wonderful. Your father was one of those strong, silent types. But when he spoke, nearly everyone listened. Your mother was ... she..." Her gaze flits toward me and then back to the Seine. "Shall I tell you the ugly truth? I was quite jealous of her."

I'm not sure how to take that. I wasn't even a year old when my parents died. Still, I can't picture Arianna Armand being jealous of anyone.

"Not only did her ability rival that of all her peers—that includes my ex-husband—she had a way with ghosts, and, since I'm being honest, men." Arianna gives me a wry smile. "It's funny what we think matters, especially when we're younger."

I shake my head, not because I disagree but because I can't form a picture of my mother. She's more of a ghost than anything.

"Darien was quite obsessed with her. At first, I didn't understand why, or, rather, I thought it was for the typical reasons a man becomes obsessed with a woman who isn't his wife."

"Arianna, please, I don't—" I don't want any of this. I don't want to know about Darien Armand and my mother. I don't want to hear about this part of her. I don't need to pull back the veil and examine my parents' lives.

"Shh." She hushes me. "It's more, and less, than what you think it is."

I wait. My throat is tight, and my eyes are watering. I brace as if I'm waiting for a physical blow.

"Your mother very much wanted to bring her father back to this plane. It was that desire that drove her, I think, to hone her skills, to join the association. You may have noticed that they're not exactly egalitarian."

"Yeah. Orson made a big deal out of it when he came to Springside."

"Yes, he would." She regards me. "In a way, you've accomplished what she set out to do. You brought Malcolm back, after all."

I open my mouth, but Arianna holds up a finger. "I know all about that. Everyone does. In fact, when things ... calm down, Prem would very much like to talk to you about it."

I nod. I would like to talk to someone about it, too, someone in addition to Malcolm. He doesn't remember his time with the entity, and our conversations about it are strained.

"But this was a special case. Your grandfather had been gone for several years, and the agreement between him, your grandmother, and the entity was complicated."

"Do you know why—?"

She holds up that finger again, halting my question. "From what I understand, it was a stopgap measure, but your mother was determined to bring him back, even up to and including sacrificing herself."

I swallow back the questions. It occurs to me that I can ask the entity about this. Oh, I could, certainly—for a price.

I ponder the timing of its visit this evening.

Again, hardly a coincidence.

I hold in my sigh and let Arianna continue.

"I don't know the whole story. There are pieces that I suspect only Darien knows, but I do know this. Your mother asked for his help, and he felt ... compelled to do so. I—" She shakes her head and then runs her fingers through her hair. The bob swings forward, the ends flirting with the corners of her mouth. "I thought that in addition to everything else, they were having an affair."

Her balcony door creaks open. Prem appears, bearing a plate of rolls, wisps of steam rising in the morning air. Without a word, he sets the plate on the table, kisses Arianna on the cheek, and then slips back through the door.

She sinks into her chair, releases a sigh, and blows him a kiss. "It doesn't make any sense, of course. You were an infant, and anyone looking at your parents could see how happy they were."

Arianna falls silent. She plucks a croissant from the plate and tears off a bite.

I work to peel away the emotions tangled in this story. My mother wanted to get her father back. What did she do? Possibly the same thing I did when I wanted to get Malcolm back.

Ask for help.

"So, my mother asked Darien if he could help her, since he's so good at catching ghosts?"

Arianna looks up from her croissant, surprise and relief playing across her features. "Yes, exactly. Darien was intrigued. Not so much with your mother, although he admired her skill, but with the entity."

Still intrigued? I decide not to ask.

"Of course, by the time I realized that, it was too late. Your parents were dead, and I found myself consoling the wrong man because of it."

Consoling?

"Here's something you probably don't know about Orson Yates. Not many people do. Unlike Darien, he's not very good at catching ghosts."

"He's not?"

She considers the croissant in her hand and picks up a butter knife. "No. In fact, he's relied on others to do the more ... menial parts of the job for all these years. It's why he almost always travels with a protégé."

"Like Carter Dupree?"

"Yes, exactly like Carter," she says. "But when it comes to deploying ghosts, to training and motivating them? There's no one better than he is. It's a highly prized skill. You know how capricious ghosts can be. No one trains them like Orson does, and the Midwest Necromancer Association rewarded him accordingly."

I'm not sure where she's going with this. I'd guessed at the one. Orson's attack ghosts are fierce, and he's both cruel and cunning with them. With a little thought, I might have puzzled out the other, but I've always figured Orson preferred to have a minion to do the grunt work.

"I don't understand—" I begin.

Arianna cuts me off with another gaze that pins me in place. "Orson deployed the ghost that killed your parents, but it was Darien who caught the ghost in the first place."

CHAPTER 4

I drop the phone again. It bounces on the bed and vanishes in a fold of the comforter. Part of me wants to grab it and demand answers. Part of me wants to hang up and pretend the last half-hour never happened.

From within the down comes Arianna's muffled voice. I search out the phone, fingers snaking through the covers. For a long moment, I simply hang on to it. Part of me insists I already knew this fact, that it was obvious from the start. I don't need to hear any more.

Arianna's voice is more plaintive than crisp. She's revealed a great many family secrets to tell me all this.

I rescue the phone and turn the screen toward me.

"Oh, thank goodness, you're still there. Katy, I know this must be a shock, but keep in mind that the Orson Yates of two decades ago was a much different man, as was Darien."

Yes. That. Another secret to keep from Malcolm—and Nigel. At this rate, I'm going to lose track.

"I can tell you this for a fact: neither man knew the ghost would end up killing your parents. I didn't understand Darien's reaction at the time. It was only much later that I discovered he had been involved." She shakes her head as if that will shake away the past. "The association has always used strong-arm tactics, but the bullying never went too far."

"Except for when it did."

She sighs. "Yes, it did. It changed Orson, for the worse, obviously. But, at the time, he was bereft. He cared for your mother. I think I mentioned she had a way with men? You look so much like her. I imagine he must have a difficult time reconciling past and present."

Is that why he gave me so many chances to join the Midwest Necromancer Association? Then I wonder something else.

"Why would the association want to scare my parents?"

"Why have they been hounding you?" she says. "The entity, of course."

"Then, my mother—"

Arianna holds up a hand. She's still gripping the butter knife, and the sight of it gives her pause. She sets it carefully on her plate before continuing. "I don't know the answer to your question."

"I haven't asked it."

She laughs, but there's no humor in it. "If your mother didn't possess the entity at the time of her death, then she knew how to invoke it. That's all I can say on the matter."

"And if she possessed it? Then, wouldn't...?" I trail off. Wouldn't the entity save her?

"The entity already had a willing sacrifice in the form of your grandfather. Negotiations would've been protracted. Both the entity and your mother were vulnerable."

Malcolm has explained that to me, how, until a pact is set, things are out of balance. "So, when my mother died—"

"The pact remained in place, with your grandfather as the willing sacrifice."

"And no one else knew the entity's name."

Arianna gives me a wry smile. "Not until you figured that out."

Of course, the problem is, thanks to Orson—and modern technology—every necromancer in the entire world knows the entity's name by now. I'm back where I started, only with a heart weighed down by sorrow.

"You might speak with Darien." The suggestion is soft. It sounds more like an invitation than a decree. "Without Malcolm and Nigel around," she adds. "He won't speak about it any other way."

"He doesn't much like me," I say.

She laughs. It's the light and airy laugh I've come to expect from her. She sounds almost like herself again. "Oh, that? That's simply Darien being Darien. He doesn't like anyone, but he did admire your mother. As I mentioned, she had a way with men. Perhaps you do as well?"

I don't dignify that with an answer.

"Oh, my dear, I've kept you up so late. I think it's time we said *bonne nuit.*" She squints at me, or perhaps at the change in the light that I only now notice. "Or, rather, *bonjour.*"

She blows me a kiss, and then my screen goes black.

I sit on the bed, not moving, and watch the sunrise touch the street beyond the window. Then I kick off the covers and clamber to my feet.

There's no sense in trying to sleep. My mind is buzzing with too many thoughts. For the first time in a week, my legs feel strong, despite the all-nighter I just pulled. I tug back the curtains and kneel next to the window.

With both hands, I push the sash all the way up so I can lean out over the porch and its green steel roof. A car is inching up the street, pausing every few houses to jettison the morning paper.

I turn my attention toward the sky. Again, I don't know why I look up—rather than down or sideways—when I speak to the entity. I only know that I do.

"You could've said something." My voice rings out, breaking the quiet of the morning.

And where's the fun in that?

"Are you going to keep feeding me caffeine or whatever it is?"

Is that what I'm doing? Are you certain?

I'm not, actually, but something is fueling my thoughts and my limbs. All I know is that I feel, if not better, then more capable—at last.

"I don't suppose you're going to give me any hints."

As I said, where's the fun in that?

I sigh and consider all I have to do today, and how I'm going to accomplish all of that alone. I hate the idea of ditching Malcolm.

I don't.

"I wasn't consulting you."

An otherworldly chuckle fills the air, the sound of it fading into birdsong and the rustle of leaves. I need to do so many things today, but first, I'm going to start with some Kona blend.

Pour me a cup, won't you, my dear?

"I'll think about it."

THE MORNING IS STILL cool and Main Street still sleepy when I pull my truck into a parking spot in front of the Springside Police Department. I suspect Chief Ramsey is already in his office. If not, he's over at the Springside Pancake House.

I think about checking, but my entire system recoils at the thought. It will be a long time before I order all-you-can-eat dollar-size pancakes again.

I slip out of the truck and ease the door closed, each movement quiet and hesitant. Instead of dashing up the steps, I lean against the driver's side door and consider whether this is the best idea.

A week ago, Nigel dug up both the police report and the newspaper articles about my parents' deaths. In all of that, there wasn't a single mention of a baby at the scene. Which means what, exactly?

Either the ghosts lied, or someone else did.

I push off the truck, but, before I tackle the stairs, I reach through the window and grab my impromptu field kit and the two thermoses of coffee I made this morning.

Inside, the reception area is quiet. Penny Wilson's computer screen is dark, files and paperwork lined up neatly to one side. The ever-present scent of charred coffee lingers, thick enough that, at first, I'm uncertain if anyone—human or supernatural—is here.

I tilt my chin and sample the air. The hint of the otherworldly is slight, but definitely there.

A moment later, a force barrels into me. The two sprites that haunt the police station dart about so quickly, I can't track their zigzags. They crash into each other—an orchestrated move—before fanning out and leaving a glimmer in their wake that looks like fireworks.

"I'm happy to see you, too," I say to them.

They whiz past, ruffling my hair and dotting my cheeks with ghostly kisses.

They were caught up in the net Orson cast over Springside's ghosts. I wonder how he managed to snag these two. They almost never leave the police station, and I was surprised to find them among the mass of ghosts I untangled in the Pancake House's cold storage unit.

"You'll have to tell Malcolm sometime," I say. "Or just be extra careful from now on. Stranger danger and all that."

They whip past again and do a lap around the station, their forms narrowing. They look like arrows, and I'm their target.

Before I can sidestep or duck, each one bullets straight for an armpit.

Oh. So. Cold.

The sensation is like a blast of ice water from a showerhead. Without thinking, I let out a yelp. A moment later, the door to Chief Ramsey's office swings open.

He surveys me, backlit by the sun filtering through the small

247

window behind him, arms crossed over his chest. He's unusually unimpressed with me this morning.

"Please tell me you haven't made a mess in the Pancake House again."

I shake my head. The sprites are burrowing deeper under my arms, and keeping a straight face is a challenge.

"Been leaving cups of coffee in strangers' homes lately?"

"Anyone complain?" I counter.

For a moment, a smile tugs at the corner of his mouth. "Your coffee? No, they probably wouldn't."

I use that as my opening and rummage in the tote at my side. The sprites don't make this easy. They're nestled in good. Now that they're calm, I detect more than elation from them.

I think they might be scared. But with Chief staring down at me, there's no time to investigate why.

"Speaking of coffee." I pull a thermos free and hold it up in triumph. "Would you like some?"

Chief remains silent, his gaze assessing me. Then he retreats to his office.

"You know I do," is all he says.

I grab two Styrofoam cups from the sideboard and follow him inside.

CHAPTER 5

I pour us both a cup. He cradles his like it's the Holy Grail, inhales the steam like he's just discovered oxygen, and sips like it's the elixir of life.

"You should really let me give Penny a few lessons," I tell him. "You'd be surprised how much better the coffee will taste."

"But then you wouldn't visit me."

I freeze with the cup halfway to my lips. I set it back down on his desk. I don't trust my hands not to tremble. I don't trust my voice either, but I want to know what he meant.

"I'd still visit you."

"Would you?" He eyes me over the rim of his cup. "Seems to me, you stop by only when you need information."

"Well, you're the police chief. You have lots of that." I go for breezy, but the comment nags before solidifying into a guilty lump in the pit of my stomach. Have I been using Chief?

The sprites beneath my arms wiggle free and zip from the office. A moment later, a jangle comes from the reception area. Chief stares past me, frowns, and then shakes his head.

"What do you need, Katy?" The gruffness is in full force—the Kona blend hasn't helped at all.

"I ... need something?"

"You're here, with coffee, at barely past sunrise, and Malcolm isn't along. You either need something or you're about to get into some very deep shit."

I open my mouth to defend myself, but shock has stolen all my words. I don't think I've ever heard Chief swear before. To be honest, I've probably given him reason to swear—most likely, several reasons.

We're renegotiating something here, but what that something is escapes me. This is brand-new territory, and I'm not sure how to navigate it. So, I decide on the truth.

"I want to know something about my parents' deaths, and I think you can tell me."

Chief's hands lock on the Styrofoam cup. I'm afraid he might crush the flimsy sides and send coffee everywhere.

After a moment, his fingers release the cup, but his grip is nowhere close to relaxed.

"I've read the police report," I begin.

"Have you, now?"

"And the newspaper articles. I want to know one thing."

"And what would that be?"

"Was I there?"

Chief blinks as if I've startled him, as if this is the one question he never expected. He recovers, quickly, his police chief persona solidifying into place.

"Why do you think you were there?"

I sag. He always manages to ask the questions I can't answer. He won't believe me about the ghosts. I'm not sure *I* believe the ghosts, which is why I'm here in the first place. Even if the entity could tell me, I want to hear the answer from a human. Specifically, I want to hear it from the man who plucked me from the ground and cradled me like a father might.

"It's just ... something I've been wondering." I grope for an explanation. "Why wasn't I in the car? Were they going somewhere without me? Was I with my grandmother?"

"Katy, this case is closed. Has been for more than two decades. The particulars don't matter at this point."

"Or maybe they just hurt."

Chief rocks back, almost as if I've slapped him. His complexion is dark enough that it's hard to detect a blush—angry or otherwise. But he stares at me as if I've just inflicted some of that hurt.

"Yes," he says, and that single word comes out like steel. "They do."

"Then, I was there?" I venture.

Chief downs the last of his coffee. Without asking, I pour him a second cup. He regards it and then tips it in my direction, as if in a toast.

"There's nothing in the police report because no one knew what to make of it, and it was easy enough to keep it out of the newspaper."

"Keep what out of the newspaper?"

He continues as if he hasn't heard me. "Your grandmother arrived long before Springside's roving reporter did. Everyone just assumed that she..." He trails off and stares past me.

"Assumed what?"

He rouses himself. "That's the thing, isn't it? A car in flames, and a baby at the side of the road, unharmed. No one thought to ask. Not the first responders. Not the reporter. To this day, I don't understand it." His gaze centers on my face and locks me in place. "You shouldn't be here, Katy."

My heart thuds so hard against my ribcage, I'm certain it will bruise. I swallow, and my throat feels tender and raw.

"Your grandmother wanted us to arrest Orson Yates, and she was quite livid when we wouldn't. If I'd known he'd show up all these years later, maybe I would have. But there wasn't any proof he was involved. He was a witness and no more."

Well, sort of.

"I was there," I say, more to myself than Chief.

What the ghosts showed me was real. I think back on that misty scene that—if I let it—might solidify into an actual memory.

"It's not something you'd remember."

It wasn't, anyway.

"You were too young," he adds. He scrubs his face with his hands. "Katy, why bring this up now?"

That's a fair question, and I've plagued Chief so much that he deserves an answer. "I think something happened between my parents and Orson Yates."

Chief goes on high alert. He leans forward, and the keen interest of an investigator chases away some of the remorse in his expression. "Do you have any idea what that something might be? Proof? Something I can actually use?"

Well, yes, but it isn't something he'll believe. I pull in a breath and go for mostly true. "He thinks I have ... something. Something they left me, maybe?" I give my head a shake and hope I'm not overdoing it. "But I don't know what that something could be, and—"

Chief holds up a hand, and I clam up, grateful I won't have to dig a deeper hole. He wakes up his computer, and in the silence that follows, I'm lulled by the rhythm of his clacking on the keyboard.

"Huh." It's half a word, half a grunt, and completely mysterious.

"Did you—?"

"I want you to stay away from him." He swivels in his chair and jabs a finger at me. "Promise me?"

I nod. This is a promise I plan to keep.

"If he comes around, call me. If he harasses you, online, in the mail, anything, call me. It might be a good idea if Malcolm—" He pauses, clears his throat. "If Malcolm continues ... sleeping at your place."

My mouth drops open. My thoughts collide, outrage warring with embarrassment. "How do you—?" I begin, and then the obvious hits me. For the last week, Malcolm's cherry-red convertible has been parked on the street outside my house, day and night.

"Promise me, Katy."

I nod again. "I don't want to see Orson again or have anything to do with him."

"Good. With a little luck, maybe we can keep it that way."

I lean forward, but I can't see what Chief has on his computer screen. "What are you going to do?"

The remorse returns to his gaze, and the lines around his eyes deepen. "Something I should have done twenty years ago."

I HEAD for my truck once it's become clear that Chief won't share his plans with me. I leave behind the thermos half-full of coffee. On my way out, the sprites dance about my head and ruffle my hair.

I hold up my hand in a wave to Penny and let them weave between my fingers.

"What's wrong?" The question is no more than a whisper, but it catches Penny's attention.

She looks up from her work, her expression bright. "Nothing, nothing. I'm fine. I'm about to make Chief some coffee. Want to stay for some?"

I open my mouth and then close it, nipping at the tail end of a sprite. I spit, and Penny's expression falters.

"Sorry, sorry," I say, trying to blow the sprite away from my face. There is no subtle way to do this. "Bug in my mouth."

I cast a sidelong glance at the coffeemaker. One of these days, I should really teach Penny how to make drinkable coffee.

"I can't." I gesture toward the door. "I have … things."

It's a poor excuse, but fortunately, it's enough for Penny, and when she goes to prepare the coffee, I conduct one last conference with the sprites.

"What has you so worried?" I ask them. "Is it Orson?"

They bob up and down, crash into each other. It's not much of an answer, but I get the gist of it. I suppose I could go all necromancer and let one of them into my thoughts. But sprites do nothing but chatter. I'm not sure it would help.

"Are there other necromancers in town?"

That's a no-brainer sort of question. Of course there are, at least in the form of Darien and Reginald. The sprites continue bobbing, adding a flourish, as if that will somehow help.

"Ones you've never seen before?"

Now they spin and twirl. I should've asked that first.

"Stay here," I tell them, "and you'll be safe."

I hope that's true. I don't like the idea of strange necromancers. Something always happens when one comes to town.

I blow the sprites a kiss and head for my truck.

Next on my list?

I'm going to go speak to one of those necromancers.

CHAPTER 6

The nature preserve is the most obvious spot to find Darien Armand.

Even in the summer, it isn't too difficult to book a reservation in the campground. The space is vast, with everything from prepared campsites to ones that are no more than a clearing of tall grass in the dense woods. Today, the spots closest to the parking lot are teeming with Girl and Boy Scouts, families, and members of the Springside Senior Adventure Club.

The aroma of wood smoke mixes with scents of breakfast. My stomach grumbles, and I regret skipping the Pancake House. Children screech and laugh. Pots and pans clatter. Someone is singing a song about campground safety.

Something tells me Darien is somewhere far away from all this —*very* far away. That means a hike. I sit at a picnic table, tighten the laces on my boots, and consider whether my legs are up to the task.

I stand and gauge their strength with little bounces on each foot. Two little girls in pajamas and sneakers rush past, spot me, and then join in. We bounce in time with a song about doing chores until the singing comes to an end.

"Is this how you catch ghosts?" one of them asks.

"Not really," I say.

"Are you sure?" She points to something behind me, and then the two of them scamper off.

I turn around. Something glimmers in the air just above my head. I reach out a hand and let my fingers touch the ethereal form. The otherworldly sensation is unfamiliar.

"Have I caught you before?"

This ghost possesses far more maturity than a sprite, but its presence is so slight that it's hardly there at all. I glance over my shoulder, searching out the little girl. She's long gone, and I regret not asking her name.

"Maybe once?" I say to the ghost.

Its only response is to ooze forward, toward a path that leads away from the established campsites with their electronic hookups, restrooms, and shelters.

The second the buzzing starts in my ear, I remember the insect repellent in my truck and consider heading back to get it. Mosquitoes swarm as if I'm the only warm-blooded thing for miles around. I slap at my neck, my arms. I keep that up until I walk straight into the ghost.

It hovers around me. It's very much like being in the cold storage unit, inside the tangle of ghosts.

"Were you there?" I ask it. "Inside the Pancake House?"

Perhaps it's trying to tell me that. Its form quivers around me, but it only moves when I do, and I remain shrouded in its mist. It takes several yards—and a trek through a gnat-infested jumble of branches—before I realize that I haven't been bitten by a single mosquito.

"Thank you," I say.

It quivers once again. This one, I think, is not very talkative. I could live with a ghost like this. It bobs once, and I think: maybe I already am.

Despite my ethereal escort, sweat trickles down my spine. Perspiration blooms on my upper lip, and, while I'm grateful for the protection, the hiking boots are baking my feet. We must be a good half-mile from the main camping area when it occurs to me that maybe I shouldn't be following this ghost, that it's a stealthy Orson attack ghost.

Except it doesn't feel that way to me.

When we reach a hill, I'm certain I won't make it to the top. My legs are aching. A wave of exhaustion hits me, reminding me that despite its otherworldly cause, necromancer flu is very real, and I'm not fully recovered.

The ghost inches forward. I follow, gripping branches and stripping them of their leaves when my feet catch on the rocks. The path is an obstacle course of ruts and jagged stones. I'm nearly positive no one in their right mind would willingly make this climb. Except that someone has, since a thin stream of smoke is rising from the crest of the hill.

I claw my way to the top and immediately sink to my knees. My ghostly companion wanders off. I catch my breath, intent on following. But when I stand, a force slams into me.

My arms flail, and I nearly tumble backward down the hill. I skid, but catch myself, and take a moment to glance around.

There's nothing in front of me. I reach out a hand but meet no resistance.

I step forward and crash into the barrier again. Only it isn't a barrier. It's noise ... sound ... words.

You have not been invited, and, therefore, I do not wish to see you.

It's a ward, or, more precisely, Darien Armand's ward. I'm certain of it. Through the thicket of trees is a clearing, and in it sits a tent. When I step away from the ward and the noise leaves my head, I can hear the crackle of the fire.

"I'd like to speak to you, Mr. Armand," I call out. I don't suppose I need to shout; the noise is all in my head. But I'm sweaty, fierce, and annoyed; shouting feels good.

I step forward again only to get knocked back by that wave of sound.

You'd think I'd take the hint.

"I have coffee," I add, equally loud.

At least, I hope I do, and that the thermos hasn't slipped from my tote on the climb up. I grope the canvas sack, and when my fingers encounter the thermos, I let out a sigh.

All at once, the crackle of the fire is louder. A log shifts, sending sparks and a hiss of smoke into the air. Tent flaps rustle in the breeze. I try the barrier again, shuffling my way through, wincing in anticipation of that blast of sound.

I step straight through and continue to the campsite. The setup is quaint—a little tent with room for no more than two, a cheerful fire with a camp stool to one side.

Darien steps from behind the tent. He's wearing cargo pants and a T-shirt and has a towel draped around his neck. There are dots of shaving cream on his face, and he's holding a straight razor in one hand.

I try to pretend that this last isn't a threat, but my gaze locks on to the blade's edge.

The barest of smiles tugs at his mouth. With great deliberation, he folds the razor shut and tucks it away inside a backpack.

"You mentioned something about coffee?" he says.

I rummage inside the tote and pull out the thermos. I hold it up so he can see it. In response, he pulls out two flat disks from his backpack. With the flourish of a magician, he pops both into cups.

If he were anyone other than Darien Armand, I might applaud.

"Extra sugar?" he asks.

"Of course." I hold in a shudder. I don't like my coffee sweet, but at least it's Kona, and I'll be able to drink it.

"It's a long walk up here," he continues. "I can't imagine it would still be warm."

I hold up the thermos again. "German-made. It will still be *hot*."

"I'll let you do the honors, then."

I pour us two cups. Despite the muggy air and the excess sugar, the Kona blend works its magic. The aroma mixes with that of the campfire smoke, and the combination is heady. Whoever coined the phrase *the great outdoors* was probably holding a cup of coffee at the time.

I take a sip to fortify myself, then dive in. "Did you help my mother catch the entity?"

Darien raises an eyebrow. "I see we're skipping the small talk and preliminaries."

He strikes me as someone who loathes preliminaries, and small talk in particular. "I didn't know you were a fan."

"I'm not. Like most social niceties, it wastes time and is generally dishonest." He regards me. "You're very much like your mother in that."

"Did you help her?" I ask again.

"If you're asking whether she came to me for help, then, yes, that part is true."

"What part isn't true?"

"In the end, she caught the entity on her own."

"How?"

"One might ask you that same question."

My mind whirls, and I think back to how I discovered the entity's name. It was no more difficult than asking Mr. Carlotta's ghost Queenie.

I don't know, for certain, how long Queenie has been haunting him—although he claims it's been since Guadalcanal. What I do know is that she's ancient, if not an actual ancient warrior.

How she knows the entity's name is unclear. She's a prickly and particular sort of ghost. It would be just like her not to share the name or how she knows it with anyone. But she did with me, and —I'm guessing—with my mother.

"Ah, so you see?" Darien doesn't smile, but his expression shifts, and I know he must've read my mind. "It may be no more than Lindstrom blood. It started, after all, with your grandmother."

"My grandmother," I say, uncertain of where he's going.

"And my father. You'll excuse me if I don't feel much sympathy for your current plight. I see it as a just payment for a crime committed long ago."

"A crime." I'm somehow reduced to echoing him.

"But that's how the entity works. It bends and twists desires, makes you betray those you claim to love. How much longer until you betray Malcolm? I'm only here to pick up the pieces and ensure the damage isn't so great that he can't recover."

My heart thumps fast and hard, and the sweet coffee turns sour in my stomach. "What are you talking about?"

"It's what Lindstrom women do. Your grandmother and my grandfather, your mother and me, and now you and Malcolm."

The clearing grows silent. No early morning birdsong. No breeze rustling the leaves. Even the fire burns silently. The only sound is blood rushing in my ears.

"I may do many things wrong," I tell him, "but betraying Malcolm isn't one of them."

We stand in the clearing, glares locked in place. I don't budge, not even to sip the coffee. I could stand here all day. In fact, I plan to. I will wait until Darien Armand tells me everything he knows.

At last, he holds out his coffee cup. It's empty. I uncap the thermos and pour him a second serving. He sips, clears his throat, and starts speaking.

"Back when the Armands were part of the necromancer community, my parents and your grandparents conspired to bring a powerful entity to this plane." He peers at me over the rim of the cup. "I don't suppose I need to tell you which entity that turned out to be."

No, I don't suppose he does.

"My father never went into much detail about how they managed that, understandably. It was meant as a cautionary tale, not one to inspire curiosity. But have you wondered why it was your grandfather who ended up as the willing sacrifice?"

I give my head a little shake.

"Your grandmother betrayed my father. You've already seen the power the entity can wield, what it can do, and what a necromancer can do with all that power. You no doubt feel the pull of temptation."

I gulp coffee in a vain attempt to melt the ice in the pit of my stomach. My limbs are growing cold, and I shiver—both from too much sugar and the idea of it. Yes. The temptation. It's like a tug against my soul. I know I could flick my wrist and make the world the way I want it to be. I also know that, as a solution, it's ultimately false.

"Your grandmother was no different," he says. Energy infuses his words. It almost sounds like he's gloating. "She succumbed to the temptation and betrayed my father, but in the end, it turned out that her desire wasn't pure enough to hold the entity. To keep it out of the hands of other necromancers, your grandfather offered himself up as a willing sacrifice, with your grandmother keeping the vigil for the rest of her life. That was the pact, and it held until the day she died, despite your mother's attempts to break it."

Darien swallows the last of his coffee and flattens the cup between his hands. "And here we are today, waiting. What's that saying? Third time's a charm?"

I fight to weave all these new ideas together with what I already know—or think I know. It sounds right; all the pieces fall into place. And yet ...

"If that's true, why would you want me to use the entity? Why did you encourage me to use it to stop Orson?"

A smirk curls his lips. He must have a devastating answer to that. But before he can speak, a thrashing comes from the path.

Darien's eyes widen. I whirl around, certain it must be Malcolm and hoping it isn't at the same time.

Instead, Prescott Jones stumbles into view. He heaves a breath, wipes sweat from his brow, and then adjusts the suit coat jacket he has slung over one shoulder.

"Yes, I agree with Katy." Prescott nods in my direction. "I'm calling bullshit on your story."

CHAPTER 7

D arien sputters, an angry red washing across his face. "How did you—?"

"Please. Like I care about your ward." Prescott picks leaves from his shirt and then inspects his shoes with a sigh. "Hand-tooled Italian leather and completely ruined. You know, Springside has a perfectly lovely bed and breakfast."

"You violated my ward!" Darien's fingers flex at his sides.

"Call for retribution," Prescott says. "Oh, wait. That's right. You don't *need* the necromancer community." He turns to me. "Is there any coffee left?"

Stunned, I pull the thermos from my tote and give it a shake. "Little more than a cup."

Now Prescott turns toward Darien. "You wouldn't happen to have a third cup somewhere in there?" He waves a hand toward the tent.

Darien's expression is filled with outrage and ice.

"Go on," Prescott urges. "You know you want to get me that cup."

To my surprise, Darien spins and stalks toward the tent.

For a moment, I can't process any of this. I simply can't pull the pieces together. The last time I saw Prescott, he was speeding away from the warehouse. As for Darien? I can't imagine him doing anyone's bidding, but the sound of rummaging from the tent tells me otherwise.

"Odd how that third cup happens to be in the same spot he keeps his attack ghosts," Prescott says, his tone bland, as if we're discussing the weather.

Attack ghosts?

"Shall we let him ready one? Or two, for that matter," he continues. "I think yes. He'll be more relaxed, and we're not scared, are we?" He winks at me.

I can taste the humidity and the wood smoke, and I know my mouth must be hanging open. My gaze darts between Prescott and the wavering tent flaps. Yes, Darien is taking a long time to find a cup.

"You're not alone in all this," Prescott says, his voice softer now.

I'm facing the man who, less than a month ago, kidnapped me. Of course, he then let me capture the entity and save Malcolm along with everyone else.

The entity's voice echoes in my head.

If you ever see him again, my dear, you must ask him why.

So I do. "Why?"

I ask without preamble or explanation, trusting that Prescott will understand. The lift of one eyebrow tells me he does.

"Ah, that. I should apologize for the ... rough handling, although, at the time, I thought ... well, I thought differently, is all."

I wait, certain Darien will emerge from the tent and put an end to Prescott's explanation.

"It's a long story, one that involves a prince and begins with *once upon a time*."

"But there's no *happily ever after*?"

He shifts the suit coat to one arm and pulls out his phone. He beckons me to step forward—within grabbing distance—and I'm compelled by some force; curiosity, most likely. That, and I'm pretty sure no one could look as mournful as he does and still be deliberately cruel.

On the screen, a man is staring up at us. The background is bright, full of blues and greens and a hot tropical sun. He is beyond handsome, possibly more handsome than Malcolm, objectively speaking, anyway. I don't think anyone could truly be more handsome than Malcolm. But the man in this photo, with his wavy dark hair and soulful, almond-shaped eyes, is a close second.

"Once upon a time," Prescott says, "I had someone who looked at me the way Malcolm looks at you. You might say my desire wavered at the last moment. I could've caught the entity. God knows I convinced myself it was the thing to do. And yet..."

"You let me do it instead."

"You caught the entity on your own. I merely stepped out of your way."

I nod toward the photograph. "Where is he now?"

"Toronto."

"Then, why are you here?"

Prescott's gaze flickers toward the tent. "Unfinished business."

"Is he a necromancer?" I ask.

"No, although he can sense the otherworldly and thinks what I do is rather amusing. Or at least, he did."

The tent rustles. Prescott tucks the phone into his trouser pocket. A moment later, Darien emerges, another flat disk in hand. He flicks it in our direction. Prescott plucks it from the air before it can soar over his head.

"Really, Darien, do I warrant three attack ghosts? I'm only here to chat. Besides, you could have thirty, and they would still be no match for the one Katy has."

Darien glowers. "What is it you want?"

"Me? I'd like to set the record straight. Or, rather, I'd like you to do so."

"I have nothing more to say on the matter."

"You forget. My mother and Katy's were best friends."

I suck in a breath, and the smoky air burns the back of my throat. I turn toward Prescott. "They were?"

"They roomed together in college. My mother was pretty broken up when your parents died." He pops open the cup and extends it in my direction. "I suppose it's loaded with sugar."

"It is, but it's also Kona blend."

"Then it will still be worth drinking."

I pour the last of the coffee into the cup. He takes a sip and sighs.

"Not even you," he says to Darien, "can ruin Lindstrom coffee."

Darien grimaces, and I feel sorry for him—almost. I wonder if he isolates himself because he truly enjoys being alone, or if it's the only way he knows how to deal with his loneliness.

I wonder if I have something in common with Darien Armand.

Prescott swirls the coffee in its cup like it's brandy or wine, or whatever it is people swirl in fancy glasses.

"So, do you want to explain the real reason Katy's grandfather ended up as a willing sacrifice, or should I?"

"There are two sides to every story," Darien says.

"Yes, but usually only one set of facts."

I'm not certain either man will speak. They stare at each other. Although Prescott is younger, I sense that, in necromancer terms, the two men are equal. The tips of Darien's fingers glow, a phenomenon that I've recently learned means he really does have at least one attack ghost.

It's only then that I notice Prescott's hands. They, too, possess an otherworldly halo.

"I've said my piece," Darien announces at last. "So, now, if you'll—"

A crashing comes from the underbrush. Darien gapes, and I

266

imagine his outrage at not one, not two, but three uninvited guests. A frown creases Prescott's brow. He sets the cup down on a nearby log and turns to face the intruder.

Only it's no intruder. Instead, Malcolm bursts into the clearing. He takes one look at Prescott and charges.

CHAPTER 8

I leap between them, arms outstretched to catch Malcolm before he barrels in to Prescott.

"Stop! Stop it! Malcolm, listen to me."

He doesn't, of course. I'm not sure he can hear anything at this point.

"He's trying to help, and if you don't stop, he'll sic an attack ghost on you."

I clutch Malcolm tight around the waist. Something otherworldly swirls between us, although it doesn't feel menacing. In fact, all this ghost does is smack Malcolm on the side of the head.

"Ow!" Malcolm blinks and glances around and then down at me. "You're okay?"

"I'm okay. More than okay."

The ghost makes a second pass. Malcolm ducks, but he's not the intended target. The ghost zips past, planting a saucy kiss on my cheek as it does.

Prescott snaps his fingers. "That's enough, Frederick."

Like that, the ethereal fades from the air, and there's nothing left but wood smoke and leaves and Malcolm's warm scent laced with sweat.

He's dressed in a T-shirt and shorts, feet clad in running shoes. His breathing is ragged, as if he's just sprinted up the hill.

"One of these days," Prescott says, "you'll get to be Katy's knight in shining armor. But that's not today."

Malcolm glowers at him before focusing on me again. "You're fine?" He strokes my cheekbone with his thumb and runs his fingers across my forehead. "The flu?"

"I feel better. The tea, maybe." Or the entity. Or possibly I'm healing on my own. The scars on my arms have faded and don't chill me quite as much.

He keeps me in the crook of his arm, but his posture and attention shift. "Nice ward, Dad."

I can't see Malcolm's face, but I'm pretty sure he's rolling his eyes.

"I value my privacy," Darien says. "That's all."

"Great. I'll give you your privacy," Malcolm says. "But I'd like to know one thing. Why did you catch the ghost that killed Katy's parents?"

I stiffen, uncertain how he knows that. I crane my neck to peer up at him in question.

"It's obvious, right?" he says. "Why else would he have been there that day?"

Both Prescott and Darien focus on us.

"When Katy was trapped inside the Pancake House, the ghosts showed her the accident." Malcolm releases me just enough to draw quotes around *accident*. "Orson was there." He zeroes in on Darien. "And so were you. There can only be one reason why."

"I did not deploy the ghost." Darien's voice is as smooth and cold as ice.

In contrast, I think Malcolm may erupt like a volcano. "But you caught it. For money."

"Which went into your college fund."

All at once, Malcolm's steam dissipates. He swears under his breath and grips me tighter. I place a hand on his back, hoping to reassure him, and my palm meets the damp cotton of his shirt.

"It's interesting, isn't it?" Prescott says. "Three generations of Lindstrom women and Armand men, and one entity. What's the common denominator here?"

"If Lena Lindstrom hadn't—" Darien begins.

"Yes, yes," Prescott says, his voice bored and dry. "We've heard the betrayal story. No one believes it."

Malcolm's gaze darts between his father and Prescott. His brow furrows. "What really happened? Do you know?"

"What I know came from my mother, who heard it from Katy's." Prescott nods at me. "What she understands of the story is this: at one time, your grandfather and Katy's grandparents conspired to bring an entity to this plane."

"Do you know why?" I ask.

"Here's the thing, according to my mother. They wanted to do good. This was the tail end of the sixties, after all. Peace. Love." Prescott lifts a shoulder. "I don't know, but it wasn't the usual prize most necromancers seek."

I only knew my grandmother as an older woman, someone who had seen a great deal of life and sorrow already, and someone who'd had the idealism knocked out of her.

"And then?" I prompt.

"And then, someone got greedy."

The words hang in the air. Malcolm shifts and pulls me closer, as if he's afraid I might bolt. The sun beats down, promising a hot day. The woods around us are still, as if the creatures there are waiting for the rest of the story.

"I think we know who that was," Darien says.

"No." Prescott brushes away Darien's words. "I don't think you do." He pivots so he can stare at Malcolm straight on. "I'm sorry. I know he was your mentor and meant the world to you, but instead of working with Katy's grandmother to harness the entity's power, your grandfather captured it."

I cast an anxious glance at Malcolm. He's standing immobile, like a statue. He gives Prescott a single nod. "Go on."

"He couldn't hold it. It would've burned through him in a few weeks, maybe a couple of months. He also couldn't unleash it into the world. There was something about this particular capture that went ... wrong. In the end, the entity accepted the offer of a willing sacrifice."

No one speaks. Above our heads, leaves rustle, the breeze skimming the tops of the trees, giving them a light caress. But there's more to it—a whisper, perhaps, an ancient and other-worldly one.

"But that's how the entity works," I say, breaking the silence and echoing Darien's earlier words to me. "It bends and twists desires. It makes you betray those you claim to love." I look at him. "Why did you agree to help my mother?"

I can imagine so many scenarios, from mere curiosity to the desire for revenge, but which it is, I don't know.

Darien's countenance is like slate. "The reasons don't matter," he says. "In the end, it was a quest that led nowhere and hurt everyone involved."

We'll never know. I sense that in Darien's stance, in his clenched hands, glowing eerily at his sides. He hasn't let down his guard. He won't. Not even to speak with his son.

Next to me, Malcolm blows out a long breath. "We're done here." He looks down at me. "Right? Is there anything left to say?"

I give my head a shake.

Malcolm kneels and picks up the thermos that has rolled to a stop next to my feet. I don't remember when or how it landed there, but I let him tuck it into the tote at my side.

"Let's go home." He takes my hand and, with great delibera-tion, turns his back on his father.

The walk down the hill is one of the longest I can remember.

~

WE'RE HALFWAY to the nature preserve parking lot when a supernatural flurry surrounds us. The air sparkles with the chaos that can only come from overexcited sprites.

"What—?" I hold out my hand, trying to gauge how many there are.

"Belinda's sprites," Malcolm says. He takes in the commotion, and a smile lights his face. It's good to see, but it's all too fleeting. "They saw you leave this morning, followed you, and then panicked after you left the police station."

"Oh, really?" I say to the air.

"They found me while I was out on my run."

Tattletales.

He falls silent. The guilt from last night's phone call and this morning's campfire chat is thick in my stomach. "Malcolm, I—"

He holds up a hand. "No, really. It's okay. It's just ... everything is starting to make sense. It's taken me a while to realize that my grandfather didn't tell me half of what I should've known about necromancy."

"You know a lot," I say. Well, he knows more than I do, at least.

Malcolm shakes his head. "I just act like a know-it-all. That's different." The grin makes a brief return. "But now I realize that he never told me half of what he knew. I wish he would've trusted me with that. He always spoke with such sadness, like a man who'd been badly disappointed."

"With life?"

"With himself. He's the one who encouraged me to go to business school and partner with a ghost. 'Be practical,' he always told me."

That, too, makes sense, in the same way my grandmother's silence about necromancy does.

He takes my hand again, and we continue our trek, the sprites dancing about like it's a celebration. They have no decorum.

273

In the parking lot, Malcolm's convertible is sitting next to my truck. He takes the tote from my shoulder and swings it up and over into the flatbed. Then he leans against the driver's side door. He curls his fingers in my direction and raises an eyebrow.

"Morning kiss?"

Yes. I think we could use one. I step into his arms, and the bustle around us fades. The sun is bright against my eyelids. The air is filled with chatter and smoke. And my business partner, Malcolm Armand, kisses me. It isn't the longest morning kiss on record, but it comes close.

At last, I rest against his chest, his hand stroking my hair.

"I missed you last night," he says, fingers gathering the strands and letting them go.

The rhythm of it lulls me. The sunlight, hot on my back, conspires to send me to sleep, right here, where I'm safe.

"I missed you."

"I called, you know."

I pull back, ever so slightly. "You did?"

"Right after I called my mother back because I forgot to mention something about her investments. It went straight to voice mail. Then, when I called you, the same."

I don't like where this is going. My mind urges me to step away and sidestep this conversation. My body, however, is cozy right where it is and doesn't budge.

"So," Malcolm continues, "I'm curious. I mean, this isn't proof you were talking to each other, but it's just the sort of trick she'd pull."

I can't tell him. I absolutely cannot. Never mind my promise to Arianna. Finding out his mother had an affair with Orson Yates— of all people—right after learning about his grandfather? No. I can't. I won't. I won't do that to him.

But I'm a terrible liar. Even when I want to lie, when it might be in my best interests, my attempts at it are weak.

"Okay, so she did call you," he says, breaking up my thoughts.

"I never said—"

"You didn't have to. Jesus, Katy, you're trembling. What did she say to you?"

I peer up at him, struggling to find words—any words—I can tell him, but the concerned look in his eyes steals my breath.

"Hey, stop that." Malcolm cups my face. Then, gently, with his thumbs, he catches the tears that slip down my cheeks.

"She asked me not to tell you."

"Which is completely unfair to you. It can't be that bad, can it?" He gives me a grin.

I open my mouth to answer, but nothing comes out. Another tear slips down my cheek, and he catches this one with his thumb as well.

"Okay, it *is* that bad." Malcolm mutters a curse and stares at the sky. When he returns his gaze to me, his expression has shifted. He looks a little bit older and a lot more determined. "You know what? I'm an adult. *I'll* ask her. It's not going to be this thing that comes between us, okay?"

I give him a tentative nod, and when he urges me closer, I burrow into the crook of his shoulder.

"Hm. That's better," he says. "So, what else did you do this morning?"

"I talked to Chief Ramsey."

"I bet that was exciting, seeing how fond he is of me."

"Actually, he wants us to keep sleeping together."

Malcolm's hands tighten on my upper arms. He eases me back to stare into my eyes. "What? He *said* that?"

"Not in so many words. He said you should keep staying at my place. He thinks Orson is up to something." I push my palm across my cheek, catching the last wayward tear. "And ... he confirmed it. I really was there, on the side of the road. He found me."

"What did you tell him about Orson?"

"That I think he wants something my parents had, and now thinks I have it."

"About as close to the truth as it comes, at least the version he'll believe." He eyes me again, his expression both abashed and amused. "He really said that, though, about us sleeping together?"

"He really did."

"It's not a bad idea. I hated being away from you last night. It's why I went out for an early run." He plucks at the T-shirt. "I probably stink."

He doesn't, not really. He merely smells more like himself, that warm, rich scent of nutmeg even stronger. I burrow closer. "I don't mind."

Malcolm holds me, chin resting on top of my head, arms secure around me. We stay like that for several minutes, not speaking, but I swear, I can feel his thoughts churning.

"Where does this leave us?" he says at last.

"I don't know."

"If we only knew what Orson was going to do next."

"You," I say. "I think he plans to hurt you."

"I don't. He had that chance. It's you he's after."

I consider that, and something Carter said to me in the Pancake House pops into my head.

"What's involved with necromancer retribution?" I ask.

"Nothing good. Depending on the offense and the verdict, the necromancer community can decide to strip someone of their ability to catch and deploy ghosts, essentially reducing them to a sensitive."

Yes, it's like I suspected. There's no glory in being a mere sensitive. "And if they can't catch or deploy, they can't make a living."

"Exactly, and they're no longer a threat, assuming they were one to begin with."

"So, you could set someone up, right? Or accuse someone of something they didn't do?"

"You could, but you'd have to convince the rest of the community. It takes a quorum. It's no small thing to strip someone of their power. They're not getting it back once it's gone."

"Huh." I consider all that, and I wonder if I've been wrong about something all this time. It's not my friends that Orson wants to hurt.

"What, huh?" Malcolm says. "Katy, talk to me."

"In the Pancake House, Carter said that Orson put out a call to all necromancers in the Midwest region, that he was asking for retribution." I pause and lick my lips. My mouth is dry, and my head is buzzing with too much caffeine. "Against me."

Malcolm's grip on my arms grows tighter. "And you're telling me this now?"

"I..." I trail off. I've been more asleep than awake this past week, and so worried about Malcolm going out on rounds on his own.

"How did you find my dad this morning?"

"There was a ghost. I didn't recognize it, but it showed me the way. I don't think it was an attack ghost. It was completely benign."

"Unless it was a spy."

Was it? I consider that and how it wandered off once I'd crashed into Darien's ward. "But—"

"This is the first time in a week you've left your house," Malcolm says.

"So?"

"You're outside your ward."

Sweat from our trek down the hill prickles my skin. Dread ices the pit of my stomach, and my fingers turn cold.

Malcolm lets go of me and wrestles his phone from a holder secured to his upper arm.

"Let me text Nigel." He taps away, waits for five seconds, and then swears. "Forget that. Let me call Nigel."

He switches on the speaker, and the phone rings and rings until it rolls into voice mail.

He scans the area, a hand shielding his eyes. "Do you detect anything?"

I lift my chin. It's only now that I realize that Belinda's sprites have vanished. "Nothing."

He tucks the phone into his pocket and then walks around my truck and his car, fingertips skimming the metal. He crouches and inspects the underside.

"You try," he says to me. "You're better at detecting ghosts."

I'm not, not really, but I go through the motions. "Do you think—?"

"I think I'm not letting you out of my sight, so it's a matter of picking the best car." His gaze darts back and forth between the two. "Mine. It's faster."

"It's really conspicuous," I say. "My truck is better."

A hint of a smile lights his eyes. "Katy, your truck is one of the most conspicuous things in Springside."

Okay, so maybe he has a point. "Do you think either one is haunted?"

He shakes his head. "No, but that doesn't mean it isn't a target."

The drive back to Springside is far less treacherous than the one to the nature preserve. That doesn't mean we should risk getting into either car.

"If I ... die before I can invoke the entity, does that mean the pact is broken?"

"I assume so. That's the way it works with ghosts, but it's risky. If you invoked the entity, even injured or near death, it could save you, and the pact remains in place."

"Then, why didn't it help my mother?"

"Are you sure it didn't?"

His words stun me. I want to probe the meaning of them, but my mind shuts down. I'm not certain I can go there, imagine that, wonder what transpired in the ravine.

"You're here, you're alive." He closes the distance between us and cups my face. "And I think that has something to do with your mother and the entity."

I nod numbly. "Should I ... should I invoke it now?"

"Do you want to?"

I shake my head.

"As long as you can speak, you're safe."

"*We're* safe."

He smiles at me, that warm, dark-roast smile I haven't seen in a while. "Yes. We're safe." He heaves a sigh. "All we need now is a plan."

"Should we leave town? Head home? Will the ward keep us safe?" The questions pop out of my mouth. The practicalities, the reality of this, are far easier to deal with than contemplating my mother and the entity.

"Maybe? I wish Nigel would answer."

"Try Belinda," I suggest. "She's off today."

He does, and again, the call rolls to voice mail.

"Sadie?" My voice cracks on her name.

The call goes through, and he counts each ring under his breath. I close my eyes and wish with all my might that Sadie will answer, that she'll reassure us, invite us over for breakfast. When her voice mail picks up, Malcolm slaps his hand against the truck's side in frustration.

"I really don't like this." He shields his eyes and scans the area again.

The summer day is growing hot. Children have traded pajamas for swimsuits. The campsite is alive with sounds: the occasional pop and hiss of soda cans, the rattle of ice-filled coolers, squeals and laughter. Malcolm and I are the only oddities here, baking on the asphalt rather than relaxing in the shade.

Then the chill of the otherworldly invades the air. It's a presence I recognize, but I can't place it, not right away. Then, it speaks.

Katrina Lindstrom, you have been summoned by the necromancers of the Midwest region. You are to submit to examination, and, if found guilty, face retribution.

Malcolm pulls me close, but his warmth can't chase away the ice that has invaded my bones.

"This is one of Reginald's ghosts," I say.

Malcolm nods. "It is."

"What does that mean?"

Before he can answer, his phone buzzes with an incoming text message.

Only, there is no message. On the screen, a single photo appears. I recognize Sadie's living room immediately, with its comfy couch, the gleaming antique furniture, and the corner that Nigel has claimed as his own, strewn with programming books.

On the couch, Nigel, Sadie, and Belinda are sitting, all side by side, all gagged, their wrists bound. A bruise has bloomed around Nigel's left eye.

I pull my gaze from the photo and look up at Malcolm.

"I guess it means"—I cough, my throat so tight I can barely force out the words—"I guess it means we're going home."

CHAPTER 9

W e're three blocks from my house when Malcolm kills the convertible's engine. He grips the steering wheel, his knuckles white as marble.

"I can't let you do this," he says at last.

"We don't have a choice."

"Yeah, we do. I have half a tank of gas and my wallet. We don't need anything else."

"But Nigel and Sadie, and Belinda—"

"Will be fine. It's only a threat meant to scare us. No one will hurt them."

I pull against the seatbelt and swivel to face him. "Orson nearly killed you, and in that alternate reality the entity showed us, he killed us both."

"He's not going to do anything, not in the middle of Springside. It would be stupid, too easy for the police to..."

His eyes light with the idea the moment it strikes me.

"The police," we both say at once.

Malcolm starts the engine and whips the car around.

"Do you think Chief will believe us?"

"At this point, I don't think it matters. Even a patrol car drive-by will help."

"Wait," I say. "Give me your phone. I have Chief's personal number on mine. I'll text him the photo and then call 911."

"I'm still driving us to the police station." He tosses the phone into my lap and floors the accelerator.

A moment later, Malcolm slams on the brakes. I let out a yelp, and both phones fly from my hands. One cracks against the windshield. The other skitters through the interior and lands somewhere near my feet.

I grope for it and my breath. My lungs feel tight, and I struggle to inhale. There's pressure against my throat, and I fight the urge to pull away some invisible hand. I touch my neck with fingers that feel like ice and peer through the fog clouding my vision.

A black sedan is blocking the intersection. Malcolm curses, throws the car into reverse, and whips us around again. At the end of the opposite intersection, another black sedan is sitting, the faces of its occupants shielded by tinted glass.

"I know you don't want to invoke the entity," he says, "but I'm thinking now would be a good time to do so."

I nod. At this point, we can't fight so many necromancers, not even with Springside's finest, assuming we could reach the police station. I don't know what it will cost me, but if everyone I love is safe, it will be worth it.

I open my mouth. The pressure on my throat grows. The fog is thicker now. I reach a hand to swipe at the windshield, but the glass is dry. I blink, but that doesn't help.

"Katy..."

I swallow—or try to. The pressure on my throat grows. That's what it feels like, too: a hand—an otherworldly hand—squeezing ever tighter. I take shallow breaths. I can't force oxygen into my lungs any other way. My vision tunnels to a single pinpoint before expanding again. I grip the dash and concentrate on getting enough air to say a single word.

"Katy..." Panic tinges Malcolm's voice.

I turn toward him. My hand flutters at my throat, and I mouth words, hoping he understands what's happening.

His eyes widen, and then he's leaning over the steering wheel and scanning the neighborhood. When he looks back at me, anger replaces the shock and panic.

"Stop it! Stop it now! She can't breathe." He unbuckles his seatbelt as if preparing to launch himself from the car. "If you kill her, I'll capture the entity. And my desire will be pure enough that I'll take the rest of you down before the entity can burn through me."

The pressure on my throat eases, but only slightly.

"Try now," Malcolm whispers.

I mouth, "Momalcurkan." The entity has a strange, nearly unpronounceable name to go along with its capricious, sometimes unfathomable nature.

The air remains still, the road steady and sure beneath us. There's no rumble. And while the otherworldly is here with us in the car, it's certainly not the entity.

"Think it, then. Think as hard as you can. Maybe that will work."

I double my efforts, both to think and speak the name. Nothing. It's almost like we're inside some sort of insulated room. I know my thoughts don't reach farther than the rag roof of the car.

That's when it hits me. We're inside a containment field. I tap Malcolm on the shoulder and then the car's top.

"Try the door," he whispers.

The handle moves uselessly. I press the button to roll down the window and the mechanism grinds, but the glass remains in place. Malcolm throws the car into gear and heads not down the road but directly for someone's lawn.

There's an alleyway behind this row of houses. I'm not sure what he has planned, and the convertible isn't exactly an off-road vehicle. But he grips the steering wheel with a determination I've never seen before. The front wheels go up and over the curb, and we rock back and forth.

Before he can tear through the yard, smoke billows from beneath the hood. It's oily and black, and its stench chokes me further. I can't cough it out of my lungs, so it lingers there, festering.

Young Malcolm, do not attempt to escape. If your speed exceeds fifteen miles per hour, the ghost that currently resides in your transmission will destroy it.

Malcolm slams the car into reverse. He inches away from the curb, and we bump back onto the road.

Please proceed to Katrina Lindstrom's house. That is where the examination will take place.

"Why?" I mouth. I don't know if he can read that single question, or understand the meaning behind it.

But this is Malcolm, and when he releases a heavy sigh, I know he does. "I don't know why Reginald is doing this. There isn't a quorum without him. There isn't retribution without him, either. He's more powerful than Orson. I just don't—"

Please proceed to the examination.

He slams his hands against the steering wheel. Under normal circumstances, the horn would blare. Now, there isn't even a squeak.

I tap him again and hold up my hand like a talking puppet. I tap him again, on the chest and then the lips.

He shakes his head, the move slow and full of regret. "I don't know the entity's name. I didn't hear you say it in the warehouse. I didn't hear Orson say it at the reception, and I kept myself from being curious. I thought it would be safer that way."

He's right. Under normal circumstances, it would've been.

"Jesus, I'm sorry, Katy. I'm so sorry—"

I place a finger over his lips. My feet scramble to find purchase on the car's floor so I can push myself far enough over the console to reach him. Then, I kiss him.

It's long and desperate and full of all the things I wish I could tell him. Stars shoot across my vision, and I'm lightheaded from lack of oxygen. None of that matters. I know this is goodbye. He cradles my face, and his thumbs can't keep up with the tears trailing down my cheeks.

Please proceed to the examination.

"Shut! Up!" He shouts the words at the sky before turning back to me. Softer now, with a tenderness that makes his voice crack, he speaks. "I love you, Katy. Nothing changes that. I will always love you. If there's a way to get us—get *you*—out of this, then I'll find it. I promise you that."

I touch his cheek and his lips, and he places one last feathery kiss against my fingertips. Then he puts the car in gear and inches us down the road.

That's when I know:

There's no way out.

THE SIGHT of a necromancer on my sidewalk has never been a good thing. Now, a dozen or so are lining the walk. They stand in between the road and my walkway, and—perhaps more importantly—they block access to the ward that surrounds my house.

What little hope I had left shrivels.

Malcolm doesn't bother to brake. He lets the car coast to a stop. It does so directly in front of my house. There, Orson is standing, and everything about the well-tailored suit, the starched white shirt, and the polished dress shoes exudes smugness. This is a man who knows he's won.

"Huh," Malcolm says. "He looks like crap."

He does? I mouth, "Really?"

"Look at his hair. It's a bad dye job, or maybe Grecian Formula. He's lost weight, but not in a good way."

I look again, and beneath the shiny exterior, I see the telltale signs of strain.

"He won't be able to hold the entity."

No, but then he couldn't before. I scan the assembled men—yes, they're all men—who will pass judgment on me and wonder which one here might be strong enough for that.

You may now exit the vehicle.

Malcolm gives my hand a squeeze. "I'll come around and get you."

The doors pop open, but there's no rush of summer air. The containment field extends beyond the convertible, maybe even encompasses my entire house. I squint at the sky, trying to discern its boundaries.

What I see appears to be layer upon layer of overlapping barriers. My gaze returns to the assembled necromancers. Each one must be contributing to the field.

Malcolm makes it as far as the front of the convertible. There, an invisible force slams into him, throwing him several feet into the air. He lands on the grass between the sidewalk and the road, his body crumpling.

I cry out—or try to. I scramble from the car, but fear and exertion steal what little air I have. I pitch forward, palms striking the asphalt. The surface tears at the tender flesh, and I tumble away from the car. I roll, come to rest on my back, and simply stare up at the sky.

"Hold him!" Orson shouts. "Both of them!"

Footsteps pound, but no one approaches me. I wheeze, breath barely whistling through my throat. When I do sit up, I see that three men are struggling to hold Malcolm, while two others are gripping Nigel by the arms and shoulders.

He surrenders first, letting his arms go limp. The men don't let go, but their stances relax.

"There's a good boy," Orson says. He nods toward Malcolm. "Now him."

"Malcolm," Nigel says, his voice rough. "This isn't helping Katy."

Malcolm yanks a hand free and swings at one of the men. There's a smack of bone on flesh, and then a flurry where Malcolm ends up on the ground, arm jerked behind him, his face twisted with pain.

I rasp another breath. I want to scream and kick and fight back, but the grip on my neck is steady and strong, and I barely have enough air to think.

"Let him go," Nigel says.

Orson purses his lips in mock consideration. "You're in no position to demand anything."

"Katy won't cooperate unless you let him go."

This is true. I've clawed my way up the side of the car, and while I can't do much, not cooperating is still an option. My gaze meets Nigel's, and he mouths a single word.

Please.

I nod and then slap the hood of the convertible to get Malcolm's attention. When I have it, I shake my head.

"But—" He squirms against the men, and I know when another spike of pain hits by how his expression contorts. I give my head another shake, and I see the moment he gives up. His body goes limp, but what's worse is the defeat in his eyes.

From the group of necromancers, Reginald steps forward. His brows are drawn together; his mouth is turned down. The men on either side inch back. Even Orson falters, although he catches himself at the last moment.

"Katrina Lindstrom," Reginald says. "It is time for the examination." He points to a spot where the sidewalk meets my walkway. I don't suppose it's likely I can make that last leap over the invisible line of my ward, land on my lawn, and insist that everyone leave.

No, I don't suppose I can. I stagger forward, and my feet drag. The neighborhood is eerily silent. No kids are playing. No one is bicycling or walking their dog. I wonder at that, at how these men have managed such a thing. Is it the containment field or something else, something otherworldly?

And while everyone tracks my progress, no one steps forward to help me. I take another faltering step, lose my balance, and land hard on my knees. I press my palms against the ground even though they sting. My lungs scream for oxygen, and the burn runs through me. It's like drowning without the final relief of giving in to the water.

The light tapping of dress shoes sounds behind me. I brace for the inevitable. A kick to the head? Some of Orson's minions dragging me across the asphalt?

Instead, those dress shoes halt next to me. Wingtips. Possibly hand-tooled, from Italy. An outstretched hand reaches for one of mine. I take it.

My legs are wobbly beneath me, but I stand. Only then does my rescuer speak.

"Do I need to remind everyone that you don't have quorum without me?"

Prescott Jones scans the crowd, his hand at my elbow. When no one responds, he gives me a sidelong glance.

"Apparently, I do."

CHAPTER 10

"We don't need you to proceed." Orson steps forward, but Reginald halts his progress with the mere lift of one finger.

"We need a quorum. There is only one other necromancer in the area who could provide that."

"Darien Armand is no longer part of the Midwest region," Orson counters.

"As you say. Also, his connection to these proceedings may be too personal for him to be unbiased." Reginald inclines his head toward Prescott. "We welcome you, Prescott Jones."

"I doubt that," Prescott mutters, but I'm the only one who hears. "Orson's grudges are never pretty. Explains the manhandling."

Yes—I cast a quick glance at Malcolm—quite literally.

"Here," Prescott continues, louder now. "Let me help you to your spot." Under his breath, he adds, "In a moment, they'll transfer the full containment field to you. If you're found guilty, they'll use their combined power to strip you of your necromancer abilities."

And if I'm no longer a necromancer, then I won't be able to hold on to the entity. Anyone might invoke it—Orson, Prescott, Reginald.

Prescott takes in my expression. "I see you understand the consequences of that."

I can't let that happen. My gaze darts from Orson and back to Prescott. I know Orson's agenda, but I wonder just how mercenary Prescott is. I consider what he said earlier, about unfinished business.

"Yes, I know. I'm not to be trusted." His smile is brief and sad. "How much air are you getting?"

I hold my thumb and index finger half an inch apart. He turns toward the assembled necromancers.

"Let Katy breathe."

Orson snorts. "What? So she can invoke a powerful and dangerous entity, one that poses a risk to the entire necromancer community? No, I don't think so."

"Call off the ghost and transfer the containment field to her. Use that to gag her." Prescott glances over his shoulder at me. "You don't have a cold, do you?"

I shake my head.

"There you go. Perfect solution."

"Yes," Reginald says. "It's time to transfer the field."

A wave washes over me, and for a moment, I can't breathe at all. Then, with a whoosh, the otherworldly presence that has gripped my throat vanishes. Air rushes into my lungs, and I nearly sob with relief. As it is, a tear travels down my cheek.

My head clears, and although I'm tethered by invisible bonds and I can't move my mouth, my thoughts are sharp again. I search out Malcolm and try to convey what I'm feeling with just my eyes.

A bruise has disfigured his cheekbone, and a cut above one eye is weeping blood. One of Orson's minions is hovering at his side, but Malcolm is stoic, like a statue on my lawn.

Reginald moves to the center of the gathering. "Katrina Lindstrom, you stand accused of endangering the necromancer community. We will hear the evidence and, as a group, decide your fate."

The invisible gag remains in place. Apparently, I don't have a say in this. Of course, if I did, at this point, I'd invoke the entity. I imagine everyone here knows that.

"Orson Yates," Reginald says, "you may speak now."

Orson strides to the center of the group. He takes time to shoot the cuffs of his dress shirt from the sleeves of his suit coat jacket. For good measure, he fiddles with the cufflinks and adjusts his tie.

Despite the fact that nothing good is bound to happen, I meet Malcolm's gaze and roll my eyes.

He squeezes his own eyes shut. I know he wants to laugh, and I know if he did, it would be that sweet, dark-roast laugh tinged with sorrow.

Orson clears his throat. "We know the checkered history of the Lindstrom women. Three generations now have tried to control an entity whose power is beyond their capabilities."

I'd like to contradict that, but of course, I can't talk.

"That is not my concern," he adds.

Really? Because, if so, it's news to me.

"What concerns me, and always has, is Katy's distinct lack of education in necromancy. Let the record show that I offered her a spot in the Midwest Necromancer Association more than once, which she refused."

"Your supporting evidence?" Prescott asks. "I also refused a spot in the association. No one's accused me of a crime."

"Not yet," Orson murmurs. "But, to your point, I do have supporting evidence."

Orson lifts his hands. A glow surrounds his fingers, the halo that means he has a ghost—or several—at the ready.

It's then that I realize that he does possess several ghosts. Their wails and cries fill the air—sad and scared. These aren't attack ghosts. They're Springside ghosts, and they emerge into what must be a containment field suspended between Orson's outstretched arms.

The field flickers, images fading in and out. It's like watching a silent movie, one where the film is scarred, the projection jittery. The first picture to solidify is of me at the Coffee Depot, speaking with the assistant manager.

I'm glad no one can hear me declare that I plan to brew him the best damn cup of coffee he's ever tasted. Not that it matters. A moment later, the industrial-sized coffee maker erupts, spraying the entire café with lukewarm coffee.

That's just the start.

It's like a coffee-soaked greatest hits reel. The next images show the damage to Sadie's house in the wake of Harold's ghost, including splatters across the walls and plaster dust that make the dining room look like an ancient crime scene. The pictures flicker again, and there I am, holding my hands against the containment field in the Springside Cemetery. I'm trying to console the ghosts caught inside. When whispers ripple through the gathering, I realize that it must look like I'm hoarding them.

The images continue to flash across the ghostly movie screen, faster now, so discerning what might be my fault from that of a particularly nasty ghost is impossible. The Pancake House. Springside Long-term Care. Even the mess left behind at Sadie and Nigel's wedding reception. All of it, my fault.

"As you can see," Orson says, his voice taking on the quality of a concerned school principal, "she is untrained and undisciplined. She has hoarded ghosts for years in Springside. To what end is anyone's guess. She is unfit to practice the craft and, as such, a threat to the necromancer community."

You could see it that way, like I leave behind coffee-stained destruction wherever I go. But then, I've never claimed to be a necromancer, either.

Maybe that was a mistake.

Reginald nods at Orson. "Thank you, Orson Yates." He turns

toward the assembled group. "Would anyone here like to speak on behalf of Katrina Lindstrom?"

Well, I would, but I don't suppose that's happening. Nigel steps forward, but Reginald gives him a sad shake of his head.

"No, my friend. Your association with her disqualifies you from speaking."

I don't see how, but apparently Nigel does. He deflates, and when my gaze meets his, he mouths, "I'm sorry."

So am I.

Then a throat clears. Prescott takes the steps up my walk and halts just inside Orson's personal space.

"Really?" Prescott adjusts the cuffs of his dress shirt with just enough of a flourish that Orson can't miss the mockery. "A threat to the necromancer community? You'd have us believe that?"

Orson remains silent. Perhaps he's not allowed to speak. Perhaps he doesn't care what Prescott has to say.

"Instead of being untrained, as my colleague claims, I would like to suggest that Lena Lindstrom was deliberate in how she educated her granddaughter." Prescott raises his hands, indicating the space around us. "Springside is small. Its ghosts, for the most part, are benign. And those that aren't?" He slides a glance in my direction. "Are dispatched with a minimal amount of fuss."

Well, sometimes.

"Katy has also formed a business partnership with a member of a well-respected necromancer family—"

"Perhaps not the best argument," Orson murmurs.

"—That provides a service to the town of Springside. A town this size needs this sort of thriving business. Strip Katy of her necromancer abilities, and you deny Springside of this vital service."

"But she can still serve Springside as a sensitive," Orson counters. "Her partner is an ... adequate necromancer."

The two men stare at each other. Prescott has his hands tucked in his pockets. I don't know if that means he has a ghost at the ready or if he's bluffing. Orson's fingers are still glowing with the ones he's trapped. In the quiet, their cries reach me, the sound so plaintive that, despite everything, my heart aches for them. No one else seems to notice.

"And I should like to remind the community of Orson's—"

"I'm sorry, Prescott Jones," Reginald interrupts. "This is Katrina Lindstrom's examination. Confine your comments to her."

Prescott presses his lips together. His eyes narrow as he takes in Orson and then the assembled group. "Then I should like to remind the community of the Lindstrom legacy, and how three generations have kept everyone"—his gaze flits toward Orson —"safer than they may realize."

It's not much of a defense. Even so, I'm grateful to Prescott. I can't move, can't speak or smile, but I stare at him with what I hope looks like gratitude. When he nods in my direction, I sense that he understands.

"Are there any others who wish to speak?" Reginald asks.

The group falls completely silent. Again, I wonder at the lack of traffic. I don't live on a busy street, it's true, but my neighbors come and go. Someone must be working from home today. I eye the assembled group and wonder at the power they wield—and what that means for me.

No one else steps forward. No one speaks. After a long pause, Reginald coughs to clear his throat.

"Then it is time," he says. "Those who wish to stand with Katrina Lindstrom may do so now."

Nigel breaks free of the necromancers holding him. He shakes the men off. The glare he gives one of them is deadly, and his fingers curl into a fist. I almost expect Nigel to return the favor of the black eye. Instead, he catches up to Malcolm and helps him limp across the lawn.

They take up a position on either side of me. Malcolm's grip is firm, one hand poised on my waist, the other at my elbow. Nigel's voice is low and rough in my ear.

"I'm sorry, Katy. I'm so sorry. So is Reginald. He had to give in to Orson's demands for an examination. It's the way necromancer justice works. He didn't have a choice."

Didn't he? I take in Reginald's passive countenance and wonder.

After a moment, Prescott clears his throat, brushes imaginary lint from his suit coat jacket as if he's brushing off Orson, and comes to stand with us.

"I apologize, Katy," he says. "I didn't think it would come to this. Otherwise, I would've prepared a better defense."

No one else moves. It's clear my three supporters don't beat the dozen or so that Orson has.

"Don't worry about the numbers," Nigel whispers as if reading my thoughts. "All it will take is for Reginald to weigh in on our side. He holds that much sway."

"Quality versus quantity," Prescott adds.

Reginald's gaze finds mine. There's something in his eyes—a message, I think, that he's trying to convey. I don't understand it. I can't even show him I don't understand. He gives me a single nod and then looks away as if the sight of me hurts him.

"I find that I must stand with the necromancer community." With that, Reginald takes a single step and aligns himself with Orson's group.

Nigel cries out as if he's been struck in the gut. Malcolm's hold on me tightens, and he draws me closer. I don't even have enough air to feel breathless at Reginald's betrayal. The only thing keeping me upright is Malcolm's hands and his warmth.

"What are you saying?" Nigel launches himself forward, his momentum cut short by Prescott's grip on his shoulders. Nigel flails, and Prescott staggers, but his grasp never wavers.

"Let it go, Nigel. Let it go."

He whirls to face Prescott. "But—"

"Let it go. It's over," Prescott says with a finality that chills me. "You can't change things."

Because that's the way necromancer justice works. No one says that, but the implication is clear. Already, the other necromancers are lining up directly across from me, well-dressed and respectable, Orson as their center. He shoots me a smug look full of triumph.

My heart thumps hard in my chest. My mouth is dry. I can't lick my lips, can't really swallow, for that matter. I can't even sink into Malcolm's presence at my side, but I soak in his warmth.

"It is time," Reginald announces. "Move away from Katrina Lindstrom."

Prescott drags Nigel toward the front porch. Nigel digs his heels in, plowing furrows into the lawn.

"I won't leave her alone, and it's not like I need my ability."

"You might," Prescott says. "Someday." He grips Nigel around the waist, and it's all he can do to hold on.

"Move away," Reginald says, his voice stronger, sharper.

Malcolm inches closer. His grip on me tightens. He's been quiet this entire time, but his voice emerges strong and sure. "Make me."

Across from us, Orson looks like he wants to do just that.

"Young Malcolm," Reginald says, and now his words carry a hint of tenderness. "You risk losing your ability as well. This won't hurt her physically."

"Really? I don't believe that. And I'm not leaving her."

If I could, I'd shove him away. One of us needs to have some ability to catch ghosts. Then again, depending on who captures the entity, that may be the least of our problems. Maybe it doesn't matter.

Maybe Malcolm has already realized that.

Reginald glances at the assembled group of necromancers and then at Malcolm. A frown puckers his brow. He turns toward Prescott with what looks like a silent command.

"Oh, no," Prescott says. He still has a hand on Nigel's shoulder. "You can do this without me."

"The community has spoken."

"This is not my community anymore. I refuse to participate."

"Very well." Reginald returns his attention to Malcolm. "The choice is yours, young Malcolm. I do not have enough necromancers present to pull you away and carry out retribution. Step away now. This is your last warning."

Malcolm is solid and warm beside me. He doesn't budge, doesn't flinch. He's stoic again, remaining absolutely still except for the thumb that swipes a tear from my cheek.

"It's okay," he says, and I know he's speaking to me and not the group. "I want to do this."

Reginald sighs, the sound heavy and full of regret. "Then we shall begin retribution."

CHAPTER 11

The air crackles around us, the scent dry and sharp. A pulse radiates from the group of necromancers. The force of it strikes me in the chest, and it feels like barbed wire has encircled my heart.

Something tugs at my insides, as if this force is trying to remove a vital part of me.

And it's working. The ability I've always taken for granted slips away. I want to cry out, but I can't. I want to shout at them, curse them. I want to...

Malcolm throws himself in front of me. All at once, the sensation stops. A strangled noise emerges from his throat. I feel a rush of returning power, a loosening around my heart. I gasp for breath, and the shock of it washes through me.

I can move my lips, my tongue, my mouth. I can speak. I bring my fingertips to my lips, testing the feel of them. At that moment, I know what Malcolm has done. To hesitate now is to waste his sacrifice.

"Momalcurkan."

A hush falls over the neighborhood, maybe the entire town.

Everything is so still. Malcolm wavers for a moment before crumpling on the lawn. No one moves, but I don't let that stop me. My knees hit the ground, and my hands search out his pulse, his breathing.

"Malcolm?" I roll him onto his back and, with careful fingers, wipe away the grime and blood as best I can. He's warm, and my hand rises and falls with each breath he takes. His pulse is strong.

I sit back on my heels. I'm about to ask someone—well, someone nice, like Nigel or Prescott—for help when I notice what's caught everybody else's attention.

In a matter of seconds, clouds have rolled in, blotting out the perfect summer sky. These aren't puffy cotton balls, either, but a thick and menacing blanket tinged green. The color reminds me of a bruise or an infection. It's the sky right before a tornado strike.

And yet, the air is so still. I can hear Malcolm's breathing and my own.

Someone coughs. A couple of the necromancers eye each other. I don't know if they doubt the entity's presence or are looking for a quick way out.

Orson raises a hand as if sensing their unease. "Hold steady. There's no need for alarm. The entity is capricious. It may not appear."

I shake my head. I know better. True, it will show itself when it feels like it, and not a second sooner. But to suggest it isn't even here? That seems foolish.

And yet.

Something that sounds like a sigh whispers through the branches. The breeze picks up again, lifting sweaty strands of hair from the back of my neck. My arms and legs tingle as if an electric current is running through the ground and into me. The air tastes like static.

A necromancer on the edge of the group takes a single step backward. He takes another. Then, emboldened, he bolts for the street and one of the black sedans parked in front of my house.

He makes it as far as the sidewalk.

His entire body jerks as if he's been struck by lightning. He collapses to the concrete, and his head strikes the surface with a sickening thud.

The remaining necromancers crowd together as if there's safety in numbers, or at least, safety in not crossing the invisible fence around my house.

"Don't panic," Orson says. "This will pass."

I'm not sure it will, not without my intervention.

"Stop it." I don't need to shout or command. I'm pretty sure the entity can hear me. Will it obey? That's something I don't know.

It hasn't made an appearance inside my head—not yet. But the air has that stale quality to it. The entity is here, even if it's playing coy.

At least, I think it's here.

Who sees it first, I can't say. Nigel has taken a knee on the other side of Malcolm and is repeating all the checks I've made. His gaze meets mine, and I see the question there. I can only shake my head. I don't know if Malcolm will wake up. I keep my palm against his chest. I count his breaths and let his heartbeat reassure me.

An urgent whisper catches my attention. As a group, the necromancers have stepped back yet again. They huddle around the bushes in front of my house, leaving Orson to stand alone in the center of my yard. Prescott is staring down the road, his skin sallow.

A block away, a man in a dark suit is strolling down the center of the street. Or, at least, it looks like a man in a dark suit. His image shimmers like he might be a mirage, a trick of the heat. His facial features are nonexistent. A pang of recognition strikes me. I know who—or what—is approaching.

His stride is deliberate and slow. A car—a black Mercedes—is blocking the most direct route to my walkway. With a finger, the almost-man upturns it. Metal creaks against the asphalt, the sound lonely and hollow. The sedan tips over, crunching its roof.

The crash makes no sound. But the footfalls, the tap of men's dress shoes against cement, ring clear.

The almost-man halts on my walkway. The swirling void where a face should be surveys the surroundings, seeming to take more interest in my house than the people outside of it.

"Your little helper is doing an excellent job with the flowerbeds, my dear," the entity says at last. "You should give her a raise."

I manage a nod.

"Of course, there is all this debris scattered across your lawn, but I don't suppose she's to blame for that."

"You don't belong at this proceeding." Orson's words emerge with surprising strength.

The entity raises a hand, palm skyward. "And yet I've been invoked."

"This is necromancer business. The pact—"

The entity holds up a finger, halting Orson's words. "And what would you know of my pact with humanity?"

"No interference in matters of justice and retribution."

A single drop of sweat travels down the side of his face, but Orson stands firm. I think there must be truth to what he said. He's too sure of himself, too sure of those words, for them to be a bluff.

"Am I interfering?" The entity gestures toward the group. "Please, continue."

No one dares, of course. Prescott looks almost amused—a half-smile lingers beneath the pallor. Reginald has closed his eyes as if he wishes to shut all of this out.

Nigel's hand comes to rest on mine. He nods at Malcolm. "I'll take care of him."

When I meet his gaze, the full implication of his words sinks in. There's only one way to stop this. I lean close to Malcolm, kiss his warm, sweet lips, and whisper words I hope he can hear.

"I love you. Don't forget that."

Then I stand. My legs feel as if I've hiked for miles, but I walk without faltering until I'm standing across from Orson, completing the triangle made up of him, the entity, and me.

I see so clearly what could be. Instead of coffee-stained destruction, I could leave behind a trail of blood. It would be easy. A flick of my wrist in Orson's direction, and all of this would disappear. The weight of it squeezes my heart. What an awesome thing, this sort of power, how seductive.

And yet, it wouldn't stop with that. Someone else would want the entity, and then someone else after that. I wonder if this is what my grandmother realized all those years ago.

I cast a glance over my shoulder and take one last look at Malcolm. I'll miss everything about Springside, but my heart will ache the most for him.

I take a step forward, breaking the symmetry of the triangle. Orson wavers as if this is something he hasn't expected.

No, I don't think he would.

I turn toward the entity, spread my arms wide, and say, "I am your willing sacrifice."

Cries go up around me, although the entity itself betrays nothing.

"You ... you ... can't be serious." Orson stares at me, naked confusion on his face.

"Of course I am," I say, and then address the entity." I can do this, right?"

"Hm. What? Yes, undeniably you can, although it's a shame to leave things so untidy." It waves a hand toward the huddled group of necromancers. "While I don't generally get caught up in human affairs, in this case?" The entity surveys the group. "I should like to see that trail of blood you have in mind."

Orson blanches. I spare him a look. It would be *so* easy.

"You're quite sure?" the entity prompts. It doesn't need to read my thoughts, although I'm sure it has. How I feel must be plain to everyone here.

"I am."

"You can't return to this plane. The one being here who might muster that sort of love has already been my willing sacrifice."

I steal another look at Malcolm and then force my gaze away.

"And while he's pretty, he's a bit dull."

"He is not!" The outburst comes automatically, even though I know better than to let the entity goad me.

It laughs, the sound tinged with a sadness I find odd.

"In any case, he no longer qualifies. You leave with me now, Katy, and you forfeit your life here. You'll never see Springside, your friends, or Malcolm again."

"And no one on this plane can invoke you or capture you again," I say. "Right?"

This needs to be ironclad. No loopholes. No tricks. I leave, and everyone I love will be safe.

"That's correct," the entity says. "I promise you. No tricks."

I resist the urge to look at Malcolm one last time. If I do, I might lose my courage, my will to do this thing. So, instead, I focus on Orson. Two bright spots of color are sitting high on his cheekbones, as if someone has slapped him. His shirt collar is soaked with sweat.

But his eyes are as sharp and canny as ever. His fingers twitch as if he wants to reach for an attack ghost or a gun. I suppose it's to his credit he hasn't cowered before the entity.

Then I think of how many people he's hurt in Springside alone. I think of Sadie and Nigel and how Orson tried to destroy them both, of Malcolm nearly beaten to death, of all the ghosts locked away and tormented.

I want to call him names, lash out, seek revenge. So easy. It would be so easy.

"Guess what?" I say instead.

Orson looks at me, a hint of doubt creeping into his eyes.

When I'm certain I have his full attention, I say the one thing I think will hurt the most.

"I win."

A burst of laughter comes from the entity, the sound strong enough to shake the earth. The air around us quakes. Leaves rattle in the trees. Car alarms blare.

"Very well, then, my dear. Say the words one more time."

"I am your willing sacrifice."

CHAPTER 12

There's a flash, and it's bright enough to blind. Then, what looks like a thousand stars streak across the sky. Darkness flows around me, and, while I can't see a thing, I sense hidden recesses black enough to wilt my soul. The air flashes hot and cold. I brace for what must be an eternity of torment.

But the air softens into something cozy and warm. I float, suspended in nothingness. Then I sink and feel the space around me solidify into something real. The sensation is like settling next to a fire on a crisp autumn day, head cushioned by pillows, legs tucked into a knitted blanket.

When I open my eyes, I discover that's where I am: in someone's den—or so it would appear. A fire is blazing on the hearth. The walls are lined with books, volume after volume. A china coffee service is sitting on an end table.

I'm alone.

I sit up and then push to stand. I pat my arms and legs, blink, tap my head, touch my nose.

I feel solid.

Shutters cover what must be a large window over the sofa. The cushions there are soft, the perfect spot for a nap, and the shutters are smooth and cool. I pull them open, expecting to meet nothing but a solid wall, convinced that this isn't a room so much as a perfect replica of one.

The shutters creak open, and I gape, transfixed. The space beyond is vast. And it truly is space, or maybe the universe, or eternity. I forget to breathe, to move, to think. I can only observe.

All at once, the shutters clatter shut. I fall back, land hard on the table, and jangle the coffee service.

"So curious," the entity says. "Always so curious. You are not ready for that, my dear. You will short circuit every last synapse in that brain of yours, and how tedious for me if you do."

Instinctively, I nod. Yes, the entity's right. Even now, my thoughts are zooming as if my mind is desperately trying to repair itself.

"What is it?" I ask. "Space? Time? The multiverse?"

The entity raises its hands, shrugs. "Yes."

I stare at the void where its face should be—only now, it's less of a void. There are planes and angles, reflecting surfaces. I see a field of stars, swirls of nebulae, pockets of endless dark and bursts of shattering light. I could stare at it for eternity.

The entity snaps its fingers. "Yes, but that would become boring." When it speaks again, its voice is softer. "It is rather marvelous, though, isn't it?"

"It is." No longer transfixed by either its face or the space outside this little room, I take a second look around. "This isn't bad, either. Where am I?"

"Think of it as your accommodations. You can adjust your surroundings as you like, but this was how your grandfather preferred things. I thought we'd start there."

"My ... grandfather?" Now I study each corner, the pattern on the rug, the books that line the shelves, as if all that could tell me more about the man I never knew. "It's like my living room, only not."

"That was our compromise. This version has enough familiarity without breeding despair." It gestures toward the coffee service. "Give it a try."

I kneel next to the table and lift the coffee pot's lid. A clink of china rings clear in the quiet room. Then I inhale. The scent of Kona blend washes over me. It strikes me like something physical, and I brace a palm against the table. This doesn't smell like something I've made, but a pot my grandmother brewed.

"Oh!" I clutch the lid in one hand and anchor the other on the end table. All I want at that moment is to be back in my kitchen, sitting on a stool, watching her concoct the perfect pot of coffee.

"Enough of that." The entity slips the lid from my grasp and replaces it.

The scent dissipates, and my senses return.

"There's a balance," it says, "with humans. Enough nostalgia to keep you sated, but not so much that you wallow."

"So, I'm a pet?"

"Oh, not at all, my dear." It shifts again, trading the suit coat for that ridiculous smoking jacket. Then it settles into a wingback chair next to the hearth. "You are my welcomed guest."

"For how long?"

"Pardon?"

"How long am I here? Until Malcolm stops..." I can't finish the sentence, so I barrel on to the next one. "Like with my grandfather and grandmother. She kept the vigil for him, and I kept one for Malcolm."

"But in this case, you were already my necromancer."

"So, there's a difference."

"A significant one."

"And that would be?" Honestly, could this thing spell it out?

"You came to me of your own free will, not under duress."

"I was under duress," I say. "A lot of it."

It chuckles, and the sound of it billows outward like pipe smoke. "Granted, but in this case, we merely shifted the locale, if you will, of our relationship. You are still my necromancer. We still have a pact. We're simply honoring it here."

"But for how long?"

"For as long as you like. Since you're human, you may want to ... let go at some point. But, my dear, we'll have millennia together if you so desire."

Millennia? With this thing?

It laughs, but it isn't that grating, metallic laugh from Earth. Like before, the sound is an endless stream that ripples through the space—rich, warm, sustaining.

"Always so charming," it says.

I ignore the comment. "But with my grandfather, with Malcolm—"

"The essential difference is that neither one was my necromancer. It's to their credit that they both knew they couldn't hold me as such. And that Malcolm had a turn?" The entity tilts its head, and the stars dance. "Fitting, all things considered."

"Are you going to tell me all those things?"

"Would you like to know?"

Really, it has to ask? I'm about to insist when a thought occurs to me. The entity must know everything, or nearly so.

"Can I ask you anything?" I say.

"You can ask. I may not answer, at least not directly."

"For instance, who really assassinated JFK?" I don't know why that's popped into my head, but it's the first thing out of my mouth. I'm not sure I really care. It's more to see what the entity says.

The entity gestures toward the bookshelves. "Over there, somewhere. Far left corner, I think. It shouldn't take you too much time to find the correct volume." It crosses one leg over the other and adjusts a trouser pleat. "Time being one of those relative things here."

"I have to look it up?"

"Indeed you do, my dear. I will not be pestered by endless questions. Plus, it will sharpen your mind, keep you engaged. Trust me on that."

I scan the bookshelves, and, as my gaze inches upward, they appear never-ending. I peer over my shoulder at the sofa. I could spend an eternity reading, and the idea of it is almost enough to make me smile despite everything.

"Your grandfather felt the same way."

"Will you tell me about him?"

The entity sweeps a hand toward the sofa. "Sit, my dear."

I do, but I take up a perch on the end table instead and pluck a china cup from the coffee service. The porcelain is cool in my hands, the pattern that of my grandmother's wedding china. Something about that hurts more than I think it should.

"Yes." It draws out the s, and something about the entity's voice soothes my heart as if the sound is a supernatural balm. "In a way, it is," it adds. "The shock of leaving your plane alone would incapacitate you, and I certainly don't want you moping about, lovesick for that young necromancer of yours."

I'm not sure I like not being able to feel the things I should. The ache is there, but it's distant, wrapped in gauze and tucked away carefully where I can't pick at it.

"Exactly," the entity says. "If you agree to leave it there, I will agree to tell you about your grandparents and how all of this started."

"And how I ended up on the side of the road?"

"That as well."

I trace the rose pattern on the china cup before setting it next to the coffee pot. Then I pull my knees to my chin and wrap my arms around my legs. I'm ready, and I give the entity a single nod.

CHAPTER 13

"Once upon a time," the entity begins, "both the Lindstroms and the Armands were very active in the necromancer community, but I imagine you've guessed that already."

I should've guessed it sooner. "Did you lead Malcolm to Springside?"

The entity raises a finger. "One narrative at a time, please." It pauses, and something brightens in the field where its face should be. "But, yes, I did. He *is* fairly easy to lead about. I'm sure you've noticed that about him."

I scowl.

The entity chuckles before continuing. "Not only were your families active, but they were also powerful, poised to rule. That ludicrous club—"

"The Midwest Necromancer Association."

"Yes, that. Either one could've assumed leadership there, but they wanted more. More is always dangerous, especially when the parties concerned don't agree on what it means."

"What did it mean?"

"To your grandparents? Peace, prosperity, a more level playing field. Their reasoning was, why should the supernatural benefit only a small portion of the world's population?"

"All or nothing," I murmur. That was so like my grandmother. "And Malcolm's grandfather?"

"Oh, he started with the best intentions, but then, so many people do. Orson Yates, for example."

I make a face.

"I believe the feeling is mutual," the entity says. It sweeps a hand, and the air in the center of the room shimmers. A hole opens up, dark and swirling at first. Then images appear.

I recognize my grandmother by the set of her jaw alone. She's so young, and every time she turns her attention to the man at her side, her face lights up and her eyes soften. Her love is so tangible that I'm certain I could reach out, capture it between my palms, and have it glow. No wonder she was able to keep the vigil for my grandfather all her life.

Malcolm's grandfather looks so much like his grandson that my heart catches. For an instant, the pain breaks through and radiates around my ribcage. I whimper, but a moment later, that soothing balm rushes in. I flatten a palm against my heart as if I could bring the pain back, because part of me still wants to feel all the hurt.

In front of me, my grandmother is conferring with Queenie, Mr. Carlotta's ghost. My grandfather is digging through the stacks at a university library, handing off volumes to Malcolm's grandfather.

They gather at night in the nature preserve, in the very spot where I've been releasing ghosts all my life. Stars fill the sky. They are wide-eyed and solemn. For a moment, it's almost as if I'm viewing myself with Malcolm and Nigel.

"Hm, yes," the entity intones. "I believe the bond was that deep, which is why the betrayal hurt so much."

They link hands and then speak the entity's name, all three of them at once. I lean forward on the coffee table and plant my feet on the floor to steady myself. Something about this is different. Something about it feels ... wrong.

The image of the entity appears. This is neither the craggy, lava-eyed version from the warehouse nor the well-heeled gentleman that currently presides over this space. It doesn't look like a being at all; it's more like they ripped out a piece of the sky and brought it down to earth.

And, oh, it is not happy.

My grandmother notices first. Her mouth is set in an O of fear, but her eyes tell the story. Nothing but sorrow and shame is lingering there. She shakes her head as if she could undo all that they've done.

But, of course, they can't.

"They hurt you," I say to the entity.

At once, the images shatter, leaving us in that facsimile of a den.

"Pardon me, my dear?"

"The three of them invoked you at once. They ripped you from ... where you live?" That must be it, I think, and there's no way that doesn't hurt.

"That is ... correct enough."

"Vendetta," I say.

We've never really discussed the entity's behavior when I first encountered it, but the pieces of that fall into place.

"That's why Malcolm was getting that vendetta vibe from you at the mausoleum." I pause, casting my mind back to that eradication. It seems so long ago, when Malcolm was merely my business partner. "He thought it was about me, though. But was it about him? Or us together? Or our grandparents?"

The entity doesn't speak, although it hasn't moved from its wingback chair. It conjures a pipe, and smoke rings billow from the bowl. The scent is insidious, sweet and calming, and not at all like tobacco.

I yawn. But I'm not on Earth, so do I really need to sleep?

"Stop that!" I say.

"Hm?"

"You're changing the subject."

Now it laughs. "I'm doing no such thing."

"You are."

The smoke curls and wanders about the space. My thoughts follow. Part of me wants to abandon the conversation, pull a volume from the shelf, and settle in on the couch.

Instead, I slip from the table and approach the hearth. There's no place for me to sit, so I kneel a few feet from the entity. This makes me look like a supplicant or a pet, but maybe that's okay, considering what I have to say.

"I'm sorry."

"Are you, now? Whatever for?"

"For what we did to you."

"You haven't done a thing, my dear."

"My grandparents did, and so did Malcolm's grandfather. So, I'm apologizing for them. If someone ripped me from Springside, I'd be pretty angry."

"It seems someone has, or am I wrong in thinking you're not currently on this plane of existence?"

"I was a willing sacrifice, remember?" When it doesn't respond, I add, "Where are you supposed to be? Here?"

"Here is adequate. When you're ready, we can explore other worlds, other universes."

"But you don't have a place where you belong."

The entity turns its head toward me. Stars shoot across the surface where its face should be. I'm relieved that I no longer see that abyss, but the vastness I do see feels just as lonely.

"That's why there was a void where your face should be. Did we take that away from you?"

"You did nothing."

"My grandmother, then, and Malcolm's grandfather."

"They merely finished something that was started long ago," it says. "But to answer your question, yes. I ... lost the place where I belong. I hope to make my way back there." It raises a hand as if it might caress my cheek. "Perhaps you'll still be with me."

The entity stands. The pipe vanishes in a puff of blue smoke. In that smoke, I see the rest of the story. Malcolm's grandfather leaps at the entity, arms wide. I can't hear my grandmother shout, but the smoke ripples in response.

Malcolm's grandfather staggers. He can't hold the entity. It rages within him, will burn him through. My grandmother steps forward and presses a hand on his heart.

Although I can't hear her speak, her mouth forms an apology. She's speaking not to Malcolm's grandfather, but to the entity inside him. She leans close, as if she might coax the entity to emerge. I know what her next words will be; I spoke them not that long ago myself.

I am your willing sacrifice.

Before she can utter the phrase, my grandfather pulls her away. He kisses her with so much tenderness that it makes my chest constrict. Then, he takes her place.

I can't hear his words either, but the lights that flash in their wake illuminate the nature preserve.

In another puff of smoke, he and the entity vanish. My grandmother collapses to the ground, hands pulling at the earth as if that will bring my grandfather back, sobs wracking her body.

Malcolm's grandfather stumbles from the clearing. He knows enough not to try to comfort her. He knows this is his fault. He surveys the sky the way I would when I was searching for the entity. He could invoke it again; he could take my grandfather's place.

He doesn't.

He walks away, very much a man who has lost something crucial.

The last wisps of smoke dissipate, and I find myself alone in front of the fire. The wingback chair is empty.

I swipe at the air as if that will let me rewind the scene.

"They didn't invoke you," I say.

Nothing but the crackle of the fire greets me.

"This was different," I continue. I don't need to speak these words. No doubt the entity can read my mind here as well as it can everywhere else. But speaking them feels important.

"It wasn't a pact. It was something else." A word pops into my head. "Leverage." I think back to when Malcolm first told me about necromancy and explained how Orson and the Midwest Necromancer Association worked, how they leveraged ghosts, harnessed them to do their bidding. At the time, I thought it sounded cruel.

Now I know it is.

I swipe the air again, and my fingers leave tendrils of blue smoke in their wake. In the wisps, I catch sight of my grandparents and Malcolm's grandfather at the moment before everything changed. Again, I'm struck with how familiar the sight is, how I can see Malcolm and myself at the nature preserve, or the three of us—Malcolm, Nigel, and me—in the office, huddled around Nigel's computer.

I return my attention to the images shimmering in the blue smoke. That could've been us.

"It was so quick," I say.

The blue smoke vanishes in the wake of my breath.

Betrayal often is, my dear.

I DON'T KNOW how much time passes. I discover that I have a never-ending pot of coffee. Once a day—at least, it feels like once a day—a treat appears on the table, although I don't need to eat, or even drink, for that matter.

It's a habit, it's comforting, and my guess is, the entity knows that.

I pull random volumes from the shelves and tumble into the past—not just of Earth. I could spend several lifetimes lost in these books. It's like reading on steroids—I feel the sun's heat and the icy rain, taste spring or gunpowder in the air, feel freshly mown grass beneath my feet.

All without leaving the sofa.

The history I want to find most is that of my mother. She must be in these volumes somewhere, because it appears that everyone is. The task is daunting. There is no index, no coherence, no alphabetical order, or really any order that I can see.

"Of course there's an order, my dear."

The entity's voice startles me. The book I'm holding slips from my fingers and lands on the floor. I'm guessing it's a floor; it looks like a floor.

The entity bends down and scoops up the volume. "Don't assume there isn't one simply because you don't understand it."

It has a point. Plus? I really don't understand anything anymore. "Where were you?" I ask.

"Someone thought to invoke me. I had to deal with that."

I'd thought maybe I'd chased the entity away with all my probing and questioning. "People can still do that?"

"They can try, but you're not only my willing sacrifice, you're also my necromancer. No one else can capture me unless you relinquish your dual roles."

"Then, why would someone invoke you?"

"Why did Orson, at the wedding reception? Why did Malcolm's grandfather betray your grandmother?"

"But I invoked you when you had Malcolm."

"And I appeared, did I not?" The entity glides across the room, pointing at books I've left scattered about. They go flying back to the shelves. "That was also the day you became a necromancer."

"I ... what?"

I think back to how the ghosts of Springside came to my rescue. "I didn't command the ghosts or deploy them," I counter. "I merely asked for a favor."

"And they agreed, and their power was enough to thwart my ...

plans for you. It wasn't quite the negotiation I was expecting. Considering you're your mother's daughter, perhaps I should have."

I latch on to that. I know I can't force the entity to tell me anything about her, but I so want to know. "What happened?"

The entity approaches the wingback chair. It hesitates, as if it can't decide whether to sit or not. Instead, it clutches the top of the chair in a manner so humanlike it surprises me.

"Your mother. Her desire was as pure as yours, although it was far sharper. Yours encompassed the whole of Springside. She focused on one thing for much of her life."

"My grandfather."

"That was her sole aim, why she trained with the necromancer association and partnered with both Orson and Darien. When your grandmother very wisely refused to reveal my name to her, she went off and found it on her own."

"Kind of like I did?"

"Indeed." The entity shakes its head, and again I'm struck with how humanlike the gesture is. "And she caught me. Exceedingly clever, your mother."

"But ... you had a willing sacrifice."

"Who refused to leave."

"But ..." I work to pull this all together. Wouldn't my grandfather want to come home? Didn't he yearn for Springside the way I do?

"He refused to let his daughter take his place, and that desire equaled hers. As a result, the negotiations became protracted—an in-between state for the necromancer and myself. Remember, in the warehouse?"

I nod.

"I could've easily been captured at that point by someone else. There were several necromancers in Springside that day. Orson Yates might have had a chance, had he been resolute enough to take it. I'm not sure he realizes that."

I think of Orson's hesitation on the side of the road, how he seemed unable to decide between the entity and the accident victims. I wonder: does that day haunt him like I think it must?

The entity doesn't need to tell me what happened next. A chase, perhaps? My parents trying to escape the way Malcolm and I did, their car haunted the way Malcolm's transmission was?

I can still hear the roar of their car engine, feel the crash in my bones, see that plume of smoke rising from the ravine.

"And in that instant," the entity says, its voice unbearably soft, "when the wheels left the gravel and met the air, all of your mother's desire transferred to you. Her one wish, her last wish, was that you would live."

And that's how I ended up on the side of the road, pinned in place, unharmed and alone.

"I didn't have to save you," the entity says.

"But you did."

"I did."

"Is that your vendetta? Is that really why I'm here now?"

"I dislike ... caring so much for something so small and puny and fragile as a human."

My heart hammers in my chest. I press my palm against it and wonder at that. Do I need a heartbeat anymore? Is it just the memory of one? The ache spreads, and I welcome it even as I try to hide the pain. I don't want another dose of that soothing balm—not yet, anyway.

But the entity has turned away from me, so perhaps it doesn't notice. Except, it notices everything, so it must be letting me hurt and cry and feel the tears scratch my cheeks.

The sorrow hollows out my belly. I'm empty inside, longing for Springside, for Malcolm, for the mother I never knew. And still, the entity keeps its back to me.

At last, I push the tears from my face and consider the coffee service. I've been using the same cup over and over again, but there are several on the tray—almost like the entity and I are some 1950s married couple, and we're expecting guests at any moment.

I pour a fresh cup and add some half and half from a little pitcher. It's fresh and cool and can't possibly be real. I approach the entity, the cup cradled in my hands.

The aroma of Kona blend must reach it first. I detect the slightest shift in its stance.

"You saved my life." I grip the cup, and the barest ripple travels the surface of the coffee.

"And now you're here."

"Well, yes, I am. But before this, I started a business and fell in love. I had a protégé and a best friend. It was a good life. And so"—I set the coffee down on a side table—"thank you."

I return to the couch and pick up the one book the entity didn't send back to the shelves. I turn the pages, more focused on the tactile experience than anything inside the book itself. I'm not sure I care about the Teapot Dome scandal.

When I look up again, the entity is gone. I find the cup empty— not even a drop of coffee remains in the bottom. Next to the cup, a puff of that blue smoke is floating. It shifts and swirls until, at last, it spells out the words: *You're Welcome.*

I blow on the words and watch the smoke shift to stars. They sparkle and shoot across the room and then fade.

I am alone. But not lonely. For the first time in a very long time, I suspect the entity isn't either.

WE HAVE A ROUTINE NOW. I know when the entity vanishes because extra treats appear. The soothing balm rushes in when my thoughts wander to Springside and especially when they wander to Malcolm.

The books on the shelves rearrange themselves, and it's as if the entity is directing my education. It's a bit passive aggressive, but it's effective. Besides, it only laughs when I complain.

There's so much more beyond this haven he's created for me. The books tell me that; my own senses do. When I sit on the couch, my feet twitch. When I felt this way in the past, back in Springside, I would brew up a pot of coffee, pull together the field kit, and go searching for ghosts.

"You're not close to being ready," it says when I broach the subject. "It will take decades, not that you'll really notice. About the time people stop invoking me. My name will fade from view, and I won't have to deal with these constant interruptions."

"Is it on the internet? Because if it's on the internet, it's never going away."

The entity laughs. "Ah, but you have to know what to look for."

"Could we go ghost hunting?" I ask. "When I'm ready?"

"Whatever do you mean?"

It knows. Of course it knows.

"My grandmother and grandfather. My parents?"

"Ah. Perhaps."

"Perhaps while we're looking for your home?"

Its posture shifts, and it settles deeper into the wingback chair. I take that as a yes.

Ours is a well-ordered existence. Nothing disturbs my daily treat. The coffee never gives me jitters. The otherworldly balm coats the rough edges whenever I feel too much. So, days ... weeks ... some time later, when something rocks the stability of the floor, I'm unprepared.

The carpets buckle. The force of the disturbance throws me off the sofa. I stare, hands planted on the table while the entity stands, its head tilted in curiosity.

A form emerges from the floor, billowing and misty. It reminds me of the chain of ghosts sewn together inside the cold storage unit of the Pancake House. The clouds expand and grow, solidifying around a central figure.

One by one, features emerge. My gaze snags on the strangest things—the set of the jaw, the lush, dark lashes against paler cheekbones, the sharp crease in the khakis, and a pressed white dress shirt.

It takes a moment, perhaps because I believed I'd never see him again.

When the clouds of mist fall away, they reveal the man who's now standing in the center of the den.

It's Malcolm.

CHAPTER 14

I gape. I forget to breathe. I know it's Malcolm. My heart is thumping too hard, my throat is too tight, and my mind is scrambling for explanations. The most dire?

He's dead. He's dead, and he's here now because ... well, I'm not sure, exactly, except he's wearing the pallor of death and hasn't moved or opened his eyes. I want to ask the entity, but I can't drag my attention away from Malcolm.

Then, all at once, he coughs. With a fist, he strikes himself in the solar plexus, and a plume of mist is expelled from his mouth. Fog rises and swirls. He continues to hack like he has bronchitis or pneumonia. As he does, his skin returns to that lovely shade of olive. His hair gleams. He coughs one last time, clears his throat, and then looks at me.

"Malcolm?"

He gives me one of those sweet, dark-roast smiles.

"But ... you can't be here. Are you dead?"

"I don't think I'm dead."

"Are you real?"

He curls his fingers in a come-here gesture. "Try me."

I leap up and throw myself across the room. This is Malcolm, and I will always run to him. I take three steps before launching myself the last few feet. I half-expect to fall through him and crash to the floor, certain this is no more than a hallucination.

He catches me. His arms are solid and sure, his nutmeg and Ivory soap scent the best thing I've inhaled in ages. He is warm and secure and definitely my Malcolm Armand.

Behind me, the entity claps. The sound of it ripples through the space, buffeting us like waves in the ocean.

"Oh, well done, necromancer. Well done, indeed. Bravo, even."

I peer over my shoulder at the entity. Malcolm keeps his grip on me, but his scowl is fierce.

"Isn't he clever, Katy? Go on, tell him just how clever he is. You know he wants to hear it from you too."

Now I frown, out of frustration. I don't get it, don't understand how Malcolm can be here, warm and alive.

"You can't be a willing sacrifice," I tell him. "Besides, I wouldn't let you."

His gaze flickers toward the entity. "I'm not the willing sacrifice."

"Then ... how?"

He points to the mist that still surrounds us. "They are."

The fog shifts once again, revealing ghost after ghost and sprite after sprite. They career around the den, rattling the coffee service, sweeping across the bookshelves, and twirling around me like an otherworldly cyclone.

"Ghosts?" Their forms collide and merge, split apart. Tracking them is impossible.

"Not just any ghosts," Malcolm says. "Every last ghost in Springside."

"Every ghost?"

Even as I ask the question, I know the answer. All at once, half a dozen sprites pepper my face with kisses—I count both Sadie's and Belinda's sprites among them. The ghost that haunts Chief

Ramsey's watering can slouches along the perimeter. The wild ghosts from the old barn push books to the floor—a Sisyphean task, as the books magically reshelve themselves.

In the corner, I detect a grumpy group that roils and simmers, but for all their discontent, even these ghosts seem placid.

"Attack ghosts?" I venture. "They came, too?"

"Would you want to be a dog on a leash?"

No, I wouldn't, especially an angry, mistreated dog, and especially if Orson were holding that leash. Still, I stare at the group in wonder. "They were able to escape?"

"They were, plus I had a little coaching from Nigel. I walked and biked every street in Springside, searched every corner, alley, and store." Malcolm grins, and he looks downright devious. "And along the way, I picked up my father's ghosts."

Oh, no wonder he looks so self-satisfied. "All the way out to the nature preserve?"

"He moved in closer after ... everything. He set up camp in Sadie's backyard."

Oh, poor Sadie and Nigel.

"And I collected Prescott's and Reginald's ghosts."

At that moment, a mischievous sprite zips by, planting a naughty kiss on my cheek. It can only be Frederick.

"And even Orson's attack ghosts," he adds.

"All of them?"

"Every last one."

"Does that work?" I ease from Malcolm's embrace, although he keeps his fingers laced with mine. I turn toward the entity. "Can ghosts be a willing sacrifice?"

The entity has fallen silent. It studies the proceedings with a hand cupping its chin as if it's deep in thought.

"There is no reason why they can't," it says at last. "Before now, they never had a means"—the entity nods toward Malcolm —"a conduit, if you will, to speak my name. And this one"—it gestures toward a single ghost making its slow way toward the hearth—"is a most welcomed guest."

Queenie. Mr. Carlotta's ghost.

"So, you what?" I turn back to Malcolm. "Swallowed all the ghosts and invoked the entity?"

"Pretty much. Queenie helped. The ghosts of Springside love you, and they listen to her. Me?" He rubs the back of his head. "Not so much."

"Now what?" I ask.

The entity still appears deep in thought. The surface where its face should be sparkles and glitters in a way I've never seen before.

"There are so many," it says, its voice both solemn and soft. "So many lost souls."

"Can you take care of them?" The magnitude of what they've done—of what Malcolm has done—strikes me, leaves me breathless. What if there's no place for these ghosts in this plane of existence?

"Perhaps not this exact plane, my dear," the entity says, "but I assure you, they will find a home somewhere. I will be their devoted caretaker, if you allow me that role. They are your ghosts, after all."

My ghosts. All of them. I extend a hand, and a group of sprites weaves between my fingers. "They would do this for me?"

"They would," Malcolm whispers.

I'm dumbstruck. Words escape me. I search the space, this facsimile of a room that I thought might be my home forever. For a fleeting moment, I hesitate. Then I find my words. In all of this, there is only one choice.

"Can I say goodbye?"

The entity gestures to its wingback chair. I sit. One by one, each ghost floats past. The sprites chatter and twirl, and the ones from the Springside Police Department collect the stray tears that wander down my cheeks. Frederick steals another kiss. I say goodbye to the rowdy ones, the quiet ones, and even incline my head as the attack ghosts pass.

The very last ghost is Mr. Carlotta's Queenie. When she oozes to a stop in front of me, all I have left to say is, "I'll take care of him. He won't be lonely." I place a hand on my heart. "I promise you."

With that, I'm done. I'm about to stand when the entity offers its hand.

"It's not often that I learn something from a mere mortal."

I wait for it to elaborate, but of course, it doesn't. Instead, I take its hand.

"You were a worthy opponent, my dear, if a somewhat dull necromancer."

"Hey!"

Its chuckle is downright demonic. "Oh, the fun we could've had together." It pauses, seems to consider something. "And it isn't often that a mere mortal either surprises or delights me. You managed to do both." The entity touches my cheek—the left one, on the very spot it marked so many months ago.

"Off with you, then. Go be with your young man. He has proven himself after all. Imagine that."

"Will you ... will you be okay?"

"You have given me quite a gift. Let me return the favor."

There's a flash, and what looks like a thousand stars streaking across the sky. The air turns cold and then hot before shifting into something crisp and cool. What feels like grass cushions me, and short, thick blades tickle my palms.

When I open my eyes, the view of my front porch at sunrise greets me. I catch a hint of blue in all the gold and pink, the darker shadows of the green steel roof. When I turn my head, I see Malcolm on the grass, his body next to mine.

"You did it," I whisper.

"We did it." His gaze is so tender. With tentative fingers, he touches my cheek, the left one. "Huh. It's gone."

"Completely?" I ask, but I already sense the answer.

"Completely."

The void rushes in, stronger than I expected. The entity is no longer connected to this particular plane of existence, or to me. It would take more than merely uttering its name to invoke it.

I stare up at the brilliant blue sky, catch a hint of smoke in the air, notice how the leaves are rimmed with red and gold.

"How long have I been gone?"

"Six weeks."

Six weeks! I'm about to bolt upright. The urge to run around and check on everything nearly overwhelms me. But I stay put, back flush with the earth. Malcolm's hand finds mine, and he inches me closer, his hold on me suddenly protective.

A shadow falls across the lawn, and it stretches long and menacing.

Orson Yates is standing on my sidewalk.

And he's holding a gun.

CHAPTER 15

Desperate, I scan the neighborhood. It's early morning, with curtains still shrouding windows, porch lights still on.

Orson takes one step and then another, a deliberate move across my ward.

"Don't move, don't scream." He aims the gun at Malcolm. "Or he'll be dead before you can take another breath."

Next to me, Malcolm tenses. His grip tightens as if he's building energy for an attack.

"Don't think about it," Orson says. "I can kill her just as easily."

"If you kill us, the police will catch you." The words emerge from my throat stronger than I think they should be.

"You've taken many things from me, Ms. Lindstrom, but not quite everything. I have ... resources, and it seems you are without any. Do you know what that means?"

I'm afraid to ask. My heart thuds, pulse roaring in my ears, and my thoughts race so fast I can't catch up to them. Malcolm grips my hand as if he, too, knows that we're out of options. Orson will shoot us. He will walk away. But before he does, he wants me to ask. So I do, if only to buy a few more seconds with Malcolm.

"What does that mean?" I say.

"It means—" That cunning and cruel smile lights his face. "That I win."

Maybe it's how his fingers are twitching that alerts me. Maybe it's his stance. The barrel is centered on Malcolm's chest. Fling myself at Orson? Tackle him around the knees? If only I had a branch, or a rake. A sword, even.

I grope the ground for something—anything—but only end up with a fistful of grass. Then Orson's own words cross my mind.

What if I told you that every time you catch a ghost, you commit an act of necromancy?

Containment fields. My imaginary tire iron that freed the ghosts in the cemetery. The sword that nearly sliced through them in the Pancake House.

I pick the tire iron and, with all my strength, picture smashing it against Orson's hand and knocking the gun from his grip.

The shot is deafening, the blood a bright red. Drops of it strike my face, the feel of it hot and sticky. A howl cuts through the ringing in my ears. My vision and thoughts clear just as Malcolm barrels into Orson.

There's no grappling. Malcolm clutches his shoulder, Orson his hand. They crash onto the lawn. Malcolm. Still alive. A burst of relief flows through me until I realize that the gun is missing—or, at least, I don't know where it is. I crawl across the grass, scanning the bushes, combing the ground, all in search of it.

Another bang rings out. For one terrifying moment, I fear Orson has found the gun and has used it. But the sound isn't as sharp or as loud.

A moment later, Darien Armand lands on Orson, followed by Nigel, and all I can see is arms and legs and the brightness of that blood. Darien jerks Orson's hands behind his back; Nigel sits on his legs.

Malcolm rolls to the side, hand clutching his arm, and stares up at the sky. His chest heaves. Pain is etched on his face.

But he's alive, and the relief comes rushing back.

I push to stand, take a step, and my foot finds the gun. I ease off it, but the last thing I want to do is pick it up.

I think someone should. I'm bending to retrieve it when Nigel calls out.

"Don't!"

I glance up.

"You don't want your prints on it."

"But—" I point at Orson.

"He's not going anywhere." Nigel shifts his weight and pulls out a phone. "We need to call for an examination."

"Shouldn't we call the police instead?"

Even now, I'm surprised one of my neighbors hasn't, but other than the commotion in my yard, the street quietly slumbers on. I glance up, wondering if there is—once again—some necromancer magic going on.

"Not if we don't have to." Nigel glances at his father, who nods.

I keep my foot on the gun, uncertain if we're doing the right thing.

"It's me," Nigel says when the call goes through. "Yeah, he made it back, and with Katy." He pauses and gives Malcolm a look filled with admiration. "You're right. It *is* damned impressive. Call Reginald. We've got Orson. Tell him it's time."

Nigel tosses the phone to me. "Hang on to that, and don't lose sight of the gun."

"But ... Malcolm?" I point again, this time indicating the blood that's seeping through Malcolm's fingers.

Nigel raises an eyebrow at his brother. "You okay?"

Malcolm rolls to face us. "I can hang on."

"Good man."

"We ... like Reginald now?" I venture.

Malcolm gives me a wan smile, one meant to reassure me. I'm not certain it does. "I'll explain it later."

So I stand there, foot on the gun, and survey the neighborhood. As far as I can tell, the gunshot woke no one else. Curtains remain drawn, doors closed. No wail of a siren fills the air. Despite this, I half-expect to see Chief Ramsey round the corner and haul us all in to the Springside jail.

Instead, a flashy yellow car rumbles down the road, followed by a Land Rover and several black sedans of the German variety.

Prescott leaps out first. He dashes up the walk, throwing me a grin as he goes.

He helps Malcolm to his feet.

Prescott keeps a hand on Malcolm's shoulder. "Steady?"

Malcolm nods and staggers over to me. His entire left sleeve is drenched with blood, and the coppery scent of it heats the air between us.

"He shot you." This is stating the obvious. I realize that. At the moment, those are the only words I have.

"In the arm," Malcolm says. He lets go of the wound for a second and taps his chest. "Not here." He leans in and kisses me, and it's hot and salty, and for a second, I think I might cry.

The sight of necromancers filling my lawn has me blinking away the tears. Like before, they assemble in a solemn row. Only this time, it's Orson's turn for an examination. Once the entire group has circled him, Nigel and Prescott let go and step back.

Orson is still clutching his hand. Beneath his grip, the flesh is bruised, an angry purple radiating up his wrist.

"I would like to state for the record that Katrina Lindstrom used necromancy to attack me," he says. "My hand is broken. She is in direct violation—"

"You were going to shoot Malcolm!" I cry out. "You *did* shoot Malcolm! I—" I glance around, wondering if this is going to be about me yet again.

Reginald raises a finger, and I swallow back my protests.

"And we might wish to lodge charges against Malcolm Armand," Orson continues, "as he's the one who has stolen all the ghosts within a ten-mile radius." He narrows his eyes at the assembled group. "You might want to check to see which ones you're missing. My guess is, all of them."

Then again, maybe this is going to be about me, along with Malcolm. Anxiety pings inside me as I study each and every necromancer. As a group, they're not just solemn, but unsympathetic. Their stances are firm, their expressions passive.

"What's a necromancer without any ghosts?" I whisper to Malcolm.

"Usually pissed off."

"Even today?"

He blows out a breath, and I hear his uncertainty in it.

Darien Armand steps forward. He casts Orson a look so cold it should cover my lawn in frost.

"I am no longer part of the necromancer community," Darien intones, "and I will not participate in this examination except to say that if you cannot protect your ghosts from a ... novice necromancer, perhaps you don't deserve the title yourself."

With that, Darien steps from my lawn and into Sadie's backyard.

"Are you sure you got all your father's ghosts?" I whisper to Malcolm.

He stares at the spot where Darien vanished. "I have no idea."

Reginald clears his throat. "Orson Yates, for too long you've been a blot on the necromancer community and its good name."

Orson snorts.

"You have already stood for examination in the past," Reginald continues. "More than once."

"And in the past, my name has always been cleared."

"That was our mistake," Reginald says. "You have been

summarily examined. We, as a community, can no longer allow you to practice necromancy. You will submit to retribution."

Orson doesn't sputter or lash out. To his credit, he pulls himself up straight, although he cradles his injured hand against his chest. "Then I bow to the wishes of the community. Do your worst."

I expect a trick. Apparently Malcolm does too. A frown clouds his brow, but then a knowing look fills his eyes.

"Money," he whispers in my ear. "He doesn't need ghosts, or necromancy, or any of that. He has plenty of money. He's set for life."

The other necromancers line up across from Orson. Prescott takes his place among them, as does Nigel. Malcolm and I don't budge from our spot on the grass. My foot is still covering the gun.

"Katrina Lindstrom. Young Malcolm." Reginald gestures toward the group. "Take your place. We need all necromancers present for retribution."

Malcolm swallows back a sigh. I still don't move. My gaze meets Orson's. In it, I don't see the man who tried to kill us—more than once—but the one who hesitated on the side of the road, the one who couldn't choose which path to take, and so had a path chosen for him.

I take a step back, and then another. I'm on the sidewalk before anyone really notices.

"Katy?" Malcolm stares at me, his gaze full of concern. He's still clutching his arm.

"Someone shot you," I say simply. "I'm going to go get Chief Ramsey."

A murmur passes through the group. A few of the necromancers shift from foot to foot before Prescott clears his throat.

"Katy, this is retribution," he says. "It's how necromancer justice works."

I survey the group one last time. So many necromancers, and all of them on my lawn. Then I know my answer.

"I keep telling all of you. I'm not a necromancer."

I turn from them and head down the sidewalk toward the center of town. A moment later, Malcolm falls into step next to me.

CHAPTER 16

P enny Wilson is holding the coffee carafe when we enter Springside Police Department. Her mouth hangs open, and the handle slips through her fingers. The pot shatters on the floor, sending coffee and shards of glass everywhere.

Then she screams.

Chief bursts from his office, scowling and perturbed. "Penny, what the hell—"

At the sight of me, he freezes. He moves a hand to his chest and, on reflex, clutches the spot over his heart. I think he might be having an actual heart attack. I can't make sense of it until I remember:

I've been gone for six weeks.

Then Chief does the one thing I didn't expect. He steps forward and pulls me into a hug.

It's awkward and weird, and I want to choke back the spate of tears that fill my eyes, but I can't. I'm reminded of the man who found me on the side of the road, who scooped me up and cradled me like I was his own daughter.

He recovers quickly and steps away, once again Police Chief
Ramsey and all business.

Between Penny's scream and the impromptu hug, Officer
Deborah Millard has stepped into the reception area. She has a first
aid kit. With the utmost calm, she cuts away the bloody sleeve and
bandages Malcolm's arm.

"You should probably go to urgent care," she says, her voice
level. "You might need stitches."

Malcolm nods, says thanks, and bestows one of his charming
smiles on her. But then his gaze finds Chief, and his eyes turn
steely.

"Can I assume this means I'm no longer a person of
interest?"

"What?" Now I gape. "You blamed Malcolm?"

Chief glances away, but that's only to gather his strength. He
spears me with a look. "You vanished without a trace."

"Well, I'm back now. I can't believe..." I trail off, all out of
words, and simply wave a hand at Malcolm.

"Standard in cases like this. We look at the ... significant other.
Mind telling me where you were for the past two months? Or is
this one of those things I won't believe?"

It is, of course, so I blurt, "Someone shot Malcolm."

"I can see that."

"It was Orson Yates, and he's in my front yard."

THE RIDE in the patrol car is fast, but not fast enough. By the
time we've returned to my house, all the fancy sedans are gone,
minus one. Prescott's yellow sports car is sitting in front of Sadie's
house. Prescott himself is on the front porch, fluttering the pages
of a newspaper.

Chief lumbers up the walk, plants his hands on his hips, and
demands, "Is Mrs. Lanca ... Armand home?"

"She's packing," Prescott says. He folds the paper and places it on the seat next to him. "As is Mr. Armand. For their honeymoon."

Chief's mouth forms a hard, thin line.

"I'm housesitting, you know, keeping an eye on things." The move is subtle, but none of us miss the nod in the direction of my place.

Some of the fierceness leaves Chief's expression. "Got a report of a gunshot. You hear anything?"

"I only woke up a few minutes ago." Prescott stretches as if his limbs are heavy with sleep. It's a fairly impressive show, but I don't think Chief is buying the act. "Must have slept through it."

When Chief turns to study my yard, Prescott winks at me.

I rush down the steps and onto my lawn. In the grass, the slightest impression of where Malcolm and I landed remains. There's a divot not too far away that—if you squint at it—could be the shape of a gun. Other than that, my yard looks well cared for and weed-free. I can't even find a single drop of Malcolm's blood, not in the grass and not on the sidewalk.

"It happened right here," I say to Chief.

Malcolm slides in next to me, his uninjured arm wrapping around my waist.

"No weapon, no suspect," Chief says. His gaze flits from me to Malcolm and back again. "No crime."

"But—"

"You know," Chief says, and now his voice turns contemplative. "I called up an old high school buddy a few weeks back, right before you did your disappearing act."

I blink and cast a sidelong glance at Malcolm, who gives his head a little shake.

"We graduated high school together," Chief continues. "He was also a friend of your mother's."

I hold very still, not daring to miss Chief's next words.

"These days, he works for the IRS. Someone has to, right?"

Numb, I nod.

Chief chuckles, and in it, I hear the echo of the entity's laughter. "Turns out Mr. Yates doesn't like paying his taxes, and the IRS would like to ... chat with him about that."

He turns from us, steps off my lawn, and heads down the sidewalk. He doesn't speak again until he reaches the patrol car.

"You two take care of each other. And for heaven's sake, go be young." He touches the brim of his hat and then slips inside the car.

Even after the rumble of the engine has faded, Malcolm and I continue to stand in my front yard. Prescott is no longer on Sadie's porch. The sun has just now crested the roofs and is painting the street in a golden glow.

"You know he arrested me after you vanished with the entity," Malcolm says at last.

"He *what?*"

"Handcuffs and everything."

"But—"

"Things were ... crazy. Orson wanted me to stand for retribution, for interfering with necromancer business." With his uninjured arm, he manages to draw little air quotes around *necromancer business*. "Chief did me a favor, really. He spent the night at the station, too. We talked until dawn." An odd smile lights Malcolm's face. "Chief's kind of deep, when you get right down to it."

That doesn't surprise me. I peer up at Malcolm. There's a bit more gray at his temples, perhaps a new crease or two at the corners of his eyes. I don't know if that's from swallowing ghosts or from the past six weeks—or both.

The magnitude of what he's done washes over me. I want to tell him everything I'm thinking, but the first thing to come out is:

"I should drive you to urgent care."

Another smile warms his face, this one richer and sweeter—a true dark-roast smile. "Yes, you should, you really should." But as he says it, he tugs me closer.

"We should probably figure out what to tell them, too." I nod toward his injured arm. "About that."

"Or we could tell them to call Chief." His gaze flits toward the street, but the patrol car has vanished. "He owes us."

Malcolm still hasn't budged, and I worry about infection and blood loss and—

His lips find mine. His kiss is so tender and sweet that it obliterates all the thoughts in my head.

"Urgent care?" I say, breathless.

"In a bit. Right now, I'm missing six weeks' worth of morning kisses, and I'd like to collect."

CHAPTER 17

W e spend the following week in the office, the gold lettering of K&M Ghost Eradication Specialists glowing in the window. Every time I see the words, my heart catches.

The phone is silent. So is our email inbox. No one has sent us a text. The implications of that gnaw away at my happiness at being back on Earth, in Springside and with Malcolm. He hasn't said anything, but then, he really doesn't need to. What are eradication specialists without any ghosts?

Out of business.

Instead, he catches me up on everything I've missed, explains how Reginald and Prescott hoped to turn the tables on Orson and use my retribution to launch one of their own against him.

"Reginald was hoping to act as a double agent, I guess." Malcolm shrugs. "That didn't really go as planned."

"He could've told us," I say.

"Not really. For it to work, he needed our reaction, Nigel's in particular. It's hard to fake that sort of response."

I think of how that felt, of how Nigel nearly doubled over as if he'd been struck in the gut.

"It was so quick," I whisper. I wait, wondering if I'll hear an echo of *Betrayal often is*. I don't, but I tip my head toward the ceiling and search for it anyway.

On Wednesday, the bell above the door chimes. For an instant, hope surges through me. A customer? Someone with a ghost? Will we need the Kona blend? I'm halfway through my mental inventory of supplies when the sight of Darien Armand brings me to a crashing halt.

"Will you grant me entry?" His voice is level and deep; his words sound measured and more formal than usual.

It's only then that I notice he has the toes of his well-worn boots on the edge of my ward.

I nod.

Malcolm doesn't sigh or roll his eyes. He doesn't squirm. He merely stands and meets his father in the center of the reception area.

"I'm leaving town today," Darien says.

"Back to South America?"

Darien adjusts the backpack on his shoulders and glances out the window before speaking again. "By way of Paris."

Malcolm darts a look in my direction but remains absolutely still.

"Your mother and I have ... things to sort through. She's happy with Prem, and I don't wish to disrupt that, but it's time we talked."

A curious look lights Malcolm's expression, but he merely nods. "Have a safe trip."

Darien grips Malcolm's shoulder. They stand like that, father and son. Then Darien nods, and in it, I see all the things he can't say.

In it, I see approval.

He's at the door, the chime ringing out again, when he pauses. He considers the entryway, then turns and considers me.

"By the way, Ms. Lindstrom, your coffee is as good as your mother's ever was."

The door whooshes closed, the bell jangling one last time.

Malcolm is standing in the center of our office, arms slack at his sides. I go to him, and it's only then that he moves and captures me in a hug.

"You okay?" I ask.

He releases a long-repressed sigh. "You know what? I am. Strange as it sounds."

"It *sounds* like you had a rough six weeks. I'm sorry I wasn't—"

"Yes, because you decided to save the freaking world, I had to deal with my parents." He cups my face in his hands. "Are you kidding me? I can hardly believe you're here right now. If I had to go through six years of that to get you back, it would be worth it."

I think he might say more. In fact, I'm positive. But he doesn't. He merely plants a gentle kiss on my forehead and tucks me closer to him.

For a long time, we stand in the glow of K&M Ghost Eradication Specialists, and I know I could never want anything more than this.

On Friday afternoon, after a week of doing nothing, we settle on the reception desk. We've never had enough money—or business—to hire an actual receptionist. The couch is more comfortable, but from here, we can admire how the letters in the window glow and follow the sun's patterns across the carpet.

"Hey," Malcolm says. "Why don't we do the rounds tomorrow?"

"The rounds?"

"Yeah, the whole town, all the usual haunts. I have an appointment at Springside Long-term Care. I'm hosting a..." He trails off and clears his throat. "A tea party."

"A tea party?"

"Well, there aren't any ghosts."

Not that he ever did actual eradications at Springside Long-term Care. It was all taste tests and flirting.

"But I hate missing an appointment, so a tea party and maybe some magic tricks."

And, of course, the magic shows. I laugh, but then I burrow closer to him. "This," I say. "This is why I love you."

Malcolm kisses the top of my head. For a moment, everything's as it should be, but that isn't this new reality. We need to confront that.

"It's over, isn't it?" I say.

"I ... yeah." A sigh rumbles in his chest. "I think it is. We don't have the cash flow to keep going, not with all this overhead and no new customers."

Or *any* customers. I consider that and all that's happened in the past year since my grandmother died.

"You know, my grandmother said she'd come back and show me how to get rid of all the ghosts in Springside. I'm not sure this is what she had in mind."

"Maybe it is. I guess she knew you'd have to face the entity one day, not to mention Orson."

"That *we'd* have to."

"She'd be proud of you."

Maybe. But that won't keep us in business. After everything, I so desperately want there to be an *us*.

Malcolm sighs again. "I didn't want to say anything today, but on Monday, I'm going to let the building manager know we won't be renewing the lease."

I swallow hard and nod.

"And talk to a lawyer about what we need to do to dissolve the business."

What then? How long will K&M the couple last if K&M Ghost Eradication Specialists is no more?

"So, tomorrow," Malcolm says. "One last hurrah. We'll go everywhere, see all the sights. Who knows, we might even find a ghost."

We might, but I doubt it. This sounds like a goodbye tour. But if it is goodbye, then I'll spend every moment of it with Malcolm.

"Let's," I say. "I'll wear my skater skirt."

"Oh, I was hoping you'd say that."

"I'll even brew some coffee, just in case."

WE START at the Pancake House with all-you-can-eat dollar-size pancakes and orange juice. Malcolm tries the coffee, just to be polite. When his face puckers in its aftermath, I shoot him a told-you-so look.

"Oh, that's terrible," he says under his breath. "That's really, really terrible."

I laugh.

In a far corner, Gregory B. Gone is sitting ensconced in a booth. He's spread all manner of papers and books on the table, and Belinda's been pouring him a never-ending cup of coffee. He's so engrossed that I don't think he notices the taste.

"Looks like he got the gig," Malcolm says.

"Gig?"

"Full-time at Springside High, Honors English and drama club advisor."

"So, he's staying ... and Terese is...?" I trail off. I've missed so much in the last six weeks.

"They went off on a long weekend for Labor Day. He came back. She didn't." Malcolm spears a bite of pancake. "I think she wanted to stay in the Cities."

I want to ask if that's what he wants, too, but I clamp my mouth shut when Carter Dupree enters the restaurant and takes a spot at the counter.

"And he's working at the brokerage firm," Malcolm says, pointing his fork at Carter.

I swivel around in the booth for a closer look. "Really?"

He picks up his coffee cup and raises it in Carter's direction. Carter responds with a rude gesture; Malcolm returns the favor.

"It's kind of crazy." Malcolm shakes his head and chuckles. I detect a grin lurking on Carter's face. "But Springside can really grow on you."

Or maybe it's Belinda. I raise my eyebrows at her as she passes. She makes a face. I turn back to Malcolm.

"This is very weird," I say.

"It is, and Jack Carlotta hasn't even shown up yet."

We decide to leave before he does.

At Springside Long-term Care, I'm sandwiched between Mr. Carlotta and Mrs. Greeley. From my vantage point, I can admire everything that is Malcolm. He's dressed impeccably, almost exactly like the first time I saw him, in a blazing white dress shirt and pressed khakis. He keeps touching his pocket as if he's making sure he hasn't lost something. It's an obvious tell, but his audience doesn't seem to mind—or notice, for that matter.

His samovar throws aromatic steam into the air. It's a heady sort of scent, and I don't recognize this particular brew.

"Oh, my, that *is* romantic," Mrs. Greeley says.

"What is?" I ask.

"The tea. Do you two have a picnic planned for later?"

"No."

I'm trying to wrap my head around the notion of tea being romantic when a gasp goes up. Malcolm has pulled silk flowers out of thin air at least a dozen times, but for the residents, the trick never gets old.

"And he's in fine form today," Mrs. Greeley adds.

She might be blind, but there's nothing wrong with her hearing. Malcolm really is in fine form, and his fan club is more than appreciative.

When the show is over and everyone's had their fill of tea, I wheel Mr. Carlotta back to his room.

He takes my hand and gives it a squeeze. "I miss her," he says.

I don't know if he means Queenie or my grandmother or both.

"Me too." I kiss his cheek and promise to visit next week.

On our way out of town, we stop at the Springside Police Department. I pull a thermos from my tote and jump from the convertible.

"This will only take a minute," I say.

"Just don't get yourself arrested."

I laugh and dash up the steps.

"I'm serious," Malcolm calls after me. "You know how he gets."

Inside, I find Penny Wilson in the reception area, contemplating the space where the coffeemaker used to sit. On the sideboard squats a sleek and shiny contraption of red and black. It looks so high-tech that you probably need a special degree to run the thing.

"What's this?" I ask.

"Chief brought it in this morning," she says, shaking her head at the sight. "Since the old pot broke, we've been getting deliveries from the Coffee Depot, but..." She raises a hand and lets it drop. "Now this."

I lean in close for inspection. The contraption will make espresso, cappuccino, steamed milk, and might just do your taxes if you ask nicely. But coffee is coffee.

"I'll stop by on Monday," I say, "and show you how to use it."

Penny gives me a numb sort of nod. I leave her to contemplate the beast and knock on Chief's door.

A grunt lets me know I can enter. I hold up my thermos to show him this is a social call.

"I guess you don't need this anymore," I say, but I set the thermos on his desk anyway. "That's a pretty fancy setup you have."

"I will never refuse Lindstrom coffee." He uncaps the thermos, inhales, and his shoulders relax. "Never."

"I'll show her how to use it," I offer, "and how to grind beans for it."

Chief waves away my offer. "You don't have to."

"No, I don't, but maybe I want to."

He assesses me over the rim of the thermos and gives me a nod. "All right. Deal."

I'm about to turn to leave when I notice his hands—or, rather, the left one and its ring finger. The wedding band is missing. Only a tender circle of flesh remains in its wake.

I close the door softly behind me and wonder what I can do for him. Nothing comes to mind until I catch sight of the black and red coffee-producing beast. I can start there.

As I leave, I pause at the door, raise my chin, and taste the air for any evidence of the otherworldly. I know I won't find it, but that doesn't stop me from trying. The air is bland, with only a hint of that burnt coffee odor, and I'm reminded that things end, even when you don't want them to.

WE SAVE the old barn for last. Perhaps it's out of hope that, of any place, a stray ghost might decide to settle here. Or maybe it's the brilliant September day—the blue sky, a scattering of fluffy clouds, the rich green of the fields, and the gold of the leaves starting to change.

It's hard to be sad here. Even so, I'm managing it.

The barn is empty, of course. Rodent tracks crisscross the cracked cement floor. Dust tickles my nose. A stall door creaks, but it's nothing more than the breeze.

Malcolm hazards a few rungs up the ladder and peers into the hayloft. He turns, catches me in his gaze, and shakes his head.

"Nothing. It's too—"

"Orderly," I finish. The air is crisp, but devoid of the supernatural.

Malcolm steps down the rungs, taking each gingerly. They groan beneath his weight but don't splinter. He approaches me, and his solemn expression sends my heart into overdrive. My palms start to sweat. I tell myself to take deep breaths, that I knew this was coming.

It's all I can do not to run out the barn doors with my hands over my ears so I won't hear his next words.

"Katy." He stops in front of me, examines the ground, then studies my face. "I've been trying—I mean, I don't know, exactly, but—"

"You're leaving. I understand. You need to find work. It makes sense." The words pour from me. Maybe if I say enough of them, his won't hurt so much.

He frowns. "What?"

"You're moving back to the Twin Cities, right? To get a job? Now that—"

"No, no, I'm not. I'm not leaving Springside. I'm not leaving you." He takes my hand. "Unless you want me to."

I shake my head so hard, strands of hair stick to my cheeks.

With gentle fingers, Malcolm sweeps them from my face. "Well, that's settled. Actually, what I'm trying to do is ask you something."

"Ask me something?" I must look dumb: mouth slightly open, eyes wide and confused. At least, that's what I think when he laughs.

"You have no idea what I'm talking about, do you?"

I shake my head again.

His eyes are dark and tender. "Just one of those things I love about you. Which brings me to my question—"

I never hear Malcolm's question. Before he can utter another word, a howl fills the space. The temperature drops by ten degrees. Goose bumps pucker the bare skin where my skater skirt ends and my over-the-knee socks begin.

We both tip our heads up and study the rafters. Swirling fog fills the space from hayloft to roof.

"It can't be," I say.

As if in response to that, a force blows through the barn, slamming stall doors open and closed, the sound so much like a shotgun that I want to cower on the floor. The otherworldly surrounds us, the flavor of it like static against my tongue.

I can't count the number of ghosts that crowd the barn, all of them unfamiliar. One zeroes in on Malcolm and cuffs him on the back of the head.

"Hey!" He whirls, but it doesn't matter. That ghost is long gone.

Another tugs at my hair and then shoves me against Malcolm. He catches me—barely. We cling to each other while chaos erupts around us. The ladder teeters and crashes to the floor, wood splintering. A group of sprites flings hay from the loft, and the presence of so many ghosts makes the dust sparkle.

"What's going on?" I grip Malcolm tight, afraid to lose my hold on him. "Where did they come from?"

"Nature abhors a vacuum." He shakes his head in wonder. "Maybe the supernatural does too."

From the entryway comes a shimmering laugh. I recognize the sound, although I haven't heard it since June, when I freed all the ghosts from the warehouse. Very few ghosts laugh quite like this one, and even fewer have the strength she does.

"Delilah?" I say. "Is that you?"

The storm she kicks up tells me it is. She circles us, embracing me in a ghostly hug, gracing Malcolm with a kiss.

"Did she...?" I begin, but can't find the words to finish.

"Bring us ghosts?" He surveys the barn. "I think she did."

"But ... why?"

"I think I told you once that you made a powerful ally by setting her free." He shrugs. "Maybe she's decided to repay the kindness."

"But—"

"Isn't this what you do?" He gestures toward the ghosts. "Isn't this what you want to do?"

"Yes, but things end."

"There's always going to be ghosts, and they're always going to need you to keep them safe—from themselves, from people exploiting them. For that matter, I need you." His grin starts a bit crooked, but it blooms into that sweet, dark-roast smile. "And with that in mind—"

Malcolm takes a step back. He clears his throat. His hand goes to his pocket again, and he pulls something from within its depths.

"I still have a question." His gaze darts to the object in his hands. "But I'm going to phrase it slightly differently."

He takes a knee in front of me.

I forget to breathe.

"Katrina Lindstrom, will you spend the rest of your life catching ghosts with me?" He offers up a velvet-covered box. Inside sits a ring with a stone that glimmers like the otherworldly.

His question steals all my words.

I should say something. Anything. Or nod. Or fling myself at him. But I stand there, frozen, the ghosts bobbing around us, quiet and waiting.

"It's a moonstone," he says. "And vintage, so it has history. I thought you might like that. I was chasing down a sprite and found it at an estate sale while you were gone."

The words jolt the thoughts back into my head. He found it, bought it, *while I was gone*. The magnitude of his love, of his faith in us, sweeps over me. I mouth a few words, but no sound emerges.

"Some people even call moonstone the ghost stone, and I thought that ... or if you'd rather have something different, or you need to think, or..."

He's babbling, probably because I haven't moved since he took a knee. Now I do fling myself at him, tumbling into his arms.

"Yes!"

"It's an art deco design, and it really is vintage, and—"

"Yes!"

"I know Nigel got Sadie that big diamond, and it—"

"Malcolm." I take his face in my hands. He peers at me, eyes wide and startled. "Yes."

He blinks. It takes a moment, but only just. He scoops me up and whirls me around. Then, with the utmost care, he sets me on my feet. He pulls the ring from its box and slides it onto my finger. The feel of it there is strange and wonderful.

The barn explodes in a flurry of supernatural activity. Ghosts zoom back and forth. Sprites shower more hay on us, and pieces of it float down like confetti.

Malcolm orders me to hold still and races to the convertible. He returns, tote slung over his shoulder, hands busy uncapping the first thermos.

The moment the aromatic steam hits the air, a ghostly cry shakes the entire structure. We let them drink their fill, placing all twelve thermoses throughout the barn. Then Malcolm swings me around again. There are so many ghosts that the air hums with their chatter, and we sway to the rhythm.

Tomorrow, I'll place an order for more Kona blend. I'll stock up on sugar and track down a new field kit. Tomorrow, we'll answer calls and scrub out the Tupperware.

But tonight, we'll dance with the ghosts. Tonight, we'll celebrate.

No matter what happens, tonight belongs to us.

All of us.

NEED ANOTHER CUP OF *COFFEE & Ghosts*? Join my Coffee and Books author newsletter and receive an exclusive Coffee & Ghosts short story (along with other books and stories in the free starter library).

https://writingwrongs.blog/mail-list/

You'll also get first crack at Season 4 (yes, Season 4!) before it's published.

WHAT THE HECK IS COFFEE & GHOSTS?

COFFEE & GHOSTS is a cozy paranormal mystery/romance that is told over a series of episodes and in seasons, much like a television series. Think *Doctor Who* or *Sherlock*.

Ghost in the Coffee Machine, which I think of as the pilot episode, began life as a short story that first appeared in *Coffee: 14 Caffeinated Tales of the Fantastic*.

Once, a very long time ago, I wrote a murder mystery that involved a ghost. During the research phase, I came across a tidbit about catching ghosts using coffee and glass jars. The novel never went anywhere, but years later, when I saw the call for submissions for Coffee, something clicked. Katy, her grandmother, and their business of catching ghosts with coffee and Tupperware (a far more practical and, frankly, safer option) were born.

Not too long later I realized that I wasn't done with coffee and ghosts—or rather, they weren't done with me. They demanded their own type of storytelling as well.

Serial fiction is exciting and fun to write. It's different from a novel in that each episode has its own story arc but also supports a larger one for the season.

I've recently consolidated the episodes into three season bundles. This makes both finding the episodes and binge-reading them much easier.

I can't tell you how much fun it was to write COFFEE & GHOSTS, and I want to thank you for reading and coming along on this journey with me.

ABOUT THE AUTHOR

CHARITY TAHMASEB has slung corn on the cob for Green Giant and jumped out of airplanes (but not at the same time). She spent twelve years as a Girl Scout and six in the Army; that she wore a green uniform for both may not be a coincidence. These days, she writes fiction (long and short) and works as a technical writer for a software company in St. Paul.

Her short speculative fiction has appeared in *Flash Fiction Online*, *Deep Magic*, and *Cicada*.

ALSO BY CHARITY TAHMASEB

YOUNG ADULT FICTION (WITH DARCY VANCE)

The Geek Girl's Guide to Cheerleading

Dating on the Dork Side

YOUNG ADULT FICTION

The Fine Art of Keeping Quiet

The Fine Art of Holding Your Breath

Now and Later: Eight Young Adult Short Stories

PARANORMAL

Coffee and Ghosts, Season 1: Must Love Ghosts

Coffee and Ghosts, Season 2: The Ghost That Got Away

Coffee and Ghosts, Season 3: Nothing but the Ghosts

Coffee and Ghosts, Season 4: The Ghosts You Left Behind

FANTASY AND FAIRY TALES

Straying from the Path, Stories from the Sour Magic Series of Fairy Tales

Lightning Source UK Ltd.
Milton Keynes UK
UKHW040315270822
407860UK00011B/54